P9-CML-272

THE GODS OF GREENWICH

ALSO BY NORB VONNEGUT

Top Producer

THE GODS OF GREENWICH

NORB VONNEGUT

MINOTAUR BOOKS

A Thomas Dunne Book
New York

A THOMAS DUNNE BOOK FOR MINOTAUR BOOKS.
An imprint of St. Martin's Publishing Group.

THE GODS OF GREENWICH. Copyright © 2011 by Norb Vonnegut. All rights reserved. Printed in the United States of America. For information, address St. Martin's Press, 175 Fifth Avenue, New York, N.Y. 10010.

www.minotaurbooks.com
www.thomasdunnebooks.com

Library of Congress Cataloging-in-Publication Data

Vonnegut, Norb.
    The gods of Greenwich / Norb Vonnegut. — 1st ed.
        p. cm.
    ISBN 978-0-312-38469-2
    1. Investment advisers—Fiction.   2. Fraud—Fiction.   3. Wall Street (New York, N.Y.)—
Fiction.   I. Title.
    PS3622.O678G63 2011
    813'.6—dc22

                                                                              2010042895

First Edition: April 2011

10   9   8   7   6   5   4   3   2   1

For my mom and dad

ACKNOWLEDGMENTS

First things first. Thanks to everyone who read and enjoyed *Top Producer.* You made *The Gods of Greenwich* possible.

Scott Hoffman is my agent and friend. This book would not exist without his sage advice and the support of Folio Literary Management—including Celeste Fine, who's been scouring the world for buyers of the foreign-language rights. Scott introduced me to my publicist, Newman Communications, where I'm in the capable hands of Mark Ratner and Tess Meyer.

Pete Wolverton is a superstar. He edited this book and made it much, much better. So did Anne Bensson, who is an assistant editor and rising talent at Thomas Dunne/Minotaur/St. Martin Press ("SMP"). I am grateful to the entire crackerjack team at SMP, including Sarah Melnyk, who is fielding a bazillion e-mails from me these days.

I have great friends, who are tireless champions. Frankly, it's a long, long list, and I can't mention everyone. Otherwise the heft of additional pages would turn this book into a doorstop. That said, I am grateful to: Alex Witt, Anita Rosner, Bob Grady, Bob Butler, Brooks Newmark, Cam Burns, Charles Bryan, Chris Eklund, Dewey Shay, Cal Shook, Dorothy

ACKNOWLEDGMENTS

Flannery, Duncan Andrews, Jan Andrews, Eric Starkman, Eugene Matthews, Faye Hanson, George Bradt, Greg Farrell, Gwill York, Paul Maeder, Jack Bourger, Selena Vanderwerf, Jenny McAuliffe, Tony McAuliffe, John Edelman, Suzie Edelman, Jon Ledecky, John Thompson, Kathleen Campion (my new best friend), Kim Morse, Mark Director, Marlon Young, James Mason, Matt Arpano, Missy Attridge, Pug Ravenel, Susu Ravenel, Peter Raymond, Peter L'Green, Vicki L'Green, Scott Malkin, Steve Murphy, Tad Smith, Caroline Fitzgibbons, Thalia von Maur, Peter von Maur, and Tim Scrantom, who is my go-to guy on many fronts—especially idea generation and endless amusement. I also have many new friends who are authors, and I would like to thank them for their warm support and guidance.

Research played a big part in *The Gods of Greenwich*. Thanks to Brad Bailey, who taught me a thing or two about mitochondrial DNA. Dave McCabe and Cort Delaney are the lawyers I call to discuss trust and estate law. Shawn Bookin helped with finance jargon. Peter Gill guided me on wine. So did Kevin Kingston and his team at Station Plaza Wine, which is a great place to examine the details, if you know what I mean. Speaking of wine, it's quite possible that oenophiles will notice a few things. I welcome your e-mails because it's always great to hear from readers. But I know, okay? I know.

Time for a little personal background. When I was a kid, my family sat around the dinner table talking about our days. The anecdotes were usually nonfiction—although one could never tell in our house. I write, in part, because telling stories is something we've always done. Thanks to: Marion Vonnegut, my mother and the force behind Jimmy Cusack (the tough kid you'll meet in *The Gods of Greenwich*); Micki and Jack Costello; Helene Vonnegut and Chris Nottingham; Wendy and Joe Vonnegut; and my dad, who could not be here, but remains an inspiration to all of us.

I could not have written this novel without the indefatigable support from Mary—my wife, my love—and our children, Wynn and CoCo. I'd like to tell you a story about how the four of us sat around one afternoon, what we said that found its way into this novel. But I suppose the story needs to wait until we meet in person. And I do hope we get to meet, whether it's at a bookstore, some public event, or your book club.

Enjoy *The Gods of Greenwich*.

THE GODS OF GREENWICH

CHAPTER ONE

"I want my money."

Jimmy Cusack gazed out the window of his office in the Empire State Building. Most days he savored the southern view of downtown Manhattan. To the east was Goldman Sachs, its Broad Street headquarters an impregnable fortress in the world of finance. To the west was Lady Liberty, her harbor a vast cluster of skyscrapers rising from the sea. New York was a city that attracted great fortunes—and epic brawls to manage them.

There were times inside his hedge fund when Cusack could taste the adrenaline. He reveled in the rush of competitors waging war from their granite towers, new-age monuments that celebrated the triumph of capital. There were no cease-fires sixty-one floors below. The struggle to win clients never stopped, and the ethos was "Kill or be killed" among soldiers suited in the battle rattle of Armani pinstripes and Gucci loafers.

Today was no ordinary day. Those four words, "I want my money," haunted Cusack's thoughts. Gone was the crooked smile. The creases around his lips, sometimes mistaken for a good-natured smirk, had long since vanished. His eyes a bitter blue, Cusack's face resembled the dark clouds outside his bluff of sixty-one stories.

The ambush was cold and ruthless. "Here's how it is," the lead investor said. "Tomorrow morning, James, you'll get a FedEx. Not the afternoon delivery, but the one at ten. Inside are eight redemption notices. Each one is signed and notarized, ready to go. I want my money. So do my friends who invested in your fund."

"Who else wants out, Caleb?"

"Everybody I put in."

"Not Whitney," insisted Cusack.

"Yes."

"What about Gould?"

"Everybody," Caleb repeated. "By my calculations, our stake totals one hundred and twenty million dollars."

"You agreed to a lockup," argued Cusack. "We're talking eighty-five percent of what I manage and—"

"My lawyers say your documents are a joke."

"You talked to Ropes and Gray?"

"What difference does it make? Just get us our money, James."

"That the way it is?" Cusack sounded hard, but he was wobbling inside.

"My hands are tied."

"Yeah. To an ax."

"I may run for governor," said Caleb. "I can't ask my buddies for contributions, not when they're losing their shirts at Petri Dish Capital or whatever the hell they call your hedge fund."

"And you think pulling your money is smart in this market?"

"Not open for discussion."

Nearly six hours had passed since then. The markets were closed. The sun was setting. And Cusack racked his brain for a Hail Mary solution, a glimmer of hope, anything to save his business from redemptions that would leave him with less than $20 million to manage.

It could take years to replace $120 million from Caleb and his fellow deserters. Until then, revenues from the remaining $20 million would not pay the light bill. Cusack had no cash left to fund operations. He had gone "all in," Texas Hold 'Em style, every chip in the pot.

With the grim reality of Caleb's words unfolding, Cusack lacked his characteristic focus. His thoughts drifted from New York's office towers to the "Irish battleships" of his youth, the three-family homes of Somerville, Massachusetts.

Jimmy had always been the scrappy kid with promise. Long ago he traded membership in Somerville's blue-collar CIA—Catholic, Irish, alcoholic— for a career on Wall Street. He was thirty-two and Ivy educated, a graduate of Columbia and Wharton. His pedigree included a one-year Rotary Fellowship in Japan and five years at Goldman Sachs. He was his family's hope for the future, the son, the entrepreneur his parents had backed.

Those were yesterday's dreams. Cusack's money-management business was going down. It was taking on water through a *Titanic*-sized hole in the hull, the lead investor's words tearing at him still. "Nothing personal, mind you."

Caleb, you made it personal.

"And we expect you for Christmas dinner, James."

CHAPTER TWO

WEDNESDAY, DECEMBER 12

The following night a biting wind roared down the street named Hverfisgata. It gusted through doors and windows, through all the nooks and crannies of the stark buildings that lined the street. The air smelled of salt and sea and the damp wrath of Arctic squalls. The windchill registered icebox-cold under the dark Icelandic sky.

Seeking cover, three Americans from Connecticut ate dinner inside Hverfisgata's 101 Hotel. The men relished their hiatus from the trading floors of Greenwich, where drip bags of gloom emptied into the markets. Their trip to Reykjavik was no boondoggle. The three had focused on business all week.

Their back-to-back meetings, insufferable at times, resembled a funeral procession of Icelandic bankers and low-ranking bureaucrats. The marathon tête-à-têtes about liquidity and leverage were benumbing. But they paid off. The fieldwork confirmed their instincts and gave shape to a scheme that had been percolating for months.

Hafnarbanki, Iceland's most celebrated bank, was vulnerable to financial attack. Headquartered ten miles south of Reykjavik, the bank had borrowed $45 billion. It was too much debt, more than twice the size of Iceland's entire economy. Much of that $45 billion came from overseas. If European depositors lost confidence and closed their accounts, Hafnarbanki would collapse under the weight of its financial obligations. It was a bank on the brink.

All it needed was a little push.

Not one of the men discussed their scheme, not at first, not during the main course of bloody lamb. They were pros, wizened hedge fund veterans, and far too wily for premature celebrations. Counting money jinxed trades. Backslapping was gratuitous. But they could taste each other's silent dreams. They could almost touch the expectations of a sure thing that would net them tens of millions.

It was not until after dinner that the three relaxed, after a $15,000 "vertical tasting" of 2001, 2002, and 2003 Screaming Eagle cabernet sauvignon. After the wine located self-control switches on two men. After a conga line of port chasers turned all three faces beet red. They split the tab and moved to the hotel's sleek bar, where conversation turned to their business in Iceland.

"Tomorrow," announced the tallest money manager, the one with the Stanford MBA, starter wife, and four kids, "I'm shorting Hafnarbanki at twelve hundred."

"Tall" believed Hafnarbanki's price was about to crash. His plan was to borrow stock and sell at twelve hundred kronur right away. If Hafnarbanki fell to five hundred, he would buy at the lower price, return stock to the lender, and book a tidy profit of seven hundred kronur per share.

"I'm in," agreed the second man. He had a Napoleonic build, MIT degree in math, and hot-action mistress. "When we're finished, these Vikings will know Hafnarbanki as Bank Hindenburg."

"If you ask me, it's more of an H-bomb," scoffed Tall. He ordered three more ports. "Cy, what do you think?"

"That you two have mouths like billboards. Keep your voices down." Cy was the most sober and the most alert, the money manager with a history degree from NYU. He smiled Joe Biden bright, his good mood at odds with instinctive caution.

"Hey, we're with you," soothed Napoleon, raising his glass to Cy. "We can't lose, right?"

Cyrus Leeser grew up in Hell's Kitchen, where he survived Irish Catholic kids and eluded "poison people." Outside his family's apartment on West Fifty-fourth, the heroin addicts were forever scratching through life in search of scag or the five-way—a cocktail of heroin, cocaine, methamphetamine, Rohypnol, and alcohol. He made it to college, graduated, and began a steady if unremarkable career as a stockbroker with the "thundering herd." Leeser left Merrill Lynch in 2000 and cofounded LeeWell Capital. That was the beginning of his spectacular rise.

Most estimates placed Leeser's net worth around $75 million. Some hedge fund insiders argued it was more. He owned a sumptuous estate and was married to Bianca Santiago, bestselling author and his trophy wife of sixteen years. He was an accomplished pilot, a philanthropist, a proud father of twin daughters attending Andover, the elite boarding school. He ran big money and recruited new investors every day, vowing never to set foot on West Fifty-fourth again.

"The only risk," Napoleon suggested, "is that three hundred thousand people live in Iceland. And they're all related."

"It's like some kind of Nordic Appalachia," Tall agreed. "Webbed feet and shit."

"These cousins can band together," Napoleon continued, "buy stock, and prop up Hafnarbanki's share price."

"Don't say the name of the bank," warned Cy. "What is it you don't understand about keeping your voice down?"

"You worry too much," scoffed Napoleon. "We're performing a community service."

"How so?" asked Tall as another round of drinks arrived.

"By shorting dumb money so it goes away." Napoleon clinked glasses with Tall and raised a toast, "To Hafnarbanki."

Cy winced as he noticed a bookish man a few seats down the bar.

Furrowed brow, sleek black glasses, Siberian-blue eyes—Siggi Stefansson pretended to read his novel. The Americans annoyed him; the bottomless drinks, the clinking of glasses, the laughter that occasionally rocked the bar. It was all he could do to concentrate.

Siggi cursed the tallest foreigner under his breath. Then he cursed his girlfriend Hanna, who always ran late. The Icelander was forever sitting in bars, alone, reading books and drinking himself into drunken stupors with people he didn't know. Or drinking with Ólafur. His second cousin was a regular at every gin mill in downtown Reykjavik.

Siggi could not help but eavesdrop, especially because the three Americans were discussing Hafnarbanki. He deposited his money there. It was the pride of Iceland, a national treasure, a legacy from a few fishermen who abandoned their nets in the 1930s for the glory of international banking.

The Americans almost seemed giddy. Siggi closed his book, taking care to dog-ear the page, and sipped his Guinness. He studied the man named Cy, who shushed the other two men from time to time.

Cy was in his late forties with deep crow's-feet and basset-hound eyes. He was an imposing figure: muscular build, five foot eleven at least, and jet-black hair that flopped over his ears and touched his shoulders. He spoke little. But he conveyed power. Siggi judged Cy to be a man who could handle himself in any bar, whether drinking, fighting, or womanizing.

The other two Americans, however annoying, intrigued him. Drunk or not, they sounded smarter than most tourists. He heard the word "short" every so often, but he was not sure what it meant. Their toast seemed friendly enough:

"To Hafnarbanki."

That was when Leeser caught Siggi's eye. "Are you from Reykjavik?" the long-haired American asked. He was all smile and bleached teeth. He spoke in a disarming manner, as though asking for directions.

"Yes." Siggi pushed his black glasses up from the bridge of his nose.

"Come on down and let me buy you a drink."

Leeser prided himself on one skill. He could read people. When he was a kid, the talent helped him duck punches, both on the streets and inside his apartment, which was a hell all its own. Within thirty-five minutes, Cy was convinced he knew everything about the bookish Icelander with the craggy face and wavy blond hair.

Siggi was the youngest of three children. He was thirty-four and engaged to be married. He had been dating his fiancée for nine months and three days. He reminded the American of a young Michael Caine.

Cy knew Hanna's name. He knew her studies were a source of conflict. Siggi wanted to get married right away. But Hanna's law degree came first as far as she was concerned. Planning a wedding, Hanna argued, was out of the question given her course load at Reykjavik University's School of Law.

Leeser's interest in the Icelander had little to do with affability. It was all about damage control. Cy wondered what Siggi had heard, whether he was a threat. Ferreting out information, though, required finesse. The American gave a little to get a lot.

At one point, Siggi asked, "What brings you to Iceland?"

"I run a hedge fund."

"I don't understand much about them," Siggi confessed.

"Few people do," Cy replied in his most disarming, empathetic voice. "In my opinion hedge funds have three things in common. We manage money. We usually charge twenty-percent fees on profits. And we're less regulated than other financial institutions, because we each work with limited numbers of wealthy investors."

"But what do you mean by 'hedge'?"

"Fair question. 'Hedge' is a misleading word. It makes us sound like money managers who protect against downside risk—in the same way landlords insure buildings against fire. I do. But not everybody does. Like I said before, hedge funds manage money for wealthy investors."

"Well, that leaves me out," Siggi noted, his voice wistful. "I have no head for stocks and bonds anyway."

Cy relaxed. And then he discovered a bonus. Siggi owned a small art gallery, two blocks away. The Icelander traveled extensively, spoke fluent Russian, and catered to an exclusive clientele of Eastern Europeans. This discovery thrilled Leeser, a true lover of art, a collector with eclectic tastes. Cy covered both his home and office walls with emerging masters from everywhere.

"Would you like to see my gallery?" Siggi offered. "We can go when Hanna gets here."

"Not me," Napoleon replied. "I'm going to bed."

"Me either," agreed Tall. "Cy's your guy. He wants to become Stevie Cohen."

Tall was referring to the founder of SAC Capital Partners. Cohen, a billionaire and king among hedge funds, owned the greats. His collection, worth $700 million by some estimates, included masterpieces by Edvard Munch, Pablo Picasso, and Andy Warhol.

"I'm small time compared to Cohen," Leeser added in a wistful, self-deprecating way. "Maybe one day."

Siggi and Cy could have yakked about art all night. But Leeser stayed on plan and forced himself to learn more about the Icelander, to ensure the art dealer was no threat.

Cy knew Siggi was a happy drunk, incapable of holding his liquor. He knew the names of Siggi's parents, not to mention his older brother and sister. He knew the Icelander felt a special affinity with his second cousin. There was only one detail Cy missed.

Cousin Ólafur worked for Hafnarbanki. He was the managing director of strategic development, the senior executive charged with mapping out the bank's competitive strategy. When hedge funds attacked, his job was to mow them down.

CHAPTER THREE
WEDNESDAY, DECEMBER 19

"You're taking too long."

"Do your job, and let me do mine." Rachel Whittier clicked off her cell phone, annoyed by his pressure. Who needed it? She had never failed her employer before. Two, maybe three more years of this aggravation, and she would tell him to take a hike. She would have enough cash and could stop moonlighting forever, or at least until she moved to Paris.

"Get your boots," a deejay advised over the radio. "There's a blizzard coming."

Rachel gazed out the window of her Park Avenue clinic. All morning the squalls had threatened. Now avalanche-white nimbostratus clouds were dusting New York City with snowy powder. It was only a matter of time before they launched a full-scale assault.

The storm would snarl traffic. The taxis would skid on rutted roads, windshield wipers slapping this way and that. The cabbies would swear and spit and smack each other's fenders, while pedestrians slipped on unsalted sidewalks and scuttled from store to store. But Rachel's green eyes blazed with gelid detachment, trancelike, in a nether zone.

She was blasé about the holiday craze in New York City. She ignored Christmas decorations and the Salvation Army ringing their handbells on Fifth Avenue. Today was the day. It was time to go.

Rachel charged out of the break room, down the marble-lined corridor, and found Doc in Reception among towering ferns and back issues of *People* magazine. New York's foremost plastic surgeon, fiftyish and too Hollywood for her taste, was braving the elements to grab lunch.

"I'm taking the afternoon off," she announced. "See you tomorrow."

Rachel was not asking. She was telling. She owned Doc. He was the one who prepared collagen syringes for her treatments. He was the one who bought lunch whenever she asked. Doc was the boss, the big biscuit in the pan. But he said yes no matter what came out of her mouth. And she doubted her honey Texan accent was the reason.

"Christmas shopping?" Doc inquired, ever the obedient dog with tongue hanging out.

"You're on my list." Rachel flipped her golden-blond hair and spun around to retrieve a purse and winter coat. She could feel Doc ogling her from behind, his eyes tracing the starched white blouse and cup of her white skirt. He appreciated her sway. She appreciated her power, the ability to milk desire for control.

Inside a private consultation room, which housed the staff's closet, Rachel appraised her figure in a full-length mirror. She approved the fullness of her breasts. She cocked her head slightly to the right, unconsciously rubbing a raised, puffy, round scar on the back of her right hand. For a moment she scrutinized her thin hips, wondering if she had put on weight.

The moment passed. It was time to get started. She was starved, already savoring the hunt.

Harold Van Nest resembled, if such a thing can exist, the poster child for grandfathers. He was seventy-two and balding, all belly and no butt, bright and boisterous with an ever-present smile. Behind horn-rimmed glasses that made him look scholarly, his soft brown eyes danced with infectious good humor.

The women at the neighborhood dry cleaners remarked, "What an adorable old man," whenever he left their shop.

Van Nest was a creature of habit. For twenty years, he had worn a red bow tie and tweedy suit—inhaler in his coat pocket—every Wednesday evening regardless of the season. He sat on the same stool inside the Harvard Club bar and sipped the same drink, always a Beefeater martini with two olives and instructions to "shake extra hard." He recycled the same stories with friends from their glory days at college, and he insisted his punch lines improved with each and every telling.

At precisely 6:45 P.M. Van Nest said good-bye to Franklin Sanborn II and William Wirt III, who was known as "Three Sticks." He patted Hayward Levitt V on the back and reminded him that poker started at 7:15 P.M. tomorrow night. They had shared the same game for the last forty years with Frederick Sterling Jr. and Samuel Harkness VI, both Yale graduates of similar vintage. Harold marched outside the club's hoary wooden halls and into a New York blizzard on loan from Siberia.

He hated the cold. It stirred up his asthma. Gave him fits.

The red awning, white number twenty-seven, was losing its fierce battle against the driving snow. Monstrous flakes pelted Harold and buried his lenses. The drifts soaked his trouser cuffs within seconds and made Harold grateful for the rubbers covering his wingtips.

The club's doorman asked, "May I get you a cab, sir?"

"Think we'll have any luck, Robert?"

"Never failed yet," the doorman replied, whistling between teeth and pursed lips. Almost at once, a lone yellow cab appeared from nowhere in front of the red canopy.

Van Nest scrambled for the taxi, the snow coating him from all directions. Robert opened the yellow door, and the older man felt a hand touch his elbow. He whirled around, sinking into the seat all in one motion, not sure what to expect. A woman with brilliant green eyes and a Paddington Bear mariner's hat was standing over him.

"Get in and scoot over," she ordered, her voice a compelling mix of sex, siren, and sergeant.

Ever the gentleman, Van Nest slipped across the black vinyl seat as instructed. He said nothing. He was dumbfounded by the sudden intrusion into seventy-two years of routine.

"Where are you going?" she asked, her voice softer and more inviting now.

"Upper East Side," he replied, stumbling over his words.

"Me, too."

"May I drop you somewhere?"

"I'm cold. I'm wet. And I could use a drink," she said.

Van Nest eyed the woman. She was in her late twenties or early thirties. He could not tell for sure. Her bold lipstick, a shade named Crimson Kiss, mesmerized him. Made him regret his standing reservation, a table for one every Wednesday at Il Riccio.

He decided his life could use a little adventure. So what if he missed the seven P.M. seating. The decision was a no-brainer. He would rather spend time with a cute young thing than eat dinner alone.

"Can you pass my inhaler?"

Van Nest pointed to the tiny canister resting on his bedside table. It was sandwiched between his alarm clock and the television remote. He had placed an inhaler in roughly the same spot for the last thirty years.

"Is there a problem?" asked Rachel, alarm registering in her voice.

There was no issue. Quite the contrary. Van Nest was savoring his good fortune. Inside the vast bedroom of his Fifth Avenue apartment, there were more important things to consider than his temperamental lungs. Chances like this were few and far between.

"I may need a puff," he replied with as much bravado as an asthmatic septuagenarian can muster. "Just in case."

"Forget it," the nurse purred. Her eyes shone the emerald hue of a Bermuda lawn. "This calls for mouth-to-mouth."

Rachel had long since shed her black woolen dress with the deep neckline and empire waist. It lay puddled at the foot of the bed. She perched on Van Nest's groin, taking great care not to rest all her weight lest she bruise the old man. He was lying on his back with no shirt but still wearing blue pin-striped boxers and black knee-length socks.

"You're quite the picture, Harold." She giggled, not in an unkind way, but with provocative, come-hither inflection.

The young nurse studied her reflection in Van Nest's cheval mirror. At twenty-seven, Rachel Whittier was beauty in bloom. Athletic, milk-pure complexion, and five foot eleven—she turned heads everywhere. She was perfect by all measures except her own. For the slightest, most imperceptible moment, she frowned at her reflection.

If Van Nest spotted the furrows in Rachel's brow, he ignored them. For that matter he ignored his white oxford, red tie, and tweedy suit spooning with Rachel's heap. Fastidious to a fault on most days, he could care less that his brown wingtips were still sheathed in waterproof rubbers somewhere in the foyer. He was wallowing in blond hair and lingerie and the sweetest perfume he had known for years.

Rachel leaned down and kissed the patient. Her touch was tender at first. Slowly, playfully, she coaxed his growing desire. With each brush of their lips she grew more fervent. She fondled his ears. She stroked his eyebrows and nuzzled his chin.

Van Nest forgot their age difference, the forty-plus years. He stopped worrying about his looks. Growing younger every second, he was lost in the moment. He was savoring the goddess on top.

"I've died and gone to heaven," he said.

"Don't rush me, Harold."

The tryst had evolved quickly—the cab, an invitation, and Van Nest's favorite bottle of burgundy. The sweet taste of wine lingered between their lips still. He remembered how it all began.

Harold: "Would you join me for dinner?"

Rachel: "Just drinks."

Harold: "They keep a table for me at Il Riccio."

Rachel: "What's wrong with your place?"

Harold: "Do you like wine?"

Rachel: "Only if you impress me."

Harold: "How about a 1996 Chambolle Musigny Les Amoreuses by George Roumier?" He doubted any woman could resist a premier cru burgundy from a vineyard named "the lovers."

Rachel: "I'm impressed."

Bottle spent and clothes more shed than not, she pulled back and sat upright on his soft stomach. Her knees were bent and feet splayed to either side. Van Nest, lying on his back, savored the sight. Her nipples strained against black lingerie, rose areolae peeking over delicate lace. He could not believe his good fortune. It was like being young again.

The drought in his bedroom had lasted three long years, a purgatory of desire even at his age. Others defined "sixty-nine" as a sex act. Not Harold Van Nest. He recalled sixty-nine as the age he last got laid. At least that was what he thought. These days he could not be certain. His mind was forever playing tricks.

No mistake this evening. There was just the here and glorious now of lace garters and black hose. A woman, young enough to be his granddaughter, was straddling him. Van Nest had discovered she was a nurse, and clearly she knew things, erogenous things, but he had no idea what would follow. The uncertainty titillated him. The more Van Nest ogled her breasts, the more he fantasized, and the more he craved his inhaler. The guys at the Harvard Club would never believe him.

Rachel caressed his stomach, pushed down hard until he tingled. She kneaded his chest, first the left side, then the right, and worked her way along his narrow shoulders. Van Nest had never been an Adonis. Under the soothing touch of powerful hands, though, he felt like Superman.

"Too hard?" asked Rachel, the gentle and caring nurse, the deft masseuse seeking feedback.

"I'm in seventh heaven," he sighed.

"Don't rush me," she repeated.

"Why do you keep saying that?"

"You're in for a surprise." She tweaked him playfully between the thighs and asked, "Do you trust me?"

"More and more every minute." Van Nest found her question odd but played the game anyway.

"Close your eyes, Harold."

"Huh?"

"You heard me."

"Okay," he complied.

"No peeking."

With a goose-down pillow cradling his head and a woman rubbing his torso, Van Nest was happy. He dared not look. At seventy-two he could not risk a sure thing, and now was no time to take chances. He allowed himself to relax, succumbing to the wine's afterglow and Rachel's steamy banter. Gone were the qualms about saggy nakedness in front of a woman half his age.

Rachel moved with a black widow's fragile grace. The mattress eased under her weight. It sprang back as she shifted positions. Two clicks to his left, two clicks to his right, and four clicks behind—she was done almost at once.

"You can open your eyes, Harold."

Her sultry voice, the timbre of innuendo, kindled his quiescent loins. It was aural sex, the way she purred and whispered into his ear. Van Nest opened his eyes and spied his inhaler. Like a turtle emerging from its shell, Adam's apple barely visible under the folds of sagging skin, he craned his neck and appraised the situation.

The sight, the sensation drained his breath. He was handcuffed to the headboard of his iron sleigh bed. He pulled with his arms toward the bars. Ankle cuffs held him fast. He lay spread-eagled, incarcerated by Rachel's carnal web, one word surging through his thoughts: kinky.

For the first time in all his seventy-two years, Van Nest would experience bondage. It felt dirty. It felt nice. It weirded him out. He had no idea what to say, but he was bound and determined to make the best of it.

"Hey, I'll cut my wrists, Rachel."

"Don't worry. The cuffs are padded," she explained, working his inner thighs. "And I know what I'm doing."

Van Nest agreed 100 percent, until Rachel stopped kneading and began rustling with a package. "What's that?"

"A girl can't be too careful," she replied, and showed him a condom, now out of the packet.

"You're kidding, right? I haven't worn one of those in fifty years."

"It's like riding a bike," she purred, unrolling the latex.

"You're supposed to do that on me," Van Nest objected.

"I got your size," she replied, not responding to his protests. "It's extra large."

"Nobody's ever accused me of that before."

"Trust me. I know what I'm talking about." Rachel touched her forefinger to the tip of his nose, the gesture a cross between impish and provocative.

"Hey, what happened to your hand?" he asked, noticing a raised white scar. It looked like a childhood accident, one of those puffy burns that make people gawk.

Rachel recoiled abruptly. Her face clouded. She hated when people asked about Daddy's little gift, the hazard that never appeared on cigarette warning labels.

Van Nest saw her flinch and backtracked away from the blemish. "I still don't get what you're doing."

His confusion—whether real or polite diversion—proved short-lived. Half naked, Rachel scooted up the septuagenarian's stomach and onto his chest. "Are you ready?"

"All yours."

She relaxed for a moment and allowed her weight to crush his asthmatic lungs. Then she wiggled from side to side, using her bottom like a rolling pin to mash out his air.

"Get up," he gasped, the words wheezing from his mouth. "I can't breathe."

Rachel moved lightning fast. A cyclone of twists and grunts, a few hellacious tugs, she yanked and jerked the condom down over his balding pate, down past his ears, over his nose, and finally down over his mouth. She cut off the asthmatic's air intake.

He could not breathe or comprehend why his good luck had soured. Hands bound, feet cuffed, lungs drained of all oxygen—he could not rip off the latex. He could barely see his inhaler through the .09 millimeters of a murky red Trojan.

"Harold, condoms increase up to eight times their normal size," Rachel explained. Bored and indifferent to his struggles, she examined her fingernails as the old man writhed.

Van Nest's panic soon gave way to a full-fledged asthma attack. His bronchi contracted. Natural spasms and man-made latex closed the oxygen from his lungs. Inflammation followed and grew progressively acute. Mucus filled his narrow airways. The padded cuffs that left no marks, pleasure toys of bondage, made escape impossible.

"Just relax, honey. It goes easier." There was a heavy Texas twang in her voice.

Rachel waited for Van Nest to stop bucking. She checked her makeup with a flip mirror and fussed her blond hair back into shape. She admired the fullness of her lips. Doc did good work.

The sweep hand on the bedside clock ticked off the seconds, then the minutes, indifferent to Van Nest's futile struggles. It did not take long. He expired, and she pulled the condom from his head. She checked his pulse just to be sure, and found nothing. He was dead beyond all doubt.

Rachel considered Van Nest's bulging eyes, which came as close to saying, "Fuck you," as a dead man can say. A deft nurse, she shuttered his lids. She tucked her four sets of handcuffs into a purse and pulled out some tunes. It was the only way to clean.

Headphone on, iPod clipped to her bra, "Satisfaction" blasting in her ears—Rachel studied Van Nest with clinical detachment. His gray face was frozen in a final good-bye gasp, his thin lips smudged with lipstick. Rachel pulled a Handi Wipe from her bag and dabbed the traces of Crimson Kiss from his mouth. Then she pulled out a second wipe, moistened it with burgundy, and patted the old man's lips once again.

"Where's your vacuum cleaner, Harold?"

An hour later, Rachel surveyed Van Nest's Fifth Avenue apartment one last time. For all her care and cleaning, she assumed there was DNA everywhere. That was the problem with ripping off clothes and jumping the bones of a man forty-plus years your senior. No Hazmat suit.

Rachel had overlooked something—hair, fingerprints, a wisp of evidence waiting to be found. She knew it. The Feds turned water into wine and trace elements into life sentences. She once read about a New Hampshire woman who went to prison even after she pulverized her boyfriend's bones with a hammer and tried to incinerate them. The investigators found shards of burnt fragments that contained enough DNA to jail the woman for a long, long time.

Van Nest's death looked like natural causes, an aging asthmatic caught short without his inhaler. But just in case, Rachel reached into her purse and pulled out a plastic bag holding brown hair from the scalp of David Sanchez: Plan B.

Sanchez was a registered "Level 3" sex offender living on West Twenty-third Street. He had been easy to find on the Web site hosted by New York's Division of Criminal Justice Services. Rachel had planned to gather up his hair at a barbershop, which proved unnecessary. Sanchez, aging and balding, shed all over a demo keyboard at the Apple store on East Fifty-ninth Street.

Inside Van Nest's apartment, Rachel tweezered Sanchez's hair from the bag and dropped it near the island counter where Harold kept his wineglasses. The Feds would find the strands if they bothered to inspect the premises. Sanchez's DNA would trigger a five-alarm alert from the federal database. She smirked at the idea of screwing with the guy's life. It served the pedophile right.

After exiting through the front door, Rachel removed her latex glove and dropped Van Nest's inhaler in the hall. She headed for the elevators and exited into the December night. She felt like ordering Chinese, sipping table wine, and listening to Édith Piaf. A few more jobs, a little luck with her savings, and she could say good-bye to nursing and move to Paris, where she would smoke cigarettes, shop at the fashion houses, and flirt with buff Euro studs in the sidewalk cafés.

Maybe she could find a gig with somebody else. All these seventy-year-olds, the men and women of the Harold Van Nest era, were too easy. It was time for a challenge. Something to generate a little walking-around money.

CHAPTER FOUR
TUESDAY, JANUARY 22

Cusack glared at the envelope on his desk. He knew what was inside: the monthly invoice for his mortgage payment of $17,507.19. He was down to his last $20,000 in cash, which was not the bank's problem. Unless they received their money, there would be late fees and dings on his credit report, maybe even a phone call—the usual flak from lender ack-ack.

His hedge fund was toast. Not yet, not officially. But it was only a matter of time. Nobody was investing new money. For the last two weeks Cusack had been smiling and dialing, anything to replace the $120 million that walked out the door per Caleb's instructions. Most everybody advised, "Call back next year after we see what happens."

Cusack could sort out his finances. He had seen tough times growing up, the way his father struggled when plumbing work was slow. Eventually, a job would come.

The immediate issue was how soon. Nobody on Wall Street was hiring. Nobody. The Dow had fallen 9.7 percent in the fourteen trading days since the beginning of the year. Market jitters were death-sucking the psyche of every man and woman in the money business.

Jimmy scanned his office. He could almost smell the despair wafting over low-rise cubicles like somebody had emptied an aerosol can of blues. His employees locked on their computer screens, their eyes riveted in Svengali mind stares, every man and woman praying for Bloomberg news that would cure their worlds.

They pretended to deal with their day-to-day responsibilities. But every one of them had circulated their résumés. One by one employees would leave, and Cusack Capital would die the unglamorous, unnoticed, unimportant death of so many hedge funds that disappear silently in the night— obscurity the sole dignity of collapse.

Even Sydney, red hair and wall-to-wall smile, looked glum. She was Cusack's personal assistant, the rock who worked hard, stayed late, and never complained. She had followed him from Goldman, loyal to the end, loyal to now.

Last week she had asked, "I know things are tough. And I promise never, ever, to leave you in the lurch. But do you mind if I talk with Credit Suisse about a job?"

Cusack needed some luck. Or he would be interviewing, too. He smiled crookedly, forcing his mood to brighten. His thoughts trailed to the single most important person in his life. She had never known financial uncertainty, though she faced hurdles he could only imagine.

Do I tell my wife or shield her from all this?

Cusack never answered the question. He picked up his phone and began dialing. Mortgage payments were one problem. He had others.

THURSDAY, FEBRUARY 7

Siggi Stefansson shifted on his stool inside Gaukur á Stöng, Reykjavik's oldest pub. He was sipping Brennivín, the local hooch, brewed from potato pulp and caraway seeds. He thought it tasted like horse piss.

Svarti dauði, Iceland's term of endearment for the liquor, means "black death." The nickname refers as much to the bottle's black label as to the lethal alcohol content of 37.5 percent. But Siggi's second cousin had insisted on Brennivín that evening. "I need to drown my troubles."

Ólafur, gone for the last ten minutes, returned from the men's room and bellied up to the bar. He looked much like Siggi; blue eyes, wavy blond hair, a few hints of white at the temples. No glasses, he was heavier, and solid through the middle. There was none of the adult-onset gut that springs from the blocks once men hit thirty-five.

Rubbing his stomach, Ólafur grimaced and said, "I'm a wreck."

"What's the problem?"

"My portfolio." At thirty-eight Ólafur was a rising star, a managing director at Iceland's most venerable bank. He believed in Hafnarbanki and bought shares whenever possible, sometimes with borrowed money. He bet big and yearned for the glory of being right.

"Hafnarbanki's shares," Siggi protested, "are trading over a thousand kronur."

"We're already down fifteen percent this year." Ólafur balled his right hand and rubbed it with the left, as though wringing out the cold.

"Ouch."

" 'Ouch' doesn't cut it. How about we go with 'I'm fucked.' " The banker drained his shot glass and signaled for another round of *svarti dauði*.

"What's wrong with Hafnarbanki?"

"Business is fine," bristled Ólafur. "But the damn hedge funds are bad-mouthing our stock and spooking everybody."

"Really?" Siggi considered next week's installation in Connecticut, remembering the first time he met Cyrus Leeser. "Do you have any proof?"

"A research analyst told me. Somebody asked him to hammer our stock. Offered him big money."

"Did he take it?"

"No."

"So what's the big deal?"

"Somebody always takes the bribe," asserted Ólafur, growing impatient with his cousin, who knew so little about finance. "It's just a matter of finding the right whore."

"I have an American client," Siggi began, "who runs a hedge fund."

"There are eight thousand hedge funds."

"My client was drinking with two other guys," continued Siggi, undeterred by his second cousin's self-importance. "They were talking about Hafnarbanki at the bar."

"What did they say?"

"Something about shorting."

Ólafur leaned closer, all ears now, no longer annoyed with his second cousin. "Who's your client?"

"He wasn't the one talking." Siggi spoke faster and faster, withering under his cousin's scrutiny. He cursed himself for blabbing. There was something foreign in Ólafur's eyes, something feral. "Cy wasn't the loud one."

"Cy who?"

"He's not a bad guy," the art dealer replied, annoyed he could not control his nerves. "Cy just bought the second most expensive painting I ever sold. His friends were the ones talking."

"Shorting what, Siggi?"

"Hafnarbanki," he answered. "What's the big deal?"

"When did this happen?"

"December."

Ólafur blinked. His blue eyes turned black, his glare sharper than a fish hook. The stare pierced Siggi's skull and came out the other side. "Why didn't you tell me before?"

"You don't discuss your clients with me, Ólafur."

"My clients don't spread false rumors."

"I had no idea—"

"Is your client," Ólafur interrupted, "Cyrus Leeser, by any chance?"

"How do you know?"

Ólafur's eyes cut through the haze of fermented potato pulp and caraway seeds. "We hear his name all the time."

"Cy's not the kind to spread rumors," Siggi stammered, defending a client through his cousin's scowl.

"His name surfaces everywhere."

"We had a few drinks. I showed Cy my gallery. There's nothing else."

"You should have told me, Siggi."

"Remember that when my clients need art loans."

Ólafur signaled the bartender for another round.

"Hanna's expecting me," the art dealer protested, rising from his stool, not too steady on his feet.

With his left palm flat, Ólafur reached over to Siggi and pushed down on his cousin's shoulder. He handed Siggi a cell phone and said, "Tell your girlfriend you'll be late." With that the inquisition began:

"What did Leeser say about Hafnarbanki?"

"Do you remember the names of Leeser's friends?"

"Did Leeser describe his fund?"

"How often do you speak with him?"

"Did Leeser discuss his portfolio?"

Ólafur signaled for one drink after another, waterboarding Siggi with *svarti dauði*. The banker's questions never stopped.

Rachel sat in her apartment on East Eighty-third, alone and surrounded by the absence of color. White curtains. White furniture. White area rug. She kept things simple and crisp.

Maybe too simple. Rachel was annoyed with her savings. They were not growing fast enough. For a while she toyed with the idea of finding a partner, somebody to source new business and figure out whether prospects were serious or just kicking the tires. A partner could land clients. A partner could negotiate contracts and get the $25,000 down payment up front. A partner could ferret out the Feds.

Or bring problems. A partner kept 20 percent of every contract, which meant $10,000 minimum. Rachel doubted the deal made sense. Ten grand was serious coin. And finding somebody reliable, somebody who would keep their mouth shut, was risky business.

Cops were always patrolling undercover. They could disguise themselves as willing accomplices and nab her. Or they could masquerade as prospects and grab the partner, who would cough her up like a hairball when threatened. Advertising through *Soldier of Fortune,* she decided, was the only way to prospect—equal risk and so much cheaper.

Rachel's existing employer was reliable. She had to give him that. His business was steady, which more than compensated for his occasional bouts of ill temper. He paid well and promised her the moon. But his assurances were talk. Empty talk. Rachel would not be satisfied until she was sifting through Parisian nightclubs for guys or chumming for adventure at the bottom of three highballs on the Rue de Martyrs. She needed to diversify.

The cell phone interrupted Rachel's reverie. She recognized the number and let it ring just to mess with the caller's head. Sipping from her glass of red wine, she punched the Talk button and greeted her employer, "I was just thinking about you, Kemosabe."

"I've got something for you. I want you to take your time and do this woman right."

The comment annoyed Rachel, who prided herself on doing everyone right. She checked her temper and said, "It almost sounds personal."

"In my business, Rachel, everything is personal."

"How old is she?"

"Does it make a difference?"

"No. But I'm curious if she's like the others."

"She's seventy-six."

"The Dead Sea wasn't on the critical list when that gal was born."

CHAPTER FIVE

WEDNESDAY, APRIL 16

Cusack was standing in line at the post office. His crooked smile curled to the right. His blue eyes twinkled. His sandy brows arched high, resembling the outer edges of half-moons. He was in good shape, 175 pounds stretched tight across a six-foot frame. He wore slim blue jeans, a white shirt, and a tweed jacket. He radiated the easy manner of success.

But he felt like a severed artery. A registered letter from Litton Loan Servicing was waiting for him at the counter. He knew all about the Houston-based company. Litton administered loan portfolios and chased deadbeats who missed their mortgage payments.

Cusack had missed the last three. With $20,000 in his checking account last January, the decision was simple. He could make one mortgage payment or parcel out the remaining cash on food, electricity, cell phone, gas, and other essentials until he found a job.

Cusack Capital was gone. The fund folded during March, not in the spectacular fashion of Amaranth Advisors, which lost $6 billion two years earlier. Jimmy never managed more than $200 million in total assets. But his company perished all the same, and like so many other would-be titans of finance, Cusack closed his doors in silent obscurity.

He had been so careful setting up his company. In order to convey financial strength, Cusack leased space on the sixty-first floor of the world's most iconic office building. To show moderation, he bought secondhand furniture at a liquidation sale and avoided the bird's-eye maple and Italian leather favored by his hedge fund brethren. Antiques were a nonstarter. He would have replaced the furnace in his mother's three-family house before spending a few hundred thousand on period pieces.

Cusack's frugal decisions no longer mattered. The Bloomberg terminals, lobby furniture, and conference table for eight were all gone. So were the Cisco phones and state-of-the-art computers, not to mention the fifty-two-inch flat-screen television. Like the legions of hedgies who crashed before him, Cusack was looking for a job. Only he was interviewing in a market where employers treated every applicant like a case of hives.

Financial organizations were spooked. The Dow's modest decline, 2 percent during the first quarter, belied the market's growing angst. In February of 2008 General Motors announced a $38.7 billion loss for the previous year. Bear Stearns self-detonated, and many hedge funds lost their shirts in the fallout from subprime mortgages and other toxic assets. There was little to cheer, except perhaps for the resignation of New York's governor, which appealed to Wall Street's cult of schadenfreude.

From Cusack's perspective there had been one bright spot, one ray of good news since December. Sydney and his former employees all found jobs, thanks to a kick-save deal he negotiated with another hedge fund. Their financial security meant that he had one less reason to flog himself for past mistakes.

Too bad he was never offered a job.

Earlier that Wednesday morning, Cusack's lawyer told him what to expect from Litton. "Most likely, it's a demand notice, Jimmy, what we call a 'forty-five-day letter.' That's how long you have to pay principal, interest, and late charges."

"What about penalties, Smitty?" Cusack knew the answer without asking his attorney.

"The bank has the right to defend its financial interests."

"Meaning I pay their legal fees?"

"Somebody does." Smitty almost sounded sheepish. "Does your lender escrow for taxes and insurance?"

"Yes."

"You need to pay those costs, too," the lawyer advised.

"What if I can't bring the loan current?"

"What about your wife?" suggested Smitty.

"Emi is a scientist at a zoo. She can't afford a three-million mortgage."

"That's not what I mean. And you know it."

"Don't go there," Cusack growled. "Just tell me what happens if I don't make payments."

"Litton takes your condo."

"I know that." Cusack's mood was growing darker by the minute. "What's the process?"

"At the start, there's backing and forthing. The lender files a lis pendens with the court and serves you a summons. You answer. They respond. We go to discovery, and they file for summary judgment. Later an order of reference. Eventually, the court signs a judgment of foreclosure and sale. That's when things get ugly."

"What could be worse?"

"A public auction and ads in the newspaper. Given your three-million-dollar mortgage, Litton will make sure everybody in New York City knows your condo is on the block."

"Great."

"Sorry, Jimmy."

"Forget it. There's actually a silver lining here."

"Which is what?" Smitty asked.

"I have forty-five days to figure it out."

Standing in the post office line, Cusack lacked his earlier confidence. He felt queasy. His stomach was rumbling, not from hunger, but from intestinal half gainers where the dives were all scored "deadbeat."

He was three people back when his cell phone rang and a woman asked, "Can you be in Greenwich this afternoon? Say three o'clock in our office?"

Cusack flipped into the icy composure of his profession. He was a finance jock after all, cerebral and calculating through any challenge. Telegraph anxiety, and you get trampled from behind. Drop your guard, and you get sucker-punched in the groin. A little bravado traveled a long way in his industry.

"Can we make it three-thirty?" he countered, his words clipped short by the twenty-five-letter alphabet of Massachusetts.

Cusack sounded steady, but his heart threatened to burst out his ribs. He clutched a BlackBerry with his left hand and fist-pumped with his right. The people in line all gawked, wondering if he had gone postal. A stout woman in a black dress grabbed her little boy's hand just in case.

LeeWell Capital was on the phone. It was the scrappy underdog of hedge funds. It was the upstart thriving among powerful adversaries like Soros Fund Management. Best of all, it was the potential employer that could fix Cusack's money problems.

Cy Leeser, the cofounder, was an emerging legend. He had never lost money, even during the rank days of 2000 when Leeser and Byron Stockwell established the firm. Their timing was the pits. LeeWell Capital opened for business just as the markets tanked. By October investors were threatening to mutiny.

The complaints exacted a heavy toll on Stockwell, who in a single sitting could suck down three Big Macs, a large shake, and all the fries within reach. At 3:59 one Friday afternoon he hung up on an irate investor and promptly suffered a massive myocardial infarction, leaving LeeWell Capital down 12 percent and one partner.

Several investors believed Stockwell was the brains behind the operation. They threatened to pull their money. The fund almost collapsed less than twelve months out of the gate.

Leeser convinced his disgruntled investors to stay the course. LeeWell Capital closed up 11 percent for the year, a jaw-dropping 23 percent recovery in the last two months of 2000. Cy never looked back. He became maniacal about secrecy, the most talked-about enigma inside all of Hedgistan. He had earned the admiration, perhaps the envy, of every money manager in Greenwich.

They knew all about his brush with failure. They admired his comeback. And now his fortune attracted space on the society pages, where he achieved notoriety for philanthropic largesse as well as his marriage to the bestselling author Bianca Santiago.

"Can we split the difference?" the woman from LeeWell Capital asked. "Can we make it three-fifteen?"

"Absolutely," Jimmy replied.

"Do you know how to get here?"

"It's all good."

Cusack clicked off his BlackBerry and stepped out of line. He abandoned Litton's registered letter and the mudslide of distractions from bad credit. He marched out of the post office, determined to ace the most important interview of his career.

CHAPTER SIX

ACROSS TOWN . . .

Hedge funds are not the only place to make a killing. As Cusack worked his way toward Greenwich, Rachel stood at the corner of Park Avenue and Sixty-second Street. No one noticed her on the busy street, the way no one notices migraines except for the hapless soul with an ice pick inside the brain. Rachel checked the time once, twice, and reminded herself not to dally. Business was picking up.

She swigged her road coffee to stay alert. Long hours of surveillance, Rachel knew from experience, could be monotonous. "About as boring as the unemployment line," her daddy used to say. The physical conditions— too hot, too cold, no bathroom—sometimes required the fortitude of coal-walking ascetics.

Not today. She needed to stay on schedule, surveillance during lunch and a Botox procedure at two-thirty. At some point before six P.M., Rachel would duck out of the clinic to make a phone call. She had tossed and turned all last night, chewing over what to say.

"Focus," Rachel reminded herself.

Across the street she eyed 564 Park Avenue, one of New York's architectural gems. Marble base and crimson brick, the building rose five stories high before culminating in a mansard roof that peaked 130 feet over the sidewalk. The Georgian structure, a yellow flag whipping outside the third-floor balcony, conveyed stability and old-world charm.

Inside was the Colony Club, an exclusive women's organization dating back to luminaries like Anne Tracy Morgan, the daughter of J. P. Morgan. Its facilities included two dining rooms, a grand ballroom two stories high, library, card room, about forty bedrooms, and an oak-paneled gymnasium. In the basement a marble-and-tile swimming pool, surrounded by European baths, measured twenty by sixty feet.

The leash laws were refreshing, perhaps comforting to the women who gathered for lunch. Men could not roam the premises untethered or at will. The club rules required members to "escort" male guests at all times.

Rachel knew the layout from top to bottom, though not as a member. Slipping inside and casing the layout had been a breeze. Several of the grand dames had even mistaken her for one of their own. She smirked at the thought of applying. How would she describe her profession?

"Cleaner."

It was the Russian word for contract killers. A cleaner, according to popular usage, got rid of pests. A cleaner eliminated the mess. It was the word she chose for her ad in *Soldier of Fortune*. Not all that discreet. The Feds knew what "cleaner" meant. But so what. There was no subtle way to advertise murder for hire.

Later that afternoon Rachel would ask questions and assess whether her prospect could pay. Or whether he was law enforcement. She had purchased a disposable cell phone and handheld voice changer just for the occasion.

The precautions annoyed her. Too cloak-and-dagger. The whole business of prospecting, Rachel decided, was hard work. There was no high, no climax, none of the executioner's foreplay that she savored in the final minutes before a hit.

Finding her existing employer had been easy. He walked into Doc's clinic one day for a rosacea treatment. He groused about his work so much that Rachel finally suggested, "Maybe there's a different kind of solution, one you haven't considered."

"What do you mean?"

"Why don't you buy me a glass of wine after we finish."

That exchange occurred years ago. Since then Rachel's savings had grown, but not enough to pick up and move. Paris had been a dream ever since she watched *An American in Paris* and pretended Gene Kelly was her father. The dancer always looked so happy and kind in the soft, sometimes smoky light of the 1951 film.

Her employer was different. He was a business decision, a guy capable of turning fantasies into reality. Nothing more. Nothing less. Rachel often found him annoying. Demanding. Prone to warlike moods. Charming when it served his purposes. But she could always count on him for assignments, his one redeeming quality.

With that thought, Rachel returned to the present. For the second time that day, she reminded herself to focus—people, exits, anything outside the ordinary routine of her target.

Henrietta Hedgecock had been a member of the Colony Club for over forty years. She sat on the admissions committee and took pride in a lineage that traced back to Mrs. Florence Jaffray Harriman of Newport, who founded the club circa 1903.

At seventy-six years and 107 pounds, Hedgecock was fit. Her figure was trim. Her hair, snow white but satiny nonetheless, extended six inches longer than fashionable for women her age. Her eyes glistened the bright blue of sapphires. And she cut a striking figure in her signature Chanel suits.

Henrietta swam at the Colony Club every day, Monday through Friday. She entered the pool at exactly 11:15 A.M., finished well before the lunchtime swimmers arrived, and headed upstairs for lunch after working out—chicken salad and cucumber sandwiches, tea, and chocolate anything. On special occasions, she ordered a glass of sherry with her meal.

There was only one exception to the routine. On Thursdays, Hedgecock began swimming fifteen minutes early. She needed extra time to walk to the Post House on East Sixty-third, where she generally ordered the Ladies Lunch for twenty-five dollars and met Walter. He was seven years younger, and at age seventy-six, Henrietta suffered misgivings about referring to Walter as "my boyfriend." She might get a reputation as some kind of grandmother cougar.

Today was hump day. Henrietta swallowed her last bite of chocolate ice cream, pushed aside her tea, and made her way to the exit where she left four days a week at 1:45 P.M. On the way down the steps of the Colony Club she saw a blond woman in a beige cardigan and white nurse's uniform crossing the street. Henrietta suspected the woman was pretty but could not be sure given the huge sunglasses covering her face.

Right on time. Rachel smiled at Henrietta and continued north on Park Avenue. The older woman looked elegant from thirty feet but vulnerable from ten, defenseless as a trailer house in a tornado. Henrietta would walk north for several blocks before turning west and heading toward Fifth Avenue. She had followed the same pattern for the last two weeks running, except on Thursdays.

At Sixty-fifth and Park, Rachel crossed to the northwest side of the corner and pulled out a compact. She looked in the small mirror and watched Hedgecock stay on plan. The stately woman turned, same as always. Rachel knew what her father would say. He brought home all kinds of expressions from the bar.

"Regular as a duck goes barefooted."

Rachel checked the time. It was 1:53 P.M., enough surveillance for one day. She would return to the clinic by two P.M., plenty of time to prepare for Doc's Botox patient at two-thirty. Once he completed the procedure, she would grab a cab and make the call from her apartment.

Stalking Hedgecock, quizzing a new prospect, and keeping up the façade at the clinic—Rachel's schedule required discipline. She managed only because of one irrefutable truth. Doc was her bitch.

Never mind the desktop quickies. She controlled the timing, not Doc. He was the one who cleaned up the mess when they spilled Purell or scattered medical records across his office. On some occasions his steamy commentary drove her nuts. "You're amazing, baby," sounded way too *Men's Health* and hairless chest for her taste. But whatever. A boink every now and then seemed a fair price for career mobility.

Rachel appreciated her daytime identity as an RN. She relished the steady income. And there was nothing like a Form 1040 and regular tax payments to hide out in plain sight. It kept the Feds off her scent. The cover allowed her to bail out the world's problems one septuagenarian at a time.

CHAPTER SEVEN
THE BEST THINGS IN LIFE ARE FREE . . .

Jimmy hustled to his garage on Hudson. His thoughts had shifted to the impending interview, and he wondered whether Leeser would go the intimidation route. Self-esteem safaris were de rigueur in Hedgistan. The funds hunted stupidity, indecision, and other big game just for kicks.

There was no better sport than job-seeker humiliation. Making applicants stammer, soak out their armpits, and slog off in disgrace—that was big time for the interviewer. It took practice. But once mastered, skewering egos yielded roughly the same satisfaction as crunching roaches under Ferragamo loafers. A cold beer afterward, and the interrogator's day was a success.

Last week in Greenwich one quant rattled off the academic degrees of his colleagues. They all sounded like "MIT squared." And then, the preening complete, he posed the following hypothetical to Cusack:

"Assume you have nine balls and a balance scale. The balls all weigh the same, except for one that is heavier. How many times do you need to weigh the balls to find the heavy one?"

"Twice," replied Cusack.

"Care to elaborate?"

"Divide the balls into three groups of three. Weigh two groups against each other. If the scale balances, then you know the heavy ball is in the third group. If it doesn't balance, then the heavy ball is obviously on the side pulling lower. Now you're down to three balls. Weigh two of the remaining three against each other and go through the same process of elimination. If the scales balance, then it's the third ball. Otherwise, it's the heavier of the two on the scale."

Logic games were never the issue. Not with the quant last week. And not today. Jimmy was crafting words to explain the defection of eight wealthy investors and his firm's subsequent collapse.

"My fuckup," as he sometimes labeled Cusack Capital, was not a problem in and of itself. Hedge funds were okay with disasters. They self-destructed all the time. The bigger issue was the reasoning behind his collapse. He needed to sound smart, sure of himself. Strut a little. Finance guys sniffed out jitters the way guillotines found necks.

As he crossed the Willis Avenue Bridge, Cusack's cell phone rang. "Alex Krause here. I'm with Chase Auto Finance."

I don't need this.

Jimmy's thoughts turned to his mother. All piss and vinegar at age sixty-six, Helen Cusack drove a black Cadillac Escalade Platinum fully loaded with a dozen running lights too many. Now that Jimmy's dad was gone, she liked nothing better than rumbling out of Somerville with her bridge club in tow and thundering up to Gloucester, where the ladies ate lobster rolls at seafood shacks, drank white wine while bragging about grandchildren who were infant prodigies, and sucked in as much of the fresh ocean air as their lungs could hold. It was like the Senior Circuit for *Thelma and Louise*.

"Everybody wants to drive with me," Helen would say. "I feel like such a smarty pants."

"Ma, your car looks like the Batmobile," Cusack teased more than once, secretly pleased. His pleasure ran out of gas, however, when money got tight and Chase Auto Finance called.

"You're leasing a Cadillac for Helen Cusack?" asked Krause in a tinny voice.

To Cusack's ear, the question crashed down like cymbals. He knew what Krause wanted. "How can I help?"

"You're two months behind. Is there a problem?"

"No." Cusack smiled crookedly, radiating charm waves through the receiver. "May I call you Alex?"

"I prefer Mr. Krause."

"Does my mom know about the late payments?"

"Not to my knowledge."

"Can we keep it that way?"

"Well, I suppose," replied Krause, "the answer depends on you." He had already smoked out Cusack's weakness.

"I've been crushed at the office."

"Tell your therapist. When do I get payment?"

"If the check's not in the mail by Friday, Mr. Krause, I'll call you."

"What time?"

"Ten A.M."

"That would be good. We have a situation here. I hope we can work together." Krause hung up the phone without another word.

Car payments were one problem. Helen's three-family house, a time-sucking money pit, was another. Two years ago it was the kitchen. Another year it was the roof. Or it was the porch. Or it was the electricity. The drafty old windows no longer opened, and the timber house desperately needed a new furnace. The existing system was forty years old and heated all three units. It chugged and clanged all winter long and belched ominous black clouds whenever the burners fired. The furnace might croak any day.

The family had discussed a financial contract for years. It was informal, no longer spoken, but one everybody understood. "We'll pay your tuition," Cusack's dad used to say. "But take care of your mother, Jimmy. And your brothers, too, if they ever need help."

"Deal."

During his six years of college, business school, and horse-choking tuition, Cusack watched his parents go without comfortable furniture or reliable appliances. Without restaurants or vacations. Without creature comforts like new clothes or decent cars. Now his mother was an early widow, and Cusack insisted she live free of financial anxiety.

Money had never been a problem at Goldman. Cusack hated the place 364 days a year, but on day 365 he collected a fat, seven-figure bonus that turned the gulag into a resort. Historically, the investment bank had given him the capacity to say yes no matter what his family asked.

Things were different now. Cusack's financial avalanche was gathering momentum. And the one person who mattered the most, his wife, probably knew the least.

The ancestors of Emily "Emi" Phelps had lived on Beacon Hill for five generations. Through successive waves of children, the Phelps of Boston swapped DNA with New England's most prominent "wasperati." They married into families with surnames like Saltonstall, Thorndike, and Blodgett. They coupled with Gardners at least three times before turning to "seeing eye" Gardiners, named for the letter *i* in their last name, for another two.

With each new batch of Phelps, the family conscripted names from their patrician marriages. Her great-grandfather was Lowell Crocker Phelps. It could have been Lowell, Crocker, and Phelps LLC. Her grandfather hit the mother lode with four names. He was Quincy Choate Peabody Phelps, but friends called him "Scooter" for reasons nobody remembered.

Not once had there been a Cusack among the dense raft of *Mayflower* Yankees. And forget about the sons of plumbers. The Phelps were not the kind to marry refugees from "Slummerville."

Until now.

Driving north on I-95 toward LeeWell Capital, Jimmy tuned to Bloomberg radio and rubbed his sandy-brown hair, trimmed short on the sides. He subconsciously thumbed his jacket lapel and fidgeted with the flag-shaped pin, a gift from his mother that he always wore.

In a tradition dating to World War II, the stars represented the number of family members serving abroad in the military. His brother Jude was frying in the sand and 120-degree heat of Iraq. Jack was searching for a six-foot-four terrorist somewhere in the mountains of Afghanistan. The three *J*'s of Jude, Jack, and Jimmy had been inseparable as children.

Cusack also displayed the pin for Emi. But that was another matter. Right now, he wondered what to tell her about Litton. He already knew how their exchange would play out.

Emi: "Did you have a good day, sweetie?"

Cusack: "I talked with Smitty about our mortgage."

Emi: "Is there a problem?"

It would be that quick. Emi's face would cloud over, and she would press for details. Cusack always tried to protect her. She always sniffed out his bullshit, which triggered strategy sessions worthy of NATO.

I'm glad she's not a spender.

For all the summers on Martha's Vineyard and the weekends in Bermuda, Emi was a trash-and-treasure gal. Her idea of fun was rummaging for Prada at TJ Maxx on Saturdays. Cusack toyed with the two-star pin, his ever-present reminder, Emi's too.

The two would sit down, and she would organize. He could almost hear Emi say, "We cut here, here, and here. We sell the condo. We plant

St. Joseph upside down in one of the ficus pots. That's what Catholics do, right?"

Emi had expressed her misgivings the first time they spotted their condominium in New York's trendy Meatpacking District. "We can't afford it."

Jimmy had driven the $3 million mistake, partly from pride and partly from ambition. He refused to live anywhere resembling his childhood. The wooden floors of Helen's home creaked something fierce, even now after being redone. And the steam pipes hissed all night during Boston's bitter, gray winters.

"What's wrong with a little racket?" Emi argued. "Steam pipes give New England character."

In the end Cusack prevailed on the condo, but only after he conceded on the Beemer. "We don't need a new car, James. Not until we pay down our mortgage."

Since they bought the condo three years ago, their blue BMW had gone downhill. The engine seldom cranked the first time. It turned over and over, never firing until the key found just the right angle in the ignition cylinder. Or until Cusack gritted his teeth and groused, "Another adventure in precision physics." Once the haggard engine choked to life, the rusty old clunker spewed great plumes of blue-black smoke and rattled like a ghost from the sleek phenom tooled a decade earlier. But at least there were no car payments, the Beemer's only saving grace.

Pulling into Greenwich, Cusack rubbed his two-star pin one last time. Not so much for luck. The gesture was more of a tribute to his brothers, recognition of their different paths. Jude and Jack had excelled in school. Both were a step faster than him on the playing fields. Had things been different, had there been more money growing up, had his parents given either one of them the nudge, Jude or Jack could be the ones interviewing today.

Cusack's crooked grin returned, radiant and unrelenting. He was far from wistful. The thought of his brothers fortified him. Jude and Jack faced tougher challenges than he would ever know in finance.

So did Emi. Maybe that was why Cusack never opened up to his wife completely. There was no need to upset her. Or perhaps he hid his thoughts from force of habit. He maintained his guard during the day, self-defense in an industry where everybody sported brass knuckles. Cusack was confident without being cocky. But he shut the door. His head was off-limits.

Same thing at night. For as much as Jimmy loved Emi, he never revealed his worries down deep. He never burdened her with his misgivings. He wanted a job, partly to avoid discussion of their money problems.

A face-to-face confession reminded him too much of the black-and-whites from parochial school. They were the nuns who still wore traditional habits, not the squad cars favored by the Boston police. Every Tuesday, the good sisters marched his classroom full of heathens off to see the priests for another round of absolution. That was not the kind of relationship he wanted with his wife.

CHAPTER EIGHT

THE INTERVIEW . . .

Greenwich, Connecticut, home to 62,000 people, is the ceremonial capital of Hedgistan. At first the community looks like many other wealthy seaside towns in New England. During sultry summer days, heat rises off the sidewalks like the double helix vapors from burning cigarettes. And convertibles become the hair dryers of choice. Towheaded kids with the occasional freckle wear faded designer colors, Nantucket red or lagoon blue, and they all look like sailors whether or not they take lessons at the Indian Harbor Yacht Club on Steamboat Road.

The town pays attention to details, perhaps nowhere more evident than Greenwich Avenue. Careful topiaries, the kind groomed with nail files, sit outside spotless shops with brands ranging from Prada to Lacoste. When the weather grows hot, baskets of pomegranate begonias hang from black lampposts that look like exclamation points for everything perfect. The street is squeaky clean and lined with hunter-green trash cans that contain one slot for recycling and one for everything else. It is the town's soul, inviting and wide enough for a two-columned parade on the Fourth of July.

Greenwich could be Nantucket or Kennebunkport. It could be Newport or Marblehead. Town shuttles offer an early clue, however, that this place is different. So do a handful of black SUVs. They are more likely to carry the names of hedge funds than the logos from Holiday Inn, Hilton, or other hotels.

Somewhere around a hundred hedge funds are headquartered in Greenwich, just thirty-seven minutes from New York City by express train. And many hedge fund billionaires live in the tony community, even if they operate their empires somewhere else. There is Stevie Cohen, who runs SAC Capital a few exits up I-95 in Stamford. Ray Dalio is another. He lives in Greenwich and manages Bridgewater Associates in nearby Westport.

The Greenwich-based funds whip around $100 billion-plus in assets. They include the investment world's nouveau elite, firms like Tudor, ESL, and AQR. Whether at the Greenwich train station or watering holes after work, there are always clusters of finance jocks swapping ideas and trading stories about payouts, spectacular divorces, or investments that returned many times their capital. Anything about money.

LeeWell Capital operated from Greenwich Plaza, part of a two-building complex that once housed lawyers, shippers, and manufacturing headquarters. In those days the two suburban buildings hardly ever bubbled with commercial frenzy. The activity, such as it was, resembled the rapid eye movement of an afternoon nap. The center stirred twice every day, when tenants strolled in around nine A.M. and when they rushed home at four P.M. That was before the hedge funds arrived.

They rolled in, and Greenwich Plaza mutated into the Mount Olympus of Hedgistan—a title subject to dispute in all fairness. Rivals might argue that 55 Railroad Avenue is the real home of the gods. "Fifty-five" sits across from the train station and is conveniently located next to a Rolls-Royce dealership that also sells classic Ferraris, Aston Martins, and other four-wheeled Viagra. Or maybe Pickwick Plaza is the epicenter of hedge funds. That's the problem when everybody wants to be Zeus. There's no consensus.

The superpowers at Greenwich Plaza included global macro, convertible arbitrage, and other obscure-sounding investment disciplines. The hedge funds stormed the building with Bloombergs and BlackBerrys and their Bluetooth headsets. They brought proprietary trading models and governed the capital markets with the proverbial two-and-twenty: 2 percent annual fees and 20 percent cuts of investment returns.

True to form, these gods of Greenwich used long-short disciplines to manage their waistlines. They installed wine cellars in their offices and amassed take-out menus. Requisite stuff to work late and get long a few extra pounds. They reserved space for elliptical trainers and stationary bikes, whatever it took to short fat and stay trim.

They arrived in limousines, chauffeured by full-time drivers in Lincoln Town Cars or full-time spouses in BMWs, Mercedes, and the occasional Lexus SUV. Or they drove performance cars of every size, shape, and color. Their Maseratis and Ferraris would never see action on the switchbacks of Monte Carlo. But the six-figure autos looked great, nesting discreetly in the parking lots underneath the two buildings of Greenwich Plaza.

Armed with fierce checkbooks, the hedge funds drove rents up and the old guard out. Only one resolute law firm remained. And now, a cryptic god patois dominated every corner of the two buildings.

Elevator bank: "I'm short volatility."

Watercooler: "We thought we were buying alpha. Got beta instead."

Men's urinal: "We flushed synthetic CDOs long ago."

Lobby: "Orthogonal GARCH is so fucked."

It was here at Greenwich Plaza that LeeWell Capital had cranked out positive returns every year since 2000. Most years, the hedge fund was up 20 to 30 percent or more. Even during the frightful bear market from 2000 to 2002, when the Dow plunged three straight years, LeeWell made money.

Cusack parked his beat-up BMW next to a glacier-white Bentley convertible. Here at Greenwich Plaza, he sought a job, stable cash flow, and a little relief from Litton, Alex Krause, and all the other creditors standing in line.

You can hang meat in this place.

Cusack noticed the temperature first thing. He ignored CNBC's newscasters, who ranted about some company missing its numbers. He overlooked the tiger-maple walls all around him. It was chilly inside LeeWell Capital, icebox cold, because the air conditioner was cranking way too early for the season.

Jimmy strode up to the receptionist, who was wearing a cashmere sweater and holding a cup of tea to warm her hands. He had read dozens of the ace-your-interview books, and they all advised the same thing: "Your job starts at the front counter."

"You need a parka," Cusack observed, bright and agreeable.

The receptionist, rosy and brunette under a high-tech headset, reflected Cusack's cordial smile with a hundred watts of her own. "Cy sets the temperature at sixty-six. Says the brain functions better in the cold."

"I can already feel the power," he replied. "I'm Jimmy Cusack."

"Amanda. We've been expecting you. I'll let Shannon know you're here."

"Shannon?"

"Cy's personal assistant," she answered while dialing.

Behind the receptionist was a large black-and-white photo, two men shaking hands and hamming for the camera. Jimmy identified Leeser at once. Everyone on Wall Street recognized the long-haired hedge fund manager, who resembled a forty-something Tommy Lee Jones. But Cusack had never seen the other man—bald, blubbery, and bespectacled.

"Who's in the photo with Mr. Leeser?" he asked after the receptionist clicked off the phone.

"Byron Stockwell. He cofounded our firm."

"Of course."

"Hey, and here's a little hint," the receptionist added. "Lose the Leeser."

"Excuse me?"

"It's Cy around the office."

"Gotcha. And thanks, Amanda."

At that instant a tall African-American man, military bearing and Ranger eyes, stepped through a glass door to the right of the receptionist. He surveyed Cusack, inspected the two-star pin on his lapel, and stuck out an enormous hand.

"I'm Shannon."

At six foot four and 240 pounds, the big black man looked three parts human and one part Mack truck. His deep voice blared like the bass horn of an eighteen-wheeler. The wide gap between his front teeth resembled an ornate grille. And his clean-shaven head gleamed brighter than any chrome bumper ever produced in Detroit.

"I'm Jimmy Cusack."

"I can see that. I'll get Nikki." With that the big man turned and disappeared into the inner sanctum of LeeWell Capital.

I can see that?

Cusack turned back to the receptionist. "Who's Nikki?"

"Cy's secretary."

"I thought Shannon—"

"No," she explained, "Cy's 'personal assistant,' as in driver and body-guard."

"It's okay," Cusack teased. "I'm not packing." He was still trying to connect with the receptionist.

"Don't mind Shannon. It's his job to check everybody out. And he's a teddy bear once you know him."

The glass door opened again. A short woman, no more than five foot two, with bobbed black hair, extended her hand and said, "I'm Nikki. Thanks for meeting on such short notice." She appeared to be in her early thirties, spoke with a voice raspy from phones or Thursday-night cosmopolitans, and wore a diamond chip in her nose.

The small stud glimmered ever so discreetly under the fluorescent lights of LeeWell Capital. It almost looked elegant paired with Nikki's trim black suit. But the jewelry was the last thing he expected to see on any CEO's secretary—even here deep inside Hedgistan.

"I'm glad to be here, Nikki."

"Cy has back-to-back meetings through the end of the month," she explained. "It was either today or late May. As it was, he canceled on his architect to speak with you."

"How long do we have?" asked Jimmy.

"Fifteen, maybe twenty minutes," she said. "Cy wants to see you right away."

Gut reaction: LeeWell Capital confused Cusack as he trailed after Nikki. He liked the photo tribute to Cy's cofounder as well as the receptionist's hints about a casual work environment. He appreciated Nikki's nose stud, a personal statement that would never survive inside most of the starched-collar corridors of finance.

The chill temperature and the iceberg-sized bodyguard—they were another matter. It was like the corporate yin and yang lacked equilibrium. Cusack puzzled over what to expect during the next fifteen minutes.

Cy's office opened yet another world. There was no sports memorabilia. There were no photos of family, save for one absolute ripper on the desk. Two tanned and tousle-haired twins, three, maybe four years old at the most, screamed little-girl happy in the mother of all Kodak moments. There were four LCD panels on a credenza behind Leeser's desk, but the room hardly looked like an office.

Paintings and line drawings, dozens, maybe even hundreds, overwhelmed the walls. This was not the office of a money Mensa who made snap decisions, buying and selling complex securities at mind-numbing speed. It was an art museum, a curator's whimsy, a vast expanse of portraits and landscapes fighting abstracts for space anywhere.

Cusack could not differentiate between expressionism and impressionism. But judging from the sheer number of works, he thought every "ism" in the history of Western civilization might be present. He assumed any one of the pieces would satisfy his $17,507.19 mortgage payment every month, probably with cash in return.

Jimmy had read the press about Cyrus Leeser: tough kid from Hell's Kitchen, now a regular at Sotheby's auctions. The art community respected Leeser's knack for recognizing and identifying new talent. Hedgistan admired the way he made money. Cusack wished he had taken art history, even one course, anything to bridge the worlds of finance and taste. Instead, he had focused on math and economics and saved English literature courses for the occasional treat.

"I'm Cy," Leeser said, extending his hand.

"Jimmy Cusack."

The two men appraised each other in person for the first time. Jimmy reminded Cy of the Irish Catholics from his old neighborhood, except that Mickey and the other guys never worked in finance. They were either dead or stamping license plates inside prisons.

Cusack had no idea how to interpret Leeser's magnetic smile. He expected a test. Cy would look for an Achilles' heel, a crack in self-confidence, anything to determine how Jimmy handled pressure. He expected Cy to zero in on the little fiasco known as Cusack Capital.

"Ginger or Mary Ann?"

"Excuse me?" asked Cusack as he sank into a cappuccino-colored guest chair. The leather seat, supple with the worn patina of old money, eased under his weight. He forgot all about the temperature set to sixty-six.

"You heard. Ginger or Mary Ann?"

"Mary Ann." Cusack wondered if Leeser expected something more cerebral.

"I'm a Ginger man," laughed Cy. "And there's nothing deep about *Gilligan's Island.*"

Cusack smiled, so wide and winning that deep creases replaced all the crookedness around his lips. "I expected you to go the quant-terror route on me."

"That shit puts people on edge," Leeser said. "You don't get inside their heads."

"I like your art," Cusack ventured, warming to Leeser and taking charge of the interview. That was the other advice inside all the how-to books: control the discussion.

"Are you a collector?"

"No. But I know you command great respect in the art world."

"Stevie Cohen is the one who commands respect," replied Cy. "I'd give anything for his Edvard Munch." Leeser spoke with the unmistakable inflection of New York's streets, a staccato rhythm like double-punching a speed bag. "Anything catch your eye?"

"Your daughters are beautiful." Cusack pointed to the photo of the twin four-year-olds.

"That's how I think of them."

"What do you mean?"

"They're teenagers now, but they'll always be my little girls."

He'd pass Emi's smell test.

"So, Jimmy," Leeser began, "why'd you go to Columbia instead of Harvard?"

"Because the People's Republic of Cambridge is seven square miles surrounded by reality. At least, that's what we believe in Somerville."

"I like that," said Leeser. "Tell me about your hedge fund."

Cusack shifted uncomfortably, and his heart beat faster.

"But before you answer, Jimmy, let's put one thing on the table."

"Okay?"

"I almost blew up in 2000. The experience consumed me, and I bet it's consuming you."

"The fast track was a crowded trade at Goldman," replied Cusack, selling and spinning, hiding from personal revelations. "I founded my company to break from the pack."

He knew the real answer. The ghost of Cusack Capital was eating him every minute of every day. But playing it safe would have haunted his thoughts forever. Cusack could almost hear his dad, the way Liam described plumbing. "I run my own business, Jimmy. You should do the same. It's not whether you win or lose. It's whether you go for it."

"Don't get me wrong," Cusack continued with Leeser. "Goldman is the Parris Island of finance. Great training."

"Yeah, maybe." Cy leaned back in his chair, hands behind his long black hair, unimpressed by the boot camp analogy. "What buried your fund?"

"Bank investments. I was down thirty percent, when my investors bailed."

"Our shop is good at one thing." Leeser's bloodless smile would send competitors reaching for their necks. "That's making money. I hire people who can't *afford* to lose."

Leaning forward, Cusack replied, "That's why I'm here."

"Why don't you reboot?"

"What do you mean?"

"Start over. John Meriwether blew up at Long-Term Capital."

"Now he's managing three billion down the road from here," Jimmy acknowledged.

"Where else can you lose four billion and stick the landing?" whooped Leeser.

"Deep pockets help."

"How much did you lose, Jimmy?"

"About sixty million. That's why I can't afford to lose."

Especially when my father-in-law was the lead investor.

It was Caleb Digby Phelps III. And it was Caleb, not Cal. In the tradition of Phelps men, Caleb attended Harvard and joined the Porcellian—an exclusive club of Y chromosomes where the members blackballed Franklin D. Roosevelt years earlier. It was there, knee deep among the elite and the effete, that Caleb honed the savage business instincts of a Grim Reaper-in-law.

According to urban legend, "Porkers" took up collections for club members who had not amassed one million dollars by age forty. Caleb never needed the help. And not because he inherited a dusty fortune dating back to the family's rum-running days during the 1700s. He was a business animal.

Caleb multiplied his trust at least ten times. He bought a nothing-special insurance business and injected new life. Phelps Financial was New England's largest insurance agency, a cash cow that funded real estate investments. The family owned properties throughout downtown Boston, including several harbor sites bordering the New England Aquarium. Caleb's losses at Cusack Capital, while significant, were modest relative to the family's holdings.

"Why should I hire you?" Cy peered at Jimmy and waited for an answer.

It was the movie scene where Hollywood cops scream, "Take the shot!" It was the moment Cusack had rehearsed a thousand times in front of a mirror and during other interviews.

"Because nobody like me will ever walk through your front door, Cy."

Leeser cocked an eyebrow and stared at Cusack. He waited and said nothing, but his body language spoke volumes. "This better be good."

Take the shot.

"Because this market is about to flush itself. There will be chaos, Cy. And while others are sucking their thumbs and hiding behind spreadsheets, I'll already have a plan. Because my bank investments buried me. And that will never happen again. Never. I can see the warning signs now, and frankly, I don't like what's on the horizon. Because I'll turn the lights on every morning and turn them off every night, and there's only one thing on my mind while I'm breathing. That's making money. Because the hedge funds that survive are coming out stronger and tougher on the other side, and they're taking market share. Mark my words. There won't be a bank big enough to hold all their cash. Because I want to get rich. And if I increase your net worth ten times, it'll be the happiest day of my life, assuming a few shekels drop on my lap. Because I'll do what it takes."

"You mean that?"

"Every word." Cusack projected the unwavering cool of an old pro. It was his turn to wait.

Cy gave no hint what he was thinking. His face was inscrutable: coal emotionless eyes, rutted brow, no smile and no frown. "What do you know about the way we invest?"

"Not much."

"Good—"

"You focus," Cusack continued, surprising Leeser, "on companies worth less than two billion. Public filings show you own a huge chunk in Bentwing Energy, where you sit on the board and are something of an activist."

"What do you think about Bentwing?"

"Some estimates say the world will run out of oil in forty years," replied Cusack. "What's not to like about alternative energy?"

"Keep going."

"I doubt you borrow much money."

"Why's that?" asked Leeser.

"Because it's too risky, and your returns are too consistent."

Leeser's eyes glimmered for the first time. "You've done your homework for a guy we called two hours ago."

"I keep my ear close to the ground."

"What don't you know about my firm?"

"How you hedge," Cusack answered. "You must invest in some asset, some kind of insurance to protect against losses."

"I could tell you, but I'd have to kill you." Every trader in the business used that line at least once.

"Do you short?" Cusack pressed.

"You don't give up," Cy observed, not in an angry way but abrupt and factual.

"Force of habit from the old neighborhood."

"I like that, Jimmy. Before we discuss my hedging model, two things need to happen."

"Okay?"

"First, you sign a noncompete."

Is this a job offer?

"I'd be surprised if you didn't ask for one, Cy."

"Good. Second, you need to apprentice for a while. I won't disclose our secret sauce to just anybody."

"Secret sauce—I like that." Cusack repeated Leeser's words by instinct, an old trick among finance pros.

Cy picked up the phone and instructed Nikki, "Cancel my appointments." Then he turned and said, "Let me explain why you're here, Jimmy."

Back in New York City, a different kind of interview was taking place. "I require twenty-five thousand dollars to proceed." The electronic voice changer turned Rachel's honey Texan tones into something robotic over the phone, impossible to determine whether male or female.

"No problem," the man countered in a diplomat's voice worthy of UN peace negotiations. "When do you need the money?"

Rachel sensed trouble. The prospect was too easy. Nobody said yes just like that. "I need fives and tens," she said, testing him. "Nothing bigger."

"That will take a while," he ventured cautiously. "Two, maybe three days."

Not a good sign, she decided. Only the Feds knew how long it took to amass five thousand five-dollar bills. "You sound serious."

As though reading her qualms, the man asked, "How do I know you won't run off with my money?"

"You don't." The voice changer felt awkward in her hand.

"Others work for less," he insisted.

"You want a bargain," she snapped, "go to Walmart."

"I'll get the money," he retreated, but still cool. "My wife is a problem."

"You don't understand what I do," Rachel interrupted. He was moving too fast. Something was wrong. She clicked off the phone. She had always followed her instincts in the past. This guy smelled like a cop, too much, too soon.

Rachel hated the voice changer. She used sex to control men, which was impossible when you sounded like R2D2. Too electronic. Even worse, there was no face-to-face. She relied on visual cues, always a problem over the phone. Now the guy was gone. Fed or whatever, he had been a miserable waste of time.

On the way back to the clinic, Rachel tossed her disposable cell phone into a garbage can at the corner of Eightieth and Park. Her March financial statement had been less than inspiring. She muttered, "I'm lucky to have one steady employer."

CHAPTER NINE

REYKJAVIK . . .

"Trading desks are waging World War Three. Which means, sir, there's only one way to make money. We fight back. We crush Cyrus Leeser and humiliate his people. Doing nothing is worse than grabbing our ankles and hoping for the best."

A little hyperbolic, Ólafur knew. But absolute conviction was necessary. Otherwise, the old man would take forever to make a decision. It was five hours ahead in Reykjavik. Ólafur's speech was still reverberating through his thoughts as he stewed at Gaukur á Stöng.

Ólafur nursed a vodka martini, his second round since leaving the office. He needed a third and maybe a fourth to soothe his nerves. The alcohol would bring calm and the clarity to dissect his one-on-one meeting with Chairman Guðjohnsen of Hafnarbanki.

Their discussion had exceeded his wildest expectations. Guðjohnsen bought the whole program. The last twenty seconds were the problem.

"It's time to demonstrate what happens to our enemies."

"What do you mean?" asked the chairman.

"Hafnarbanki is trading at eight hundred and fifty kronur. We're down twenty-nine percent since December, because of LeeWell and its lies. We can't hide and close our eyes. Those bastards won't go away. Nor will their cronies."

It was risky speaking to the chairman like that. But Ólafur, ever hawkish, took the chance. Guðjohnsen owned more shares of Hafnarbanki than anyone else in Iceland. He stood to lose or recover the most as the stock price roller-coastered.

"Are you recommending legal action?" asked the venerable old man, his brow wrinkling under a shock of silver-white hair.

Ólafur spotted the puzzled expression. He had waited for this moment, rehearsed his lines for hours. "Courts take forever. There's only one solution: shore up our defenses and fight."

"Exactly what do you mean?"

"We get our Qatari friends to buy shares of Hafnarbanki."

"What makes you think they'll invest, Ólafur?"

"We'll lend them the money."

The chairman said nothing.

"On a nonrecourse basis," the younger banker added. If the Qataris defaulted, in other words, Hafnarbanki could not sue for losses. It could only repossess its shares.

Guðjohnsen's eyes narrowed into slits. "They have all upside and no downside."

"Exactly."

"You think this risk is acceptable?"

"I have absolute faith," replied Ólafur, "in your vision and our bank's future." What would Guðjohnsen say—that he lacked confidence in his own leadership?

Again, the chairman's eyes narrowed, as though he were calculating the impact on his portfolio. "I like the idea of helping our stock price."

"That's step one."

"What else?"

"We attack the single biggest position in LeeWell Capital's portfolio the same way they attacked Hafnarbanki."

Ólafur had studied the hedge fund since February. From public filings, he estimated its stake in one company equaled 15 percent of total assets. Maybe more. Bentwing Energy Group traded under the ticker symbol BEG, and Cyrus Leeser sat on the board. It was the core position in Leeser's portfolio.

"What's the purpose?" objected Guðjohnsen. "We're not in the revenge business."

"We'll make money on the trade and send a message to the enemy."

"Which is what?" the chairman asked.

"Fuck with our stock, and we'll bury you."

"You think this message is important, Ólafur?"

"Like I said, we're at war. Unless we strike, every hedge fund in Greenwich will short our stock until it falls another thirty percent."

Guðjohnsen said nothing for a moment. He was known for manipulating subordinates with awkward pauses. "What can go wrong?"

"My sources say LeeWell Capital hedges risk with a secret, no-fail technique."

"But you're not convinced?"

"It's impossible to eliminate all risk. 'Risk-free' sounds too good to be true."

"And what else?" the chairman asked. "I hear something in your voice."

The younger banker hesitated. "I think LeeWell Capital is borrowing way too much money."

"But?"

"I can't prove it. And if I'm wrong, we'll lose money betting against Bentwing."

"You think we should take this risk?"

"Yes, because the Qataris are on our side."

The chairman raised his eyebrows, both surprised and pleased by his subordinate's homework. He said nothing.

"If we both dump shares of Bentwing," Ólafur continued, "we're more likely to win. The stock will fall from all the selling, and we'll make money on our short. That's my quid pro quo with the Qataris for making a nonrecourse loan."

Chairman Guðjohnsen looked at Ólafur with an undecipherable expression, something between shock and awe. The older man's brow creased, and he didn't speak at first. He finally broke the silence and said, "Now I understand why your nickname is 'Mr. Ice.'"

The chairman's words sounded like a compliment. But that's when their conversation soured.

Halfway through his third martini, Ólafur didn't feel like "Mr. Ice." Cerebral and rational at the office, he soothed his colleagues when they groaned about the bank's share price.

"Don't worry. It's just the markets at work."

The words sounded good. But deep inside, Mr. Ice hated risk. He owned way too much of the bank's stock on margin. Every 3 percent decline rattled him, and the rebounds turned him silently euphoric. Of course, there had been few celebrations with Hafnarbanki down 29 percent since December.

Ólafur's daily regimen of hangovers masked his inner angst. It was easy to appear calm when you felt like shit. The banker wondered, however, whether this technique would continue to work. That afternoon he had doused himself with a brand-new risk. His career was on the line.

Guðjohnsen said, "Make the loan to the Qataris and start trading."

"It's the right thing to do, sir. The Qataris will buy Hafnarbanki shares right away. And we'll take our time shorting Bentwing. We'll do it right."

The chairman's approval should have been cause to rejoice. But as he left, his hand on the doorknob, he destroyed the feel-good moment. "There's just one thing, Ólafur."

"Yes, sir."

The white-haired chairman, wizened and cool during the storm, stated with the coldness of a shark, "You've done great work."

"Thank you."

"But if our war goes bad, you're fired." The chairman paused and added, "And your job may be the least of your problems."

"Meaning what, sir?"

"If anybody learns about our loan to the Qataris, you're going to jail."

"But—"

"I'm not taking the fall, Ólafur."

Mr. Ice ordered martini number four. Finding courage in the vodka, he considered the Romans. They destroyed Hannibal, raped the women of Carthage, and poured salt onto the city's ruins. He could use their help with LeeWell Capital.

CHAPTER TEN

THE INTERVIEW . . .

Cusack had hated interviews ever since college. The talk was boring, two people united by a common desire to be anywhere else except a dental chair. The interviewer was digging. He was selling. And the job hinged on whether the interviewer was digging what he was selling.

Interviews usually ended flat. "We'll get back to you" meant a letter two weeks later that started, "Thank you for your interest." After the decency of a paragraph break, the sender continued, "We are sorry." The words sounded nice, but they translated, "You're joking, right?"

The alternative was just as bad. Callbacks equaled another round of digging and sniveling as necessary. The whole process struck Cusack as an assault on the brain, possibly exceeded by reality television. But even there, it was debatable which was worse.

This interview was different. Cy dispensed with the artifice. "I need help growing my business." He leaned across the desk, and his manner changed. He was no longer the interviewer. He was the decision maker, the star quarterback urging a teammate to join his huddle. "You can take us to the next level, Jimmy."

"How much money do you manage?"

"Eight hundred million, give or take."

"With your track record," Cusack observed, "it should be double."

"Agreed. But I need a pro to handle our investors."

"I'm hungry."

"Have you ever considered sales?" asked Leeser.

It's a career graveyard for fuckups.

"I manage money," replied Cusack, avoiding the urge to say, "No way."

"Don't kid yourself. We all sell. Besides, you know how to listen. I bet people whisper shit in your ear all the time."

"Tell me what you have in mind, Cy."

"You raised two hundred million right out of the gates."

"Some of that was performance. We made money the first year."

"Doesn't matter. You're a born salesman, Jimmy."

"I was building a company."

"Which is why I want you on the team at LeeWell Capital."

You're good.

"You'll be involved in most portfolio decisions," added Leeser. "We're a small shop, and everybody wears different hats."

"How many people work here?"

"Sixteen in all. We have a kick-ass trader named Victor Lee. There's Nikki, my assistant, Amanda, our receptionist, and several other people in accounting and finance."

"Why the bodyguard?" asked Cusack, referring to the big man with the gap between his front teeth.

"Shannon is a key player."

"Do you have security problems, Cy?"

"We all make stupid money," Leeser explained. "My receptionist drives a sixty-thousand-dollar car. It's just inviting trouble."

"But—"

"You know what happened to Eddie Lampert at ESL Investments," Cy continued. "He was kidnapped in the parking lot outside his office."

"I still can't believe he negotiated his own release."

"I don't leave anything to chance, Jimmy, which is why you'll be a great addition."

Cusack could feel himself yielding—Cy's flattery and Litton's ever-present drumbeat. "You said I'd be involved in 'most portfolio decisions.' What do you mean?"

"I do all the hedging," Cy replied. "But with time we can talk about that, too."

"The secret sauce," Cusack stated, lingering on the words.

"You think Coke's senior guys learn the formula day one?"

"Is this an offer?"

"We need to talk money," replied Leeser.

" 'Stupid money.' "

"There are never any complaints on bonus day. Nobody leaves Lee-Well."

Cusack smiled crookedly but said nothing. He felt his face redden and hoped it did not show. That was the problem with adrenaline, veins, and fair Irish features. Try as he might, he could never hide his emotions. Bluffing was out of the question. At Wharton, his friends referred to him as "ATM" whenever they played poker.

"It's like this," said Leeser. "Pay peanuts, and you get monkeys. I don't want monkeys."

The interview progressed. There was more discussion, more give and take. The two men finally circled the all-important topic of money.

"I'll pay you a salary of two hundred and fifty thousand and a minimum bonus of one million dollars. Subject to one condition."

Cusack considered the offer for a moment. After tax, his take-home salary would not cover mortgage payments. Everything was riding on his bonus. "How would you feel about refinancing a three point one million mortgage?" He had added $100,000 to the existing balance on his mortgage, just in case. He still faced late fees and penalties from Litton.

"Five and three quarters." Leeser never blinked.

"Interest only with one annual payment?"

"Done," Leeser agreed. "But let's make the first payment due in February. That's when I pay bonuses."

"Speaking of which, what's the condition?"

"Our portfolio needs to be up ten percent," said Leeser. "Otherwise, I don't pay bonuses. Not to you. Not to me. Not to anybody."

"What if I bring in two hundred million?" objected Cusack. "That's twenty-five percent of the portfolio. That's great performance."

"Doesn't matter. One bad year, and we're toast. In our business, everybody is a redemption or two from shutting down."

"Don't I know," Cusack said. "Don't I know."

Forty minutes later Cusack headed out of LeeWell Capital with a job offer sketched out on the back of an envelope. Literally. The proposal was not perfect. But it might work.

After saying good-bye to Nikki, and Amanda the receptionist, Cusack shook hands with Shannon, who stared him out the front door. He never met Victor Lee, the head trader at LeeWell Capital. It made no difference. Job offer in hand, Jimmy smiled broadly, crookedly, and from ear to ear.

Down in the lobby Cusack headed past a chest-high sculpture of disembodied wings. The artist named the work *Pegasus* after the horse from Greek mythology whose father was Poseidon the god of everything underwater and whose mother was the snake-headed Medusa. Jimmy thought the lineage a fine choice for a building full of hedge funds.

On the way home Cusack stopped at a drugstore and bought a scratch-and-win lottery ticket on principle. His luck, it seemed, had changed for the better. And now he had a decision to make.

Sure, there was downside. Cy's offer thrust Cusack into a career crossroads—sales versus portfolio management. Everything was riding on performance. If LeeWell Capital missed the 10 percent hurdle, Cusack would forego a bonus and default on his annual mortgage payment. The offer, however, beat the registered alternative waiting for him back at the post office.

CHAPTER ELEVEN

Cusack burst out of the elevator and bounded down the corridor. His building, on Gansevoort Street just under Little West Twelfth, once housed brawny men in blood-soaked aprons who spent their days hacking great racks of butchered beef. Everything changed in the 1990s when developers arrived with legions of carpenters.

Now a different kind of butcher occupied the building. Lawyers and investment bankers kissed their spouses good-bye each morning. They traded the soaring ceilings, exposed brick, and designer kitchens for cubicle farms, where they spent their days slaughtering opponents from rival firms.

In the crook of his left shoulder, Jimmy cradled lemon-colored roses. He had chosen the shade in tribute to Madame Olenska, the heroine who receives yellow roses in Edith Wharton's classic *The Age of Innocence*. Cusack had always appreciated Olenska's irreverence, the way she flouted society's expectations during the 1870s. It made no difference that she was a fictional character.

The bouquet was huge, petals everywhere, two dozen roses in all. Cusack rapped on the door with his right hand. He had keys but waited for his wife to answer anyway. Surprise, showmanship, a spray of long-stemmed roses—panache was everything in the romance business. Cusack checked the two-star pin on his lapel to ensure it was visible.

Seconds later the door opened. Emi resembled so many other New England women from the wholesome tribe of L.L. Bean and the great outdoors: slim, athletic, and not much in the way of makeup. Her brown hair gleamed like brushed satin when she pulled it back in a ponytail. Her blue eyes sparkled with the light, perhaps the distortion, of a thousand sapphire prisms. Emi stood two inches shorter than Cusack in her bare feet, nudged him by a hair when wearing clogs, and completely dwarfed him in heels.

"Hello?" Emi asked, betraying her usual control.

It was not, "Hello. I love you. How was your day at the office, James?" Most of the time, Emi addressed Cusack as "James." So did Caleb.

It was not, "Hello. I'm aching for you. Let's get naked, Bevis, and go to bed five minutes ago."

Cusack was not "James" all the time. When they were holding each other, Emi called him "Boris" or "Bluto" or some other phantom lover just to be provocative. She liked *B*'s in bed for some reason. It was her joke, Emi's buoyant banter with her beau.

And it was not, "Hello. Who the fuck are you?" Emi was too good-natured, far too kind to bark at anyone. But there was no "dear" included, no hint of Barclay or Blythe or even Brady. No recognition whatsoever.

Jimmy had seen her blank look before, those confused eyes that struggled with identities. He had heard the same "hello" many times, the unmistakable hint of doubt. And he loved his wife without reservation.

Cusack never heard of "prosopagnosia" before Emi. He discovered the word the hard way, early during their relationship in college. They passed on the street, and she did not recognize him. Had no clue who he was. Walked right past without so much as a wink. Left him slack-jawed in the middle of a busy intersection. Made him wonder what he had done wrong. That was after several weeks together and a string of happy *B*'s.

"Prosopagnosia," Emi later explained, "is sometimes called 'face blindness.' We can't distinguish the features of people we know, even friends and family."

"You can't tell who I am at a dinner party?"

"Short term, I'm okay. It's the next day that's a problem. I forget faces."

"You wouldn't recognize Hugh Jackman?"

"Probably not."

People with prosopagnosia can distinguish among eyes and noses and different kinds of chins. Assembling the pieces, however, is like distinguishing among rocks sanded smooth by weather over long stretches of time. Nearly impossible.

Emi's case was not severe in a clinical sense. Her struggles were imperceptible to most everyone other than Cusack. But they were real. She sometimes failed to identify him, especially in crowds.

Because of these recognition problems, Emi opted for a career with reptiles and worked as a herpetologist at the Bronx Zoo. She loved reptilian colors and textures. Their shapes were easy to distinguish, their markings no problem for her particular case of prosopagnosia.

Through the years she developed many tools to identify her husband, who lacked the multicolored stripes of Gila monsters or the red-and-green webbing of Tokay Geckos. She depended on his voice. His scent. His square jaw and cockeyed smile. The faint cleft in his chin helped, but Emi used one other no-fail trick to identify her James.

Emi spotted the two-star pin on Cusack's lapel, and her smile widened enough for the world to forget Mona Lisa. She hopped straight up and wrapped her long legs around Cusack's lean torso and the two dozen roses. She squeezed with all her might, oblivious to the thorns digging into her thighs and his chest.

Cusack carried his wife into the condominium. He lurched this way and that, padding through their foyer on the Oriental rugs from Turkey. Her clogs dropped to the floor as he struggled to keep his balance. She had morphed into a giant octopus, all arms and eight-foot legs, suction cups everywhere. She gripped and groped, consuming her husband from all directions at once.

"What's this all about?" asked Cusack, surprised by her fervor.

Emi smothered the words as her husband spoke. She kissed him once, twice, the second time sloppier than the first, and pulled back. She inspected his face, gently caressing his cheeks and chin with the deft touch of a lover who had been there before. She finally relaxed her thighs and slid to the floor.

"Yikes," he teased, "let me know when the coast is clear."

"The roses are beautiful." Emi took them from Cusack, and the two walked into their kitchen appointed with granite counters, imported tiles, and the other accoutrements of a bloated mortgage. "What's the occasion?"

"Who said they're for you?" Cusack asked with an impish smile. Then he added, "I have some news."

"Me, too," Emi replied. She glowed. Her blue eyes twinkled, more breathtaking than all the stars of New England.

In that instant Cusack decided Emi's ivory-snow complexion had never looked so pure. There were no worry lines on her forehead or subtle crow's-feet extending from the corners of her eyes. None of the body's evil tricks that surface in the thirties, gain momentum in the forties, and raise all-out hell during the fifties. Even as Emi arranged the roses in a vase, cutting here and fluffing there, she radiated the unusual blend of peace and energy.

"You first," Cusack said, parentheses framing the corners of his mouth. He grabbed an Australian cabernet from their sleek galley kitchen, poured one glass, and started to pour the second.

"None for me," Emi interrupted. No more than an ounce of the Wolf Blass had splashed into her glass.

Cusack's brown eyebrows arched with surprise. Emi never drank to excess. Nor did she go without. She always nursed a glass of wine when they unwound together in the evenings. "So what's your news, Em?"

"I just told you."

"Boy gawd, girl," he teased in the Somerville dialect of his youth. "You don't make it easy."

Emi said nothing. She burrowed into his eyes with her sapphires. She sparkled from ear to ear, happy and cryptic all at once. "I just told you."

Cusack blinked once, then again. He sipped his cabernet and studied the second wineglass, mostly empty. All of a sudden, he got it.

"Hah," Cusack cheered. "You're pregnant."

Emi nodded yes, her face as soft and serene as a mountain lake on a still summer night.

"How long?" he asked, placing his glass on the counter and hugging Emi again.

"Six weeks. Seven tops."

Cusack kissed her on the lips. She tasted like a cross between red lipstick and something sweet. He tasted like cabernet.

"Did you win the lottery?" she asked.

"No. And what makes you think I bought a ticket?"

"There's scratch-off goop under your fingernails from one of those games." Emi cocked her left eyebrow and tilted her head slightly to the right. She saved her Sherlock Holmes face just for these occasions.

Emi Cusack saw everything—errant eyebrows, stained cuffs, nervous tics—everything except faces and bills. The invoices that originally went to the office now landed in a PO box. Her powers of observation, Jimmy decided, compensated for the prosopagnosia.

"Next time I'll use a quarter to scratch," Cusack confessed to Emi. "And no, I didn't win the lottery. It's better."

"Okay?"

"LeeWell Capital offered me a job."

"Hah," she whooped, echoing Cusack from before. "Are you taking it? I want to hear everything! How come you didn't call from the car?"

"I have my reasons."

Cusack had deliberated about his career and mortgage woes all the way home from Greenwich. His misgivings about sales, however, no longer mattered. Emi, beautiful and slightly broken, was six or seven weeks pregnant. He was a dad.

LeeWell offered Jimmy Cusack a fresh start, a chance to ring the cash register. He could make big bucks at LeeWell. More money than three blocks of Somerville plumbers, carpenters, and bus drivers earned in aggregate. More money in one year than Cusack's father earned his entire career.

"I want you focused on one thing," Leeser explained earlier that day. "More money and more growth for LeeWell. I want you thinking about our company in the shower, not your mortgage payments."

"There are a few details," Cusack replied to Emi, "we still need to work out." He tried to sound nonchalant. Force of habit from finance. "It's more of a sales job than what I've done in the past. But LeeWell Capital is a small shop, and I think my role will grow over the long term."

"You'll be great," she said, sensing hesitation. "Dad says you can sell ice cubes to Eskimos."

"Door-to-door at the igloos if Caleb has his way."

"Oh, stop it," Emi scolded playfully. "Grab your wine, Barney, and tell me everything," she ordered, leading him to the bedroom.

"You want a purple dinosaur?" he teased. "I'll show you a purple dinosaur."

"Let's go with Buster."

CHAPTER TWELVE

Cy Leeser cruised the rolling hills of Greenwich in his cream-colored Bentley, top down. Past the stone border walls that never end. Through the area known as "Mid-Country," where newer mansions abut the roads and stately 1920 homes hide at the rear of the properties. He glanced at Judge Judy's sprawling summer estate on the south side of Round Hill Road and shook his head.

The *New York Post* dubbed her manor "Judyville." The 24,000-square-foot residence resembled a transplant from Normandy, but without the fine patina of wear and tear that makes the French countryside so charming. The *Post* was unfair, Leeser decided. Sure, the house included ten hand-carved marble fireplaces and ceilings that soared two stories high. But there were only thirteen bathrooms.

Judyville was nothing compared to Valery Kogan's proposal. The Russian billionaire intended to erect a 27,000-square-foot super-mansion, complete with twenty-six bathrooms and enough flushing power to drain the Atlantic. Kogan's architectural plans included a Turkish bath, Finnish bath, and even a dog-grooming salon. Now, that was a Greenwich theme park.

Give the judge a break, Leeser thought.

Judyville required only five hundred lightbulbs. Paul Tudor Jones, the hedge fund billionaire, put up fifteen thousand Christmas lights every year and synchronized their flashes to a four-minute loop on FM 90.5. His holiday display required a small army equipped with scaffolding and extension ladders just to hang everything. He was the one who needed the arrow at his front gate. The sign pointed left so visitors would not mistake his fiefdom for the Belle Haven Club next door. Judge Judy was not the one with a problem.

The reality: Leeser never deliberated whether any Greenwich estate was excessive. He regarded each as a logical conclusion. He understood Judge Judy, Valery Kogan, and Paul Tudor Jones. He understood why the founder of SAC Capital owned a Munch and built an ice rink in his backyard. The *New York Post,* by lampooning members of the Greenwich über-rich, missed the point.

With its mix of Russian oligarchs, old-line fortunes, and hedge fund money, Greenwich was a living, breathing philosophy debate. These neighborhoods, in Cy's opinion, were not the happy endings of too much money. They posed a twist on the classic question: "If a tree falls in a forest and no one is around to hear it, does it make a sound?"

Greenwich raised the same issue about wealth: "If no one sees your money, do you have any?"

Bianca Santiago Leeser stared out the kitchen window, waiting for her husband and wondering if they could make it through the night without an argument. With dark Brazilian hair and latte-cream skin, she wore white jeans and a Tory Burch top. Bianca was one of nature's anomalies, slender but big breasted, short but statuesque. Stunning at forty-seven.

She stood five foot two in stocking feet, with legs sculpted better than any slab of marble inside the Louvre. When Bianca wore stilettos to the charity circuit dinners, men forgot she was tiny. They forgot their rubber chicken meals, and they gawked. Even Cy could not help but stare.

The sixteen-year marriage had been good at the start. Bianca cranked out romance novels in their West Village condo, and Leeser cabbed downtown to Merrill Lynch. In those days they met for lunch all the time. Sometimes, the couple's stolen nooners found their way onto the steamy pages of her novels. And romance fans everywhere agreed that Bianca Santiago set the bar when it came to passion.

Now Bianca wondered what had gone wrong. Why their marriage had soured. She wasn't bitter about putting her career on hold. At least she didn't think so. She was the one who opted to stop writing, take care of the girls, and support Cy's career all the way.

When the family moved to Connecticut, it was her decision to embrace the demanding schedule of a Greenwich housewife: Pilates before breakfast to keep husband's interest; children off to Greenwich Country Day no later than seven-thirty; Starbucks grapevine afterward, hold the chocolate cake doughnuts; shopping at Patricia Gourlay Fine Lingerie to strut trim figure and low-fat diet to husband; and a $49.95 lunch consisting of three-bean salad and white wine with other moms before picking up the kids.

Or maybe Bianca played the game for reasons other than choice. Maybe she capitulated to the incessant pressure from Cy. "Look, Bianca, appearance is everything in my biz. I can't have you disappearing into your hole ten hours a day to write books. Your job is to be dumb, dark, and decorative."

Their problems escalated with the twins. Around the time Cy turned forty, he began to keep score with babies. Family size, as far as he was concerned, conferred status in the Greenwich league of hard-charging couples.

Five, in Cy's opinion, was the perfect number of kids. Five legitimized women who stayed home to raise their families. Five turned wives into CEOs, especially with nannies, maids, cooks, gardeners, drivers, personal trainers, and other employees cycling through the homes. Five was a career. Any less was a copout. Any more bordered on freakish, perhaps a religious thing. Above all, five was an obsession that spawned painful cracks.

Cy: "We have seven bedrooms, Bianca. Are you waiting for something?"

Cy: "So much for Brazilian factory output."

Cy: "Louise and Chip have five. Sally and Penn are adopting just to make their numbers."

Leeser's perspective confused Bianca. "My husband thinks five kids are the new Birkin," she once complained to several girlfriends. Brazil had its share of large families, but children were never a status symbol. More often than not, the number of kids correlated with the level of poverty.

Five was one obsession. Blond was another. When the twins turned eleven, or maybe it was twelve, Leeser arranged for a hairdresser to visit the house under the cover of dark. He never discussed his scheme in advance, the "miracle bleach from the sun" that tied his wife in a knot.

"It's exactly what they need, Bianca."

"The twins are already beautiful," she objected, horrified by the notion of their daughters going blond from a bottle. "Young girls don't need help."

"The guy can do your hair, while he's here," Cy hammered away, widening the ever-growing fissure between their values.

"What is it with you and blondes?" objected Bianca. "Not everybody in Greenwich is blond, you know."

"But everybody *looks* blond. I just want to give our girls a nudge."

Bianca never forgot the incident and resolved to protect her daughters at any cost. It broke her heart to send them to Andover when they turned fourteen. Distance shielded the twins from Cy's crazy expectations, however, not to mention the constant sniping between mother and father.

Leeser turned onto the chip-stone driveway of his estate—19,000-square-foot home, five acres of manicured lawns suitable for ultimate croquet, and enough wetlands to moisten the eyes of conservationists. For a moment, he stopped and savored the twilight shadow. American elms, sawtooth oaks, and star magnolias—gracious boughs, all heavy with spring leaves, saluted his arrival and thanked him for sparing them from backhoes. He admired his rock-solid house, its stone walls hewn from a quarry in Peru or Chile or some remote place littered with ancient ruins.

Not too shabby, Leeser decided. He didn't have the flashy résumé of other hedge fund tycoons. He never played hockey at Harvard, like Phil Falcone from Harbinger or Tim Barakett from Atticus. What was it about banging heads and losing teeth that incubated great money managers? But he had done okay.

"For a starter estate." That was what his mother would say. She never saw his spread. He could almost hear her, though. "How come you didn't buy the joint next door? It's so much bigger." And deep down, when Cy was relaxed and honest with himself, he knew she was right.

Leeser eased the Bentley down the drive toward a five-bay garage. Bianca had insisted they dine at home tonight. She was cooking pasta, always an adventure.

Her Bolognese tasted okay, nothing special. Nobody could botch a pound of ground beef, can of pre-sliced mushrooms, and jug of ready-mix sauce from the grocery. Throw the ingredients in a pot and stir the Ragú.

The problem was Bianca. She spiked the sauce. The last batch had been a disaster. She broke into a crate of 1961 Chateau Latour.

"To plump up the sauce," explained Bianca, ten-minute chef who insisted on a healthy pour.

Cy paid $390,000 for five cases; $390,000 for the dark garnet color with a "full-bodied nose." *Wine Advocate* called 1961 Chateau Latour "one of the Bordeaux legends of the century." Just thinking about the bottle, Leeser could almost smell its big-time aroma, the wisps of vanilla and smoky oaks, something wild and gamey to the scent. As far as he was concerned, it was not "one of the Bordeaux legends." It was *the* wine of the twentieth century.

"Wine eases acidity," Bianca said, defending her choice.

"So do Tums," he countered. "Why don't you stir in a roll?"

Leeser winced as he remembered that night, the verbal firefight that escalated through the months. When Bianca's dachshunds one-two peed on his $800,000 Chinese rug, things only got worse.

He parked the Bentley and headed inside, wondering what to expect. Mr. and Mrs. Cyrus Leeser always dined at the local restaurants: Rebecca's when the markets soared and the Elm Street Oyster House when they tumbled. The couple could afford a full-time chef. They could even rotate a few with different specialties through the kitchen. But in public they avoided the endless skirmishes that erupted in the privacy of their home, confrontations he labeled as "Shelter Skelter" when working out with guys at the gym.

Inside their kitchen Bianca pecked Leeser on the lips with a détente kiss— civil, practiced, and acceptable for public photo ops. "I have a surprise," she announced.

Freddy and Ginger, the dachshund dance duo, ripped around the corner and barreled into Leeser. He was their lord and master. His presence indicated they were about to be fed. Or maybe all the sniffing and snorting and scrambling around meant they shared Bianca's secret.

"Did our painting arrive from Iceland?" Leeser asked expectantly.

"Yes," she confirmed. "But that's not my news."

"What do you think?" Cy asked excitedly, referring to his latest purchase from Siggi.

"It's still in the crate."

"Why didn't you pull it out?"

"You hate when I get into your things." Suddenly, his wife sounded weary.

"Oh, right."

"Siggi wants his U.S. team to install the painting tomorrow," reported Bianca.

"What's your surprise?" Leeser asked, noting her waning interest.

"I'm going back to college."

"That's great," Cy remarked, reaching deep to sound enthusiastic. "Where?"

"NYU."

"How'd you swing that?"

"Why the surprise, Cy? I wrote ten bestsellers."

"How'd you explain what happened in college?"

Bianca's face clouded from the question, and Leeser immediately braced for trouble. His cell phone rang, though, a random gift of fate that spared the couple fifteen rounds of Fight Club in the kitchen. He studied the caller ID and said, "I need to take this. Can you fetch a Mollydooker Boxer 2005?"

Bianca bristled at the word "fetch" but headed toward the cellar as Cy marched into their great room.

Leeser did not care if the entire sixty-dollar bottle of Mollydooker ended up in the Bolognese sauce. He forgot all about his Chateau Latour with the "big nose." He missed the fury in Bianca's brown eyes.

Out of earshot, or so he thought, Cy whispered into the telephone, "Now is not a good time."

"Not my problem."

For a moment Leeser said nothing and listened. He gazed at an empty space to the right of a seven-foot fireplace. He forgot all about Siggi and the new painting. He ignored the dogs sniffing their favorite spot on his $800,000 rug. He tensed, listening to a familiar voice on the other end.

Two steps down the stairs to the wine cellar, Bianca stopped and whistled for Freddy and Ginger. They came ripping to the door, and she held out her left hand for them to sniff. It kept the dance team from yapping. With her right hand, Bianca pulled back her hair and cocked an ear around the corner. She could not help but eavesdrop.

Bianca Santiago was a natural-born voyeur. Before Cy, or "BC" as she said, preternatural curiosity drove her rise as a bestselling romance novelist published in thirty-eight languages including Farsi, Tagalog, and Turkish. Before Cy, Bianca Santiago wanted nothing more than to turn her romance novels into a Hollywood soap opera.

"I can't talk," Leeser whispered into the cell phone, turning his back to the cellar door, secreting the conversation from his wife. Cy's face reddened. His eyes widened. His nostrils flared. He could do without this partner.

Bianca strained to hear. The dogs lost interest in her fingers and broke for the rug, paws slipping on the glossy wooden floors as they scrambled. Cy's body language, Bianca decided, could only mean the one thing she had long suspected. The late hours, the whispers, and the lack of interest in bed—she knew what was wrong. Cy was having an affair.

A few muffled whispers, and Leeser finished on the phone. His body language went limp, which made Bianca wonder how any woman exercised that kind of power over her husband. It was impossible.

Bianca whirled around and hustled down the stairs. In the dim light of the wine cellar, she clenched both fists and decided her husband's infidelities required something extra, something special. Her beloved Dorothy Parker had said it best:

"It serves me right for keeping all my eggs in one bastard."

"Are you sure this will work?"

"I've got it under control," Leeser whispered into the phone.

He paused, suppressing his anger as his partner spoke.

"I've got it under control," he repeated, doing his best to sound emphatic. "Cusack's taking the job. He's in financial trouble."

"How do you know, Cy?"

"I ran the credit reports."

Leeser paused again, wincing at his partner's reply and checking for Bianca. He was oblivious to Freddy of the lifted leg, this time sniffing around the carton from Iceland.

"Give me a few months," said Cy, "and Cusack's father-in-law will be eating out of my hand. I bet we get Caleb Phelps as a client."

Leeser hung up and felt his shoulders slump. Nobody ever made him feel this impotent. Not even Bianca, who required ten times the care and maintenance of his Bentley. He headed into the kitchen to check the Bolognese sauce, eager to knock back a glass of Mollydooker and forget about his partner.

Cy arrived just as Bianca tipped 1961 Chateau Latour into the sauce. By her calculations every ounce she poured, every gulp and gurgle of the dark garnet perfection, added $256 to the pot filled with five bucks of Ragú.

"Not again," Leeser muttered, wondering if he could list his wife on eBay.

"Freddy, Ginger," called Bianca. "Who likes Bolognese?"

CHAPTER THIRTEEN
SHE'S A KILLER . . .

The next morning, Rachel turned east at Sixty-ninth and Madison, careful to avoid a direct path between Doc's clinic and the Colony Club. Repetition was careless in her profession, careless even here in New York. The city salted everything with two measures of chaos and a big dose of the unexpected.

At Lexington and Sixty-fifth Rachel spied a woman, probably a nanny, screaming at her little red-haired boy. He wailed and bawled his eyes out, trying desperately to rip free from her clutch. She had lost it, her face bloated by exasperation or exhaustion, her free hand raised to strike.

Rachel put her mission on hold, passed to the left, and hip-checked the nanny. The young woman lost hold of the boy's hand and skidded to the pavement, scraping her chin on the curb.

"Are you okay, little man?" Rachel asked the boy. He said nothing and sucked his thumb, not bothering to wipe the tears streaming down his cheeks.

"Watch where you're going," the nanny hissed, struggling to sit up, rubbing blood from her chin.

"The kid comes with a warranty," Rachel warned, pulling the woman to her feet. "Mine."

With that, she continued down Lexington before turning west on Sixty-fourth toward Fifth Avenue. The nanny gaped, her jaw hanging slack. Rachel never bothered to look, though. She had crossed into the kill zone.

"We have a date, Henrietta."

By eleven A.M. Henrietta Hedgecock traded her Chanel suit for a black, one-piece Speedo. She tucked long white locks inside her swim cap, blue with a Nike swoosh across the front, and appraised her arms and upper body over the cool chop of the pool's water. Hedgecock approved of what she saw. All her efforts—clothes, exercise, and trips to the salon, not to mention a thousand different moisturizers—paid off.

Even at age seventy-six, Henrietta turned heads among New York's haut monde of high-minded philanthropy and abused livers. Which was why she regarded the Colony Club's pool as a safe house. Men never swam in it, and members seldom ventured into the basement. No hard stares of appraisal. No need to worry how she looked.

Henrietta relished the temporary respite. She was not wearing jewels from Tiffany or makeup from the ground floor of Saks Fifth Avenue. She was wearing spandex from the Sports Authority. She did not trail sophisticated scents from perfume boutiques lining Madison Avenue. Henrietta reeked of chlorine. She loved the solitary pleasure of her morning workout, her translucent hands already wrinkling from the water.

Hedgecock folded against the edge of the marble-and-tile pool, splashing water on her shoulders, prepping for thirty laps. In the adjacent lane a young woman glided through the water. With effortless strokes, she covered the length of the pool and executed a perfect flip turn at the far end.

The maneuver looked impressive, the fluid motion of an elite athlete. Suddenly, the woman bugged Henrietta. It was partly the intrusion. Hedgecock could not remember sharing the pool with anyone during morning laps. It was also the damn flip turn.

Hedgecock had attempted flip turns, on and off through forty years of laps, but never perfected them. Water filled her nostrils every time, either choking her lungs or making her sneeze. Even Hedgecock's personal trainer had given up. He no longer tried to teach Henrietta the move. That was over ten years ago. And here in the Colony Club basement was a swimmer, violating Hedgecock's one-woman, one-pool sanctuary and flipping with ease.

The woman paddled closer, her freestyle flawless and smooth, her kick powerful. She touched the side of the pool in the adjacent lane, stopped for a breather at the edge, and smiled at Henrietta. Her eyes shone a brilliant green. A nasty round scar, top of her right hand, bulged with puffy white tissue. It looked like a cigarette burn.

Henrietta averted her eyes. She fought the impulse to stare at the intruder's damaged right hand. She never noticed what the woman was holding in her left, a curious piece of plastic that did not belong in a lap pool. For that matter, the object did not belong anywhere close to a seventy-six-year-old woman who prided herself on weighing 107 pounds dripping wet.

The green-eyed swimmer, cute and buxom in her late twenties, wore a navy blue swimsuit and white cap. Pretty, but Henrietta knew one thing for sure. The woman was not a member of the Colony Club.

"You must be a guest?"

Henrietta spoke in her most charming and winsome voice. There was no accusation to her tone whatsoever. She was earnest and friendly, a big smile for the guest.

"Yes," replied the woman. A few ringlets of blond hair peeked through her swim cap. "And this pool is fabulous."

Henrietta wondered how to ask, "Whose guest," without being rude.

Rachel, who had learned much about the membership by walking through the clubhouse, read the older woman's thoughts. "Liz said I would love it down here. She was right."

"You mean Liz Southwick?" Henrietta immediately approved of the woman with green eyes and navy blue swimsuit.

"Are you friends?" Rachel asked with enough charm to take gloss out of a photo.

"Liz and I meet for lunch every Friday," replied Henrietta. "Which reminds me, I need to start my laps. Otherwise, I'll never finish in time."

"I need to finish a few things myself."

Henrietta started a steady breaststroke, which unlike the freestyle did not require flip turns. She loved the water. The pool invigorated her, chased the cruel aches that accompany seventy-six years and one false hip, turned her sixteen again if only for brief and glorious interludes. As she swam, however, Hedgecock decided there was something odd about the other woman.

Rachel watched Henrietta's steady cross. When the older woman covered a third of the pool, Rachel launched in hot pursuit. Her freestyle, a casual stroke to the bystander, was lightning fast. She easily passed Henrietta, executed a perfect flip turn, and drove off the side of the pool like a shark tasting blood.

Kicking. Gliding. Hunting. Rachel rammed her syringe needle into the septuagenarian's skinny thigh. Her thumb mashed down the plunger, and one hundred units of insulin gushed into Henrietta Hedgecock's 107-pound, nondiabetic body.

Ever the nurse, Rachel preferred Apidra for these occasions. It worked faster, in her opinion, than the competing brands of insulin that required fifteen minutes to take effect. Some diabetics could inject Apidra with no delay whatsoever. They gauged their intake—like one unit for every ten carbohydrates or five units for a combo of sweet yogurt and a granola bar—and gave themselves a shot before eating.

Rachel did not calculate the carbs. She injected a hundred units of Apidra, which was a whopper shot by any standard. Hypoglycemia would start soon enough: rapid heartbeat, blurred vision, irritability, and the eventual loss of consciousness. She liked what the military called "redundant systems" in this hit. If Henrietta did not die from the diabetic coma, she would drown in the pool.

"Ouch," shrieked Henrietta, screeching to a halt, grabbing her thigh, tears streaming from her eyes.

Palming the syringe, Rachel asked, "Are you okay?"

"What was that?"

"I'm blind as a bat without my glasses, Henrietta."

"It felt like you pinched me. And how do you know my name?"

"I broke my fingernail," replied Rachel in a soothing voice, not bothering to answer the question. "Come over to the side of the pool."

They paddled to the edge, where Henrietta said, "That really hurt. Do I know you?"

"We've never met."

"I feel funny." Henrietta's tongue already sounded two times too fat for her mouth. Her skin, once translucent from age, clouded to a sallow gray. Her brow beaded with moisture, either from the pool or the adrenal medulla secreting epinephrine in a desperate effort to check plummeting sugars. "How do you know my name?" she asked again, garbling her words.

"I'm so sorry," soothed Rachel, concern in her words, demonic gleam in her eyes. "Walter will be disappointed when you miss lunch. But if you ask me, he's a little young for you."

"Listen," Henrietta struggled to say. Now it sounded like there were two tongues in her mouth, struggling for space, bullying each other for room. "I feel funny." She pulled out of the water, arms trembling from the effort, but all strength had quit her body. Hedgecock collapsed, just barely hanging on to the pool's edging.

"Do you feel your heart racing?"

"Listen," Henrietta garbled a second time, head bobbing, eyes twitching.

"Are you hungry?"

"Listen."

"You know, Henrietta, sugar lows make people do the oddest things. I once heard about a guy who ran outside, jumped on the hood of his boss's car, and peed all over the windshield."

Rachel loved this part of her job. She felt like an alley cat toying with a trapped mouse.

"You won't pee in the pool, will you?" Subconsciously, Rachel rubbed the puffy scar on her hand. "The Colony Club girls will pull the plug if they ever find out."

"Listen," Henrietta said for the final time. Her head dropped forward and banged hard against the pool's edge. She slipped down, gray face forward, not reacting as water poured into her lungs.

For good measure Rachel pushed the old woman into the center of the pool. "Good night, Henrietta," she whispered, checking that they were still alone in the cavernous room. "I may join Walter for lunch."

As she pulled out of the pool, Rachel noticed Henrietta's purse sitting on a nearby chair. She smiled and rifled through the contents, hoping to find a bottle of CoCo Chanel. "Ah, this is exactly what I need," she said to no one in particular, surprised that Tasers came in pink.

Rachel rushed to the changing room. She dressed quickly, donned a raincoat, gargantuan sunglasses, and a floppy hat. She exited the building without inviting so much as a casual glance, savoring how good it felt to work in public. There was less mess to clean.

Outside in the April drizzle Rachel sighed audibly among the pedestrians, the hard-charging New Yorkers accustomed to grunts and ambient sound effects. The laps in the pool that morning had been a nice perk. The killer buzz, juiced by exercise endorphins, had been more potent than all the opium of Indochina. She checked her cell phone's clock. It was time to get back to the clinic.

CHAPTER FOURTEEN

"I'll crush you, Leeser. I'll punish you in public. I'll make you beg until the world recognizes what you really are. An insipid little man with an insipid little hedge fund and an insipid little brain that would jump ten IQ points from a lobotomy performed by crowbar."

Alone in his Reykjavik office, Ólafur was talking to himself and scanning stock prices. Hafnarbanki was not the problem. The bank was trading at 907 kronur. Not great. But at least the shares had rallied 6.7 percent since his meeting with Chairman Guðjohnsen. The Qataris were already buying, and it was good to show early results.

The problem was Bentwing. The problem was patience—his. Bentwing had also rallied, and on Friday its shares closed at their high for the year. Buoyed by soaring energy prices, the stock would probably break through $62.31 today. The gain was acceptable only because of the banker's promise to Guðjohnsen:

"We'll take our time shorting Bentwing. We'll do it right."

Ólafur wanted to attack Bentwing now. But prudence dictated otherwise. The blitzkrieg, the all-out hell and destruction, would begin once Ólafur recruited Siggi and turned the mild-mannered gallery owner into a spy. It was only a matter of time, weeks, maybe even days, before Hafnarbanki and the Qataris opened fire and bet against Bentwing. Not much longer until they shorted the company's stock and its price dropped like a rock.

Over the weekend Ólafur's best source told him that a new guy, Jimmy Cusack, had joined LeeWell Capital. Ivy educated. Goldman Sachs pedigree. He was starting today.

Ólafur recalled his first days at Hafnarbanki thirteen years ago—all the promise and expectation. He shook his head and said with only a hint of remorse, "Congratulations, Cusack. Welcome to your life as *hákarl*."

He was referring to fermented shark. The Icelandic cuisine is not so much a delicacy as an ordeal to be endured. Traditionalists prepare *hákarl* by gutting a shark, burying the headless carcass in sand, and allowing the remains to stew in their own uric juices for twelve weeks. The meat is exhumed, sliced into ribbons, and hung out to dry. Several months later the strips are scraped of their brown crust, cubed, and served to those who dare. *Hákarl* smells like the ammonia used to clean public bathrooms and tastes about the same.

This process, Ólafur decided, was the perfect way to cure employees at LeeWell Capital and other hedge funds.

Five hours behind Reykjavik, Jimmy pulled into the Greenwich Plaza parking lot underneath the buildings. He parked his battered blue BMW, 250,000 miles and climbing, between a spanking-new Mercedes on one side and a two-tone Maserati on the other. He retraced his path to the entrance ramp and walked past the taxis outside the Metro North platform to his left.

The train was easier than driving—and less embarrassing. But Cusack was in sales. He needed the flexibility of a car for impromptu client meetings. He also loved to blast Roy Orbison out the windows. He decided to drive until he found his groove at LeeWell Capital or grew tired of "You Got It."

Jimmy could already taste the sweet-and-sour backwash from day-one jitters. LeeWell Capital offered a new beginning. He was the unofficial apprentice of Cy Leeser, an emerging legend inside Hedgistan.

Sweet: If the markets cooperated, Cusack would solve his money woes by February—the month bonuses were paid. With a little luck, if he tripled LeeWell Capital's assets under management, he would join the legends. He would lay claim to his rightful seat among the gods of Greenwich.

Sour: Cusack had no formal contract. Emi's father knew nothing about his mortgage woes or handshake deal with Leeser. But Caleb was forever preaching, "Get it in writing." Cusack's mind was playing tricks, and he suddenly doubted whether Cy would keep his part of the bargain.

Litton had gone MIA since mailing their certified letter. Alex Krause, however, was a migraine with a mouthpiece. The collections agent from Chase Auto Finance called twice, each time asking the same basic question: "When are you paying us back?"

As Cusack walked into LeeWell Capital, his first time as an employee, Amanda boomed, "Good morning."

"We're glad to see you," added Nikki, radiant face with a throaty voice.

Both women wore light cardigan sweaters in the office, sixty-six degrees and chilly. Nikki had replaced her diamond-chip nose stud with a blue stone, flashier than before and far less elegant, but alluring and mysterious by all measures.

"Good to see you," he said, rolling out the twisted smile, shaking each woman's hand. Cusack had forgotten Nikki was so short, no more than five foot three. Or maybe he hadn't noticed during the interview haze.

"Cy's been telling everybody how great you are," Nikki said.

"Are you kidding? I'm thrilled to be here."

"Come on back. Cy wants to see you first thing."

Leeser rose from his chair with the easy confidence of a boxer who'd decked his opponent thirty seconds ago. His long black hair draped over his shoulders. He thrust out his hand, which was blue-collar gnarled and turned up slightly in a welcoming manner. "Welcome aboard, Jimmy."

"Glad to be here."

"Sit down and relax. You can work your ass off later."

Cusack surveyed Cy's office, again struck by all the art. There was not an inch to spare on the four walls. Paintings occupied every nook, every corner, every flat surface that could hold a hook. Jimmy would have called the style "bric-a-brac" had the artwork not looked so expensive.

"Let's discuss your mortgage," Leeser said.

"Right to business," Cusack replied agreeably, hoping to disguise his angst.

"Our real estate attorney can close this morning. All we need are transfer instructions, and we'll wire three point one million where you tell us. No problem, right?"

Cusack wanted to scream. He wanted to drain his lungs with one monster sigh of relief. Instead, he confirmed in his most nonchalant voice, "No problem from my side. What about the title work?"

"Done."

"Terms same as we discussed?" asked Cusack, leaning back in the leather chair.

"Interest only at five and three quarters. Done."

"That's great, Cy."

"There's just one catch."

"Okay?" Cusack avoided the temptation to say, "There always is."

"If you leave LeeWell Capital for any reason, whether you're fired or you take a job with a competitor, I want my money. Your mortgage is payable in thirty days."

"Is that negotiable?"

"Not one comma, Jimmy. The loan documents are standard."

"Where do I sign?"

"Shannon will drive you."

Twenty minutes later Shannon parked Leeser's glacier-white Bentley on Greenwich Avenue outside the lawyer's office. The big man said a total of three words during the short drive: "Hi" and "Let's go."

Cusack pulled out his cell, phoned Smitty, and asked the lawyer, "Can you get my payoff figure?"

"Through when?" the attorney stammered, surprised by the question.

"Ten minutes from now."

"That's awesome, dude."

"Thanks," replied Cusack, thinking Smitty should strike "dude" from his vocabulary. "Text me the payoff number."

Smitty sensed something else, something in the way Cusack hesitated over the phone. "Anything else?"

"Call Robby and tell him to overnight a listing agreement."

"That's crazy. Why sell your condo when the pressure's off?"

"I'll never be this vulnerable again, Smitty."

Last night Emi had agreed to put the condo on the market. She supported the idea of raising their family in the suburbs. Cusack liked cutting their debt. The first payment on his new mortgage from LeeWell Capital was not due until February. But interest was still accruing at 5.75 percent on $3.1 million. That was $14,854 ticking away every month like a time bomb.

"But the market—"

"Just do it," Jimmy interrupted. It was time to move on and leave the condo mistake behind.

CHAPTER FIFTEEN

DAY ONE AT LEEWELL . . .

The first time Jimmy saw Victor Lee, the head trader had his jaws wrapped around one-third of a cheeseburger fully loaded with mushrooms, bacon, and some kind of brown-red barbecue sauce. There were probably pickles and lettuce, maybe even some diced onions. Cusack was not sure because Victor never dribbled the trace elements—not even a drop of the blood-soaked grease that would have soiled the chins of lesser men.

Lee had a broad mouth, his double-wide face big enough to swallow half the cheeseburger in one bite. He opted for fries instead, wedging them between cheeseburger and cheek and grunting over the phone mid-swallow. From the distance, Victor's guttural sounds could have been mistaken for walrus sex had he been somewhere else than Greenwich Plaza.

The head trader took one look at Cy and one look at the new guy. Victor garbled something into the phone that was either "gotta go" or "get stuffed." It was impossible to tell with him scarfing down the five-inch-high cheeseburger.

"Victor Lee," he announced, ripping off his ultralight headset, tossing it against a wall of three thirty-inch LCDs, and thrusting out his hand.

He blinked several times through horn-rimmed glasses. His spiky, jet-black crew cut stood straight up. For a guy in his thirties, he looked like a throwback to the 1950s.

"Meet Jimmy Cusack," said Leeser. "He's the new face of sales."

Cusack shook Victor's hand. "I've heard great things about you."

"Over there," Leeser continued, "that's Bill. And Adam. And that's David. They all trade with Victor."

Cusack shook hands with each of them.

"You any good?" asked Lee, no smile, no humor.

One of the junior traders rolled his eyes. The others watched Jimmy. They had seen Victor in action before.

"We don't want anybody who sucks, Cusack."

Lee's clipped accent betrayed long years on the crowded streets of Hong

Kong. He stood five foot six and 165 pounds, not an ounce of fat. He looked like a preppy fire hydrant, open at the throat and blasting testosterone rather than water.

"I do okay," Cusack replied.

From experience he knew the one technique for taming blowhards: rope-a-dope. Take the punches while they talk themselves into exhaustion. Then land a few smart-mouth combos. He had seen his share of "Victor Lees" at Goldman Sachs and other shops around the street. Jimmy counterpunched with the best.

"You have any idea what we do here, Cusack?"

"Make money."

"Hey, Cy," Victor said, grinning for the first time. "I like this guy."

The head trader turned back to Cusack. "What else, newbie?"

Jimmy hesitated and glanced at his boss. Leeser never said a word. He watched his employees with less expression than a cantaloupe.

"I haven't seen the portfolio," Cusack started, "but I know that Lee-Well concentrates its bets on a handful of companies. That you buy huge blocks of stock without running up the price. That Cy sits on the board of Bentwing Energy, where he's not afraid to rattle the cages."

"You don't have a fucking clue," Victor snapped. "That's the right answer."

"Excuse me?"

"Nobody knows what we do," announced Lee, pausing for the silence to punctuate his words. "We don't tell anybody anything. Otherwise, every dickhead in Greenwich would follow our lead."

Cusack took the shot and waited.

"Nobody makes money," Lee continued, "if we're all hosing our mothers for each other's trades."

"You available for client calls?" Jimmy asked, speaking without any trace of sarcasm. "You're perfect for the college endowments. Harvard, Yale, Princeton—we'll make a road trip out of it. Stop by a few pension plans, maybe a family office or two along the way."

"Victor's no HR department," Cy interceded, stifling a smile while slapping his trader on the back. "But he has a Ph.D. from MIT and knows how to trade. That's why I want him on our team."

"I look forward to working with you." Cusack flashed a thumbs-up sign to the three junior traders, who returned the signal.

"Can you guys join Jimmy and me for a drink after work?" asked Cy.

Before Victor could reply, his phone interrupted the group. The incoming number displayed on his console, and he said, "I need to take this." He donned his headset and asked, "What do you have?"

As Victor Lee listened, he fiddled with the claw of a sixteen-ounce Estwing hammer. Tools were out of place in most office environments. It was anything goes with traders, though. They were always fiddling with something—bats, hackie sacks, you name it. Anything to release the nervous energy.

Coiled and alert, Victor scanned one LCD display to the next. He searched charts, flashing tickers, and scrolling news as though evaluating his caller's market advice. Finally, he announced, "Don't waste my time, pal," and clicked off.

Cy flashed a wan smile.

Lee gripped the hammer claw, pointed the handle at Jimmy, and said, "Just remember, Cusack. There are two kinds of people in the world. The ones who make money."

"And?"

"Oxygen thieves."

Cy and Jimmy continued their tour of LeeWell Capital. The offices—a lavish, largely accidental hash of technology, hedge fund chic, and frathouse Shangri-la—included an eight-by-ten cool room for computer racks and a roomy billiards lounge complete with drop-down lights over a massive table. Cue sticks lined one wall. A fifty-two-inch flat-screen television was tuned to Fox Business on the other.

"Nice pool table," Cusack observed.

"Snooker," Leeser corrected, selecting a pool stick from the wall. "The table's bigger, and the balls are smaller."

LeeWell's kitchen housed an open-flame range for grilling steaks, Le Cache wine cabinet racked with 160 bottles, and another fifty-two-inch flat-screen television. This one was tuned to CNBC. A huge copper-and-brass cappuccino maker engulfed an entire kitchen island. The machine contained two gauges, one digital display, and at least three spigots. On top, a spread-winged eagle scanned the horizon for stray coffee beans.

"Shipped it direct from Italy," Cy announced with the pride of acquisition in his voice. "I insist on good coffee." He was still carrying the pool stick from the billiards lounge.

Jimmy struggled to show respect. He remembered his firm's Mr. Coffee machine, the one Emi bought at Walmart for $19.99. "I bet you can make moonshine in that thing."

"Our coffee is stronger," Cy replied, "and it tastes better."

The workout room contained a stationary bike, weight machine, and another fifty-two-inch screen. Using the pool cue, Leeser pointed to a door at the rear of the room. He explained, "Back there we've got showers, lockers, and a sauna big enough to host client meetings."

"Do you laminate the PowerPoint handouts?" Cusack deadpanned.

"No place like a sauna to close the sale," answered Leeser, choking the pool cue with a gnarled grip. "Just turn up the steam and serve martinis."

Over the next thirty-two minutes Cusack met two accountants, several junior research assistants, and Kennedy from Compliance. He visited with Nikki, who sat outside Leeser's office, her head hidden by a computer screen and a bank of chest-high files surrounding the workstation.

"Let me know if you need anything," she offered. "I'll book flights and catch your phone during the day, if you're not around."

"Thanks, Nikki. You're the best."

"And this is your new home, Jimmy," said Leeser, gesturing to a door next to his own office.

At that moment Shannon's huge bulk filled the frame. "All clear," he advised Leeser, not looking at Cusack.

"Good," Cy replied.

Shannon glanced at Cusack's two-star button, the big man's expression colder than a gouty piranha. He turned and asked, "You need anything else, boss?"

"All set," said Leeser, and Shannon left.

"What's 'clear'?" Jimmy asked.

"Your office. We sweep for bugs."

"You're kidding."

"Our competitors will do anything to get an edge, Jimmy. Even if it means bribing employees or sifting through the trash."

"Ever have a problem?"

"Not yet. Our bonuses keep people honest."

"You were relaxed," countered Cusack, "when you hired me."

"You waited a few days before starting."

"So."

"You checked out just fine." Leeser smiled broadly. His brown eyes gleamed.

Cusack suddenly felt violated. He tried to mask his reaction. But the crooked smile came too late.

"What can I say?" asked Cy with a matter-of-fact voice. "People in our industry will do anything to be right one time."

"What do you mean?"

"What were your fees?"

"Two and twenty like everybody else," said Cusack.

"Your fund was two hundred million. If you're up fifty percent in one year, you keep twenty million dollars. You can break the rules once, retire, and tell the world to kiss the sand off your ass."

"It works in reverse, Cy. One bad year, and we're out of business."

"Loyalty is fucking extinct," Leeser agreed wistfully.

"Hey, you can't quit now," pressed Cusack, half in jest. "I just started."

"Don't worry about me, Jimmy. I love this game." Passing the pool cue back and forth between hands, wielding it like a relay-race baton, Leeser added, "We're creating long-term value at LeeWell Capital."

On his first day, Cusack began working in earnest forty-five minutes after the markets closed. He sat alone in his office, eyeing a stack of papers and bubbling with optimism. He felt safe but refused to kick back.

Cusack sifted through his pile and found LeeWell's portfolio of stocks. Within thirty seconds his eyes widened, his jaw dropped, and he whistled under his breath:

"You've got to be kidding, Cy."

CHAPTER SIXTEEN

Bentwing Energy totaled 30 percent of LeeWell Capital's portfolio. It was a huge stake, especially when many consider 5 percent a full position. Every swing of one dollar in Bentwing's share price added or subtracted $4 million to the fund.

The stock was like a toddler near the swimming pool. Cusack checked for company news first thing in the morning. When talking on the phone, he found his eyes drifting toward the ticker symbol BEG. And with a black marker, he scribbled *Bentwing $78.79* on an envelope and taped it to his computer LCD. That was the share price necessary to get a bonus.

The calculation, Cusack knew, was far from perfect. The rest of the portfolio could do almost anything—rise, fall, or trade sideways. "Bentwing $78.79" kept him focused, however, on the single biggest factor in the portfolio's health. And unfortunately, the stock had already fallen $1.14 since his first day on the job. Every downtick at BEG, no matter how modest, kindled his growing curiosity about "the secret sauce" and how Leeser minimized risk.

Did Cy stumble onto something brilliant?

Cusack had barely taken the job. He could not reveal his doubts. Not to Emi, who shouldered her own issues. Not to colleagues, who heralded him as the new champion on their team. And certainly not to finance buddies, who trolled for weakness and snatched clients every chance they got.

During his first week at LeeWell—"Bentwing $78.79" forever in the background—Jimmy fielded a staggering number of phone calls. Fellow alums from Columbia, Wharton, and Goldman all wished him "good luck."

"I heard you got carried out," said Peter. He meant carried out on a board, as in the carcass of his deceased fund. "Glad you're back."

"The guys are calling you 'Cool Hand Cusack,'" Sam reported. He worked at Wexford Plaza, another outpost of the gods, otherwise known as a "hedge fund hotel" because the tenants were all hedge funds.

Bill and Doug called. So did Rick, which was bizarre because they had not spoken since sophomore year. Fred invited Jimmy for drinks at Barcelona, a mecca for girls'-night-out dinners. "We'll pound beers and check out the cougars. Last time I was there, a woman whipped out her boobs and dunked them in a couple of martini glasses."

Even Sydney, Jimmy's former assistant, telephoned to say congratulations and gossip about the hedge fund she joined. "My boss is a stitch. He put signs in our bathroom that say 'Employees must wash hands after touching the money.'"

Where would I be without Bouvier?

It was Jean Bertrand Bouvier, to be precise. The New Orleans native hired the entire staff from Cusack Capital. He bought all the phones, computers, and furniture, even the old prints of Boston, despite early protests that he would rather "eat dice and spit snake eyes."

Bouvier bargained hard through February and March and scratched for every dollar, a lethal blend of Cajun charm and filed teeth. But in the end he took everything and everyone prepackaged and ready to go, assembling a shake-and-bank hedge fund in one fell swoop.

The deal saved Cusack from personal bankruptcy. Like other entrepreneurs in New York City, he personally guaranteed all his firm's rent obligations. Bouvier subleased the space at the Empire State Building and took over the $50,000 monthly payments, which totaled $1.2 million through the end of the lease. Crisis averted, problem solved.

Except for Smitty—his lawyer had to know—Cusack confided his near brush with bankruptcy to only one other person. Even there, his words were more hint than outright revelation. Neither Emi nor his brothers knew. His mother was out of the question.

For all their good wishes during week one, Cusack's friends would have picked him clean with less remorse than dead men. They were competitors. Hedge funds hired Ivy Leaguers in part for their networks. Grads partied together and swapped ideas back and forth. They talked to friends, always fishing for the next trade to generate big bucks.

So many had traded the ideology of their youth for a shot at private jets and beach retreats in the Hamptons. They had accepted Hedgistan's un-written code that money trumps friendship. They understood the rules and dismissed backstabbing and betrayal as occupational hazards. It was all part of the game.

Dimitris "Geek" Georgiou was different. While others pressed for de-tails about LeeWell, Dimitris guided Cusack through the wilds of Hedg-istan. The two had been best friends ever since Wharton, where they joined the same study group, commiserated over the Boston Red Sox, and forged an enduring alliance through late nights and the pressures of rigorous aca-demic schedules.

"Maybe we can start a company together," both of them said on more than one occasion.

Dimitris grew up on Columbus Avenue in Boston. His childhood home, wedged midway between South End gentry and West Roxbury gangs, ob-scured the family's finances. As a kid, he had no idea whether they were rich or struggling to make ends meet.

The uncertainty was gone. Dimitris employed a full-time driver, who chauffeured him to a large, Greenwich-based hedge fund every day. He owned a sun-drenched co-op downtown with a 360-degree view of Man-hattan, a choice deemed reasonable by other gods given his bachelor sta-tus. And the Boston native now frequented poker tournaments in Monte Carlo. According to the rumors, he won a million euros one night from a wealthy Middle Eastern businessman.

Rail thin, wavy black hair and outsized nose, Coke-bottle glasses—Dimitris stood five foot eight with stand-tall inserts stuffed inside his Gucci loafers. His Wharton classmates nicknamed him "Greek" for a few months. Dimitris was, after all, the son of first-generation immigrants from the Hellenic Republic. He claimed to be the third cousin of Steven Demetre Georgiou, who later changed his name to Cat Stevens.

"Greek" gave way to "Geek," perhaps because he wore pocket protec-tors inside his rumpled Armani jackets. Or maybe it was the short-sleeve shirts, forever stained no matter what the laundry tried. Geek's polos be-longed in labs with bubbling beakers rather than in offices brimming with Bloomberg terminals and LCD displays. Except for one thing. The shirts cost $350 each.

There was also the matter of language. Geek, a Yale double major in math and computer sciences, spoke an incomprehensible language cobbled together from physics, finance, and words nobody used. Cusack some-times wished his friend came with subtitles.

"I'm closing my fund," Cusack informed him back in February.

"Why, what happened?"

"Bank stocks, among other things."

"Did conformal invariant deformations get you, Jimmy?"

"Yeah, if Caleb Phelps is a 'deformation.'"

During Cusack's first week at LeeWell, the two spoke by phone every day. It was Geek who helped Cusack work through his silent misgivings. "Your head trader knows how you hedge. Right, Jimmy?"

"Of course. Otherwise, Victor can't execute on strategy." Cusack sounded confident but his answer was a guess. He was afraid "Dunno" might sound stupid or naive—unacceptable no matter how loyal his friend.

"That's a good sign," concluded Geek. "Your boss has an inner circle. Once you bag a few clients, he'll tell you how he hedges."

"How can I sell what I don't understand?" Cusack shifted awkwardly. "It's a chicken-or-egg problem."

Geek immediately detected the uneasy vibe. He pressed forward any-way, long aware of Cusack's reticence. "Will Victor tell you?"

"No way. The guy's a loose cannon."

"Then it's simple," said Geek. "Make sure Cy attends your pitches. He can finesse the tough questions from prospects. After a while, he'll need you more than you need him."

"That's good thinking."

"I got your y-axis."

"What are you talking about?"

"Your back, Jimmy. I got your back."

WEDNESDAY, APRIL 30
BENTWING TRADING AT $60.49

Leeser brooded inside his office, drumming his fingers and eyeing a chart. The door was closed, and he was annoyed. His fund was outperforming the Dow. But so what. The index was down 3.2 percent, and his portfolio barely in the black. Something was wrong. The way Bentwing had traded off its highs. The way Hafnarbanki had rallied.

"Shit," he said, recognizing the caller ID on his cell phone.

"How you doing, Cy?"

He hated his partner's drawl. For that matter he hated the South, and its stinking heat and all the fuss about mildew plantations like New Orleans or Charleston or any of the other Southern cities. Cy never crossed the Mason-Dixon line. It was too damn hot down there. "What's up?"

"Have you met Cusack's father-in-law?"

"Are you crazy?" Leeser snapped. "Jimmy hasn't found the bathroom yet. Let's stick to our plan."

"You're wasting time."

"Who asked you?" he bristled.

"Funny you should mention that. It's time we discuss a few things."

"Like what?" Leeser grimaced, fully aware of what was coming. His partner held all the cards.

"My share."

Twenty minutes later, Cy clicked off his cell phone in the blackest mood he had known in a long, long time. "I don't need this shit," he muttered under his breath. Over and over he echoed his partner's words:

" 'I want. I want. I want.' "

CHAPTER SEVENTEEN

TUESDAY, MAY 6

BENTWING AT $61.61

"I'm scared."

Those words were not how Cusack expected to wake. Most workdays his alarm clock shrieked, and he smacked it silly with the palm of his hand. Most workdays he mumbled something groggy and ugly, usually one letter for every hour slept. Which can be a problem when you hit the sack at one A.M. and the clock is glowing five A.M. and your sleep-startled wife wonders what the fuck happened when "darn" is not the four-letter expletive that comes to mind or mouth. Today it was Emi who nudged her James awake.

Cusack had fallen into a rhythm of long days at LeeWell and short nights with his wife. The couple had not spoken since yesterday morning. Emi was already asleep Monday when he returned from a strategy dinner with Cy and Victor. Something was eating the boss last night, while the three were eating the $125 Akaushi Kobe shell steak at Polpo, a restaurant in Greenwich.

Now something was eating Emi. She was lying awake in their tan-and-white bedroom, wrestling with her fears. She jostled Cusack a second time and then a third. He jolted awake, consciousness whisking his brain like a potato peeler.

Did Emi figure out our finances?

"What's wrong, sweetie?" asked Cusack, blinking awake, steeling himself for trouble.

"What if I don't recognize our baby?"

Cusack breathed easier. He reached over and rubbed his wife's belly. Emi was not showing, but he could feel the thickness of her stomach. When she crossed the three-month mark with no problems, they would both heave a sigh of relief.

"Trust me, you'll know Yaz." Cusack had nicknamed their unborn baby after the Red Sox slugger Carl Yastrzemski. "You'll know the way he smells. The way he moves and searches you out with his big blue eyes. Moms clobber prosopagnosia every time."

"What makes you so sure?"

"I know these things," he said, fully awake, confident and reassuring with the crooked smile sometimes mistaken for a smirk. "Besides, if there's ever a problem, we'll tattoo a pair of red socks under Yaz's belly button."

Emi eeked and hit him with a goose-down pillow. "We're having a girl. And no tattoo shop is touching my daughter."

The girl-versus-boy banter, Cusack knew, comforted Emi and eased her fears about prosopagnosia. Most workdays, Emi fell back asleep after their playful discussion. She left around 7:30 A.M. for the Bronx Zoo and life among the reptiles—feedings, habitat checks, research.

Emi's fears were growing more acute, though. The insomnia was new. And Cusack, despite his words to the contrary, had no clue whether recognition would be a problem.

During his glory years at Goldman, Jimmy would have purchased a Tiffany baby bracelet engraved with YAZ. It would be her sign, a tool similar to the two-star pin. Cusack had sworn off all discretionary expenses, though. He was hoarding every spare dollar in case LeeWell failed to earn 10 percent. Bentwing, at $61.61, was only a few dollars higher than the $59.09 where it began the year. The stock was losing ground on the $78.79 target taped to Cusack's computer terminal.

Emi stayed awake instead of rolling over and falling back asleep. "We need to talk about something else."

"Is there a problem?"

"My parents invited us to visit this weekend."

"Oh."

"I know that 'oh,' and I don't like it. It's time you make peace with Dad." Cusack said nothing.

"Mom and I can't figure out how to get you guys to talk. You know Dad won't take the initiative."

"That's like asking Darth Caleb to abandon the Death Star."

"Not funny, James."

MONDAY, MAY 19
BENTWING AT $66.30

Ólafur was tired of hanging back. He had better things to do. And as far as he was concerned, patience was a euphemism for cowardice. Over a month had elapsed since Guðjohnsen approved the attack on LeeWell Capital. Still no action on that front.

Some days the banker fantasized about cornering Leeser in a room, punching the guy's spleen, kicking his groin, and kneeing his back where neck turns into spine. That was to get started. The Icelander was furious at Leeser for shorting Hafnarbanki. The shares had only climbed seventy-six kronur since the Qataris started buying.

Ólafur dialed Snorasson, Hafnarbanki's chief economist. "When will energy prices break?"

"Soon," he replied. "Soon."

"Same answer I get every week." Ólafur clicked off the phone, grumbling, "Screw it," as his receiver banged the cradle.

He had been careful. And careful bugged him. There was no such thing as a risk-free trade. There were casualties in all wars. Virgil may have been a pacifist, but he was the one who asked, "Why should fear seize the limbs before the trumpet sounds?" Aggressors, the guys who pounced during uncertainty, prevailed in the capital markets.

Ólafur scowled as he envisioned Cyrus Leeser gloating about Hafnarbanki. Maybe, just maybe, Leeser was bragging to other hedge funds. Encouraging them to short Hafnarbanki. That's why the Qatari purchases had not juiced the bank's stock more.

Enough, the banker decided. First, he dialed the Qataris. "Let's get started."

"Are you sure, brother?"

"It's time to defend your investment in our bank. It's time we send a message to hedge funds everywhere."

After the two men finished, the banker dialed Siggi on his cell. He went right to voice mail. But the attack had started. Once Siggi wrangled more information from Cy, Ólafur and his Qatari allies would pour it on.

THURSDAY, MAY 22
BENTWING AT $64.33

"This one's a personal favor."

"Favor as in freebie?" Rachel asked, yawning, annoyed her employer was calling during lunch break.

"You'll be compensated. Same as always."

"Whatever," replied Rachel in a monotone. She had not slept well and felt lousy.

"'Whatever'!" The listless response confused her employer. "You're the one pushing for more work all the time."

"I need a break."

"Take a vacation."

"That's easy for you to say, Kemosabe. I work two jobs. I'm saving my money." She paused before adding, "But you know all this."

"Why don't I send you somewhere and pick up the expense? We can talk about the assignment when you get back."

"No thanks." His largesse surprised her. She had never trusted generosity. It made no sense to her. It struck her as calculating and manipulative. What did he want?

"Surely there's someplace you'd like to go."

"I'm partial to Paris," she admitted, feeling her resolve weaken.

"Have you ever stayed at George Cinq?"

Within five minutes, they worked out the arrangements. She'd give Doc a heads-up, which was a formality more than anything else. He said yes no matter what she asked.

Kemosabe was a different story. There were times when she could not figure him out. Like today—he was brilliant. It took him five seconds to unearth exactly what she needed, and lo and behold he delivered the trip to Paris on a silver platter. Savvy on his part. Rachel would work twice as hard for him when she returned, which was probably what he calculated.

There were other times, however, when Kemosabe seemed like the kind of guy who banged his head in the shallow end of the gene pool. Not all that bright.

CHAPTER EIGHTEEN
WEDNESDAY, MAY 28
BENTWING AT $61.98

By late May tensions were spreading through LeeWell Capital. The signs were subtle, the way poison ivy surfaces in one spot before it spreads and itches everywhere. Bentwing's share price hit a high of $66.30 on May 19. Since then the stock fell to $61.98, not a collapse, not exactly. But the downward momentum fed sour dispositions and an insatiable need to scratch.

Victor Lee sat in the epicenter of the outbreak. He was the head trader, the guy renowned for his finesse buying and selling stock in companies worth less than $2 billion. Most hedge funds built their businesses around traders, their special skills. And his mood infected the small fund of sixteen employees.

The problem was money, which Victor guzzled three zeros at a time. He owned a 15,000-square-foot cottage in the Belle Haven neighborhood of Greenwich, just the right size for a bachelor. He rented a house in the Hamptons year-round, $75,000 per month, where he installed $125,000 in stereos and flat-screen televisions because there was too little technology to suit his taste. He parked a $250,000 Ferrari underneath Two Greenwich Plaza and spent at least $300,000 on spas and resorts every year, which he justified by taking it easy on clothes. He never spent more than $15,000 on fashion and accessories, though he treated himself to six-figure watches all the time and reckoned his collection was worth at least $2 million.

Like others in Hedgistan who depended on whopper bonuses, Victor spent beyond his means 364 days a year. Budgets, he decided long ago, were for retirees. Spending was more about touch and feel and how the markets felt, good or bad.

"Who the fuck is leaning on Bentwing?" he stormed. It was the last Wednesday of May. He knew somebody was selling the stock, puking it out and sending the price lower. The junior traders never bothered to look up. They had grown accustomed to their boss ranting and raving.

Victor stopped talking to himself and scanned his e-mails. A buddy at SAC Capital forwarded an article with the title "Market Volatility Tied to Testosterone."

Lee, ever curious, read that testosterone prompted risk taking. That guys, awash in hormonal flood zones, doubled down when prudence dictated otherwise. That women made better long-term investors. That estrogen was more cerebral than testosterone. That women's hormones showed no reckless tendencies.

"People study this shit?"

"Study what?" replied Cusack, who happened to be walking through the trading floor.

"Fuck you, newbie. Don't talk to me unless you're bringing in the assets," Lee barked. "Know what I mean, jelly bean?"

"Hey, Victor."

"What?"

"Can I trade you for door number three?"

Victor looked up from his three LCD panels. He blinked through the lenses of his horn-rimmed glasses. After a few seconds, he finally removed them and said:

"I take it back, Cusack. Unfuck you."

Back in his office, Jimmy replied to a few e-mails. He tried to forget Victor's jab: "Don't talk to me unless you're bringing in the assets." But the head trader was right. Cusack had joined a team of thoroughbreds, high-strung to be sure, but talented and capable nonetheless. This stable never lost money. They had until December 31 to earn 10 percent. Seven months for Bentwing to hit $78.79. It was time to deliver.

With the drumbeat of bonuses in the background, Cusack focused on gathering assets. He scheduled investor presentations around ten A.M. and asked Cy to keep the time slot free. The two tag-teamed prospects and grouped them into three broad categories: pension plans, university endowments, and elephants, which was jargon for folks with lots and lots of money.

Afterward, Cusack fell into the routine of hedge fund ennui. He worked out during lunch and returned phone calls and wrote letters and studied portfolio positions and answered e-mails and ate dinner with clients or prospects because there was always an excuse. Monday through Thursday Cusack seldom returned to his condominium before ten P.M.

Long hours seemed a small price to pay for resurrecting a career. The daily grind could have been comforting except for one problem. Jimmy still had no idea how Cy hedged.

Bentwing's share price exacerbated his concern. The stock should have been soaring. Oil broke through $135 per barrel on May 22, and Goldman Sachs forecast a price of $200 per barrel and no end to the commodity's climb. Bentwing developed wind farms, a hot sector in a world with an insatiable thirst for fuel. The shares, however, were trading down.

The phone rang as Cusack speculated how LeeWell Capital reduced its risk. "I want to bounce an idea off you," said Leeser.

"I was just about to call."

Cusack was sitting in Leeser's office. A massive desk separated the two men like the thirty-eighth parallel between North and South Korea. Every once in a while, sonar pings from the computer announced incoming e-mails.

"What's up?" asked Cy.

"We're meeting with the Retirement Fund for New Jersey Sheet Metal Workers in thirty minutes. What should I tell them about Bentwing?"

"What's to tell? It's our largest position. We already made three times our money."

"That's old news," said Cusack. "Bentwing's shares are trading like crap, and energy is up fifteen percent since March."

"People take profits," argued Leeser.

"You should discuss how we hedge a thirty-percent position."

Cy frowned. Then he asked, "You think the pension plan wants to hear about my foray into B-grade zombie movies?"

"What are you talking about?"

"I produced *Night of the Living Dead Heads* in 2003. It's a cult classic. All about a rock band of zombies. Ticket sales bailed us out."

"Is cash flow how you manage risk?" asked Cusack. Hedge funds dabbled in Hollywood all the time. They partially financed *The Pursuit of Happyness*, *Blood Diamond*, and *Borat*. Despite the precedent, he could not believe his ears.

"No, but the movie worked before I perfected my algorithm. And that's all I'll say. I've got to protect my trade secrets."

"Please don't mention zombies," said Cusack, not amused.

"Here's the deal." Leeser leaned forward, confident and commanding. "These guys don't want to hear numbers. Their eyes will glaze over. There's a better way to field questions."

"Okay?"

"I sit on Bentwing's board. If I can't comfort New Jersey Sheet Metal about our earnings, who can?"

"Fair point," Cusack admitted. The rock-solid confidence of an insider made perfect sense.

"So are we good, Jimmy? We don't have much time, and I need to speak with you about something else."

"What's up?"

"Your father-in-law is Caleb Phelps?"

He's more of a cadaver-in-law.

"Who told you?" asked Cusack.

"One of our partners," explained Leeser. "I'd love to meet Caleb."

"He's funny about investing with family."

"I'm not family."

"You know what I mean," said Cusack. "Besides, Caleb and I have a complicated relationship."

"I don't care if he's dead to you," replied Leeser. "It's good business to spend time with successful people."

Nikki, Cy's assistant, interrupted and said, "The guys from New Jersey are here."

"Just think about it," Leeser said. "That's all I ask. Just think about it."

The last thing Jimmy wanted to do was "think about it." Instead he remembered Geek's advice about breaking into Leeser's inner circle: "Once you bag a few clients, he'll tell you how he hedges."

"Okay," Cusack replied to Leeser. "But let's reel in these guys from New Jersey Sheet Metal."

CHAPTER NINETEEN

MONDAY, JUNE 2
BENTWING AT $60.08

"No. No. No. Forget it."

"Hear me out, Siggi."

"The answer is no. I'm not discussing Cy Leeser."

Ólafur was dumbstruck. Siggi never argued, never threw a punch in his life. He was the family ambassador, the one weaned on pureed olive branches. Siggi searched for graceful resolutions to conflict, even if it meant saying yes when he wanted to say no.

The two men were sitting on red stools inside the bar named Hverfisbarinn. They each sipped Red Bull and Turi, a syrupy vodka distilled according to a centuries-old Estonian recipe. Siggi removed his black glasses and swept back his wavy hair. He drained the contents of his glass and double-clinked the counter for another round, bracing for what he was about to say.

"You're obsessed, Ólafur."

Siggi was a happy drunk on the days he drank, which were more often than the days he went cold turkey. But tonight he shouldered the discussion with Ólafur like an anvil-sized tumor.

"Obsessed with what, Siggi?"

"With Cy. And when you're not obsessed with him, you're obsessed with Hafnarbanki. And your share prices. And your portfolio. Why don't you obsess over a girlfriend?"

Siggi stopped there. He wanted to say: "Before you drink away all your good looks, Ólafur. You look like shit." But he resisted the urge, even though the banker could use another session at the clinic. His nose was a mess. There were capillaries sprouting everywhere.

Ólafur morphed into Mr. Ice. He was the field general who reassured colleagues. He was the combatant who stayed cool and methodical in the heat of battle, the one who roused a doddering old chairman with demands for Cy Leeser's head. He was cold-blooded and a ruthless warrior. He could shake hands with the enemy one minute and rip off their faces the next.

He was also a soldier with secret misgivings. Ólafur's career depended on making Hafnarbanki go up and Bentwing go down. He knew what to do about his bank. The Qataris were buying stock. He had no idea, however, whether LeeWell Capital could make Bentwing climb in price. If so, Leeser would crucify investors who bet against the energy stock. And Ólafur knew better than to underestimate his enemy.

He put his arm around Siggi—swaddling the art dealer with body mass—and asked, "What's the problem? You can tell me."

"Forget I ever mentioned Cy Leeser's name, okay?"

"I need your help, cousin."

"You're asking me to slit my throat, Ólafur. Cy's my best customer."

"Was."

"He may buy another painting," Siggi added, not catching the significance of Ólafur's one-word reply.

The banker suddenly turned full-tilt toward his cousin and leaned in close, his body language reassuring. "Tell me about it."

"Why do you ask?" Siggi eyed his cousin suspiciously.

Ólafur ignored the question. "What's the painting worth?"

"Four million in U.S. dollars."

"Is that a fair price?"

"No," the art dealer snapped, his voice a mix of authority and exasperation. "Six million is a fair price."

"Then why sell so low?"

"The market's a joke."

Maybe it was the Red Bull and Turi. More likely it was the topic. Siggi relaxed as they discussed art. He had the home court advantage, rare when dealing with his cousin. Ólafur always, always got the upper hand.

"Does Leeser want the painting?" asked Ólafur.

"Probably. But he's holding out for a better price."

"Your ship just came in, cousin." Ólafur glowed with enough alcoholic wattage to light Laugardalsvöllur, the national stadium of Iceland.

"That's easy for you to say. Hafnarbanki's shares are trading over nine hundred kronur again."

"Forget my shares," Ólafur barked.

The mild-mannered art dealer started from the rebuke, annoyed about letting down his guard.

"I have a deal for you, Siggi."

"The answer is no."

Ólafur persisted, a veteran of ax fights in finance, undeterred by meek protests from his cousin. "The owner of the painting makes money. Cyrus Leeser makes money. You make money, and that's not the half."

"You must have corks in your ears, cousin. I said no."

"Your newest client can buy Cy Leeser one hundred times over." The banker paused and added, "At least one hundred times."

"And who would that be?" Siggi sounded skeptical. He raised an eyebrow.

"Tomorrow we're calling Qatar together. You're meeting Sheikh Fahad Bin Thalifa over the phone."

"He's the one who bought five percent of Hafnarbanki's shares?" asked Siggi.

"The same."

Siggi started to smile, his stress whistling free through a steam valve. But then his eyes narrowed, and his look grew far too sly for a gallery owner. "What's in it for you, cousin?"

"I told you. I need information."

"What makes you think I can get it?"

"Oh, you'll get it."

"You sound so confident, Ólafur."

"Cy won't realize he's telling you."

"I'm confused. I thought you said he'll make money."

"He'll make money," said Ólafur. "You'll earn his trust, and then—"

"And then what?"

"I bury that *asni*," Ólafur replied, using the Icelandic word for "asshole."

"I can't."

"Relax, Siggi. Cyrus Leeser will never suspect you of anything."

CHAPTER TWENTY

THURSDAY, JUNE 12

BENTWING AT $59.70

"We'll start with forty million."

"Thank you," Cusack replied into his wireless headset. He was calm and methodical, professional to the core. His inner euphoria never trickled through the mike. Jimmy spoke with all the emotion of a tollbooth attendant, one who had gone without coffee, radio, and much by the way of oxygen, one who was down to the last thirty minutes of an eight-hour shift.

In the privacy of his office, however, Cusack sprang from his Aeron chair and knocked over café au lait fresh from the kitchen. He ignored the foamy suds surging from his toppled cup and victory-danced the twist like John Travolta in *Pulp Fiction*. Cusack heard the music. He had just landed an account with New Jersey Sheet Metal.

"I'll FedEx the paperwork, Buddy."

"Great, Jimmy. And remember one thing." The union rep spoke with an Oklahoma accent, curious for a guy from New Jersey. "There's more money behind the forty million."

"We value your trust."

"Don't screw up," Buddy said, and clicked off.

Cusack started toward Cy's office but, eyeing the coffee, thought better of it. He grabbed a few paper towels and attacked the spill, soaking up the coffee and milk. He was still twisting to the inner beat of "C'est La Vie" when the phone rang. It was Robby, his real estate broker.

"Don't tell me," Cusack boomed, "you sold our condo." He was fired up. In his experience good news always arrived in threes, which meant two positive surprises on the way.

"Afraid not," the real estate broker replied, his tone flat. "It's time to cut our listing price."

Cusack's good humor collapsed like a punctured lung. He paused for a long moment and finally replied, "No can do. I say we jack up the asking price."

As Cusack spoke, he typed an e-mail to Cy: *New Jersey Sheet Metal in for forty. On phone now. Debrief in five.*

"Are you nuts?" Robby shot back. "There aren't any buyers."

BEG ticked up to $59.80. Cusack sighed with his crooked smile, wondering how long it would take for Leeser to reply.

"Keep looking," Jimmy replied to his real estate broker. "Somebody out there is dying to buy our condo."

"I'm telling you. It won't sell."

"And I'm telling you, Robby, forget about dropping the price. I'm not taking a check to the closing."

Cy replied, via e-mail: *You're a fucking Whartonite stud. New Jersey will be our biggest client.*

Thanks, Cy. I think, thought Cusack.

"What do you mean, 'a check to the closing'?" asked Robby.

"Document stamps, real estate taxes, lawyers, your commission, and of course, the mortgage—they all add up."

"How much did you borrow?"

"Three point one," replied Cusack.

He typed: *FedExing docs overnight. New Jersey wants in as soon as possible.*

" 'Three point one,' " Robby echoed. "How do you live with that?"

"I cut a great deal."

"How great can it be if you're on the hook for that kind of money?"

"Interest only and one payment a year—"

"But at five percent," Robby interrupted, "you pay at least one hundred and fifty thousand a year. Is that comfortable?"

A second e-mail arrived from Cy: *Great fucking work.*

"It's comfortable if I get a bonus," Cusack replied.

"I don't get how you live with the pressure." Robby sounded skeptical.

"Keep my head down."

"So do ostriches," Robby said. "Is LeeWell making money this year?"

"Put away your abacus," replied Cusack, drawing the line, "and sell my condo."

Victor Lee sent an e-mail: *Nice work, dickhead.*

Cusack typed back: *Don't lose it.*

"Well, I hope you get a bonus," Robby persisted. "You're gonna need it, because this market sucks."

"I won't drop the listing price."

"You got monster nads." The real estate broker whistled under his breath.

"Do you think," snapped Jimmy, "that LeeWell Capital will foreclose on my condo?" He was growing tired of his broker's pushback.

"It happens."

"I talk to our clients every day."

"Well, that's pretty damn ruthless," Robby observed.

"The last thing Cy needs is to lose his head of sales." Cusack regretted his words immediately. The money had not even arrived, and the forty million win was going to his head.

At that precise instant, a third e-mail arrived from Cy. *Get me in front of your father-in-law, and we declare victory this month.*

"Monster nads, Cusack," Robby repeated with clear admiration. "But there's only one way to raise the price on your condo."

"Which is?"

"Spring for a new master bathroom, something nice, no expense spared. You know what I mean."

BEG ticked down to $59.60.

"That's better than solving P versus NP," said Geek.

He was referring to a famous problem from computer science. In 1971 Stephen Cook posed a question that no one has been able to solve, even though there is a $1 million reward for the right answer: If computers can *verify* solutions quickly, can they also *compute* these solutions quickly?

Cusack had just told Geek about the $40 million commitment, without disclosing the name of New Jersey Sheet Metal. Best friends or not, the two were still competitors. They discussed business situations in general terms and steered clear of the details. Discretion was the only way to protect their relationship, which is why Geek's follow-up comments came as a surprise: "You're just in time, too."

"What's that mean?"

"Asymptotic implied volatility of the second order."

"You're killing me," said Cusack. "Translation please."

"Danger under every rock. I hear things about Bentwing."

"Like what?"

"How much you own," replied Geek. "Potential problems with the company."

"What can I say?" Cusack refused to discuss LeeWell Capital's concentration in the stock. "Alternative energy is the world's future."

"We've been friends a long time, Jimmy."

"Ever since Wharton."

"I'd use this win to maximize your leverage with Leeser. Time for you to get your arms around how he hedges."

"Do you know something I don't?" asked Cusack, feeling his stress rise.

"Nothing that's public," replied Geek, using the one word guaranteed to stop further discussion—public. "Do yourself a favor. Snoop around the office. Keep your ear to the ground. Anything to get the full picture."

"Thanks for the heads-up."

Then, with astonishing clarity for a guy who sprinkled "jump-diffusion" references into everyday conversation, Geek blackened Cusack's mood with a single warning:

"Don't get stuck on stupid."

FRIDAY, JUNE 13
BENTWING AT $59.30

Following the big win, Victor treated the entire office to "Lunch on Lee" from Greenwich Pizza. The big show of team success was the trader thing to do. Caffeine, cholesterol, comfort food—sacrificing arteries warded off bad markets. And with the Dow off about 8.4 percent halfway through the year, there was no better time to indulge.

No one needed a reprieve more than Lee. He cheered as assets grew to $897 million by mid-May. He grimaced as they pulled back to $800 million, making LeeWell Capital flat on the year. No gain. No loss. The retreat spawned Victor's cancerous funk, which slowly metastasized throughout the office. He was ready to embrace good news, any hint of a market rebound and better times ahead.

Surrounded by pepperoni and mushrooms, the conference room air glorious from victory and garlic, Victor almost sounded affectionate when he praised Cusack's big win with New Jersey Sheet Metal. "Our dickhead does good work."

"Thanks. I think," replied Cusack, which made everybody laugh.

During "Lunch on Lee," the people of LeeWell Capital came together and rallied around the conference room table. From mouth to paper plate, every employee stretched cheesy strings three inches long. It was a tribal gathering, a ritual feast, except there were no grass skirts or belly dancers. Everyone wore sweaters, given the temperature was set to sixty-six degrees. Even Cy broke from a solitary lunch at his desk to join the troops.

Amanda the receptionist, sated from fresh mozzarella and Diet Coke, proposed the unthinkable. Not at first. She took her time and worked up to the ask. "Hey, Cy. This is a big deal. We're celebrating Jimmy and his victory. And it's true, I don't know much about the portfolio. I answer phones."

She paused for a moment, savoring all eyes, flirty and fully aware she was rosy and cute and blessed with a hundred-watt smile. A few people giggled. Nobody interrupted. Cusack could hear a pin drop.

"What I'm saying," Amanda continued, "is that LeeWell Capital never loses money. Never. And I understand the markets are shaky, but I bet we make money this year. Big money, because we're managing new money. So please, sir, I want more heat. Please, sir, maybe sixty-eight degrees, sir."

Amanda pleaded with Oliver Twist eyes, half in jest, half in earnest. In that moment, she would have traded either porridge or pizza for two more degrees from Con Edison. She sometimes complained to Nikki in the ladies' room about the temperature set to cold feet and goose bumps.

Nobody uttered a word. The employees of LeeWell Capital, expectant and full of good humor, eyed their boss. Cy Leeser always said the right thing. He always chose words that made employees redouble their efforts. And so far, he had always been successful, given the hedge fund's unblemished investment returns. That Friday the thirteenth, fifteen employees waited in silent expectation for encouragement from their fearless leader, who would make everything better.

Leeser scanned the crowd, aware his company was waiting. He finally faced Amanda and said one word: "No." He walked out of the room, with Shannon close behind. In their wake, the two men left behind the nervous silence of air hissing from a balloon. With that one word, "No," Jimmy's feel-good moment from a $40 million win ended. It was that fast.

CHAPTER TWENTY-ONE
MONDAY, JUNE 16
BENTWING AT $60.00

Shannon operated in one gear—snarl. The big man seldom revealed the gap between his front teeth, the grillwork smile without good humor. He just cleared rooms over and over to the point of annoyance, fat butting into Cusack's business like a cross between Genghis Khan and an Orwellian Big Brother:

"What time are you leaving, Jimmy?"

"Who's Geek and why does he call so much?"

"I need your list of prospects."

"What for?" the head of sales demanded, hearing the last request.

"Background checks."

The response put Cusack over the top. "He'll scare off our prospects," Cusack complained to Cy.

"I don't care," Leeser replied dismissively, almost yawning. He picked up the phone and said, "Nikki, I'd kill for a latte. Jimmy needs one, too."

"You're kidding," Cusack snapped, wondering whether he heard right. "You don't care?"

"No," Cy answered, his voice cool. "You ever hear the expression 'broker of the day'?"

"Rookie stockbrokers who get incoming calls. What's this got to do—"

"Hear me out. When I was at Merrill, the receptionist put through a call from a guy named Sal DiLeonardo. He asked to meet and threw out numbers about his portfolio. Five million here. Ten million there."

"I'm listening."

"Big Sal was a member of the Gambino crime family," explained Leeser.

"Merrill connected the dots, and I canceled the appointment. DiLeonardo got the message."

"You never met him?"

"No," confirmed Leeser. "Years later, Big Sal turned state's evidence. He's either dead or in witness protection."

"Our prospects don't fit the profile."

"Don't kid yourself," cautioned Leeser. "Nobody ever sees wise guys coming. And I don't need mob goons seeping into my fund."

"Whatever you say."

"Good, because we'd be lost without Shannon. He's a one-man dynamo when it comes to background checks or corporate espionage."

"Sounds like Kroll in a box," Cusack observed in a neutral tone, annoyed, referring to the company known as Wall Street's private eye.

"Funny you say that. Shannon worked at Kroll."

"How'd you find him?"

"He found us."

"I'm surprised," observed Cusack.

"Why's that?"

"I thought he was a friend from way back."

"He's one hundred percent loyal," said Leeser.

"How can you tell?"

"Remember my employment criteria—people who can't afford to lose?"

"I'll never forget."

"Shannon can't afford to lose." Leeser's expression showed absolute conviction.

Does he have mortgage problems, too?

"Why's that?" asked Cusack.

"Kroll fired his ass for background omissions."

"Such as?"

"Shannon's brother has a fifty-eight-page rap sheet," explained Leeser. "He's doing time in ADX Florence for manslaughter."

"How's that affect Shannon?"

"He can't get a job in security. Would Cusack Capital ever hire somebody with criminal links?"

"Not now," Jimmy replied.

"You get my point," said Leeser. "If you ask me, Shannon's background makes him better at his job."

"Why's that?"

"He's an insider."

"Great."

"He knows the criminal mind-set."

"Everybody's friend on Facebook," Cusack replied, unable to curb his sarcasm.

"You need to forget Shannon," Leeser said, half command, half request. He leaned forward, his brown eyes burrowing into Cusack. "And concentrate on getting me in front of your father-in-law."

"Just give me time, Cy."

"Make it happen."

TUESDAY, JUNE 17

BENTWING AT $60.22

It was Rachel's last full day in Paris, and she was on a mission. Slouchy blazer, long tank, and loose shorts—at seven A.M. she was already dressed for the day. Chunky shoes and cute to beat all hell.

First, Rachel would eat breakfast at George Cinq's sculpted French garden. She preferred it to the hotel's indoor dining rooms, which were too rococo for her taste. Then a massage from Pierre. How was a Balzac body attached to such gifted hands? Afterward, she would hit the fashion houses, starting with Givenchy.

The cell phone rang as Rachel left her suite. She knew the number. She thought it odd her employer was calling. He generally waited until the afternoon. "I'm surprised to hear from you this early, Kemosabe."

"My work is never done. How do you like George Cinq?"

"Overwhelming," she admitted. "But I can get used to it."

"Enjoy your last day, because I want you good and rested when you get back to the clinic."

"I may never leave Paris."

"Stick with me, and you'll own Paris."

Rachel's ears pricked up. "How so, Kemosabe?"

Five minutes later, and Rachel got it: the risk, the opportunity, and the prevailing market conditions. She found it odd that people could make money whether a stock was going up or down. Time to keep her head down and focus on the new target, a guy named Conrad Barnes from Bronxville. She was still trying to understand the new tone in Kemosabe's voice, a curious mix of salesmanship and unbridled fury.

I bet he's wearing war paint, she thought.

WEDNESDAY, JUNE 18
BENTWING AT $61.22

"Cy, have you given any more thought to the Goncharova?"

Siggi was referring to a painting by Natalia Goncharova. A Russian painter, she lived from 1881 to 1962. The art dealer reckoned that his biggest client would appreciate her Cubist leanings.

"No, in all honesty," replied Leeser. "Too busy running my business. You know how it is."

"I totally understand. I don't mean to pressure you."

"Not at all," Leeser said. "We've been dancing around this one for how long?"

"Two months. But it's okay."

"No, it's time I make a decision."

"It's okay," Siggi repeated.

Leeser's eyes narrowed. He twirled his long black hair with an index finger. Was it desperation in the Icelander's voice? Or was it opportunity? Cy detected something but could not tell what. "Will your seller take three million?"

"The estate is firm on four."

" 'Estate.' What do you mean?"

"I've said too much already."

"You can tell me," pressed Leeser, detecting a nervous timbre from the art dealer, or so he thought.

"The family patriarch was a good friend. And he's turning over in his grave because the heirs are splitting up his collection."

"It's just business."

"It's the legacy of a man's life," argued Siggi, "which his kids don't appreciate. They want to dump the Goncharova. It makes me sick to my stomach."

"How come they won't take three?" asked Leeser, ignoring the Icelander's sick stomach.

"Because somebody else has an interest."

Siggi leaned back in his chair. He waited for Reykjavik's damp ocean breezes to whip through the open windows and rearrange the dust inside the tiny office of his gallery. Then he cast a line with enough live bait hanging from the hook to snag a big one.

"Somebody else with an interest in excess of four million." He yawned, his voice quivering ever so slightly. "Maybe as much as five."

"What happens if I wire you four million in five minutes?" asked Cy.

"The Goncharova is yours."

"You think I can flip it to the other buyer?"

"Probably an eighty percent chance," replied Siggi, inspecting the half-moons of his fingernails.

"I'd love to make a quick buck."

"It's perfect for the other guy's collection."

"I'll take it," said Leeser, "under one condition."

Siggi's enthusiasm waned, his shoulders slumped, and his casual veneer disappeared. There was always a catch. "What do you mean?"

"I want a put option. You have one year to flip the Goncharova at a profit to me. Otherwise you buy it back at four million."

"Why would I do that?"

"Commissions. First when you sell it to me and then when you flip it to the other buyer."

The art dealer paused for a long moment. He said nothing, the silence between phones darker and deader than the middle of the night in central Iceland.

"Are you there, Siggi?"

"I'm thinking."

"It's okay if you can't handle that kind of action," Leeser said, baiting him back. "A four-million put option is a bunch of money for anybody."

"I'm still thinking."

"That's the funny thing. When money is on the line, everything comes into focus."

"Okay, Cy. We have a deal."

Ólafur erupted when his cousin hung up. He raced around the art dealer's desk and slapped his cousin on the back. "That was beautiful, Siggi. You belong on the stage. Better yet, why don't you come work for us at Hafnar-banki?"

"Beautiful for you, cousin. See that piece?"

Siggi gestured toward a whimsical line drawing of a kneeling green figure. The corpulent belly jutted forward, a cocky, aggressive stance. Elbows akimbo, spindly arms lined in bold black, the figure had no head. A plume of wispy gray smoke billowed from the neck.

"I see it."

"That's how I feel right now—headless."

"Are you kidding? Our plan is perfect."

"Your plan," Siggi corrected Ólafur. "You think the Qataris will pay five million for the Goncharova?"

"It's a done deal."

"I hope you're right. I don't have four million dollars."

"Forget it, cousin. The Qataris are rock solid. And you're fantastic."

"I didn't do anything," Siggi replied, relaxing in the wake of his cousin's praise. "Cy structured the deal."

"That's the thing about finance guys," said Ólafur. "We're always telling people what to do. Even at meals."

"Meals? What are you talking about?"

"Cyrus Leeser just told us how to stuff his balls down his throat."

CHAPTER TWENTY-TWO
WEDNESDAY, JULY 2
BENTWING AT $59.87

"We need to talk."

"I hate that expression," Leeser growled at Siggi. "Can't you say, 'I'd like to bounce an idea off you.' Or ask if I have a minute. Or come up with some other expression than 'We need to talk.'"

The rant stuck four inches out of Siggi's back. It was cold and edgy. It was utterly confusing to the art dealer. "I don't understand."

"My wife says 'We need to talk' when there's a problem."

"Has Bianca ever wired you five million dollars?" asked Siggi.

"The Goncharova?" Leeser knew exactly where this conversation was headed.

"You sold it."

"But I haven't taken possession."

"You forced a decision, Cy. It's perfect for the other bidder's collection."

"And I'm up a million bucks on the trade." Leeser glowed from inside out, savoring the sweet, swift score. "Minus your commission, of course?"

"Yes and no," Siggi replied. Ordinarily, he never toyed with his customers. This time he could not resist.

"What are you talking about?" Leeser's good humor vanished at once. Inside, he berated himself for dropping his guard. "What's the catch?"

"No catch. You're up a million bucks. And there's no deduction for my commission."

"Nobody works for free, Siggi."

"Who said anything about free? I sold the Goncharova net. The other party paid my fee."

Leeser blinked, processing Siggi's words. He surveyed his office walls, every square inch graced with urbane musings from gifted artists. And he finally erupted, not in God-speak but in language from the streets: "Shit hot. You know what I'm saying? That's shit hot."

"It's not much money in your world but—"

"It's a down payment on a new helicopter," interrupted Leeser, his voice drooling with anticipation. He had his eye on a Bell 430, fully loaded and currently owned by a Swiss industrialist.

"I'm working on something new. Something big."

"You got my attention."

"I need to work out a few details before we talk."

"Tell me when you're ready," said Leeser.

"Done. Where do I wire your money?"

"I'll put Nikki on the line. And by the way, keep your eyes open for a package from me."

After they hung up Ólafur said, "We've got his trust, Siggi. Now it's time to find out whether there's any substance."

On Saturday morning, Jimmy forgot the markets and his schedule for the following week. The unanswered questions about Cy's hedges never entered his mind. Nor did Shannon, Victor Lee, or any of the usual suspects. Saturday was his day to cook, his turn to feed Emi and Yaz—their baby now four months in the making. His turn to create fantasy breakfasts.

Cusack was serving crispy bacon, which was a risk. Pregnancy had turned Emi's taste buds fickle. She might love it. Or she might go, "Eww." But he was okay with risk even in cooking. Cusack believed the weekends required bacon. It had been that way ever since his childhood in Somerville.

He was serving scratch biscuits, none of that pop-and-regret crap from the supermarket freezers. And the pièce de résistance—he was serving caramelized apple omelets complete with sugar and sour cream and splashes of dulce de leche because Emi craved sweets more and more all the time.

"Smells like donuts," she said, passing him the business page of *The New York Times*.

"Your breakfast," said Cusack, pretending to be miffed, "is not on the menu at Dunkin' Donuts."

"Oh my God, this is good," Emi garbled with full mouth and biscuit-loaded cheek.

"Nice," Cusack mumbled, pretending his own mouth was chockablock. He noticed a headline toward the bottom of the *Times*. "I can't believe it."

"Something wrong?" Emi had swallowed her first bite of the omelet. Even without a verb, she sounded more articulate this time.

"Caleb paid Hartford two hundred million for one of their divisions. Cash."

"He never told me," Emi observed, loading her fork with more omelet. "I wonder why."

"He can't."

"Can't what, James?"

"Discuss a deal involving a public company. It's too easy to run afoul of securities laws."

Emi placed her fork on the plate and blinked hard. "Any idea how long my father was negotiating?"

"Knowing Caleb, I bet nine months. Maybe longer."

"That's what I think," agreed Emi. "He was probably negotiating with Hartford back in December."

The couple reached the same conclusion at the same time. "Caleb needed money," said Cusack, "to close the deal with Hartford. He shut me down but couldn't breathe a word."

"That's a game changer."

"It still sucks, Em."

"But you get it."

"Yes," Cusack conceded. "I get it."

"Maybe you can declare a truce," she offered hopefully.

"Maybe," he agreed. "And it sure would make Cy Leeser happy."

"What do you mean?"

"Pass the bacon, and I'll tell you about it. Want some orange juice?"

TUESDAY, JULY 8
BENTWING AT $57.50

Eddy was on the phone again. He was a trader on the team that managed Merrill's relationship with LeeWell Capital. He knew Leeser from way back, from the time when his client was a stockbroker at Merrill. Because of their history together, Eddy worked with Cy to shepherd his loan requests through Merrill's chain of command.

The two men were not especially fond of each other. Nor were they especially civil. But the relationship worked. Eddy booked his trades, and Cy booked his loans.

"Your loan balance is over two hundred and sixty million dollars."

"Is there a problem?" asked Leeser, cool at first.

"That's a bunch of money."

"Number one," Leeser said, opening and closing his right fist, "it's two hundred and sixty-three million. Don't call me unless you get your facts straight. Otherwise, you're wasting my time. Number two, our loan balance is thirty-four percent of total assets. Last I looked you guys lend up to sixty-five percent. Which leads me to number three. What the fuck do you want?"

"Bentwing is down thirteen percent since mid-May," the trader replied, remaining calm. His job was to please clients, no matter how difficult. "I hope there's not a problem."

"I sit on the board. And as an *insider*," Leeser paused to let the word register, "I can tell you straight, we're knocking the cover off the ball. I can disclose every detail about Bentwing, every number, every order, every dollar saved, anything you want to know, even down to our expense cuts in the ladies' room where we opted for a cheaper brand of air freshener." Trading sarcasm for cyanide, Leeser added, "Afterward we can jump for joy on each other's stomachs when we're summering together in Leavenworth."

"Aw, come on, Cy. The market's got us spooked." In full retreat, the trader added, "I'm just saying," like the phrase was a peace offering.

"I'm hedged. And by default, so is Merrill Lynch."

"We can't see your hedges. I don't have anything to show my boss."

"Show him the commissions I pay. My trades bought his wife's face-lift, Eddy. My trades paid tuition for his kids."

"I'm just saying—"

"Morgan Stanley wants my business," interrupted Leeser. "So does Goldman. But UBS will get it. They do a great job executing my hedges. So, Eddy, are you asking me to pay back your loan?"

"You're too important a customer. I'm giving you a heads-up."

"Margin call—yes or no, Eddy?"

"No."

"Then get off my phone." Leeser slammed down the receiver, scattering poison pheromones every which direction and leaving the trader with dial tone. "That guy gives infanticide a good name."

Cusack, with the timing of a two-dollar watch, rapped on the door and caught his boss on the wrong side of a portfolio down 4 percent since the beginning of the year. "Gotta minute?"

"What. What. What," Cy snapped. "Don't bother me unless we have an appointment with your father-in-law."

CHAPTER TWENTY-THREE

The movie theater was dark inside. The noise was not deafening so much as it was annoying—the shuffling, the getting situated, and the backing and forthing on cell phones. Who the hell cared? The cleaner closed her eyes, trying in vain to shut out the hubbub from seniors on date night.

Rachel considered her employer's words from earlier that month. She understood so little about the stock market and her finances. But one thing was for sure. His analysis of her profession was right on target.

"You have a problem, Rachel. Your business doesn't scale."

"What do you mean?"

"What's an average job cost?" he asked, sounding much like a Socratic philosophy professor.

"Fifty thousand, give or take." She grew wary, uncomfortable and acutely aware he was her only client. "Plus expenses. I always get expenses up front."

"How many jobs a year?"

"Not including you, Kemosabe?"

"That's right."

"Four or five," she answered. She thought these numbers sounded impressive.

"So it takes four years just to save a million bucks," he said. "I don't see how you're ever going to retire in France unless—"

"Unless what?"

"Unless we work together and get it right."

The guy's smooth, Rachel decided. Her employer was Mr. Charisma, a regular George Clooney when he tried. She had seen his pain-in-the-ass side, too. But she was giving him the benefit of the doubt ever since Paris.

With cool air blasting full tilt inside the theater, Rachel snugged her white cotton cardigan over a beige sundress with spaghetti straps. The sweater and cinched belt, she decided, eased the seductive cut of her neckline. Toned it down, because tonight called for a modest look. Rachel even wore flats so other women would think her shoes nothing special.

And forget her.

The 6:45 show in Bronxville attracted the oldies, especially on Thursdays. Rachel staked out a back row in the theater, expecting the surveillance to be peaceful if somewhat mundane. But oh my god, this crowd was a crabby lot. Or hard of hearing. Or something.

A seventy-something woman blasted into her mobile phone. "Herbert, we're in the back. On the right. Would you hurry? Have you parked the car?" It was like she paused every few words to catch her breath or ratchet up the volume. "I'm hanging up, Herbert."

Given her decibels, Rachel wondered whether the woman needed a cell phone to be heard outside the building. "I'm hanging up," she repeated as though Herbert missed what she said the first time.

More seniors doddered past. One man in his seventies—hair migrating from scalp to bushy white unibrow—lumbered past and seated his wife a few rows up, near the aisle. He asked in a voice loud enough for the entire theater to hear, "You want something to eat, Marge?"

"No, Conrad. And neither do you."

"I'm getting some popcorn," he insisted, asserting his male independence via the overpriced concessions.

"You just ate."

"What can I say? The Bronx Zoo makes great hot dogs."

"Keep your voices down," somebody shushed from up front. The aging crowd behaved more like the fans of World Wide Wrestling than moviegoers.

Amid the noise Rachel decided Conrad was a gentle old man. She would rather do Herbert's wife. That old bird was a grouch. She deserved to get "done," something other than a random act of fate like going to bed one night and not waking up. Herbert's wife deserved something more creative. Maybe two or three corks stuffed down her throat. But hey, a contract was a contract. Even if it meant trekking out to the suburbs.

Conrad was turning into a royal pain in the ass. For one, the train ride from New York City took thirty minutes. For another, the hit was all wrong, too close to the Colony Club.

Rachel, of all people, a cleaner for chrissakes, feared that erratic patterns and pieces would fit together. That clues would beckon hotshot detectives to come sniffing and asking questions, always lifting their legs in her direction.

She needed "operating leverage," whatever that was. She still didn't understand what Kemosabe meant by the expression.

The biggest problem was Mrs. Conrad Barnes. For all her seventy-something aches and pains, Marge could not leave her husband the hell alone. It was like she camped out on his shirttails. She was always there: his shopping expeditions, his errands, and every Thursday when they hiked around the Bronx Zoo together.

You're getting in the way of my retirement plan, thought Rachel.

Once the movie began, Rachel considered sneaking out of the small theater. A few doors down, on the other side of the wine store, there was a bistro that advertised a mean skirt steak. All the chomping and chewing inside the theater, the slurping of Coke until air gurgled through straws, made her hungry. Somebody was taking forever to rip off a wrapper.

Too risky to leave, Rachel decided. She was on the job, watching Conrad and learning his habits. And, unfortunately, she was watching a stupid movie with crusty old cranks who grazed like cows.

Tonight was about perfection and flawless execution, not errors. She could not afford to leave clues. Or succumb to steak frites and a French red, only to be recognized later from good times at the bistro. Tonight was about surveillance.

Without thinking, Rachel rubbed the puffy blemish on her hand. It was always that way whenever her thoughts drifted to food. She remembered that night with the chocolate layer cake. Her daddy screamed, "I'll beat the wax out your ears."

"Damn him," Rachel muttered.

The theater, she decided, would not work for an insulin hit. There were too many people around, not just Marge the ubiquitous, but every moviegoer within a five-mile radius. And there was too much candy, enough to fish Conrad Barnes out of a diabetic coma a hundred times over. No wonder these people got all grouchy and loud. They were probably suffering from sugar highs.

After the movie, Rachel abandoned Marge and Conrad; enough stalking for one night. She walked through the parking lot across the street from the theater. She headed down into the tunnel leading to the southbound side of Bronxville's train station. She wandered along the platform until she found a concrete bench, then plugged in her earbuds and listened to Josephine Baker, the American-born singer who moved to Paris in the 1920s and became "La Baker" to all of France.

The music was sultry but Rachel hardly drifted on the humid summer night. With exacting precision, she mentally probed the lives of Mr. and Mrs. Conrad Barnes. What they did. Where they went. Whom they knew. Their patterns were her blocks, the pieces she assembled for a successful hit. Rachel found herself returning to one place, a venue that stretched her lips from ear to ear, which was how her daddy said, "Smile." Conrad Barnes was a regular at the Bronx Zoo, an endless stream of intoxicating possibilities.

CHAPTER TWENTY-FOUR

MONDAY, AUGUST 4
BENTWING AT $49.25

Most Monday mornings, sixteen employees packed inside LeeWell's conference room and jockeyed for eleven of the twelve available chairs. One seat was sacred. Nobody ever sat in Cy's throne, which had achieved a hallowed status equal to several Vatican relics. He made the decisions. He paid the bonuses. He decided who was exceptional and who was expendable.

During these company-wide meetings, employees buzzed from caffeine transfusions and the innate optimism that follows two days off. Leeser encouraged his entire team, from accounting to reception, to trade ideas about the markets or the office. Whatever was on their minds. Discussions were frank with no holds barred.

Today was different. On Friday Bentwing closed under fifty dollars for the first time since January. The doors were shut, and there were only eight people in the conference room. Those eight said nothing and avoided eye contact, all except Victor. He looked ready to strangle someone. Cy sent e-mails that morning asking other employees not to attend.

Cusack, Victor, and his three junior traders gathered round the table. Nikki sat at the far end, poised to take notes on her steno pad. Shannon stood, arms folded, with his back against the wall. Nobody said a word. All eyes fixed on Cyrus Leeser.

"Since the beginning of the year," Leeser said, "we have lost over one hundred million dollars." He parsed his words and spoke with a slow, methodical cadence that slapped the blues onto every face in the room.

Silence in response. A hush hung over the conference room. It was heavier than L.A. smog and produced roughly the same results. Heads ached. Hearts pounded. Throats turned dry.

Leeser appeared calm, but his coal-black eyes burned with the fire no one had seen in a long time. His clothes were rumpled, the wrinkles totally out of character. And Cusack thought there was the faintest hint of grass stains on his shirtsleeves.

"Victor," Cy continued. "Get us started."

"The shorts are all over Bentwing."

"Tell me something I don't know," snapped Leeser. "Who the fuck is attacking us?"

Victor recoiled and squirmed in his seat to the right of the throne. His hands fussed across the table, uncomfortable without his sixteen-ounce Estwing hammer. "If I had to guess, it's an institution in the Middle East or Europe. Maybe a combination."

"I don't pay you to guess," bellowed Cy. "Find out. You got that, Victor? You find out, and you get back to me."

"I'm on it." The head trader sounded calm, but his eyes blinked over and over behind horn-rimmed glasses. His junior traders scanned the room for a place to hide.

"What about Hafnarbanki?" pressed Leeser. "We're giving back our gains. Why?"

"A royal family in Qatar is buying stock," Cusack volunteered. He had seen the press releases. He had scrutinized every position in LeeWell's portfolio. Intensive research was the only way to compensate for the nagging question he could not answer: *How does LeeWell hedge?*

"The family owns more than five percent of Hafnarbanki," added Victor, still nursing his ego.

"That's fucking goofy," snorted Leeser.

"Maybe not," countered Cusack.

All eyes in the room turned to the head of sales. Even Shannon, who had not displayed much interest, focused on him. Cy raised his eyebrows and voiced what they were all thinking:

"What do you mean?"

Before Jimmy could respond, Victor recouped his hogshead of testosterone. "You think Hafnarbanki is a buy, Cusack?"

Nikki glanced up from her pad. Shannon frowned, which was how he handled all situations. Leeser's reaction was the worst. He waited and watched. He said nothing.

"No," Jimmy replied to Victor. "I'd go all cash. I'd sell everything in the portfolio and take our profits on Hafnarbanki. I'd get safe in this market."

Cy's eyes widened.

"All cash," Victor scoffed. A vein in his forehead throbbed angry and indigo blue. "We're not a goddamn money market fund."

"Focus," growled Leeser, exercising his authority. "What's the interest in Hafnarbanki?"

"Follow the money," Jimmy explained. "If the Qataris buy stock, the chairman is the single biggest winner. He owns more shares than any other investor."

"You think he talked the royal family into buying?" asked Victor.

"How many times do we flush before this fucking bank goes away?" Leeser was growing agitated.

"I bet Hafnarbanki's management made a sweetheart loan with no downside to the Qataris," said Cusack. "Bankers have all kinds of tools. Low interest rates. No personal guarantees. They can structure almost anything."

"But why make it easy on the Qataris?" argued Cy.

"With my net worth tied up in one stock," Jimmy answered, "I'd figure out how to prop up the price."

"Me, too," agreed Leeser. Then he added, "You think they know we're short?"

His question betrayed the classic paranoia of short sellers. Betting against companies creates the opportunity for finite gains—and unlimited losses. If investors short stock at ten dollars and the price goes to zero, the gain is ten dollars. If the same ten-dollar stock rallies to one hundred dollars, short sellers lose ninety dollars per share. And the stock price can always climb farther.

"They know somebody is short," said Cusack. "But why us, Cy? We don't know who's shorting Bentwing, right?"

"But when I find out," Victor threatened, rebounding from Cy's earlier rebuke, "I'll fucking drill the Bentwing shorts."

Does Victor know something I don't?

"How will you drill them?" asked Leeser. He leaned forward with elbows on the table, chin resting on his thumb and knuckles pressed against his nose. He disappeared into a nether world of concentration as the whole room watched and waited.

"We back up the truck," Lee answered, "and buy, buy, buy until the price skyrockets. Until we crush any dickhead who bet against Bentwing. It's time LeeWell shows some balls." And then he added gratuitously, "Which may be a problem for Cusack over here."

"Who the hell are you?" asked Jimmy, taking the bait.

"I'm the guy who makes money. You must be the other guy, Cusack."

"Knock it off." Leeser leaned back in the throne and wrapped his hands behind his head.

"It makes no difference who's shorting," urged Victor. "I say we attack by adding to our position in Bentwing."

"My thoughts exactly," agreed Leeser.

Cusack avoided the temptation to roll his eyes. He suppressed his crooked smile, which resembled a smirk and might enflame tensions in the war room. "Buying more shares of Bentwing takes cash. How much do we have?"

"Forty million and one pizza lunch less than you promised," taunted Victor. "New Jersey Sheet Metal fucking missed the June closing."

Lee was referring to a common industry practice. Most hedge funds, including LeeWell Capital, accepted new money at the end of every quarter. This custom simplified the accounting.

"We missed June by one signature," explained Jimmy. "The guy was on vacation. We'll get the money."

"You're paid to close," the trader growled, "not to find excuses."

"New Jersey is rock solid," Cusack observed, calm on the outside, not taking the head trader's bait this time. "They'll fund our September closing."

"Knock it off, Victor," interrupted Cy. Then he turned and said, "Victor's right, Jimmy. We don't run from fights here."

Cusack's ears grew red but he said nothing.

"When you get back to your desk," Cy instructed Victor, "buy Bentwing in size. Put the word out. I'll worry how we fund." Then he addressed Jimmy: "What about your other prospects?"

"Plenty of people in the pipeline. But half of them are at the beach."

"Buy some fucking sunscreen."

Now Cusack's entire face reddened, but not from ultraviolet rays. "Got it."

"We all know what to do," Cy concluded. "Get to work."

The eight filed from the conference room into the corridor, where Leeser was waiting for Cusack. "Would you stop by my office, Jimmy?"

"Sure, Cy. When?"

"After your nap, your meds, whatever else you do all morning."

"I'll be right over."

Cusack sat ramrod straight. Leeser's leather guest chair felt cramped and uncomfortable today. It reminded him of a medieval pillory—his arms locked, his head on display.

Cy came out swinging. "You a short-timer?"

"What are you talking about?" The question flummoxed Cusack.

"We lose one hundred million. And you're ready to go all cash."

"You asked my opinion. Oil prices have cracked, and they're taking down alternative energy with them. That means Bentwing and thirty percent of our portfolio."

"We've never had a down year, remember?" argued Cy.

"Yesterday's news. I have no idea how we hedge. All I see is money disappearing down a rat hole."

"Leave the investing to me," Leeser barked, "and do your job."

"Nobody around here ever bagged a forty-million client before."

"Tell me when the money arrives, Jimmy."

"I have no idea what we're selling." Cusack regretted his outburst at once.

"Damn that Nikki," snapped Leeser, squinting and feigning anger. "You never got my memo on trade secrets?"

In the eye of Leeser's sarcasm, Cusack decided to stand down. "Sorry."

"I told you day one," pressed Leeser, "you need to apprentice before I demonstrate how we hedge. The problem here is loyalty. Yours. I'm not sure I can trust you."

"'Loyalty.' What are you talking about?"

"Caleb Phelps. How many times have I asked for an introduction?"

"We don't speak. I keep telling you our relationship is complicated."

"Then let me help," offered Leeser, suddenly magnetic from an epiphany. "My daughters aren't close to getting married. But I hope their future husbands make good. You know what I'm saying?"

"Yes."

"Let me brag about you to Caleb. Trust me. Every father wants to hear good things about his son-in-law." Leeser picked up the baby picture of his twins as though to punctuate his comment.

"Caleb just bought a major division from Hartford. It put some things into perspective."

"Okay?"

"I need to mend fences. But Caleb is closing the deal over the next few weeks. And afterward Anne and he go to Bermuda. They go the last two weeks of August every year."

"Anne?"

"My mother-in-law."

"Of course. Let's shoot for something in September. Maybe he can come to the event at the Museum of Modern Art."

"What event?"

"MoMA is honoring me." Leeser flashed a bright smile.

"Wow, that's exciting."

"Anybody can get an award, Jimmy. Just donate a few million."

"It sounds so simple."

Alone in his office, Leeser reflected on Cusack's words about Hafnarbanki's chairman: "I'd figure out how to prop up the price."

The kid only got it half right, Leeser mused. He should have said, "I'd figure out how to prop up the price and fuck my enemies." But who would know LeeWell shorted Hafnarbanki?

"Everybody," Leeser cursed. His allies from the two other hedge funds, Tall and Napoleon, were always running their damn mouths. "Damn them."

His mood black, Leeser phoned Eddy at Merrill Lynch and shifted to the bigger issue. "We're buying more Bentwing Energy."

"It's off twenty-five percent from the high. Are you sure?"

"Business is booming, Eddy. The stock's on sale."

"Is the window open?" asked the Merrill trader, referring to regulations that govern when board members can buy stock in their companies.

"Everything's fine. No problems with anybody. And that includes the SEC."

"How are you paying for the stock, Cy?"

"We're borrowing the money from you."

"Shit," Eddy exhaled. "Didn't you hear me the last time? We're getting tight on loans."

"Get it done. And one other thing."

"But Cy . . ."

"But nothing. Find out who's shorting my stock."

Cusack drummed the top of his desk and considered Leeser's words: "Since the beginning of the year, we have lost over one hundred million dollars." Unless the portfolio rebounded 23 percent, there would be no bonus. There would be a collection letter instead, this one from LeeWell Capital.

Leeser was growing more erratic by the day. He had long protected his technique to manage risk with paranoia worthy of Joseph Stalin. The Russian dictator once said, "I trust no one, not even myself."

Cy apparently shared the sentiment. He was buying more Bentwing. But instead of explaining his rationale, he repeated the same words over and over: "We don't lose money at LeeWell Capital."

My mother has blind faith. I don't.

Eyeing the number $78.79, Cusack fantasized about how good it would feel to resign. How good it would feel to march into Leeser's office and say, "I quit, motherfucker." The daydream was delicious, especially the motherfucker part, but it lasted all of twenty seconds. The word "mortgage" kept wedging into his thoughts.

Cusack Googled, "I hate my job," hoping for a catharsis from the forty-three million hits. He reviewed seven of them. Most proved to be self-help posts from tripe-mongers. "Be a better worker" pushed him over the edge.

He stopped surfing ten minutes into the session, annoyed by the bloggers and a job market with few alternatives.

Cusack phoned Emi. When all else failed, he could grouse to the spouse. He reached her voice mail, which was just as well. He had no business transferring his stress to her.

"I was thinking about you, sweetie. Say hi to Yaz for me."

Cusack left the message but never put down the phone. He became a salesman. He smiled and dialed prospects, convinced that a little more focus would fix his mess.

After Leeser finished with Merrill Lynch, he called his partner. He expected another tough exchange, but now was no time to hide. "I'm meeting Caleb Phelps."

"When?"

"Next month."

"Dammit, Cy. You're a human rain delay."

"Phelps is buying a company," Leeser explained.

"So what?" his partner objected.

"He's buried in closing details."

"And what happens after you meet him next month, Cy? Do we wait another four months? I'm losing my patience."

"And I'm living happily ever after. I keep telling you, we're on plan. Cusack is helping in ways we never dreamed."

CHAPTER TWENTY-FIVE
WEDNESDAY, AUGUST 6
BENTWING AT $50.75

Long after the markets closed, Cusack gazed out his office window at the train station below. The forecast called for wet weather. But nothing this sloppy. When the Metro North trains arrived and opened their doors, the Greenwich-bound commuters bolted for cabs and double-parked SUVs stacked two and three deep. The downpour pasted hair to heads. It wrecked shoes. The rain gusted great sheets of dry-cleaning bills—a backlog of soggy suits and saturated skirts growing among those who ran for it.

Storms were a way of life in Greenwich. They toppled trees and downed power lines, sometimes blacking out electricity for days. They littered limbs and leaves across the perfect lawns and sometimes crashed heavy branches against the perfect homes. The garbage and debris served as Post-it notes from heaven, each one with the same revelation: There were complicated, sometimes feverish lives behind the stone walls guarding properties. There were messy affairs and messy substance addictions and messy teenage behavior, the occasional murder or intervention that could take place in any American community. The difference was that Greenwich had more square footage than most and more hired hands to clean up the mess.

It would have been easy for Cusack to dwell on the inclement weather. But his thoughts inevitably returned to Cy Leeser. The boss's interest in Caleb Phelps was bizarre. Jimmy wondered whether the fascination was linked to the family's real estate interests. His father-in-law owned most of the waterfront property surrounding the New England Aquarium.

What's the connection between Bentwing and real estate?

In that moment, Cusack returned to December 2007. To Caleb's ambush and the FedEx package containing eight notarized redemptions. To the forty-five-day letter from Litton Loan Servicing. To the eureka moment when Cusack read about his father-in-law's deal with Hartford. Jimmy picked up the phone and dialed the sixty-first floor of the Empire State Building.

"Sydney here." Ordinarily, she put the fizz in a can of Coke. Not today. She mouthed the words, all flat and languid and full of an aftertaste that sounded like trouble.

"It's Jimmy. What's wrong?"

"Oh my god, does it show?" Sydney turned up the cheer and reverted to the human dynamo. Her instant change was like a personality refund. "I'm miffed about staying late."

"I don't buy it, Syd." It was 6:34 P.M. She never left before seven when they worked together. "Something's eating you, and we both know it."

"Work is kind of tense these days."

Cusack's heart skipped a beat. His thoughts jumped the rails to Jean Bertrand Bouvier. "What's the problem?"

"I'm not sure. Jean is edgy these days. He snaps at everybody. None of that pralines-and-cream glop from before."

"Client problems?" asked Cusack.

"Maybe. He met with some woman the other day behind closed doors. Everybody in the office could hear them screaming. But she didn't act like a client."

"Banker?"

"Blonde," Sydney replied. "That's all I know. He scheduled the appointment, and our shop hasn't been the same since."

"Did you ask him what's wrong?"

"You betcha." Sydney could charm charging cattle. "I asked if he took a beat-down in there."

"And?"

"Jean said, 'I got tattoos on the roof of my mouth.'"

"What does that mean?" Cusack scratched his head, wondering what language Southerners spoke.

"The hell if I know."

"That's weird."

"You're telling me, Jimmy."

"Has he lost any clients?"

"No," Sydney replied.

Cusack felt the tension in his neck ease.

Then lowering her voice even more, she said, "I have to go. Jean's coming back."

"Do you want to—"

She was gone before Cusack could finish. And his phone started to ring.

Geek called first. "My Bayesian networks say if you're drinking at the Ginger Man tonight, there's a ninety percent probability it's with me."

"Not tonight."

"We can ride out the storm over a few beers," Geek pressed.

"I want to see Emi before she falls asleep."

"How is she?"

"Glowing and growing." The crooked smile swept over Cusack's face. He could hardly wait to be a dad, no matter how daunting the prospect.

"Is Emi still working at the Bronx Zoo?"

"Stops in October," said Cusack.

"Wish we could do that, Jimmy. The markets always blow up in October."

"Tell me about it."

"Rumors are flying around Greenwich." Geek was a hit-and-run thinker. Not reckless—but after examining issues and firing off conclusions, he often changed the subject without notice.

"About what?"

"Your boss." Geek waited before adding, "And his wife."

"There are no secrets over the long run," answered Cusack, somewhere between philosophical and claustrophobic inside the gated community of Hedgistan. "It's a regular Peyton Place around here."

"Cy Leeser could use a loss-aversion utility at home."

"Try that in English," prodded Cusack.

"His wife threw all his clothes out the window."

"What are you talking about, Geek?"

"A buddy from Lone Pine Capital told me. He was driving down Round Hill Road and watched Cy's clothes flying from the second story. Shirts and pants and about a thousand shades of gray everywhere. There was probably enough Armani on the lawn to open a store."

"How did your friend know the clothes belonged to Cy?"

"He stopped and was watching from across the street. That's when your boss pulled up in the Bentley. Cy hopped out of the car and ran into the house like a man possessed."

"Well, there's a mess," observed Cusack.

"I'll say. Cy Leeser could use a Gaussian copulation rhythm."

"Only you could say that." Cusack knew the reference was a play on Gaussian copula algorithm, but after that he had no clue what Geek meant.

The phone rang, interrupting their repartee. Cusack recognized the Rhode Island area code but not the number. "Somebody's on my other line. I need to go."

"Jimmy Cusack."

"Graham Durkin here. I'm returning your call."

In that instant Cusack's spine tingled. His body temperature warmed ten degrees. The next thirty seconds, he knew from both instinct and experience, could change his career forever.

Last Monday, according to *The Wall Street Journal*, Durkin sold his medical device company to one of the big pharmaceuticals for $1.3 billion. All cash. He was the perfect prospect. Cusack dialed him after reading the article, and left a message. He never really anticipated a return phone call. He expected to chase Durkin like all other prospects.

"Congratulations on your deal," Cusack said, trying to walk the fine line between flattery and nonchalance. He stood while speaking, an old sales trick to summon energy as needed.

"Don't tell me. You manage money. And now, you're my new best friend."

Tough audience.

"Your phone must be ringing off the hook," Cusack admitted. "That's the downside of hitting the ball out of the park."

"I'm listening."

"LeeWell has been in business since 2000. I'd like to meet you and describe how we invest."

"Why you?" asked Durkin.

"We've never lost money."

"Fifty financial advisers have called. Goldman. Morgan Stanley. Every Merrill Lynch guy on the East Coast. What makes you different?"

"Those are investment banks. I work for a hedge fund."

"I mean you personally."

Weird question.

Cusack paused, considered where to begin, and then swung for the fence. "There are a hundred thousand guys on Wall Street, Graham. I'm one of the few who's ever run a business and struggled to make payroll. I know how hard it is to make money and how easy it is to lose. If I didn't believe in LeeWell Capital, I wouldn't be here."

"What's your minimum?"

"Ten million." Cusack hesitated, thought about what he had just said and added, "But frankly, I'd put money in bonds before investing the first dollar with us."

"Do you manage bonds?"

"No, but—"

"You said it's Jimmy?"

"Yes."

"Are you wasting my time, Jimmy? Why are you sending me to your competitors?"

Cusack flashed his crooked smile and replied, "I'm giving you my best advice. At some point, you'll want growth capital. And I'll be there no matter how long it takes, no matter when you add risk assets to your portfolio."

"I like that," Durkin said. "My secretary and you can arrange a time to meet. You have other business out in Providence?"

"Always."

The conversation was that quick. Thirty seconds later Jimmy finalized arrangements to meet Durkin in Rhode Island. He had just bagged an appointment with a billionaire, a feat he had never accomplished at Cusack Capital or with the gilt-edged panache of Goldman. He should have been elated. He should have been pumping his fist.

Cusack sat with his hands wrapped behind his head, though, pensive and reflective. He faced Sophie's Choice without the kids: his family's welfare versus selling out. He was exposing a guy he just met to a firm he no longer trusted. Jimmy considered what he'd said, words intended to convey honesty and integrity. "If I didn't believe in LeeWell Capital, I wouldn't be calling you."

He flip-flopped between defending Leeser and crabbing about him. Cy was odd, which did not mean bad. Or evil. Maybe paranoid. But there was no certainty that his boss was anything other than a hard-charging entrepreneur with marital problems and some kind of fixation on Emi's father.

One truth, Jimmy realized, was growing clearer with every passing day. There would be no 2008 bonus at LeeWell Capital—and probably no jobs anywhere else in Hedgistan. The portfolio would never clear the 10 percent hurdle, not with Bentwing dropping day in, day out.

The game was survival now. Bagging new clients was the only way for Cusack to save his job and negotiate, maybe, just maybe, a little relief on his mortgage. There was another conclusion Cusack could not escape, try as he might. And for a guy whose pride was a problem with his own father-in-law, the realization tasted like rotten clams.

Cy owns me.

Cusack drove home after the rain stopped. He arrived at eleven P.M. and wedged his BMW into a parking space on the street, kissing bumpers front and rear the way he learned in Somerville. He locked the rust bucket, which was odd, because most nights he never bothered. It was too ugly to steal.

Three hours more, and the meatpackers would rumble through the neighborhood. Every night they arrived in convoys, somehow coexisting with Kiss & Fly, Level V, and the other nightclubs. Heavy trucks creaked across the cobblestone streets, gears grinding with every shift, motors laboring from the loads. Swarthy men, their white aprons blood-splattered from sawing animal flesh, would push beef and lamb carcasses from low-rise warehouses. At that hour, the air stank like death. And blood from the slaughter ran down the cobblestones in rivulets that beckoned blowflies long before the opening bell rang at the New York Stock Exchange.

Upstairs Emi nestled inside her cocoon of sheets, no covers. Cusack tiptoed through the bedroom, shed everything except his boxers, and slipped between the sheets, spooning and savoring his wife's great, ponderous belly. He started to drift with the unsettling notion that Yaz would inherit her gene for face blindness.

Emi stirred and said in a voice caked with sleep, "I tried to wait up."

"Late call from Providence," he explained. "I'm driving up to Rhode Island in a few weeks."

"Is it important?"

"Big prospect."

"That's nice, James."

He started to fade again, when Emi whispered through her own sleepy haze, "Is Geek okay?"

Cusack's eyes rolled open. "I just spoke to him. Why do you ask?"

"Some guy called today. He's doing a background check."

"On Geek? Did you get the guy's name?"

"Daryle something. I wrote it down in the kitchen."

"What did he want to know?"

"Whether Geek went to Wharton. How long we've known him. If we spend time with him." Emi sounded more alert now, somewhat irritated to be awake.

"That's odd."

"You're telling me. A few questions were about us."

Emi's comment set off the alarm bells. "Did he ask for a social security number?" Cusack suspected identity theft.

"Nothing like that. But it still felt," Emi paused momentarily, "intrusive. I told him to call you."

"Good. Did you get a phone number?"

"In the kitchen."

Cusack bounded out of bed. He found the message pad with a 646 area code and assumed it belonged to a cell phone. But he froze at the sight of the caller's name. Emi had written *Daryle Lamonica* on the pad.

No way.

As long as mankind exists, there will be only one Daryle Lamonica. Cusack knew the name well. Lamonica, known as "the Mad Bomber," quarterbacked the Oakland Raiders in the late sixties and early seventies. His playing days ended two years before Jimmy was born.

Cusack's dad disdained Lamonica. Every fall when Oakland whipped his beloved New England Patriots, Liam barfed out expletives that most plumbers hid under the lid around their families. He beseeched St. Patrick to rain hell on Raider Nation. He asked that misery follow the seed of every scumbag who played for the "Silver and Black." He cursed on and on.

The diatribes started with Daryle Lamonica. They gained momentum with Kenny Stabler, who replaced Lamonica. They reached a fevered pitch with Jim Plunkett, the Benedict Arnold who defected from the Patriots and led the Raiders to two Super Bowl victories.

Lamonica was the name, however, that triggered the harangues. Cusack's parents once fought bitterly over the star, a scene that left the indelible print of Lamonica's name in family folklore. That was the time seven-year-old Jimmy Cusack asked his mother, "Is Daryle Lamonica's middle name Fucking?"

Liam Cusack burned bright red. Busted.

Helen Cusack, Jimmy's mother, gasped. "Jesus, Mary, and Joseph."

Jude, Cusack's older brother, stated with the indignation of a Sunday morning preacher, "You're sinning, Mother."

"I'm not sinning," Helen Cusack snapped in her Irish brogue. "I'm praying for the strength to clobber Jimmy. And maybe your father, too."

Her sharp rebuke scared Cusack's younger brother, Jack. Four years old—he started to cry.

Liam soothed, "It's okay, son."

Whereupon Jack wiped his moist eyes and announced fiercely, "I'm praying to Jesus, Mary, and Joseph so Mama doesn't have the strength to clobber anyone." Ever since, the episode always made for a good laugh at Thanksgiving dinners.

Back in bed Cusack asked Emi, "Was 'Daryle Lamonica' one of my brothers?"

"Don't be silly. They're not prank-calling you from the war. And besides."

"Besides what?"

"Daryle had the world's deepest voice. Nothing like the way your brothers sound."

"Would you recognize it?"

"Of course. I never forget a voice." That was the thing about prosopagnosia. Through the years, Emi had developed many tools for recognition. "Go to sleep, James."

Cusack was wired. He decided to call Daryle Fucking Lamonica first thing in the morning. He hated when his career followed him into bed. It was one thing to lay awake at night thinking about the markets, whipping yourself for investment decisions that looked stupid in the rearview mirror. But background checks on his friends by people who left fake names—they were another matter.

CHAPTER TWENTY-SIX
THURSDAY, AUGUST 7
BENTWING AT $50.16

In grade school one year, Jimmy wrote an essay titled "Mornings Are Purgatory." Somewhere he added, "One step away from hell." Sister Rosario smacked his knuckles with a ruler and sent him home with a note asking his mother to do the same.

Through the years Cusack's opinion never changed, which was a problem in an industry where the reading, the yakking, and the osmotic flow of ideas all took place before the market open at 9:30 A.M. Bacon, egg, and cheese offered some relief to the rise-and-asinine hours of money management. But most of the time, Jimmy struggled to self-medicate with coffee.

Not today.

Cusack kicked out of bed at 5:30 A.M. No groggy start—he showered with purpose. Getting up was one part anticipation. Emi and he were celebrating their fifth wedding anniversary today. She mattered above everything else. Four months from now so would Yaz.

Getting up was one part relief. He had tossed and turned all night, flopped on his stomach, rolled on his side, turned the infomercials on, turned them off, and tried everything except Ambien. He checked his alarm clock at least a thousand times during the early-morning hours.

And getting up was ten parts foul temper. Financial problems were one thing. The intrusion into Cusack's life was another. The phone call to Emi was both bizarre and invasive. He vowed to learn the real identity of Daryle Lamonica. If it were Cy or Shannon, they had gone too far.

Cusack hopped into his BMW. He turned the key, gritted his teeth to find the right angle in the ignition, and the cranky old engine rattled to life like Chinese New Year. Forty-five minutes later he pulled into Greenwich Plaza, already bustling with the citizens of Hedgistan.

Jimmy passed Victor Lee's station en route to the screaming eagle cappuccino in the kitchen. The trader had not arrived, odd for seven in the morning. His three screens were still blank, on sabbatical from the red, yellow, and green tickers that would follow during the day. Cusack hoped the market rally would continue. LeeWell Capital's portfolio had crept up 2 percent since Monday.

There was a computer printout on Victor Lee's desk. It was the same one Cusack had seen before, "Market Volatility Linked to Testosterone." This time the passages were highlighted so manically that only bits of white paper showed through the fluorescent yellow.

Great. My bonus is 20 percent away. And Victor's buried in weird science.

Cusack closed his office door and dialed Daryle Lamonica's 646 phone number. The phone rang. He wondered what to say if the Raiders legend answered.

No such luck. An automated voice responded tinny and robotic, none of the rich bass tones Emi had described. "Please," pause, "leave," pause, "a message." Beep.

Cusack thought about saying, "Daryle, this is Tom Brady. You suck." But rather than fuel a rivalry, he said, "Jimmy Cusack here. I understand you have a few questions about Dimitris Georgiou. Call me."

Next, Cusack phoned Geek. "Are you changing firms?"

"We have asymmetrical variable input here."

"Just answer the question."

"Before our year-end bonus," Geek exhaled in a nasal voice. "Are you nuts?"

"Some guy called Emi at home. He's doing a background check on you."

"You're kidding."

"I'm telling you," Cusack continued, "the guy asked all kinds of questions."

"Like what?"

"How long we've known you. Whether we spend time together. That sort of thing."

Geek paused for a long minute. Cusack could almost hear his friend blinking behind the Coke-bottle glasses, piecing together his thoughts and figuring out what to say. After seconds that stretched to the point of awkward, Geek asked, "Maybe somebody is investigating you?"

"What makes you say that?"

"The way those questions are phrased. The guy probably learned things about Emi and you."

It was Cusack's turn to pause. "Emi said he felt 'intrusive.'"

"Did he say anything else that seemed strange?"

"Yeah. His name is Daryle Lamonica."

"Who's that?"

"Have a few minutes?"

Geek finished with Cusack and surveyed the Long Island Sound from his office window on Steamboat Road. Today the waters were gentle, not much chop around the sailboats at anchor, a contrast to the way he felt inside. Dimitris Georgiou was not one to deliberate. Or seethe. But right now he was furious and dialed 974, the country code for Qatar.

He reached the offices of his lead investor, Sheikh Fahad Bin Thalifa, on the first ring. "Somebody is investigating me. And I don't like it."

"What are you saying, Dimitris?"

"A guy named Daryle Lamonica phoned Jimmy Cusack's wife and pummeled her with questions about me."

"Slow down, Dimitris. Who's Jimmy Cusack?" asked the Qatari.

"My friend at LeeWell Capital."

"Okay. Who's Daryle Lamonica?"

"The name's a fake," Geek reported. "It's some kind of signal."

"I still don't understand the problem."

"Somebody's on to us, and they're alerting my friend." The Geek speak had all but vanished.

"It doesn't make sense. Lamonica calls an employee's wife. Why wouldn't he warn the founder of LeeWell Capital? Leeser's the problem."

"Maybe Cusack has a friend. I have no idea."

"But why alert an employee?" the Qatari persisted.

"I don't know. I don't care. I'm caught in the crossfire with a friend. And I don't like it."

"Not my problem," the Qatari said. "I've got money at risk. And bankers to please."

" 'Not my problem'! Is that all you can say?"

"No, Dimitris, there is one other thing. Our next opportunity to redeem is September 30. I can say that."

The threat silenced Geek. Investor redemptions brought down Cusack Capital. With one phone call the sheikh could do the same to Geek's firm—all by himself. For a while, neither man spoke.

"You know what we need," the Qatari finally said. "Hurry up and get it." Then he hung up, leaving Geek to ponder how the game had changed from theory to brass knuckles since graduation.

It was 8:30 A.M. Jimmy Cusack sat alone in his office, troubled by Geek's conclusion, fuming, unable to work. The more he thought about the mystery phone call, the more he suspected Shannon was the culprit.

"Daryle has the world's deepest voice." Emi's description fit the head of security at LeeWell Capital—dark, observant, a bad mood with biceps. Shannon seldom spoke. But when he did, his voice resembled a bass violin.

And Geek made the more troubling remark: "Maybe somebody is investigating you?"

Is it Cy again?

"Move to the ball, Jimmy." Cusack's coach screamed those five words all the time during football practice at Columbia. They still made sense. Cusack grabbed his notebook and headed for Leeser's office. He was armed with a cell phone, a twisted smile, and an opportunity in Rhode Island. He needed answers.

Who called Emi and why?

Surrounded by a netherworld of paintings, the whims of artistic fantasy, Cy studied a yellow line graph on his thirty-inch computer screen. The line's shape resembled the cast from a fishing pole. It arced up, peaked, and dropped steadily, inexorably, moving down, down, down, and farther right as though searching for a sandy bottom. The cast was Bentwing's share price—little changed even though Victor was "backing up the truck" and buying more Bentwing every day.

Leeser leaned back in his chair, hands behind his head and fingers locked. He muttered, "This sucks."

Cusack hesitated at the door, hoping Cy would sense his presence. Leeser concentrated on the screen, however, oblivious to anyone and everyone. From behind her bank of lateral files, Nikki signaled for Jimmy to knock.

"This sucks," Leeser repeated to himself, uncoiling his fingers and leaning forward.

"Do you have a minute?"

Cusack rapped on the door, surprising the boss with his presence, not in the startling way that makes people flinch, but surprising nonetheless to a guy grumbling, "This sucks," to himself.

"I've got a couple of things to go over, Cy."

Leeser swiveled in his chair and said, "Come on in and have a seat." There was no trouble in his voice, just the staccato beat of street speak from New York City. "Futures indicate a higher open," he boomed, radiating confidence, unaware that Cusack had heard "This sucks" not once, but twice.

Cusack avoided small talk. He had no stomach for it today. He began with a flanking strategy—delivering good news before asking what the hell was going on with the Mad Bomber from Oakland.

"On Monday *The Wall Street Journal* profiled a medical device company. Did you see the article, Cy?"

"The company that sold for one point three billion?"

"That's the one."

"Nice fucking trade." Leeser focused, all ears.

"The founder is a guy named Graham Durkin. He pocketed one billion plus from the sale."

"There's a guy you should be calling."

"We have a meeting in Providence the week of the eighteenth," Jimmy said.

Leeser's expression morphed from concentration to euphoria. He sprang from his seat and pumped Cusack's hand. "That's fucking awesome." It was an attaboy for the ages.

After Leeser sat, Cusack said, "I could use some help with the pitch."

"Do you want Victor to go?"

Are you crazy?

"Cy, I mean you."

"I'm on the Vineyard all that week. You can handle it."

"On most things."

"But what?" demanded Leeser.

"We get one chance with Durkin. One chance, Cy. I want to show him how we reduce risk. What hedging is all about. The steps we take to protect his money. I want you to tell him war stories from your days at Merrill, while I tell mine from Goldman. I want to scare him about Enron and WorldCom and other big companies that went belly up. And to discuss the conflicts at investment banks, because those buzzards will snatch this business the first opportunity they get. I want you to talk about Peloton. They earned ninety percent last year. Now they're dead, and two billion is gone. Toast—and 2008 isn't over. You're the founder, Cy. I want you to look into Graham Durkin's eyes and explain why we won't be another Peloton, even with all the Bentwing we own." Cusack stopped talking. He could have continued. He thought his speech sounded pretty good.

"Not happening. It's the only week I'll see the twins this summer." He straightened the photo of his twins to emphasize the scheduling conflict.

Shit.

"Nothing more important than your kids," Cusack observed.

"While you're here, any word from Caleb?"

"We're on target for September." The truth was they had not spoken.

Cusack hoped the white lie would not bite him later. "Anne and Caleb are in Bermuda through Labor Day."

"Why don't we hop a flight to Bermuda?"

"You like game fishing?"

"I get seasick," Lesser said.

"Knowing Caleb, he's spending all month strapped to a fighting seat with a fishing pole."

"I can't do business over a barf bag."

"Then go with your strength, Cy, and wait for your big night at MoMA."

"Did you want to discuss something else?"

"It's awkward."

"Spit it out," coaxed Cy.

"Are," Cusack started before pausing, "are you investigating me?"

Leeser's eyebrows arched high in surprise. "Why do you ask?"

"Emi received an odd call yesterday. Some guy said he was investigating a friend of ours."

"What's that got to do with me?"

"The questions were too personal. More about Emi and me than our friend. That's why I thought—"

"I never sanctioned an investigation," said Cy. "But Shannon's job is to provide security in whatever form it takes. Did you get a name and number?"

"The caller left a name. But it's a fake."

"How do you know?"

"Long story," Cusack said. "Just trust me on this one."

"What about a phone number?"

"I think it's Shannon's cell."

Cy picked up his receiver and punched four buttons on the console. "Shannon, I need you in my office. Now."

Thirty seconds later the big man arrived. He wore a starched white shirt, no jacket, sleeves rolled up, military bearing. His biceps bulged every time he bent his arms. He glanced at Leeser. He glared at Cusack.

"Have you been investigating Jimmy?" asked Cy.

"It's my job to watch everybody." Shannon's bass tones filled the room.

"Did you call Emi Cusack yesterday?" Cy continued.

"Why would I do that?" replied Shannon.

The big man's evasive answers had no impact on Leeser, never fazed him. "Do you have your cell phone?"

Shannon reached into his shirt pocket, pulled out a small mobile, and placed it on the table. He said nothing.

"Is it on?"

"Always, boss."

"What's the number, Jimmy?"

Cusack read the 646 number from his notes. Leeser dialed. Nothing happened.

Shannon flashed the big gap between his front teeth. His expression was half smirk and half gloat, more screw-you than smile. The big man picked up the phone and showed the display to both Leeser and Cusack. No silent ring.

"Anything else, boss?"

"No thanks." With that, Shannon exited Leeser's office. "There you go, Jimmy."

"I'm ready to crawl into a hole."

"Forget it," Leeser said, changing the subject. "I need a favor."

"What can I do?" asked Cusack, drowning in a sea of embarrassment.

"Wife-sit tonight."

CHAPTER TWENTY-SEVEN

TAKIN' CARE OF BUSINESS . . .

L'Escale was hopping by six that evening. The popular restaurant overlooks six hundred feet of private docks on Greenwich Harbor, where captains from neighboring ports sometimes anchor for meals before powering out. Happy hour on the outdoor patio draws the gods and their disciples, otherwise known as groupies or divorcées and definitely not to be confused with moms on ladies' night out.

The drinks are strong and the bartenders discreet. The sea breezes are always a refreshing change from the frenzy of trading floors. When happy hours stir restless libidos, a five-star hotel beckons from next door. Suites at the Delamar generate grist for the local Greenwich gossip. And they feed the enduring loop of bar, bedroom, and bar that appeals to so many in the cocktail crowd below.

Cy asked Jimmy to meet Bianca for no more than "1.5 drinks" at L'Escale and promised to relieve him from wife-sitting by seven P.M. sharp. Cusack insisted on "sharp," because he was celebrating his fifth anniversary tonight with Emi.

Bianca, however, was nowhere to be seen. Sitting at a pentagon-shaped bar, its teak gray from the elements, Cusack sipped a glass of cabernet. He said hello to a few buddies and made small talk. Mostly, he chafed while listening to the ambient sounds of bar talk among guys without ties and women dressed in their summer uniform of white jeans.

Hedge fund god: "Frank's been hogging the Presidential for six months. I wish he'd wrap up his divorce so I can move in and get mine started." The man, in his early fifties, was referring to the $1,800 suite at the Delamar.

Cougar cub: "This rosé is all the rage on St. Barth."

Bartender: "Uh-oh, trouble. That's the guy police Tased a few weeks ago for urinating here in public."

Brunette: "We're canceling NetJets."

Redhead in reply: "Oh, you poor dear."

The crowd ordered scotch rocks or white wine, "Just a full glass please." Some of the gods wore earbuds and treated their BlackBerrys like prosthetic brains, capable of delivering double-digit investment returns with a few clicks. Every so often, one of them walked down the dock to take a call in private.

How did Cy talk me into this?

Cusack knew. Leeser dropped a five-letter F-bomb, the birthright of bosses everywhere, and asked for a "favor." He said, "Bianca needs company, and I need to make my meeting," which Jimmy translated to mean, "I'm sick of my clothes flying out the window."

Airborne Armani was less the issue than job security. Cusack was still sweating over Monday's blowup with Cy, and today's confrontation with Shannon only exacerbated his fears. It paid to say yes these days, no matter how annoying or inconvenient the boss's request.

Cusack could wife-sit Bianca and still make it home by nine P.M. There would be plenty of time for a fifth-anniversary celebration, the candles and romantic dinner on their terrace. Wine for him and maybe a taste for Emi. They would discuss diapers and debate "boy or girl," because Emi insisted

Yaz was a girl. After dinner Cusack would rub his wife's stomach and whisper stories to her navel, which he called the "Yaz hotline." He wanted to be home now.

Leeser had been so convincing. The man could sell. No surprise for a guy who started the year with an $800 million hedge fund. It was down to $700 million now, but market losses probably made him a better salesman, all things considered.

"I have an appointment at five, Jimmy. Bianca will meet you at six. I'll be there at seven or so. And you'll be home with an hour to spare. Guaranteed."

"Just meet Bianca at seven," Cusack suggested helpfully. "I'm not sure why you need me."

"Date night. My wife will pitch a fit if things don't start at six."

"Don't get me wrong, Cy. I want to meet Bianca. But tonight?"

"I need a favor," the boss replied. "It's important."

Cusack perched on a stool and nursed his drink. He recalled the subtle grass stains on Cy's sleeves last Monday. He understood Cy's urgency. It was a good idea to court favor with the boss given a shit storm of no bonuses on the horizon.

From time to time a thirtyish woman, leathery smoker's tan and teeth power-bleached to match her hair, glanced in his direction. Checked him out once over. Liked what she saw. He flashed his wedding band to throw her off the scent. His watch read 6:20 P.M., and he was growing more agitated with each passing minute.

Jimmy had never seen Bianca in person. He knew Leeser's wife was in her late forties, short with dark Brazilian hair and lots of it. That morning he saw her photo, the one Leeser locked in a desk drawer with rubber bands and printer cartridges. But the picture was eight years old and Cy's description sounded more elk than spouse. "Great legs, big rack. You can't miss her."

Five minutes later a busty woman strutted through L'Escale's back deck. Dark features, she wore a white denim skirt and darted blouse open one button too many. It was a good look for a breezy summer night. Cusack guessed the woman to be in her late thirties. But he had never been a strong judge of age.

The woman sauntered directly toward Jimmy, hips rolling and body rocking. Men and women gawked. Hedge fund managers looked up from their BlackBerrys and forgot who was long this or short that. The cleavage, the clothes, the long swinging strides—there was a little something for everyone.

Cusack sipped his cabernet and noticed her platform sandals, the extra three or four inches of height. Leeser was right: "You can't miss her."

"I'm Jimmy Cusack," he said, standing and extending his hand.

Bianca never answered. She tripped on the deck and, arms extended, flipped face-first toward the floor. The crowd froze with wide eyes and gaping jaws.

Cusack thought fast and bent low. Elbows facing down, palms facing up, he grabbed Bianca's torso and broke her fall with a Willie Mays basket catch for the ages. He also discovered, to his growing consternation, that he had shagged Bianca's weighty left breast. It was no way to "say hey" to the boss's wife.

"Are you okay?" he asked quickly, pretending not to notice, pulling Bianca to her feet, feeling his face go red. She had been drinking.

"Nice hands, Jimmy Cusack."

"Greenwich is no country for old women," observed the midthirtyish woman with power-bleached teeth.

"Did Cy ask you to wife-sit?" asked Bianca, smart and sassy with at least one drink under her belt. She smoothed her outfit and fussed her hair into place. Then she climbed onto the bar stool next to Cusack.

"He's joining us at seven." The corner of Jimmy's mouth eased up from force of habit. He never addressed the dig about "wife-sitting."

"No need to protect Cy," Bianca chided, not in a caustic way but canny and perhaps even coquettish. "We go too far back."

"May I get you a drink?" asked Cusack. It seemed the ambassadorial thing to do.

She reached over, squeezed Cusack's cheek, and said, "You have great dimples."

"Er, thanks."

"Tom, do me a favor," Bianca said to the bartender. "Bring us two vodka martinis, Grey Goose, plenty of lemon twists. Shake 'em hard."

"Coming right up, Mrs. Leeser." Tom, twenty-something with the boyish good looks of pool bait, winked at Bianca like an old friend.

"Nothing for me," Jimmy said.

"What makes you think I ordered one for you?" Bianca asked, cocking her right eyebrow.

"On second thought," Cusack replied, turning on the charm and pushing aside his cabernet, "I'm glad you did."

"Thought you'd come around." In that moment Bianca looked radiant: the twinkle in her eyes highlighted by the crow's-feet Cusack found so alluring; the warmth of her sun-blanched, coffee-bean coloring; and the beacon blush from whatever she had been drinking that afternoon.

At 6:35 P.M. Cusack willed himself to relax. The evening was back on schedule. Cy would arrive in less than thirty minutes, and Jimmy would be home before 8:30. "Guaranteed."

Between sips, Bianca told Cusack her life story and proved to be an engaging conversationalist. Native of Brazil. Retired romance novelist, who put her career on hold to support Cy and take care of her girls. She had a "love-hate thing for Dorothy Parker," and was getting her degree at NYU. Never explained why she didn't finish college in the first place. She was a mother who missed her daughters. The twins were spending another week at camp in Maine.

Bianca played the society game for Cy. "I'm organizing his big night at MoMA next month."

"Emi and I will be there."

But she hated the glitz. "Survivor Greenwich is not my thing."

Bianca wore no jewelry. When a human ad campaign for Pilates and Tory Burch walked by, the two-and-twenty crowd ogling every loose-limbed step, Bianca announced, "I may pack on twenty-five pounds just to piss off Cy and stir things up around here."

She proved to be an engaging, inquisitive listener. "Your fifth anniversary! Why aren't you home with Emi?"

"It's a long story."

And later she asked, "Is Yaz your first?"

Cusack appreciated Bianca's husky voice. Her sultry tones could have been tobacco cured, though she never reached for cigarettes. Her voice could have been pickled, though she purred with sultry sweetness, none of the coarse croaks that sometimes riddle the larynxes of heavy drinkers.

At 6:50 P.M. Bianca hijacked Cusack's martini. He preferred not to drink and drive anyway. The evening was going fine. Or so he thought. By 7:10 P.M. Cy still had not shown. Nor had he called.

Cusack decided to leave at 7:30 P.M., no matter what. He changed his mind around 7:15 P.M. when a revelation from Bianca made him forget Emi and their fifth-anniversary date.

"You like working at LeeWell Capital?" Bianca was slurring more than purring. "Tom, bring me another martini, easy on the vermouth."

It's a monkey house.

"Cy's a great mentor," replied Cusack, ever the ambassador.

"My husband can be a bear. Not a market bear," Bianca clarified, referring to investors who bet on falling stocks. "The kind that's a pain in the ass."

"You follow the markets?" Cusack refused to take the bait and dump on Leeser. Never a winning strategy with the boss's wife, no matter how drunk or sober.

"I read everything."

For a moment, Bianca's tipsiness disappeared. Her eyes were clear, her gaze bristling with conviction. The strength of her declaration, "I read everything," made Cusack wonder why the force.

"He's got the Midas touch," Cusack said, falling into work mode, employing practiced lines from the office.

"That's a joke," Bianca scoffed. "He's got the coyote touch."

"What do you mean?"

"Did you ever watch Roadrunner cartoons, Jimmy?"

"Of course."

"Wile E. Coyote had better outcomes."

"What's that mean?" asked Cusack.

"Beep, beep," Bianca snorted, impersonating the bird.

"Have you looked at Cy's performance numbers?"

"Wile E. Coyote," she tittered.

"Not funny." Cusack felt the barometric drop of a hurricane on the horizon.

It was 7:15 P.M.

"Did Cy tell you about the time he bet against oil?" continued Bianca.

"No."

"Lost his ass."

"You're kidding."

"Did Cy tell you about *Night of the Living Dead Heads?*"

"Yeah, the movie was a windfall," replied Cusack.

"Windfall," she scoffed. "Those zombies bit him in the keester."

"What are you saying?" Cusack made no effort to hide the edge to his voice. Leeser had reported the opposite, boasted how the movie's cash flow solved LeeWell's performance problems in 2003.

"Cy lost his ass," Bianca said. "The crew's still in court."

Cusack had no idea what to think. These revelations were either the bitter meandering of a drunken spouse, or Cy had lied. One or the other. Jimmy grew angry. He grew confused. "Are you sure?"

"Twenty million down the sink," Bianca confirmed with swizzle-stick tonsils. "My husband has one thing going for him. Luck. He's really lucky."

"What do you mean?"

"LeeWell Capital almost collapsed in 2002."

"Don't you mean 2000, the year Cy and his partner founded the business?"

"There was that, too," Bianca slurred, not bothering to explain. "I don't get how somebody can be so wrong, so often, and still make money. I'm not sure Cy can add."

Cusack sickened. Bianca was losing the war to vodka and vermouth. But she just posed the smartest question he had heard in a long, long time. Leeser's boasts now sounded hollow, one in particular:

"We don't lose money at LeeWell Capital."

It was 7:40 P.M. No sign of Leeser. No phone call either. That was when Bianca quoted Dorothy Parker:

> *I like to have a martini,*
> *Two at the very most.*
> *After three I'm under the table,*
> *After four I'm under my host.*

"Guess what," Bianca advised, "I'm on number four."

Cusack's cell phone rescued him. "Sorry, big guy," Leeser apologized. "Tough meeting with one of our partners. Tougher than I anticipated."

Why didn't you include me?

"Can I help?" asked Cusack without thinking. "Maybe I should drive Bianca home."

"How many martinis?"

"Four at L'Escale." He whispered, "Not sure about the warm-ups."

"Oh, shit. I'll be there in five." Dial tone.

Bianca knew it was Cy. And something made her crack. Maybe it was the four martinis. Or emotions finding daylight after sixteen years of marriage. Her self-restraint gave way to more information than Cusack ever expected to hear while wife-sitting.

"It's not about me," she started. "It's the twins."

"He adores them, Bianca. You should see the photo on his desk."

"That photo is eight years old," she argued. "He treats our twins like a to-do list."

Cusack watched Bianca's face cloud. Suddenly, without forethought, he felt a greater need to soothe her than to defend his boss. "You should know something."

She tried to button her blouse without much success. "Yes?"

"There's a meeting in Providence on August twenty-second. The week your family is on vacation. It may be the biggest opportunity we ever see as a company. And I need Cy to be there, really need him."

Bianca picked up her martini from the bar, her eyes inviting Cusack to continue.

"He refused." With a deft motion, smooth and deceptively quick, Cusack removed the glass from her hand and returned it to the counter. "Your twins are the reason. Nothing's getting in the way of his father-daughter time, not even a guy with a billion in cash who can take our company to the next level."

Bianca grabbed the martini glass back. She took a sip and replied, "I wrote ten novels, Jimmy. I know something about heroes. You think *you* came from nothing? You had a family," she asserted. "They got behind you. Cy Leeser came from parents who beat him. From a dad who spent more time in jail than at home. From a mom who slept around to pay the rent. And now look where he is. If anyone wants to believe in Cy, it's me."

"I'm sorry," was all Cusack could say.

"I envy you, Jimmy. You have a life. I remember what it was like."

"I'm sorry," Cusack repeated, shifting on his stool. He cursed himself for crossing the line.

"Look what happened to us. My only job now is to protect the twins from drowning in our sewer." Bianca's eyes dampened but she did not cry.

Leeser arrived at 8:05 P.M. He wore faded black jeans and a sweaty NYU sweatshirt, with the sleeves cut off above the elbows. Pre-shower, not post. His hair was wet and slicked back, the style more boiler room than hedge fund magnate. He carried a navy blue polo shirt in his right hand and navigated the patio bar with purpose.

"Sorry, Jimmy," he apologized.

"You've been through the wringer," Cusack said.

So has your wife.

"You have no idea." Leeser motioned the bartender to close out the bill. "This fucking partner insists on a three-mile run every time we meet."

"Have I met him?" Jimmy asked.

"No. And tonight it was six miles, not three," Leeser said, "of riding my ass."

"Look at you," Bianca snapped. "We can't eat dinner with you looking like that."

Leeser inspected his jersey with an expression that said, "Oh, right." With that, Cy shocked everybody in the bar: Bianca, Cusack, Tom the bartender, and the crowd that had changed several times over since six P.M. He ripped off his sweatshirt, not in the tearing sense but really fast, and began pulling on the polo shirt.

Around the bar's pentagon elbows, the power-bleached woman eyed Leeser's flat stomach and started to clap. He kept things tight. A few of the gods laughed and clapped, too. The one with bulging, thyroid eyes hollered, "Hey, Leeser. It's too late for the swimsuit edition."

Not everyone in the bar found the quick change funny. Bianca growled, "What's wrong with you, Cy?"

"I need to fly." Cusack shook Cy's hand and cheek-kissed Bianca good-bye.

It was 8:20 when Cusack jiggled the ignition of his car, always an "adventure in precision physics." Once, twice, it took three times before Cusack found the right angle. The old clunker fired. Or rather it deigned to fire. The car performed like a teenager doing him a favor.

Cusack arrived home at 10:45 P.M. The condo was dark. The lights in the kitchen were off. The house smelled flower fresh, a welcome respite. For the last two or so hours he had been listening to the blues. That was the good part.

He had also been sucking on exhaust fumes. That was the bad part. Ordinarily, the drive home took forty-five minutes. Cusack hit a major snarl, however, on the West Side Highway. It backed traffic all the way up the Henry Hudson.

When he called from the car, Emi said, "Just get home."

He was finally standing in the dining room, surrounded by shadows and guilt from missing his date. He flipped on the light to find a plate waiting on the dining-room table. There were mashed potatoes, pounded veal and mushrooms, and almond green beans all covered in plastic wrap. Easy enough to nuke in the microwave. There was a glass of red wine, uncovered, breathing long and hard with enough kick to take out some nerves. And there was an envelope marked *James* across the front.

Cusack was not sure what to expect. Emi had listened to his breathless excuses earlier, the booze, the boss, the Beemer in traffic. He ripped open the envelope, a mix of curiosity and apprehension pasted across his face.

The note said, *James, I can't wait up any longer. Xoxo, Emi.*

The tone was flat. Cusack never understood the whole "xoxo" thing from women. And right now those mystifying *x*'s and *o*'s were the only hope he had not checked into Emi's doghouse.

Cusack slumped down on a leather chair in front of the television. Alone. He drank the wine and ate his dinner. Alone. He never even bothered to microwave the plate, a lousy end to a lousy day where the Sturm und Drang of late-night news resembled an uptick.

CHAPTER TWENTY-EIGHT

By late August, Victor's financial strategy showed the promise of a poolside tray holding a pitcher of margaritas, a bottle of sun cream, and an empty bikini. As LeeWell bought more Bentwing, slathered it on, the portfolio recouped fifty million of its losses. Employees turned optimistic; everyone except for Cusack, who watched as promises drained his bank account.

Two days ago he had written an $8,990 check to cover tuition for Jude's two kids. He paid another $12,330 for Jack's three. As enlisted men, they could never afford private education for their kids. And Cusack's mom would raise hell over public schools. She had always insisted on a Catholic education for her grandkids.

Though he stockpiled cash every paycheck, without a bonus Cusack could never make the $148,542 interest payment in February—ten months at 5.75 percent. It was like waiting for a guy wearing a black hood and holding a rope to hear the word "Pull."

Ever since the night at L'Escale, Cusack had been mulling a comp strategy born on Wall Street and perfected in Hedgistan. Renegotiate the package. Top producers, the best salespeople, could squawk and bitch and threaten to leave until they got what they wanted and said they deserved. All it took were revenues.

Graham Durkin, an entrepreneur with over $1 billion in cash, could generate monster fees for LeeWell Capital. Bagging Durkin as a client, Cusack knew, would change the balance of power between employee and boss. Leeser might not explain how he hedged. But he would talk turkey when it came to Jimmy's mortgage, no doubt about it.

Cusack boarded Amtrak 2150 north for Providence. He marched through several cars and found the first-class cabin. After hefting his travel bag onto the overhead rack, he grabbed an empty seat next to the window and pulled out his presentation materials.

Executives jammed the 8:03 A.M. train, which continued all the way to South Station in Boston. From force of habit Cusack surveyed the car. Several suits pounded away at their laptops, pausing every so often to talk Yankees baseball. Others busied themselves with BlackBerrys. A few sported wireless headsets, the models that suck one ear like electronic ticks that have grown fat from hanging on. Amtrak's first-class cabin was the perfect place to prepare for Durkin—loads of space and few distractions.

Cusack grabbed a coffee from the food car before opening his pitch book. He had reviewed it at least a thousand times. He proofread every word and double-checked sentences to make sure the sales material told a logical, easy-to-follow story about LeeWell. He suspected Graham Durkin knew little about hedge fund alchemy, the longs, the shorts, the correlations, the leverage, and the relentless quest for "alpha," god patois for outperforming indices like the Dow.

Why should he understand what we peddle?

Durkin never worked in finance. He never whipped securities around the exchanges or suffered the ritual humiliation of Wall Street's sacred ceremonies. Durkin sold a medical-device company to Johnson & Johnson. Nobody ever scissored his tie to celebrate a first trade and the coming of age.

As the train railed toward Providence, Cusack visualized his presentation. He played what-if games and tried to anticipate questions, projecting a response for each one. That was when he noticed an envelope peeking from his pitch book.

Sometimes Emi buried love letters in his luggage. Wrote provocative things like, "I'm aching for you, Bluto." Not this time. The letter was addressed to "Jimmy Cusack," not "James." Nor was it Emi's handwriting. Block letters, no script.

Cusack ripped out a letter, folded in neat thirds, penned in the same labored style as the envelope. There was no greeting. No "Dear Jimmy." No date. Cusack's eyes raced to the bottom of the page.

It was signed "Daryle Lamonica."

Ólafur stewed at his desk.

He was hungover and pissed off. He craved "hair of the dog." A shot of Reyka vodka and a beer chaser at Vegamot would do the trick, that and a bacon burger drowning in béarnaise sauce. The bistro's monkfish was out.

So was his hip flask. Empty. Buried in the middle drawer of his desk, behind business cards and staples, the pewter medicine bottle offered the right antidote for most every ailment. These days, Ólafur needed refills all the time.

Last night the Reyka flowed nonstop. But vodka shots hardly explained the banker's foul mood. He had grown accustomed to headaches and cottonmouth, the need for coffee-and-Advil cocktails at the office. Days came. Days went. But hangovers remained the same. They were reliable, their consistency comforting in a perverse way. They masked his anxieties about, well, everything: no wife, no kids, and, as of late, no money.

Ólafur owed his crabby mood to Hafnarbanki's stock price. The shares were dropping like anvils. He had first spoken to Chairman Guðjohnsen when Hafnarbanki traded around 850 kronur. The shares rallied over 900 with the Qatari purchases but were now trading just over 750.

Guðjohnsen called again that morning, just as he had called the day before and every previous day since the end of July. He always asked the same tedious question: "Do we have a problem?"

"No, sir."

"Our shares are trading lower than when we started," asserted the chairman. "Perhaps you declared war on me."

Ólafur bit his tongue. "You know how many shares I own, sir."

It was all Ólafur could do to refrain from telling the old man, *"Farðu í rass-gat."* Icelandic for "Go fuck yourself." A career-limiting gesture in any language.

"Yes, of course," the chairman replied. "What about our problem?"

"It would help if the Qataris double their position."

"Yes, it's time."

"Then you approve the loan increase, sir?"

Chairman Guðjohnsen hesitated for sixty seconds, an eternity of dead space on the phone. Ólafur waited, knowing the older man expected him to break the silence. "Yes," the chairman finally said. "How soon can you start?"

"Yesterday."

"Good. And what about your hedge funds?" the chairman asked.

"Time to rip out their eyes and piss in the sockets."

"Save the venom," Guðjohnsen advised. "Just get our share price up."

Alone in his office now, 1:15 P.M. in Reykjavik, Ólafur dialed the sheikh's office and told the family's chief investment officer, "I need your help."

"Same deal as before, brother? No recourse if Hafnarbanki shares blow up."

"The same." Then Ólafur clarified: "That includes our attack on Lee-Well Capital and Bentwing Energy."

"Agreed."

"Has your man in Greenwich learned anything?"

"Not yet," the Qatari replied.

"Can you turn up the heat?"

"Of course. We're the largest investor in the fund where Dimitris works."

"Excellent. I'm about to turn up the heat myself," Ólafur said.

The two men clicked off the phone, and for the first time that day, Ólafur felt okay. Once the Qataris resumed their purchases, the slide in Hafnarbanki's stock price would stop. Maybe the shares would hold steady this time.

Ólafur dialed Siggi and asked, "What are you doing for lunch?"

"Nothing."

"Have you ever tried boilermakers?"

"No."

"Good. Meet me at Vegamot in fifteen minutes. I'll introduce you."

"What for?"

"Remember how happy Leeser was about the Goncharova painting?"

"How can I forget?"

"It's time for phase two, cousin."

Rachel Whittier slipped into her white coat, the cotton soft and familiar. Through the years she had grown fond of the clinic's unique morning scent, a cross between French roast coffee and the antiseptic bouquet of hand soap. It was 8:30 A.M.

Doc's practice woke slowly during the dog days of summer. RNs often lingered in the kitchen, chatting over bagels and savoring the whatever of

August ennui. The morning commute siphoned their energy, left them clammy from humidity and vulnerable to the artificial chill from air-conditioning.

Soon the pace would soar at the Park Avenue clinic. There were three liposuctions scheduled, including Robinson. Fatty face, beefy belly, and chubby chin, he was getting the works. His butt required two hours minimum.

"Never seen anything that big without a John Deere stamp on it."

Rachel could almost hear Daddy, his Texas accent and the aw-shucks twang that hid a sot's violent rage. He once had an opinion, a funny colloquialism for everything and, unfortunately, for everyone. That included Rachel. He rode her hard for years, really hard, about forty pounds too many:

"It takes you two trips to haul ass."

The taunts turned vicious more often than not. And Rachel still winced at the burn scar, Daddy's home remedy for losing weight. After guzzling a bottle of Jim Beam one night, he snuffed out his cigarette on her right hand. "Lay off the feed bag," he warned, "or I'll tattoo the other one same way."

Two weeks later Rachel turned sixteen, and no one was there to celebrate. Her mother had died long ago. Her father was camped out back in a chair, listening to AM radio and dining on his nightly supper, the six-pack and a toothpick that he labeled a "seven-course meal." When he discovered a half-eaten chocolate layer cake, the one Rachel baked for herself, all hell broke loose.

"You got two hogs living in your jeans, girl." His face crimson and bloated from beer, he slapped Rachel. Hard. Really hard. Held nothing back.

Rachel pushed the drunken old man. Anger. Self-defense. Whatever. He fell backward, rolled down the stairs, and landed at the base—neck broken, head cocked at an angle from *The Exorcist*.

To her great surprise, Rachel discovered she liked what she saw. Her father broken. Powerless. No longer a threat. The vision intoxicated her. Standing over his lifeless body, she crowed, "I got the rigor-mortis touch, old man."

Rachel's extra rolls were gone, all forty pounds of cellulite and blubber. But the burns from childhood still seared. The puffy white blemish haunted her every minute of the day. Rachel rubbed the damaged flesh, her mood souring with each stroke of the index finger.

There was only one way to cheer up—she knew from experience and two-hundred-dollar-per-hour sessions with her shrink. He was always saying, "Compartmentalize. Find something that gives you pleasure."

"Like my night job," Rachel mumbled, alone in a consultation room of the Park Avenue clinic. She pulled out a cell phone and dialed the number she knew by heart.

"Conrad Barnes," she said, referring to the seventy-plus target from Bronxville, "is proving tougher than I thought, Kemosabe."

"Not my problem."

"Bad mood?" she purred, more mocking than sexual. "Maybe *you* need a vacation."

"No."

"I can't shake Conrad's wife," she reported. "They're inseparable."

"I don't need details, just results."

His abruptness surprised her. Their relationship had almost been cordial since her trip to Paris. The thought reminded her of what she wanted most, not so much retirement as the opportunity to shop for clothes and build the carefree life she had never known as a kid.

"You have things under control, right? It's nothing personal, Kemosabe."

"I keep telling you. In my business, everything is personal."

Cusack stared at the Daryle Lamonica signature. For the second time that morning, he stood and surveyed the Amtrak cabin. Recognized no one. The occupants were just suits heading up to Providence or on to Boston. They were guys carrying briefcases chock-full of sales propaganda and other lies. Nobody appeared capable of impersonating the storied quarterback from Oakland.

He reread the short note. The block letters were rigid and penned in black ink. He had not seen such crisp handwriting since second grade. The message was short, absent any emotion, and to the point.

It read: *Get out while you can. Beware the Greek, and whatever you do, watch your back. There will be no further warnings. Daryle Lamonica.*

Cusack forgot all about Graham Durkin and the big sales pitch for LeeWell Capital. Instead, he read the letter over and over. He dissected every word, comma, and space. He tried to envision when and where someone slipped it inside his pitch book. His trip to the food car had been the only opportunity.

After a while, Cusack packed up his computer and began walking the train. He checked for faces, anyone he might know, not sure where to look or what he would find. He opened three bathroom doors in as many minutes, which prompted one suspicious conductor to ask, "What are you doing?"

Looking for the "Mad Bomber."

"Returning to my seat," he replied, squeezing past the conductor in the narrow aisle and heading back to the first-class cabin.

CHAPTER TWENTY-NINE

PROVIDENCE . . .

"Glad to see you, Jimmy."

Graham Durkin extended his right hand. He stood Ranger straight at six foot two, buff for a guy in his fifties. His dark eyebrows were thick but trim, his head shaved like guys thirty years younger. Durkin's brown eyes radiated an appealing mix of energy and curiosity. In person he exuded warm intensity, the kind of guy who reads *Peanuts* and can still finish crossword puzzles in the Sunday *Times*.

"Thanks for meeting with me." Cusack forgot Daryle Lamonica and focused on Durkin, who could move the dial at LeeWell Capital.

"Do you have other meetings today?" Graham gestured Jimmy to sit, and took control of the meeting with practiced ease. Through the years, the entrepreneur had grown accustomed to being in charge.

"We have clients in Providence," replied Cusack, measuring his words. "But I came to see you."

"Oh."

"I have no expectations," Jimmy continued, "either positive or negative." It was important to put Durkin at ease. Pressure spooked prospects the way bad reviews emptied restaurants before restaurants emptied wallets. "Thank you for meeting with me."

"You brought pitch books?" Durkin glanced at Cusack's briefcase. "You finance types kill too many trees. Goldman is the worst."

"I remember," Jimmy agreed, smiling wide and revving up the charm. "I spent two years at the gulag."

Cusack pulled out two presentations, one for himself and one for Durkin. He inspected the covers one last time. All the hours, the research, and the PowerPoint gymnastics—they had come down to this moment. And it was a moment, regrettably, where Jimmy missed the billionaire's cues as he handed over a work of art.

Durkin eyed the presentation like it was fresh dog shit in the middle of a busy sidewalk. He grabbed the booklet anyway and said, "Let me have yours."

"It has my notes."

"You don't need them."

Daryle Lamonica's warning was still buried inside Cusack's copy. Jimmy fished it out and jammed the letter inside his jacket pocket. He handed over the presentation book, unsure what to expect.

With the flourish of a Barnum & Bailey ringmaster, Durkin dropped both presentations into his trash can. "Let's just talk." He leaned back in his swivel chair, hands behind his head as though to punctuate the unspoken message: less show and more substance.

For an instant Cusack lost his voice. His head cocked to the side. And then he recovered. "We can talk. We can do that." Jimmy instinctively liked the billionaire's casual indifference to convention.

"Charts get in the way," said Durkin. "You know what I mean?"

The two men built a quick rapport over the next two hours, in part because they fed each other's good-natured irreverence. Cusack grew increasingly comfortable but reminded himself not to drop his guard. Too much was at stake.

"What do you think about hedge fund fees, Jimmy? All this two-and-twenty nonsense?"

"Sometimes the letter K, as in ka-ching, is the only difference between money and monkey business. Unless, of course, you know what you're doing."

"Does LeeWell Capital know what it's doing?"

"If I didn't believe it, I wouldn't be here." Cusack paused at the comment, pensive and introspective. "But I'd put a big chunk of your money into bonds before you invest the first dollar with me."

"You said the same thing over the phone. Is this some kind of anti-pitch?"

"Self-defense."

"What's that mean?" the billionaire asked.

"If you invest primarily in safe securities, then you won't pull your money from me the first sign of trouble. It's not easy finding new clients." Cusack wished he had given Caleb the same advice long before last December.

"I thought LeeWell Capital never loses money."

"There's a first time for everything," replied Cusack.

"It sounds like you don't care whether I invest with your firm."

Cusack knew investors associate indifference with prosperity. And so far, he deserved an Oscar for best man. He had feigned success and acted the part of a god from Greenwich. He never revealed his inner distress, never betrayed the tension growing louder and louder like bagpipers approaching from the distance. Fear—wanting something too bad—was the quickest way to scare off money.

It was time to send the billionaire a new message. Cusack leaned forward and riveted into Durkin's eyes.

"Don't get me wrong, Graham. I want you as a client. But let's start the right way, so we work together a long, long time." There it was. Cusack asked for the order. It was Durkin's turn to move.

"You hungry, Jimmy?"

"Starved. Didn't eat a bite on the train."

"Good," Durkin said. "Let's grab a burger. You can tell me more over lunch."

"Great."

"There's just one thing."

"What's that?" Cusack asked.

"Is there a problem with your firm?"

"Say what?" Cusack shook his head, puzzled.

"Do yourself a favor, Jimmy, and never play poker with me."

Cusack and Durkin scarfed cheeseburgers at the Capital Grille. Graham called them "too high," because there was no way to trap all the sirloin, bacon, Havarti, and jalapeño-onion marmalade inside. Not that it mattered. The two men used fries to mop up whatever dripped out the sides.

"My burger," said Durkin between mouthfuls, "could make guys like you forget sushi."

"And I suppose you think I'm a Yankees fan, too," protested Cusack.

During lunch the two men forgot all about LeeWell Capital. They spent more time discussing ProShares Short Dow30. It was a blah and benumbing name for a public fund with perhaps the greatest ticker symbol of all time.

Trading as DOG, its shares tumbled when the Dow advanced. They climbed when the Dow fell. And these days DOG was off to the races, the stock price increasing more and more every day.

That discussion took place thirty minutes ago. Durkin was returning to his office, as Cusack walked toward the train station. Cloudy and damp, a soggy breeze rolled off the harbor as the gray summer skies misted across downtown Providence. The city's sturdy brick buildings, many from the 1700s, defied the ravages of time. The structures extolled craftsmanship from days gone by. But the historic views were lost on Cusack as he dissected the conversation from lunch and wondered what his boss would think.

No need to wait for an answer. The phone rang. Cy was on the line.

"What happened, Jimmy?"

"Do you want the good news or the bad?"

"Go with the bad."

"Graham won't invest," reported Cusack, "until he learns more about our hedges. He used the word 'transparency.'"

"Tell him to buy some fucking Saran Wrap. What's the good?"

"He wants to meet in Greenwich, Cy."

"So what."

"He's nibbling," explained Cusack.

"He should. You showed him our returns, right?"

"Here's the deal," explained Cusack. "There's a revolving door into Graham's office. Morgan's been through it, Goldman, everybody. The guy needs a thirty-four-inch bat to defend himself. But he's coming to see us. That's good, right?"

"Okay," Leeser replied, softening. "Why don't you invite him to my deal at MoMA?"

"No offense, Cy. But I'd rather he visit our office, where we can focus on business."

"Do both. Get him to stay in the city on Thursday, and we'll meet with him the next day."

"Good idea."

"Are your in-laws coming to MoMA?"

"Working it, Cy."

"You're starting to piss me off. You said—"

"I said," Cusack interrupted, "that I'll deliver Caleb during September. We're on plan."

"Make sure we are," Leeser snapped, and clicked off the phone.

Something was wrong. For the last four hours, Cusack had labored to stay cool and avoid the cardinal sin of sales—wanting something too much and showing it. And here, his boss was obsessed with Caleb Phelps.

Cusack could have dwelled on the thought. But his cell phone rang again. *What now?*

"This is your lucky day." Most of the time a Boston accent returned Cusack to the days when three brothers pigged out on "Hoodsies," the small cups of half vanilla, half chocolate ice cream that come with flat wooden spoons. Only now the voice evoked images of Shannon and the embarrassing confrontation in Leeser's office. There was also the warning from Daryle Lamonica: Beware the Greek.

"What's up, Geek?"

"You're in Providence?"

"How'd you know?"

"Called your office, Jimmy. I have an offer you can't refuse."

"The Red Sox aren't in town until next weekend."

"It's better than Sox-Yankees."

"That's a pretty high bar," Jimmy replied. "You'll lose all credibility if this isn't good."

"We're hitting the casino tonight."

It was as though the C-word, "casino," burst a balloon. "I can't," slipped from Cusack's lips before he checked the rest of the sentence. He almost said, "I can't afford that shit."

"I won't take no for an answer," replied Geek. "You, me, and a couple of traders from UBS. Foxwoods is comping the suites."

"I thought Monte Carlo was your thing. Since when do you slum the casinos of Connecticut?"

"They know me at the blackjack tables," Geek explained.

"I'm due back in New York." Cusack felt his interest roller-coaster. Geek was sure to put on a show. His prowess at the gaming tables was legendary inside Hedgistan, fun to watch. Cusack, however, could not gamble. It would be like going to a high school dance on crutches. And he sure as hell had no interest in explaining what happened.

"The casino is on your way home," persisted Geek.

"I'm painting the condo this weekend."

"Bad case of cryptorchidism."

"What's that?"

"In plain English," Geek began, "it means no balls."

"Bite me," Cusack laughed. "I promised Emi."

"Tell her it's a night out with the guys. A few steaks. Some time at the blackjack tables. You'll be home by midday tomorrow."

"But—"

"Believe me, Emi understands man's innate need to roam. It's who we are."

"You don't understand."

"That's right," Geek snapped. "You'll be home tomorrow afternoon."

"Let me call you back in five. Emi's on the other line."

" 'No' is not in my lexicon, Jimmy."

"Yeah, right."

"James, guess what we're doing." Emi's voice bubbled with excitement.

"You got the wrong number, lady. This is Boris."

"Quit horsing around." In that whisper of a second, Emi changed the topic. "How'd it go today with Durkin?"

"Not great. I think the technical answer is 'work in progress,' " Cusack replied. "So what are we doing?"

"Flying to Bermuda."

We can't afford it.

"Three days, all expenses paid, James. You hop a flight and meet me in Hamilton tonight."

"Staying with your parents?"

"They rented a villa," Emi confirmed. "It has plenty of room."

Cusack wrestled with the idea. The seconds ticked away. No one said anything, like a husband and wife trying to remember who spoke the last sentence and used the last period.

I'd choose Abu Ghraib over Bermuda with Caleb.

"Are you there?" Emi assumed she had lost the connection.

"I'm thinking."

"James," she said, and paused for the gravity of silence, "you need to reconcile with my father."

"I know. I know. But three days with Norman Bates is more than I can handle."

"Knock it off."

"All it takes are a few Bloody Marys, Em. Then it's 'Petri Dish Capital' this. And 'Petri Dish Capital' that."

"Dad drinks dark and stormies in Bermuda."

"You get the point."

"What about Cy? It'd be a great time to tell Daddy about MoMA."

"I understand why Caleb pulled his stunt last December," Jimmy replied. "But I don't like it. And reconciling with him has nothing to do with my job."

"Your feud is hurting my relationship with Dad."

"I know, Em. I know. Part of the problem is that Geek just invited me to a guys' night at Foxwoods, and I'd love to go."

"So meet us Saturday and come back Monday night."

"I'm not comfortable taking time away from the office," said Cusack. "I've only been on the job four months. And I won't fly to Bermuda for one day on Caleb's dime."

"You think Foxwoods is a better offer?"

Uh-oh.

"It's not like that, Em."

Their conversation had turned into an afternoon with *War and Peace*. Every sentence was a challenge. After an extended pause, she finally said, "I'll make you a deal."

"I'm all ears."

"You go to Foxwoods, and I'll go to Bermuda. Under one condition."

"I'm all ears," he repeated.

"You spend time with my father when I tell you. Where I tell you. No questions asked. Otherwise, you deal with Mom and me."

"You'd make that trade?"

"I don't want to ref squabbles all weekend."

Cusack swallowed hard and agreed. "Done."

"You owe me, Bubba."

"Is this Jimmy?"

"Speaking." The phone rang as he finished with Emi.

"It's Bianca Leeser," she announced with intonation that could have translated, "I'm here. I'm happy. And so are you."

"What a nice surprise."

"I'm double-checking our guest list for MoMA," she said. "Cy will buy tickets for your prospects."

"There are a few folks with New Jersey Sheet Metal, and Graham Durkin, the guy I met today."

"Get me the names, and I'll take care of the cost. That goes for your father-in-law, too."

"Cy mentioned him?"

"I look forward to meeting Caleb." On a scale ranging from light to coquettish, the timbre of her voice registered a notch below inviting.

"You got it, Bianca."

Cusack thought they were finished. He was about to hang up, when Bianca said, "There's one other thing."

"What's that?"

"I want to thank you."

"For what?" he asked.

"That night at L'Escale. I was a mess and—"

"You helped more than you'll ever know, Bianca."

"I bet you missed your anniversary date because of me."

"It's okay," he replied, letting her off the hook.

"You are some kind of hug, Jimmy Cusack."

"Hey thanks, right?"

"Oops, there's Cy," Bianca noted. "Gotta go."

Her swinging cadence sounded cheerful. And her choice of words, calling Jimmy "some kind of hug," turned Bianca warm and oddly affectionate. There was energy about her, the kind of perkiness found in coffee beans and substances that come with twenty-year sentences. But after five seconds of dial tone, which were three more than necessary, Cusack decided things were still tense in the Leeser household.

"I'm in."

After a quick discussion, Cusack clicked off the phone with Geek. For the moment he forgot Durkin and Leeser's secret sauce. He put Shannon and Victor out of his mind, as well as the warning from Daryle Lamonica. His attention shifted to the business of renting a car and driving to Foxwoods.

Cusack had no idea he was being shadowed. He never trained with the CIA or FBI, the Delta Force, or countless other organizations where individuals acquire the special skills to observe, evade, and hunt. He never jumped from an airplane or shot a gun.

Talk—that was Cusack's job. He ate lunch with prospects. He lived inside a shark tank filled with numbers, either billions or basis points. When Cusack saw .25, he said "quarter." He never heard the expression "deuce five" or interpreted .25 as the caliber of a gun. He lacked the espionage skills to spot surveillance or pick out a "pavement artist" from the crowd.

The tail knew how to make himself invisible. He knew how to extricate himself from messy situations. And he knew how to crush larynxes with his bare hands. He had stabbed, punched, and gutted his enemies under the cover of night. He once dropped a man in broad daylight with a sniper shot of four thousand feet, hardly the longest strike ever, but respectable nevertheless. Long ago, his hand had molded to the grip of an M9 Beretta. The tail pulled triggers the way Cusack ran spreadsheets.

The tail was not the only person with special skills. That Friday afternoon Rachel called her employer. Something in his voice that morning had troubled her. Anger. Venom. Something not right.

Emotions were a problem in her business. Mistakes accompany tempers—his spats of fury could cost her big time. It was that simple.

"You sure everything's under control, Kemosabe?"

"What are you, some kind of fucking therapist now?"

"I'm here if you need some help. That's all I'm saying." She had always controlled men, even Doc, and had never succumbed to the bad-boy moodiness that aroused other women. Any more guff, and she would tie his ears in a bowknot.

"Do they ever shut up on your planet? Leave me alone, Rachel, and focus on Conrad Barnes."

CHAPTER THIRTY
MONEY FOR NOTHING . . .

Foxwoods Casino is Oz, orgy, and Thunderdome all in one. There is anticipation, the never-changing lust for jackpots and greener pastures. There is consumption, the nonstop sating of desire no matter what form it takes. And there is conflict worthy of *Mad Max*:

> *Two men enter.*
> *One man leaves.*

The men entering Foxwoods are Jackson and Hamilton or any of the other faces printed on U.S. currency. Dead presidents find it tough to escape the 4.7 million square feet of casino games, luxury hotel rooms, and shops that hawk everything from carats to computers. The forefathers that find daylight are only a fraction of their former selves.

Restaurants are everywhere. They wrap around the slots and craps like boa constrictors squeezing the few remaining dollars from outmanned wallets. The house can take everything, unless, of course, you know how to play the game.

Cusack checked into the MGM Grand, where the staff greeted him like Julius Caesar. They made a big fuss and acted as though he belonged. They asked for his credit card but only to cover incidentals. The hotel, they explained, had comped Mr. Dimitris Georgiou's party of four. The staff never referred to him as Geek.

The tail checked in twenty minutes later under the alias Brandon Anderson. He paid cash, slipped two Franklins to the bell captain, and said,
"You have a guest named Jimmy Cusack. Call me if he leaves the hotel."

Inside his suite on the fifteenth floor, Cusack dialed Emi and left a message
on her cell phone. Geek and the traders would arrive around seven P.M.,
summer beach traffic on I-95 permitting. The four already agreed, after
swapping e-mails on their BlackBerrys all afternoon, to drink tequila and
heat up the blackjack tables until all the other gamblers dropped.

Who am I kidding?

Cusack came to watch and hang with the guys, not drop money at the
tables. He had seen his share of hose-jobs at Goldman—the times when
traders bet wrong, blew their year-end bonuses, and avoided eye contact
afterward. Jimmy pitched his stuff on the bed and ventured downstairs into
a jungle of slots, where he identified one major difference between Foxwoods
and his day job. The bells from thousands and thousands of one-armed ban-
dits sounded like an electronic seizure. Trading floors were serene by com-
parison.

A woman in her late sixties, sallow and oblivious to the racket, caught
Jimmy's attention as he drifted through the great hall. She wore three
money cards, dog-tag style, with extra-long chains that allowed her to plug
into a trio of slots. The woman gazed at lemons and cherries, locked in a
Svengali trance, her nose only a few inches away from the tumblers. With
her left hand she worked one machine's arm. With her right she worked the
other two. Three machines gorging her money at the same time. Cusack
counted not one but two cigarettes dangling from her lips.

She should start a hedge fund.

Just once, Cusack sensed a presence among the retirees strolling the casino in stretchies and tennis shoes. He detected a shadow, a person, someone,
somebody standing behind two roundish couples eating ice cream cones,
somebody eyeing him with more than casual interest. When Jimmy checked
again, the focused eyes were gone.

Meandering through Racebook, Foxwood's world of horse and grey-
hound racing on big-screen televisions, Cusack heard an unmistakable
voice over his shoulder. "Since when are Yankees fans allowed in here?"

It was Geek giving him grief, a good-natured jab from one Red Sox fanatic to another. With the UBS traders on either side, he added, "I thought we'd find you here."

Fifteen minutes later the four men hovered around a blackjack table. The traders grabbed two chairs to Geek's left. And Geek gestured for Jimmy to sit to his right. Dimitris was on a mission. The consummate casino man, he was teaching his flock and showing them the ropes. It was the one place on earth where people got him.

"Geek, you're the pro. Let me watch for a while and see how you do it." Cusack had been practicing his excuses all afternoon. The truth was he had no stomach for sitting down at the $500 minimum table with $148,542 due in February. He knew the consequences, however. The traders would roast him for standing on the sidelines.

"Sit down," pressed Geek. "I'll tell you what to do."

"This seat taken?" asked a pretty brunette, Hollywood body without the airbrush.

Before anyone answered, the brunette parked herself in the chair to Geek's right and winked at the UBS guys. It was a stroke of luck for Cusack. Because now the table was full, and the traders would rather flirt than tell him to man up and play cards.

"I guess that settles it," observed Cusack.

"Suit yourself." Before joining the game, Geek added with intense eyes magnified by Coke-bottle lenses: "Just remember I can always help."

What's that mean?

Geek was a thing of beauty at the tables. First he ordered $50,000 in chips. "That's to get started." Then he played with the panache of James Bond in *Casino Royale*.

Other players began to take notice. Geek won three out of the first five hands, adding $5,000 to his stack in less than five minutes. Ten minutes later he pulled two aces, split them, and blackjacked with a king of spades and ten of diamonds. That hand raked in another $8,000.

Within the hour Geek doubled his money, pausing every so often to nurse his tequila or check on Cusack. The UBS traders gawked at Geek's growing stack of chips. And spectators gathered round the table to witness the diminutive hedge fund maven, who made blackjack look simple.

"Damn, Geek," whistled one of the UBS traders.

"Yeah, damn," agreed the brunette, who appeared ready to adopt Dimitris.

Cusack broke from the action only once. Emi texted, *Here, safe, and I have good news.*

He always felt better when she checked in. Not that prosopagnosia was debilitating. It was more like annoying background music that never stopped. *Tell me, tell me,* he texted back.

Dad is coming to Cy's MoMA event.

Roger that.

You got any money left, Bert? she sent back.

When Geek's winnings hit $75,000, he ordered a bottle of champagne and asked if anyone at the table wanted a glass. "My usual," he instructed the waitress. "And bring back a carving knife with it."

The pit boss looked up.

Three minutes later the waitress returned with a bottle and a sixteen-inch carving knife. "Here you are, Mr. Georgiou."

"That's a seven-hundred-dollar bottle," observed one of the UBS traders.

"Make way," Geek ordered the small crowd round the table.

He ripped the foil from the champagne bottle and twisted off the wire safety holding back the plastic cork. With deft motions he pointed the bottle away, grabbed the knife, and ran the flat side of the blade hard against the seam of the bottle. The knife whacked the bottle's lip with a resounding clink of metal against glass. The crowd stopped buzzing, and one woman gasped.

Off flew the lip. Cork and glass collar sailed together in one clean break. Out shot the champagne. It sprayed harmlessly into the aisle, fizzing over Geek's hand. Up stood the brunette, who clapped and cheered along with everyone on the sidelines, including Cusack.

"Anyone want a glass?" asked Geek in his most casual voice.

"What was that?" asked the first trader.

"Sabering," explained Geek, "is how Napoleon's armies celebrated their victories."

"Not with seven-hundred-dollar bottles," protested the second trader.

"Seven hundred wholesale. And that kind of money is the only way I get away with this shit," explained Geek. "Now, who's hungry? I'm starved. And I'm buying."

"Are you leaving?" objected the brunette. She winked at the traders again and said to Geek, "Why don't you help me lose a good night's sleep."

"Damn, Geek," repeated the trader.

"See ya," said the other UBS guy.

"Hang on," replied Geek. He collected his chips and whispered something in the brunette's ear. She smiled ear to ear.

En route to David Burke's steakhouse, where elongated glass udders with Dali-like proportions hang from the ceilings, Cusack asked Geek, "What did you say to that woman?"

"I gave her my cell number." Geek blinked through his thick lenses, still charming but not so powerful as at the table.

"You make it look easy."

"Go ahead," Geek instructed the guys from UBS. "We'll catch up." Then he whispered to Cusack, "Like I said before, I can always help. You know what I'm saying?"

"No. What are you saying?"

The answer came later that evening. After two rounds of port that followed three bottles of $1,200 cabernet that chased vodka martinis, which flowed like tap water. Somebody recalled tequila shots during the procession of drinks and enthusiastic choruses: "Lemon, salt, and suck." But nobody was sure.

By the time dessert arrived, Geek abandoned his self-appointed role as host extraordinaire, casino insider, and camp counselor. The answer came shortly after he made a big show of paying the tab from his $75,000 payday and asked, "Now what?"

The UBS traders looked at each other, then at Geek and Cusack. And with no further ado, they replied in unison, "Strip club."

"I know the place," said Geek.

The answer was not what Cusack expected. Nor did he notice the guy who had checked into the hotel as Brandon Anderson. The tail was recording everything.

CHAPTER THIRTY-ONE

WORKS HARD FOR THE MONEY . . .

"Ten dollars," announced Danny Bag, which is what members called him at the club. His official title was "Danny Bag of Doughnuts." At 350 pounds the big man was a crowd of one inside the small theater-style ticket booth. He wore his white oxford shirt like a diaper, cinched tight to rein back the overflow.

Cusack, Geek, and the two UBS traders paid Danny Bag and became guest members for the night. That arrangement would never work at the Belle Haven Club back in Greenwich, a place where members dined on the deck and gazed at boats moored sleepily in the harbor. Or they admired waterfront estates belonging to hedge fund legends. It was there at the Belle Haven Club that a cannon roared every dusk as diners stood at attention while staff lowered the American flag over all Hedgistan.

One by one, the foursome pushed through an iron turnstile and entered a different kind of club, not in Greenwich, but just outside Providence. No flag. No cannon. And not much by the way of clothes among women. The Foxy Lady was hopping at one in the morning, well worth their forty-five-minute pilgrimage in a stretch limo.

Home to "Legs and Eggs" every Friday at breakfast, the Foxy Lady had been Rhode Island's strip club of choice for forty years, more or less. Ever sensitive to its clientele, the bar tended to all details starting with credit cards. It billed as "Gulliver's Tavern," bump the Lilliputians, because the name "Foxy Lady" would shut down expense accounts from most stockbrokers and a few lawyers.

Dancers lived year-round in the surrounding areas and led modest lives away from work; not modest in the sense they kept their clothes on, but modest as in no frills. These dancers were not the tour girls, who played Vegas and moved on. The Foxy Lady was their way of life. It was territory to defend as they crawled over laps and made men happy, whatever it took to supplement a husband's salary, pay down a second mortgage, and make ends meet.

"Nice tramp stamp," observed one of the UBS traders. He pointed at a Goth pole dancer with bat wings tattooed on the flat of her back.

Cusack's head was spinning from fog of drink and thump of music. A thirty-something woman, blondish and sheathed in gold lamé, winked at him through the crowd. By now, Cusack had forgotten whatever Geek said that seemed so important earlier. Or so bizarre. He couldn't remember.

"Personally, I'd prefer thongs," opined Geek, "something with the bat wing up front. The problem with tattoos is you can't change them." He was more sober than the others and spoke with authority.

"You're missing the point," scolded the first trader, slurring his words.

"Tramp stamps are reading material," finished the second.

"Maybe we should stay an extra day," ventured Geek, "and explore the artwork around here. You can get some ideas, Jimmy, for painting your condo."

"Hey, is that a shot?"

Geek flashed a knowing smile. It was the smile of a guy who knows a deep secret—something too dark and sub rosa for even the closest confidant to know. The look lasted no more than an instant. Then nothing. It faded, and he returned to the thump-thump of music and the foursome's safari to the dark side.

The traders never noticed Geek's expression. Nor did others in the club, where well-oiled patrons savored the sea of implants that came in large, extra-large, and McDonald's supersize. Even Brandon Anderson, watching from the shadows through black wraparound shades, missed the look. After twenty years of inspecting doors and windows for gunmen, he noticed everything. But not tonight. No one noticed.

No one but Cusack. After all the wine and earlier choruses of "lemon, salt, and suck," he saw the look. Wondered what it meant. Not that he cared. That was the great thing about hanging with Geek and the guys, about pounding drinks. After a few belts nothing mattered. Everything came with rock-solid explanations until the next morning.

Cusack started to speak, unaware the stripper with a bat-wing tattoo was marching toward their table. Focused and battle ready, she was on a mission. There was no stopping her advance.

The stripper with the bat tattoo leaned forward and spread her wings around the UBS guys. Cleavage at eye level, she invited the four men to check out her cave. "You boys on business?"

"That's some tat," said one trader, attempting the difficult jump to urban cool but landing like a dumpy white guy from Wall Street. "Reminds me of Batgirl."

"Wait till you see my superpowers." She crinkled her nose and cocked her head halfway to come hither.

"I have powers all my own." The trader thought it was a damn good line, especially when Batgirl boob-nuzzled him tight.

She thought him boorish. She heard the same joke night after night and sometimes during the matinee shift.

"Batgirl has gadgets," argued the second trader. "She doesn't have special powers."

"Take me into the VIP room," the stripper purred, shoulders thrown back and breasts thrust forward like the nose of a 747, "and find out what disappears." Her fingers drifted over to his chest, where she traced circles on the hair peeking from his collar. "You know what I'm saying, big boy?"

"Done," woofed the first trader. "Lap dances on me."

"Jimmy and I need to talk," Geek announced. "Give us a few minutes, and we'll join you."

"Are you holding out for something inflatable?" The second trader was incredulous. "The swap king of UBS just hit the bid, Geek."

"No rough stuff," warned Batgirl, suddenly anxious. "You hit my bid, and Danny Bag will kick your ass."

"It's not like that," the second UBS guy soothed. "'Hit the bid' is how we talk about spreads."

"I do spreads." She brightened, feeling more at ease.

"We'll be there in a minute," Geek said. "You guys go ahead."

"Talk about what?" asked Cusack.

Cusack waited until Batgirl and the UBS guys were gone. He had worked his buzz hard all night, and now the Geek wanted to talk business. "Why so serious?"

"Remember what I said, Jimmy?"

"I remember you putting seventy-five K in your pocket."

Geek signaled for another round. "I can help."

"You're hard enough to understand when I'm sober," said Cusack, doubting that clarity during intoxication was his superpower. "What are you saying?"

"I ran the numbers, and your life sucks. Is that clear enough for you?"

"Are we playing buzz kill?"

"You've got a three-million mortgage, right?" Geek's eyes grew intense.

"Since when are my finances your business?"

"That's one fifty in interest, minimum."

"I pay once a year," admitted Cusack, not sure why he answered.

"You pay eleven thousand for your mother's car and twenty-one thousand in tuition for your nieces and nephews."

"How do you know? Every time I turn around, somebody's doing a background check on me. First Cy, then Daryle Fucking Lamonica, and now you. Maybe Batgirl wants to probe further." Cusack realized Geek had not touched his drink.

"You finished?"

"You're giving me a hangover," said Cusack.

"How long have we been friends?"

"If this is a money intervention, we probably could have done without the three bottles of cabaret back at Foxwoods." Cusack was growing angrier by the moment.

"That's cabernet."

"Whatever."

"Your expenses," continued Geek, "are at least one hundred and eighty thousand. That doesn't include food or travel or the cost of being a dad. It doesn't include insurance or lights or the money you spend on your mother's renovations in Somerville."

"Did you hack my bank account?" snapped Cusack. "How do you know this stuff?"

"I bet you're netting one fifty after tax, which means three things. One, your cash flow is negative. Two, you can't cover expenses without a bonus."

"What's the third?"

"You're fucked, Jimmy. You're running out of time, because this market is the pits. You won't see a bonus. You won't make your mortgage payment. And you won't sell your house, because you need cash to close."

"Okay, you win. I feel like shit."

"I can help," Geek repeated.

"What do you mean?"

"Find out how LeeWell Capital hedges," he explained, "and tell me." Now Geek was uncomfortable. His right knee pumped like a piston under the table, a tic that traced back to Wharton.

"You want me to spy on my company?" asked Cusack, growing sober.

"I want you to stay on your feet. Your boss pissed off the wrong people. And your firm looks like Cusack Capital part two."

"Cy picked a fight with somebody?"

"Seen Bentwing's stock price recently?"

Cusack paused for a long time, growing more alert every second. When he finally spoke, his words hailed from the enlightened mix of philosophical musings, grapes, and José Cuervo. "I guess everybody has a price. You, me, everybody."

The diminutive hedge fund maven blinked through his Coke-bottle lenses. He had been so powerful in the casino, but now he was tense— waiting for Cusack to play his hand. He stared at his drink with no interest.

Cusack's eyes narrowed, a look just shy of assault and battery. "Who paid you for a lap dance?"

"Aw, come on."

"We can two-and-twenty all we want, Geek, but it's money that pulls the strings."

"It's not like that."

"I got a Ph.D. in getting fucked," Cusack continued. "Your lead investor get to you?"

"Forget the sheikh. You need a friend."

"Listen, pal, you're the one who needs a friend. Some pushover that coughs up info so you can torch Bentwing and make money on the way down." Cusack's head was spinning. It took some time, but he finally grasped Geek's words. "Who's your sheikh? We never picked a fight in the Middle East."

Geek said nothing.

"Who?" demanded Cusack. And in that instant, under leggy shadows from topless dancers working their poles, he understood.

Geek stopped blinking. He reverted to his poker-face mode, the one that sparked legends about his exploits in Monte Carlo. Even the piston knee was under control.

"Your big investor is the Qatari sheikh buying Hafnarbanki," Cusack called out, his stomach sour from booze and betrayal. "The sheikh thinks you can use our friendship to crush Bentwing."

Ordinarily, Cusack was a happy drunk. A guy reliable for good times and discretion when buddies drank too much and said more than they should. Only now, he was not happy. And he was trying hard not to be drunk.

Neither man was sure how much time passed. The two sat in silence, their thoughts drowned by the boom and bass of clothes coming off. Geek finally said, "Make sure you back the right team."

Almost on cue the two UBS guys returned, Batgirl in tow along with three other women. None of the strippers wore tops. One of the traders said, "Guys, come on back to the VIP room with us."

"I'm leaving," announced Cusack.

Geek blinked.

"Don't be a party pooper," Batgirl pleaded. On her command, all four women swarmed Cusack. One sat on his lap. Two others wrapped themselves around his head, sandwiching his face between their breasts. He was lost somewhere in the waves of silicon and nipples, the naked flesh and areolae of all sizes and colors, the pierced parts and tattoos.

"We're like the Canadian Mounties," one of the strippers announced. "We always get our man."

In the shadows the tail sat alone and watched the spectacle, his small camera rolling. It was not the kind of device likely to be noticed, given the DDs and other man-made distractions of a strip bar. At first the man's face was a mask, stoic, sunglasses even in the dark, no expression and no drink to draw attention from a club full of working girls.

When the four strippers tore at Cusack's shirt, Shannon, a.k.a. Brandon Anderson, smiled from ear to ear. "Gotcha, Cusack. Why are you spending so much time with Dimitris Georgiou?"

CHAPTER THIRTY-TWO

Leeser sat alone in his office with the door closed, shut since he arrived at 7:45 A.M. His ear was glued to the phone. His black eyes glowed like the charcoal on a grill. He tapped an email to Nikki: *Tell Victor to run strategy without me. I won't be at the meeting.*

All his life he had fantasized about an opportunity this size. Monster trade or inside information—a random twist of fate could change anything. This conversation, however, was no dream. He was negotiating immortality in real time.

At first Cy had thought Siggi was calling to thank him. In keeping with a tradition dating back to the epic battles of Zeus, the hedge fund kingpin had shipped a case of 2005 Sine Qua Non the 17th Nail in My Cranium to Iceland. All the Olympian gods celebrated their triumphs with drink. In ancient paintings, the winged goddess Nike carried a cup just for those occasions. And as far as Cy was concerned, a million-dollar payday called for a few belts.

"Seventeenth Nail is a classic, Siggi. Impossible to get."

"Thank you. My girlfriend and I will raise a glass in your honor."

"I owe you the thanks," said Leeser. "You can send me trades all day long."

"Too bad," sighed the art dealer.

"What do you mean?"

"I have something. But it's not a quick flip."

"Tell me anyway," urged Cy.

"This situation is long term. It's the kind of opportunity every collector craves, but few see."

Despite his mounting curiosity, Leeser played it cool. He had heard thousands of sales pitches through the years. "Long term" sounded like a big down payment with uncertain returns. "I'm not sure about my appetite for tying up money."

"Maybe you're right. The High Renaissance isn't your thing anyway." The art dealer, an old veteran in the cat-and-mouse game of taste, knew the power of an antipitch. "Sorry to bother you."

Across the other side of Siggi's desk, Ólafur's jaw dropped. All his coaching and their hard work—the careful plans were about to unravel.

"Are you nuts?" the banker mouthed in silence.

Siggi read Ólafur's angst. He extended his hand, palm down, and dropped it like a slow-motion anchor.

"Let me judge what I like," Leeser growled. "What do you have?"

"What do you know about Raphael's *Portrait of a Young Man*?" That simple question changed the tenor of their phone call.

"Raphael Sanzio?"

"No, Cy, I mean *the* Raphael. Raphael of Urbino."

"I know the Nazis snatched one of his paintings. It's still missing?"

"It was."

On August 26, 1939, the German army invaded Poland. Within months the Gestapo unearthed a cache of paintings in the small Polish town of Sieni-awa. Among the paintings were three masterpieces: Leonardo da Vinci's *Lady with an Ermine*, Rembrandt's *Landscape with Good Samaritan*, and Raphael's *Portrait of a Young Man*.

The paintings belonged to the Czartoryski Museum, located in Kra-kow. But Prince Agustyn, who ran his family's museum, had relocated them for safekeeping as war erupted across Europe. His efforts were to no avail. The Nazis unearthed all three as 1939 came to a close.

The German army shipped the treasures to Dresden, which touched off a fierce struggle within the Third Reich. Everyone, it seemed, coveted the masterpieces. Leonardo da Vinci. Rembrandt. Raphael.

Hermann Göring controlled the paintings. But there were constant challenges. Adolf Hitler's personal dealer, Hans Posse, demanded all three for the Führermuseum. Posse, it seemed, was speaking for Hitler. Yet somehow, the masterpieces found their way back to Krakow in 1940. It was there that Hans Frank, the Nazi governor of Poland, displayed them.

The paintings, under Göring's command, traveled to Berlin in 1941. They backtracked east, however, as Allied bombs fell closer. Eventually,

Hans Frank regained possession. He maintained control until his arrest in May 1945.

Military forces found the works by Leonardo and Rembrandt. But they never located Raphael's *Portrait of a Young Man*. Hans Frank guarded the location until his death, when he was hanged for crimes against humanity.

Through the years, there have been few clues to the whereabouts. Frank destroyed documents and the Nazi paper trail. His subordinates, like Wilhelm de Palézieux, the "art protector," never talked. Frank's art restorer, Ernest Kneisel, once claimed to have seen the Raphael in Palisieux's possession. But in 1965, Kneisel changed his story, saying in effect, "I was mistaken."

"It was."

"What do you mean?" Leeser asked Siggi.

"Ernest Kneisel restored art for the Nazis. He was the last person known to see *Portrait of a Young Man*." Siggi paused before adding, "Until now."

"Have you seen the painting?" Cy's back grew clammy, which had become his leading indicator for a good trade.

"Maybe." Siggi yawned, playing coy and hooking Leeser. "Our banks maintain discreet relationships with clients. Especially customers from Eastern Europe."

"You're killing me," Leeser confessed, unable to restrain his curiosity.

"Times are tough. Not just in Iceland, but all through Europe. Art surfaces when people need money."

"What did you see, Siggi?"

"A treasure lost to the world since 1945. A treasure that could stay lost in the vaults of an Icelandic bank for generations to come."

"What's this have to do with me?" Leeser asked, growing wary, street smarts taking control.

"The painting requires a special kind of buyer."

"No shit," Cy scoffed, "somebody will claim ownership the minute it surfaces."

"No."

"What do you mean no?"

"The title is clear. Years ago, the current owner settled with the Czartoryski Museum in private."

"Keep going," pressed Leeser.

"Now he needs, shall we say, to diversify his assets."

"Why not auction it through Sotheby's?"

"The owner insists on absolute discretion. And as we both know," the art dealer added, "confidentiality gets lost inside big sprawling corporations. The Nazi links are awkward in my client's world."

"They're no cakewalk in mine."

"You're missing the point, Cy. Recover a painting lost to the world. Fix a Nazi sin that's generations old. And you live forever in the annals of art. Who's that hedge fund manager you always mention?"

"Stevie Cohen?"

"Suddenly, Stevie Cohen wants to be you." Ólafur watched with wide eyes, riveted as his cousin manipulated Leeser.

"How much is the painting worth?" asked Leeser.

"High eight figures under ordinary conditions. Maybe more."

"That's strong." Cy hated to admit $80 or $90 million would tax his resources. It felt like he was always playing catch-up. "And now?"

"Hard to say. The price is negotiable."

"How do I know the painting's real?"

"I have experts, Cy. Plus, there's paperwork signed by Hermann Göring and Hans Frank."

"Göring!"

"I had his signature verified by three separate experts," the art dealer replied.

"Let's say I get comfortable—"

"We can work something out," Siggi interrupted, anticipating the money discussion.

"What do you mean?"

"The owner wants some cash up front."

"He'll take a note for a portion of the purchase price?" interrupted Leeser, unable to stifle his excitement.

"With the right security arrangements."

"What kind of security?" asked Leeser, his expression growing wary.

"Pledge your stock in LeeWell Capital. Assign a percentage of future earnings until the note is paid. These are things you need to arrange with him, not me."

"It's too easy," Cy objected. "Something's wrong with this picture."

"Easy," Siggi cautioned. "You're dealing with a thorough man."

"What do you mean?"

"Before my owner takes security in your business, his team will inspect your operations, your profitability, and how you manage risk. They're not turning over *Portrait of a Young Man* without decent security."

"We've never lost money."

"Tell the owner. And remember this. You won't become a legend until his people know everything about your hedge fund."

"Not happening." Instinctively, Leeser recoiled at the thought of sharing trade secrets.

"You'll need to explain your techniques to my owner."

"Not happening," echoed Cy.

"No problem," Siggi replied. "I can always find someone with more money."

"Let me think about it," Cy reversed, feeling the needle.

"You know where to reach me. But there's one thing."

"What's that?"

"I can't wait forever."

Siggi placed the receiver on its cradle and sighed.

"What did Leeser say?" demanded Ólafur.

"He'll get back to me."

"When?"

"You heard me," growled Siggi, no longer cool and in command. "I told him, 'I can't wait forever.' "

"What's the problem?" Ólafur asked, noting the change in his cousin's temperament.

"Cy might call our bluff," the art dealer snapped. "That's the problem."

Siggi had been so smooth on the phone. Now the calm veneer was gone, his agitation mounting by the minute. Ólafur started to speak.

"What if he wants to meet in Reykjavik?" Siggi interrupted, growing sarcastic. "Maybe we show him *Portrait of a Young Man* in an art history book."

"Agree to meet," Ólafur soothed. "The 'owner' is our fiction, who does what we say. He can develop cold feet at the last minute."

"It won't be the first case of seller's remorse," acknowledged Siggi, understanding the concept but not buying into it. "Your game is stupid, cousin. Cy backs out. Or we back out. I don't see what it gets you."

"Knowledge," countered Ólafur. "The next call is critical. If Leeser concentrates on price, then his investment secrets are real."

"Why?"

"I know this guy, Siggi. I've read everything about him in print. Cyrus Leeser will swap formulas for immortality in a heartbeat—especially if he thinks there are tens of millions to be made in the process."

"And if the secrets aren't real?"

"He'd never risk exposure," explained the banker. "Trading desks are like war."

"How so?"

"It's all about deception," Ólafur said. "He won't expose his flank."

"Well, I wish you'd stick to your securities, cousin, and leave me and my art business out of your war."

"Your art business is our advantage. Leeser is patrolling foreign soil."

Cy surveyed the walls of his office. For a moment, his gaze settled on a line drawing by Picasso. The piece, no more than meandering scribbles courtesy of a sardine and sangria lunch, was inexpensive as Picassos go. But the hedge fund titan liked what he saw.

The Picasso equaled success. The drawing validated Leeser's decision to leave Merrill Lynch and take a chance that landed him as lord and master of 19,000 square feet and a five-acre estate on Roundhill Road. There was glory in risk.

The spoils of the market—Picasso or Bentley—accompanied uncertainty. "So long as you win," Leeser reminded himself. "Poor losers are poor because they lose."

Now, Leeser had a similar decision to make. A similar chance to take. Because stick figures from a master like Picasso would not bring immortality to the founder of a hedge fund with less than one billion under management. It took at least ten billion, maybe even twenty, to live forever.

Cy imagined his fame from uncovering priceless Nazi plunder. He visualized a dream scene at Sotheby's—flipping the Raphael, taking a check, and wallowing in glory. There had to be a way, he decided, to finesse the opportunity without jeopardizing his business.

Leeser could have dwelled on the thought forever. But Cusack knocked at the door and poked his head inside. "Sorry to interrupt, Cy. Can you give me five?"

"Is it important?"

"I know who's shorting Bentwing."

"Who?" bellowed Cy, suddenly rising from his chair like a white-hot ember.

"Remember the Qatari sheikh I mentioned?"

"The one in cahoots with Hafnarbanki," confirmed Leeser.

"He's signaling us to leave the bank alone."

"How do you get there?" Cy's face grew curious.

"Retaliation. Our bet against Hafnarbanki hurt his portfolio. He's pissed. So he's shorting Bentwing to get even."

"Send the fucker a peace offering, maybe a pound of bacon."

"I think we should take profits," replied Cusack. "But you already know where I stand."

"How's he know it's us?" Leeser asked, ignoring the market advice.

"I pieced together a few comments from my circle of friends. It's more hunch than anything."

"Who?" Cy repeated.

"What difference does it make?" Jimmy knew his friendship with Geek would never be the same, doubted it would survive. But ratting out Dimitris Georgiou rubbed him the wrong way.

"Suit yourself," said Leeser, before changing the subject. "Is Caleb Phelps on for MoMA?"

"Done deal. I confirmed it Friday."

"Good work. Now leave me alone. I have a call to make."

Cusack left the room wondering "good work" for what? Was it "good work" for exposing the Bentwing shorts? Or was it "good work" for delivering another guest to the party?

Leeser phoned Siggi forty-five minutes later. "You were right the first time," he told the Icelander.

"What do you mean?"

"High Renaissance is not my thing."

"No, but money is," the art dealer insisted. Suddenly, he was onstage again, cool and confident, the consummate actor. "I'm surprised you would pass on an *opportunity*."

"Not my thing," Leeser repeated. Right now, everything from Iceland felt toxic.

"The discount will be substantial. It's a forced sale."

"Not interested."

"What's wrong? You're the one who wanted to see deals from me."

"Not interested," Leeser said again.

"You haven't seen the painting."

"Probably better that way," Cy noted. "I need to stay focused on my business." His tenor grew cold and distant.

Siggi knew just what to say. "Have it your way. I won't show these opportunities going forward."

"You have others?" Cy asked, now revealing the first hint of remorse.

"Good-bye." Siggi hung up. It was that abrupt. He looked at his cousin. The curtain had dropped. The mild-mannered art dealer was no longer onstage. He blinked once, then again. "I feel sick."

Ólafur put his arm on his cousin's shoulder, a gentle reassuring gesture. "I know just what you need. What's the name of that wine Leeser sent?"

"You mean the 2005 Sine Qua Non the Seventeenth Nail in My Cranium? It came in a wooden case with a nail through the center of the lid."

"That's the stuff. Why don't you pull out a couple of bottles? We need to celebrate."

"Celebrate what, Ólafur? I'm not in the mood."

"A couple of glasses and you'll be fine, cousin."

"You sound giddy."

"That's because," the banker said, "I'm about to hammer the seventeenth nail from that case into Cyrus Leeser's cranium."

"That's sick, cousin. That's really fucking sick."

"Relax, Siggi, it's time for me to pour on the pressure. And you know what von Clausewitz says."

"Military history is more your thing than mine."

" 'Blood is the price of victory.' "

CHAPTER THIRTY-THREE

Summer left like a three-time loser who just made bail. The morning after Labor Day all of Hedgistan returned from homes in the Hamptons or Martha's Vineyard. Most money managers were tanned and focused, reinvigorated from the salty ocean breezes. Their heads were clear, their bodies lean. They were ready to grapple with the troubled markets, down 13 percent since January.

The beaches failed to reinvigorate anyone at LeeWell Capital. Bentwing was down 16 percent over five ruthless trading sessions, over one fugly week of the stock falling lower every trade, day in and day out. Employees attempted brave faces. But as 2008 headed into the final stretch, every man and woman suffered private cases of fear. It was bad form to express anxiety in public.

No one knew what to expect come bonus time. Or what to expect from the head trader. For all his expertise with small-cap stocks, no one suffered choppy markets worse than Victor Lee. And historically, no one harangued other employees with more serpentine venom. No one.

Victor walked past Amanda, already manning the reception desk. "Good morning," she ventured, jittery he would blow a gasket without provocation.

"Nice blouse," he grumbled. "It suits you."

"Thanks," she said, thinking his comment surprisingly civil. Like everyone else at LeeWell Capital, she knew Bentwing was poised to open down. Again.

At his trading station, Lee wiped crumbs off a black chair. He was wired from two Starbucks ventis, sipping a third, and not eager to sit. He plopped down anyway and inspected his jar of Premarin. The container was one-third full of pills, the 1.25 mg dose. It was sitting next to his hammer, underneath three thirty-inch LCD screens flying over his desk like the Green Monster of Fenway.

"Estrogen makes for good business," Victor said aloud.

Ordinarily, his team of three traders, all guys, ignored his remarks. They had grown accustomed to their boss mumbling and talking to himself. Today, he puzzled them.

Lee pulled out his calculator and ran the numbers he knew by heart. He multiplied $800 million by .93 percent—the annual cost savings, according to UK and Swedish scientists, from women traders who hold positions longer and pay less in commissions. A few more keystrokes, and he discovered LeeWell Capital could save $37.2 million in trading costs over five years with the right workforce.

Victor's brow furrowed, as it always did when he ran the numbers these days. He was no longer trading an $800 million portfolio. With Bentwing down so much, the savings would only total $28.1 million. It wasn't chicken feed so much as it was depressing. The portfolio now equaled $605 million in assets. Lee grabbed his hammer and called Numb Nuts, the trader who worked for Eddy's team at Merrill. All the while, Victor stared at his bottle of pills manufactured from the urine of pregnant mares.

Since Cusack joined LeeWell, New Jersey Sheet Metal was the only thing that had gone right. Plan B—renegotiate the package—was looking more certain every day as his only hope come February. Unless he bagged New Jersey and other prospects, however, Cy would never discuss his mortgage.

Cusack picked up the phone to call Buddy at the New Jersey pension plan. An e-mail arrived from Leeser. The subject read, *Caleb Phelps*. And in the message, Cy asked, *Can we move up our meeting with him? I'd like to get started*.

The request was bizarre. Not just the wording. Leeser had better things to do than chew the fat with Caleb Phelps. "Like hedge our stupid portfolio," Cusack muttered to himself. There was no way he would ask his father-in law for a favor. "No way."

Working on it, Cusack e-mailed back, before calling Graham Durkin to keep the ball rolling. All the while, he wondered one thing:

"Started" on what?

Ólafur studied two charts on his computer terminal. He liked one. Bentwing had fallen 30 percent from where it started the year. Sure, alternative energy offered some hope for a world running out of carbon fuel. What did he care? Iceland would always have heat. His country possessed a vast network of subterranean geothermal springs. There were more important issues bedeviling his thoughts—like the kronur in his brokerage account.

The attack on Bentwing started back in April, when Chairman Guð-johnsen approved the assault. It was slow at first, methodical, a few shorts here and a few shorts there. The campaign had since changed. The markets were souring, investor outlooks growing bleak. Oil prices were plummeting from their July peak. And the strike on LeeWell Capital's single biggest position was gaining intensity.

Every time Bentwing's share price recovered, Hafnarbanki and the Qataris shorted and drove prices down. Ólafur shorted in his personal account. The Qataris enlisted the support of their associates in Greenwich, London, and Moscow. Bentwing's stock price dropped every day, down, down, down, falling victim to the financial blitzkrieg.

Ólafur relished the sweet ruin of LeeWell Capital—hedge fund, upstart, and Greenwich parvenu that dared attack his bank. He had always respected Plato's take on conflict: "Only the dead have seen the end of war." Before long, Leeser and his employees would see no more. The Icelandic bank would terminate their war with brutal finality, an experience similar to gutting a fish, and a bit more satisfying.

Even better, Ólafur had recouped some personal losses. His gains totaled over $2 million from shorting Bentwing Energy. With help from the Qataris, the allied forces would continue their assault.

"And force Greenwich to leave us the hell alone."

There was one problem: the second chart on his LCD display. Hafnarbanki's shares were trading at 704 kronur, down 40 percent since January. And Chairman Guðjohnsen's warning still rang in his ears: "If our war goes bad, you're fired."

Ólafur willed himself not to worry. The share price was the temporary setback of battle. The Qataris were buying Hafnarbanki shares. The shares would turn. "Someday, I'll be commander in chief," he mused aloud.

Leeser sat inside his office with the door closed. He was squeezing a tennis ball with his left hand, keeping rhythm to his clenching jaws. Nothing good ever happened on a Friday afternoon. Clients called to complain. Trading errors surfaced. Lenders called to deliver hard news about their loans. As Cy spoke on the phone, his office at Two Greenwich Plaza felt less like Mount Olympus and more like a crematorium.

"I'm trying to imagine you with a brain, Eddy."

"Let's do the math," replied the Merrill trader, ignoring Leeser's dig. "You started the year with just over two hundred and fifty million in margin debt. You added thirty million during early August alone. That doesn't include the previous seven months."

"That makes me a good client," Cy interrupted dismissively. "Now I need more money."

"Don't you get it?" asked Eddy in exasperation.

"Bentwing's stock price is a joke, and we both know it."

"Irrelevant," the Merrill trader shot back.

"If you were worth a shit, you'd help me fight Sheikh Bin What-the-fuck."

"It's official," Eddy decided. "You don't get it."

"Who else is shorting Bentwing?"

"Who isn't?" replied the Merrill trader.

"Is Hafnarbanki on my ass?"

"You know the game. Everybody attacks the weak sister, and right now that's you."

"Let's cut to the chase," barked Leeser. "Why'd you call?"

"Your debt totals three hundred million."

"Your point, Eddy?"

"We have our own issues, Cy. Which means we're scrutinizing borrowers, including you."

Leeser dropped his voice, making the Merrill trader strain to hear. "Fine, I'll take my commissions elsewhere. Tell your boss to hoard cash and pull his girls out of boarding school."

"That game's over, pal. Nobody's lending on the Street. The Dow's off twelve percent, and we're all scared that's the tip of the iceberg."

"We're not close to a margin call," snapped Leeser.

"It's a demand loan, Cy."

"I've been through this drill. Right after my partner died."

"So you know how it works. We demand. And you pay."

"Is this a margin call? Are you demanding payment? Are you telling me to sell assets? Is that why we're speaking?" Cy punched out the questions like he was smacking a speed bag. His voice grew louder with every word.

"Not officially. But one——"

"Get off my phone. And don't you ever threaten me with a margin call again," Leeser screamed. He slammed down the receiver, sending dial tone and a big "fuck you" to the Merrill trader. And throughout LeeWell Capital, in the pool room, across Victor's trading floor, in the kitchen with the screaming-eagle cappuccino machine, every employee including Cusack heard two words:

"Margin call."

CHAPTER THIRTY-FOUR

MONDAY, SEPTEMBER 15
BENTWING AT $30.71

Early in the morning an unattended computer at KfW Bankengruppe wired out 300 million euros. It expected 426 million dollars in return, a routine "foreign exchange swap." The German bank soon discovered, however, that it had flushed the money down a toilet of bankruptcy litigation. Or driven 2,130 Ferraris off a cliff. Or taken a wrecking ball to Petco Park, home of the San Diego Padres.

Lehman Brothers, the other side of KfW's trade, failed that day. Most citizens of Hedgistan, bright faced and talcum fresh in their late twenties and early thirties, had never seen such a powerful institution fail. Nor had they ever seen the resulting loss of confidence in the capital markets. The world was on edge. No one, god or wannabe, trusted anyone or anything. Not even their beloved technology.

Victor gripped the handle of his sixteen-ounce Estwing hammer. He stared at the three thirty-inch LCD displays. He would need more Premarin soon. He put down the hammer and rubbed his chest. It hurt like a bastard.

Nothing, it seemed, had helped Victor's trading. Early mornings and late nights—long hours made no difference to trading desks around the world. Securities were indifferent to work ethic or pharmaceuticals. The markets would do what they would do. There was no good news anywhere.

Victor's eyes gleamed red and moist behind his horn-rimmed glasses. "It's a shit show," he had whined to Cy that afternoon. His voice lacked the usual confidence, none of the cocky, testosterone-infused bravado.

"Hang in there," replied Leeser, resolute and with no hint of the Friday afternoon blowup with Merrill Lynch.

With fifteen minutes to go in the trading session, Lee grabbed the sixteen-ounce hammer with his left hand, then his right. He repeated the motion over and over again. He was watching history. A few more minutes and the Dow would close under 11,000, a drop of 4 percent–plus in one miserable day.

The phone rang. It was Numb Nuts, Eddy's sidekick at Merrill. "You guys have a new boss," said Victor. He was referring to Bank of America's surprise acquisition of Merrill Lynch, announced that morning. "How's it affect us?"

"You heard about Eddy's call with Cy on Friday?"

"Yeah. A page right out of the seagull school of relationship management."

"What's that mean?"

"You squawk, shit all over the place, and fly out."

"We're serious, Victor."

"You're serious about losing a client."

"Not sure we care," Numb Nuts countered. "It's B of A. Their people are crawling all over our shop, examining our books, loans, anything."

"Are you nuts?" Victor asked. "Whatever happened to the long-term perspective?"

"I don't know what to tell you," Numb Nuts said, not so much hesitant as distant. "Your account is dropping like a rock."

Victor blinked through his horn-rimmed lenses. He rubbed his forehead with both hands. He hated debt. He hated to lose. At this rate, his beach rental in the Hamptons would go the way of Lehman Brothers.

"Don't do anything you regret." Face flushing red, Lee swigged from a big can of Diet Coke and added, "I gotta go."

On the LCD screen, LeeWell's stocks continued to fall. Victor averted his eyes, his focus drifting to the sixteen-ounce Estwing hammer. He looked back at the portfolio. And in one brief, insanely glorious second of absolute clarity, the trader realized what he must do.

Victor grabbed the hammer and pummeled the middle screen, full of cratering stocks, with all his might. The screen exploded on contact, shards of metal and plastic and all the internal electric organs sailing through the air and showering the junior traders. In a frenzy, he beat the left screen. He bludgeoned the right. Over and over he clubbed the displays, fury etched across his features. His glasses sheltered his eyes from the circuit shrapnel exploding everywhere.

Nikki, Cusack, Shannon, and Cy—they all heard the explosions, the shattering circuits. They raced to Victor's trading station. They stared, wide eyed and slack jawed, as Victor looked at each and every face. At all the bewildered expressions. At his three junior traders, who watched him lose it.

In that one instant he buried his face in his stubby little hands and sobbed with big wheezing gasps, "I'm so ashamed." The head trader, Cusack realized, was succumbing to the pressure like everybody else.

A hammer was not the only weapon of choice. Nor were LCD screens the only targets.

"I've solved the problem with Conrad Barnes," said Rachel.

"I don't need the details."

The employer's brusque reply annoyed Rachel. It was time for her to take control. "Conrad and his wife go to the Bronx Zoo every Thursday."

"What is it you don't understand about 'I don't need the details'?"

"Well, it's not like I can pop by for coffee and Danish, Kemosabe."

"What do you want?"

"I've been watching Conrad for two months," she said.

"Don't say his name on the phone. I keep telling you we need to be more discreet."

"Do you have any idea, Kemosabe, how many hours go into a stakeout?"

"Is this call about money?"

"I'm working two jobs to be this poor. I need a raise."

"Raise! You can't make what I pay you anywhere else."

"Remind me when it's cash," Rachel countered angrily.

"You don't have shit without me."

"Then treat it like manure, Kemosabe."

"What the hell does that mean?"

"Spread the money around a little more. And see what grows. You know what I'm saying?"

CHAPTER THIRTY-FIVE
WEDNESDAY, SEPTEMBER 17
BENTWING AT $32.01

"Get Bianca on the line, Nikki."

Leeser shut the door and stormed back to his desk, bracing for another round with his plastic-faced wife, whose hair would feel like hardened concrete tomorrow night at MoMA. He had no choice but to double-check her work before the black-tie fund-raiser. Bianca missed details all the time.

Cy wondered how she pissed through the days with her damn dachshunds and the effete toothpicks who drank too much coffee at Starbucks and read *Vanity Fair* while working out on ellipticals. Which is what they all did when not stretching at Pilates or fingering through trunk shows at Randolphs, the clothing store on West Putnam Avenue that specialized in excuses to buy Isaia, Alberta Ferretti, Magaschoni, and other multi-vowel designers that could savage ten grand in a single blink of unbridled credit-card fury.

Bianca's head was not in the game. It would take her thirty seconds to propose counseling—for the hundredth time that week. Cy had neither the time nor the patience to enter therapy with a guy named Alfredo who charged seven hundred bucks per hour to watch husbands and wives fling acid at each other. The shrink, Leeser decided, got the better side of that trade. Most spectators paid to watch, not the other way around.

"I have your wife on the line," said Nikki over the phone. "May I put her through?"

"Make my day."

Leeser reminded himself to be careful. He needed Bianca to pick up laundry. He needed her to trowel on the game face for MoMA. He had one chance to make a good first impression with old man Phelps. And frankly, it was equally important to shine in front of tomorrow's crowd. His public persona was all about the execution of perfection.

"Hi there," said Bianca. "How are things?"

"Another day in paradise," he replied. "Is everything set for tomorrow night?"

"All done," she replied, cheery but without the annoying self-satisfaction that follows a completed to-do list.

"Did you invite Jeff and Lizzy?"

"They RSVPed yes two weeks ago."

"Did you pick up my black tie from the cleaners?"

"It's hanging in your closet," she said. "Along with your shirt, starched just the way you like."

"Great. What am I missing?"

"You need to call Paul and twist his arm for a check."

"Oh, that's right," Leeser said. "I almost forgot."

"How about your speech? Do you need any help with it?" offered Bianca. "I'm pretty good with words."

"No. I'll figure it out."

"Any chance you can make it home early?" She sounded hopeful but tentative.

"I'm drowning at the office."

"I was hoping," Bianca began earnestly, "we could pick up our discussion about Alfredo."

Cy checked his watch. He had underestimated his wife's reserve. She waited forty-five seconds to mention counseling. And he knew what would happen without some care. Their discussion would start slow, gain momentum as it soured, and his tux would land on dachshund piles in the front yard just in time for tomorrow night.

"Sweetie, let me get through the fourth quarter. And then," Leeser paused a beat, "we'll start working on us."

"We need some affection back in our lives, Cy." Bianca spoke without bitterness, even though she had heard the same excuse before.

"Just another quarter. I promise."

Leeser smiled when they hung up. His tux was ready, and there had been no verbal fisticuffs. He would rather sit through a root canal than discuss affection with a guy named Alfredo. Bianca could get herself a pool boy and hose a romance novel for all he cared.

There were bigger problems at the office.

This year was a disaster. Leeser faced three major problems, the first being the environment. Things were bad—so bad that "toxic" and "transparency," the trendy new buzzwords of finance, were outpacing F-bomb usage by a factor of two to one. And 2008, to the universal regret of everybody who made their living from the markets, was far from over.

Bear Stearns was gone, sold to JP Morgan. Merrill Lynch was gone, sold to Bank of America. Lehman was gone, the carcass picked buzzard clean and sold to Barclays in a deal announced that morning. The government, according to CNBC, was seizing control of AIG. And it appeared Morgan Stanley would be the next financial institution to take a dive.

The financial institutions reminded Leeser of the poison people from his youth, always scuffling for their next fix. The big institutions, saddled with their own problems, were indifferent to everyone and everything in their endless quest to find capital.

Eddy had been crystal clear last Friday. No more money. Merrill Lynch would not help shore up Bentwing's stock price. More likely the investment bank would force LeeWell to dump assets at fire-sale prices in order to pay off debt. Losses would be huge, and investors would jump.

LeeWell's hedges were Cy's second problem. They protected against risk. They were working. But not fast enough. Nor big enough. Cy never anticipated losses of $350 million. If the markets stayed this bad, he would be playing catch-up for months, maybe even years. And at least one of his partners was an absolute pain in the ass when it came to hedging.

Jimmy Cusack, to Cy's way of thinking, was *the* solution. The kid offered access. He offered size, important now that Bentwing was dropping like a rock. But the kid was slower than cross-town traffic in Manhattan, always dragging his feet, always finding some excuse to whine and bitch about his "complicated" relationship with Caleb Phelps.

"That shit stops today. And I know just how to make Jimmy dance."

The third problem was that Qatari sheikh. He rained crushing hell on Bentwing, which traded under thirty dollars for a few minutes on Monday. Leeser was no longer running a hedge fund. He was running a triage unit where everything was hemorrhaging all at once.

The sheikh's wrath almost felt personal. But why? And how did the sheikh connect Hafnarbanki to LeeWell? Cy had been stewing over the question ever since late August.

After hanging up with Bianca, Leeser checked Bentwing's share price. Still north of thirty—that was good. His thoughts turned to Hafnarbanki. Nobody knew about LeeWell's bet against the bank. Nobody outside the company—that is, except the reps from Merrill, not to mention Tall and Napoleon, his partners in crime.

Only one other person was present that cold December night in a Reykjavik bar. And he made no sense. He was bookish and financially naive. He called with great deals, one that landed a million-dollar payday. And he just might be the walking colonoscopy behind Leeser's troubles.

Cy picked up the phone and dialed Iceland. There was nothing like Bentwing hovering over thirty dollars to focus his thoughts.

"What a pleasant surprise," Siggi said. "I've been thinking about you."

"I bet you have."

"What's that mean?"

"Let's cut to the chase," snapped Leeser. "Who do you know at Hafnarbanki?"

The mild-mannered art dealer said nothing at first. Mentally, he struggled for something, anything, to throw Leeser off the scent. The Icelander had worried about this moment. He knew the day would come when Leeser linked him to Ólafur. And he cursed himself for not prepping ahead of time.

A pause was all the confirmation Leeser needed. "Who?" he demanded.

"I don't know what you're talking about," the art dealer stammered.

"What the hell was that Raphael about?" persisted Leeser.

"An opportunity. That's it. I swear."

"Who'd you tell, Siggi? I don't have time to play games."

"Tell what? What are you talking about?"

"Me shorting Hafnarbanki." Leeser knew the Icelander would break. Rapid-fire interrogation, unrelated questions zinging from every direction, always flustered the battle-scarred CEOs of public companies. He would wipe the floor clean with a third-rate gallery owner who spent his life shuffling around that volcanic afterbirth of an island.

"I don't know what shorting is," pleaded Siggi.

"Bullshit," bellowed Leeser. "Tell me, or I'll be knocking on your door five hours from now."

"No. You've got it all wrong."

"Five hours. And you'll wish you disappeared with the Nazis instead of that painting. Who do you know at Hafnarbanki?"

"Ólafur Vigfusson," cracked Siggi.

It took Google .40 seconds to find him and Leeser another ten to scan the Web hits. "So, who is this managing director to you?"

"My cousin."

"Give him a message for me."

"I'm afraid to ask," confessed the art dealer.

"Twenty-four hours."

"Twenty-four hours for what?"

"To start buying Bentwing," barked Leeser, "or Hafnarbanki gets a barbed-wire enema that sends the stock price to sewage treatment."

"Cy—"

"Give your cousin my phone number if he has questions. And tell Ólafuck I know about his sweetheart deal with the sheikh." The words were a total bluff, a best guess, but worth the shot with Bentwing trading at $32.01.

Ultimatum delivered. Dial tone.

After he hung up with Siggi, Cy conference-called his partners in the Hafnarbanki short. He never mentioned Bentwing. Tall and Napoleon would kick sleeping puppies, not to mention a stock reeling from the coordinated attacks of powerful financiers in Qatar and Iceland.

Leeser focused on the Icelandic bank. "Time to go for the jugular. Let me tell you what our friends at Hafnarbanki are doing in the Middle East."

Thirty seconds later Tall asked, "Do you know this for a fact?"

"What difference does it make?" said Leeser.

The two other gods chuckled.

Leeser asked Napoleon, "Do you still operate the International Institute for Financial Transparency?"

"Whenever it's necessary," the squat hedge fund manager affirmed. "I know where you're going, Cy. Give me two, maybe three days, and I can whip out fifteen pages."

"Make it two days," instructed Leeser. And then he said to Tall, "Can you get addresses of the people we met in Iceland?"

"He said what?" screamed Ólafur.

"You have twenty-four hours to buy Bentwing or else."

"Or else what?" the banker asked Siggi.

" 'Hafnarbanki gets a barbed-wire enema that sends the stock price to sewage treatment.' "

"Did he say anything else?" Ólafur could feel his blood pressure rising.

"Something about your sweetheart deal with the sheikh."

"I have no idea what he means," Ólafur lied.

Leeser's threat was a bluff. It had to be. No one else but the chairman and the Qataris knew about the nonrecourse loan from Hafnarbanki. And the paperwork was hidden inside a maze of dummy entities. The only way to fight deception, Ólafur knew, was through deception. "Do you still have the case of wine Leeser sent?"

"I don't get you, cousin. My client just threatened to take down your bank, and you want to drink?"

"Who said anything about drinking? I want the crate."

"For what, Ólafur?"

"To hit him where it hurts."

"What are you talking about?" Siggi asked. "And spare me the warrior quotes about castration."

"Leeser's ego is where it hurts. Get me the crate."

Cusack brooded in his office. He doubted the market would continue yesterday's 142-point rally. There was no confidence anywhere. And every trading session was wood-chipping his bonus, possibly his job, into saw-dust.

The phone rang, and Cy asked, "Are you free at four?"

"What's up?"

"Just swing by my office at four."

"Roger that," Cusack affirmed. "Do you have a few minutes now to discuss something else?"

"What's on your mind?"

"Help me craft a script about how we hedge. No trade secrets but enough to pacify curiosity." Cusack paused a beat. "Then we make calls, you and me on the line. Get out in front of the problem, because one thing's for sure."

"What's that?"

"Clients will call us if we don't call them."

"Anything else?" asked Leeser.

"Level with me about our margin debt."

"What makes you think we have issues?"

"The whole building heard you screaming at the guy from Merrill last Friday."

"You finished?" Cy sounded testy, his tone steely and distant. "Because if you want to whine and snivel a little more, don't let me interrupt."

"Yeah, I'm finished."

"I've got the margin under control. That's my job, not yours. And you're the employee, remember?"

Cusack said nothing and waited. He could hear himself perspiring. He could feel his ears growing red.

"Tell investors," Leeser continued, "what we always say. LeeWell uses a proprietary trading mechanism to hedge. It's highly reliable but simple and easy to replicate. If others learn what we do, we'll lose our competitive advantage. And remember, I sit on the board at Bentwing. We're knocking the cover off the fucking ball."

"I'm telling you," Cusack resisted, "your black box won't work. People are scared, Cy. They need something tangible."

"We did just fine before you arrived."

"The world changed."

"Then say our gate is up," Leeser barked. He was referring to a clause in the subscription agreements. If investors tried to redeem 25 percent or more of the money in the fund's assets, then LeeWell Capital could close the "gate" and limit investor payments until times got better.

"Do our redemptions total twenty-five percent?" asked Cusack, alarmed and incredulous.

"No."

"I won't lie. That's where I draw the line, Cy."

"Who's lying? If you don't follow my instructions, we'll have the twenty-five percent. Besides, you work for *me*."

"We can fix that." Cusack refused to back down.

"That's right. We can," Leeser pressed. "Good luck finding a three-million-dollar mortgage in this market."

"Don't threaten me, Cy."

"Hang up, cool off, and we'll pick it up again at four." Threat or not, Cy sounded smug.

Dial tone rang in Cusack's ears. He slammed down the receiver and started to fume. He could have fumed all day but there was no time. Client calls poured in as the market opened anchors aweigh—down, down, down. The dashboard of his phone resembled Times Square on New Year's Eve.

One after another, the clients of LeeWell Capital regurgitated what Cusack already knew. "We're pulling out if you lose our money."

When the Dow finally closed at 10,609, a drop of 4 percent on the day, Cusack answered one call before heading to Leeser's office. The next five minutes ranked right up there with a double-barreled case of food poisoning.

"We're putting our forty-million commitment on hold." It was Buddy, the chief investment officer from New Jersey Sheet Metal.

Shit.

"The market's less rational every day," protested Cusack. "Now's the time to make real money."

"How much lower is it going?"

"I don't know. Which is why we take your forty million and feed it into the market a little every month for six months."

"I have a better idea," the pension officer rejoined.

"Which is?"

"We speak eighteen months from now." Buddy hung up.

At 4:06 P.M. Cy barked at Cusack over the phone, "You're late, girl-friend."

CHAPTER THIRTY-SIX

4:08 P.M. . . .

Cusack walked into Leeser's office, where the air smacked of a death sentence. Cy sat behind his desk. His hair was the color of coal. His eyes glowed like bonfires, and his grimace resembled lethal injections. Shannon glared from one of the guest chairs. The big man said nothing, no emotion and no expression. His head had taken the shape of a hangman's noose.

I'm getting fired.

Cusack recalled the flare-up that morning: "Don't threaten me, Cy."

The words sounded insubordinate in retrospect. With Shannon present, Jimmy assumed his outburst had crossed an unspoken line. Security people always accompanied pink slips at investment banks. Bosses fired employees, and guards escorted them out the door. Cy probably borrowed a page from the HR playbook at Goldman Sachs.

"Four o'clock was eight minutes ago," snapped Leeser.

"I was on the phone with New Jersey Sheet Metal."

"What do they want?"

"Out. New Jersey pulled its forty million."

Leeser's face blew a crimson gasket. "I suppose," he said, mocking and venomous, "you still insist on a script for investors. Maybe we should gin up something for prospects. Or better yet, let's invite the ladies over for tea and finger sandwiches because you're too fucking skittish to close business."

"I don't need a script for one piece of advice."

"What's that?" asked Leeser, taunting Cusack and inviting him to take his best shot. Shannon watched impassively.

"For you to wake up. The phone is ringing off the hook. Your investors are scared stiff."

"Forget the investors," ordered Leeser, "and tell me why you're free-lancing." He swept back his long black hair with both hands and reclined in his chair, at ease after landing a knockout punch.

"What are you talking about?"

"Providence last month."

"I saw Graham Durkin. You know that."

"What else were you doing, Jimmy?"

"What's your point?"

"I'm the one asking questions," barked Leeser. "Who's Dimitris Georgiou?"

"A classmate from Wharton."

"What does he know about LeeWell Capital?"

"The market's melting down and you're asking about a guy named Geek?" Cusack glanced at Shannon. His head had gone from noose to garrote, his expression taut, tight, and plenty keen to get the job done.

"The shorts are circling," explained Cy. "We're down over a hundred million on Bentwing. And you've been hanging out with that clown since day one."

"How do you think I found out about the Qataris?"

"Now you tell me," scoffed Leeser. "Remember what you said three weeks ago, when I asked about your source?"

"No," said Cusack.

"You said, 'What difference does it make.' "

"Yeah, and I still mean it. You know who's attacking us. Geek is immaterial."

"I'm losing money, Jimmy. You haven't invested one dollar in my fund. And now you're blowing it with prospects. It makes me wonder whether you're a plant for our friend Dimitris."

"That's crazy. Money is tight in my home. That's why I haven't invested."

"You the bagman for Dimitris?"

"I haven't spoken with him since Providence."

"Selling out cures cash flow problems every time," persisted Leeser.

"You want deception?" asked Cusack rhetorically. "Bianca said you lost your ass on that zombie movie. *Night of the Living Dead Heads* is about the stupidest thing I've ever heard."

Jimmy regretted the outburst at once. His job was gone. There was no doubt. He had also dropped the mother of all husband-wife quarrels onto Bianca's lap. It was a dumb mistake.

Shannon watched intently. He was waiting for a ringside bell to send the men to their corners. No such luck. Leeser continued to throw combos. "My wife is a plagiarist and a drunk. Her bedside table is better stocked than most of the bars around town. She has no idea when or how we make money."

"Plagiarist?"

"Stick with 'drunk.' Bianca doesn't know what she's talking about."

"Your movie was a flop," argued Cusack "I Googled it."

"We'll discuss your disaster movie in a second, Jimmy. Who paid for your room at Foxwoods?"

"It was comped. And what do you mean, my 'disaster movie'?"

"Dimitris paid," translated Cy. He ignored Jimmy's question. "Who paid for meals?"

"Geek."

"Just as I thought," blasted Leeser. "Your friend financed the whole damn affair."

"You don't understand," Cusack protested.

"Why are you protecting Dimitris?"

"Geek is immaterial, Cy. I told you about the Qataris the next day."

"It's been three weeks since this guy plied you with a faceful of tits and who knows what else."

"What are you talking about?"

"Did you fuck me in Providence?" screamed Leeser. He shotgunned accusations faster than Cusack could return fire.

"I prospected a billionaire."

"You didn't close Durkin. We had forty million in the bag with New Jersey Sheet Metal. And you fucking blew it."

"Graham's a businessman. He's been around the block too many times to invest after one meeting."

"I pay you to bring in assets, Jimmy. Not to make excuses."

"Graham's attending your party at MoMA. And we're meeting him on Friday. What more do you want?"

"Close some business. Or maybe you're killing time at LeeWell until you get a better offer from Burger King."

"Nobody's putting new money to work unless it's a sure thing. Which is why I keep asking you about the hedges."

Leeser glared at Cusack. Then he glared at Shannon. For a moment, Jimmy believed Cy had run out of gas. He was wrong.

"There will be a day," Leeser started, "when your three-million-dollar mortgage seems like chump change."

When I sell the condo.

"But if you ever cross me again," Leeser continued with mounting anger, "I'll cram your teabag up your nostrils."

"Damn," Jimmy uttered without thinking. There had been countless threats back in Somerville. This one was new.

"I insist on confidentiality," Leeser bellowed, his anger gaining momentum. "Shannon, show Jimmy his 'disaster movie.'"

The chief of security opened a Mac laptop on the corner of Cy's desk. Knee-deep in hostilities, the office a rancorous morgue and the paintings all headstones—Cusack missed the computer earlier during the meeting. Shannon said nothing, clicked the track pad several times, and waited for a movie to start. The images flashed fuzzy at first, the sound scratchy from voices and a heavy beat in the background.

It was the Foxy Lady, the strip club in Providence.

No one said anything. The three men huddled over the fifteen-inch LCD screen. The camera zoomed through the crowd, grainy images growing clearer by the second.

There was Cusack, surrounded by four topless women. One of them pulled his head into her heavy breasts. And the twisted smile, the one that could be mistaken for a smirk or something more lurid, crossed his features in one spectacular splash of implants.

Shannon clicked the touch pad, and the movie froze. The frame caught Cusack's smile. It caught him in all his glory, plunging nose first into the stripper's breasts.

"What the fuck, Cy. Where'd you get that?"

Shannon said nothing.

"There are all kinds of surprises in my wheelhouse, Jimmy. Be a shame if Emi saw this."

"Are you threatening me?" Cusack asked again, seething. "Send her a copy. She won't care."

"Maybe not," smirked Leeser, "but Caleb's coming tomorrow. I wonder what he thinks. His daughter is pregnant, and you're at the Foxy Lady?"

Cusack looked at Shannon, who said nothing. But he smiled for the first time, flashing the big gap between his two front teeth. That's when Leeser landed the final blow:

"My journalist buddies say Caleb may run for governor. Kind of a public thing. Clean living. Family values. You know the drill. You think the tit video will help Caleb Phelps or your marriage?"

"Why are you doing this?"

"We win this year by surviving, Jimmy. You survive by delivering Phelps. And I'm getting to next year with or without you. Now get the fuck out of my office."

Alone in his office, Leeser wondered when Bentwing would hit the twenties. The next three months would be tough. Two separate beat-downs, first Siggi and then Cusack, had been the only bright spots in his day.

They were exactly what he needed to clear his head. They might even get things back on track. Ólafuck would buy Bentwing if he had half a brain. And Jimmy would deliver his father-in-law pronto.

The kid's a bonehead, thought Leeser, alone, gloating in his office, surrounded by paintings and other trophies from past financial victories. The video from the Foxy Lady would never see the light of day. Cy would never undermine Caleb Phelps, either his gubernatorial campaign or his business interests. He needed the Bostonian too much.

"But Cusack won't call my bluff," Leeser said aloud, confiding to the photo on his desk, the one of his twin daughters before grade school. Irrational behavior is a beautiful thing, he decided. Volatility, lack of restraint, all the screaming and threatening until others cower and cave—nobody really knows when a madman will pull the trigger.

CHAPTER THIRTY-SEVEN

Cusack was lying in bed. He stared at the ceiling, his thoughts bouncing from outrage to disbelief over a threat that bordered on the surreal. He struggled to avoid revenge fantasies that were almost Pavlovian, like cranking Leeser's head in a shop vise until his boss coughed up the video.

Emi was asleep, no surprise there. She could hibernate through heavy metal concerts. She found comfort in dreams, however distorted or Tim Burton they might be. Dreams were the one place where Emi recognized everyone.

There were no dreams to comfort Cusack. Not that night. He had already told Emi so much. Maybe too much. But he held back on some info, and now he wondered if the omissions had been a mistake. The thing about confessing to priests is that you can feed them a little at a time. He was unsure whether the same strategy worked with his wife.

"Are you crazy?" Emi never lost her temper. "You want to tell my father?"

"That video can blindside him."

"Make sure it never surfaces," she warned.

"Nothing happened."

No one said anything. Cusack looked at Emi. She looked at him. The seconds passed like a kidney stone. And he finally said, uncertain how to make things right, "I was leaving the Foxy Lady."

"You planted your face in a lap dance."

"She grabbed my head, Em."

"I've been struggling since December to bring you chowderheads together. You hold grudges, James. And I get over your hard feelings, because in your core, you're kind. And you're honest. And you always screw up doing the right thing. Your messes are why I love you. But guess what. My father's grudges date back to the *Mayflower*. Lose his money—he'll get over it. Botch his politics—he'll never forgive you."

Hands on hips and belly thrusting forward, Emi stared a hole through her husband's forehead. She added, "Our child won't grow up in a divided home. You make peace with my dad."

For the second time that evening, Cusack said nothing. Not at first. The silence was his place to think, more of a demilitarized zone than Weapon of Marriage Destruction. During the pause Cusack considered Leeser's creepy fascination with Caleb Phelps. He considered personal finances on the brink, problems still hidden from his wife. He smiled crookedly and finally said, "I know what to do, Emi."

"Don't play games."

"You're looking at LeeWell Capital's model employee."

"What are you talking about?"

"I worked hard before. I work harder now. I suck up and say all the right things, to Shannon, who gives migraines a good name. To Nikki and Amanda. Even to that whack job Victor."

Emi double-checked the two-star pin.

Cusack noticed the glance. "It's me, Emi. I support Cy and say yes whenever his ego needs a backrub. Even if it makes me barf later. I become a knight at Cy Leeser's round table of goons."

"Where are you going with this?"

"I keep my eyes open until I find and destroy that video from Foxwoods. And once it's gone through a digital shredder twice, I'm out of this monkey house."

"You need to find that Mac computer?"

"I need to find the video and all the copies, wherever they are."

Emi's hands relaxed from her hips. She rubbed the two-star pin on his jacket lapel, before resting her hands on his shoulders. "Where do we start?"

"Tomorrow night at MoMA."

"I'll meet you there. I'm working a little later than usual," she said.

"What about Caleb?"

"Same thing. He has a full day."

For a moment the two said nothing. Emi broke the silence and asked, "Remember when you landed the job with LeeWell Capital?"

"Like it was yesterday."

"You were happy. The markets were better."

"Markets aren't the problem," Cusack said, shaking his head. "I discovered the difference between my office and hell."

"Which is what?" she asked.

"We have Bloomberg terminals."

"Wait here for a moment. I have something for you."

Emi disappeared into their guest bedroom, which doubled as an office. He could hear her rifling through papers, but just for a moment. She returned with a printout, black and grainy on a single sheet of paper.

"Is that what I think?" asked Cusack.

"Put Yaz up in your office," she confirmed, handing him the sonogram. "He'll help you through the days, the way he helps me."

"He?" Cusack forgot LeeWell. Emi always claimed their baby was a girl.

"I peeked during my ultrasound."

Jimmy looked at Emi's swollen belly. At Yaz. At his wife's kind face. Gently, he touched her cheek with his right hand and kissed her full on the lips.

"Does that mean we still like each other?" asked Emi. She added coquettishly, "I'm fatter than a walrus, you know."

"You're beautiful."

"Just do me a favor," she said.

"Anything."

"Next time I ask, suck up to my dad in Bermuda."

Cusack listened to the rhythmic sounds of Emi's sleep. He watched Yaz rise and fall with every breath. He wondered whether his wife would be so forgiving once she grasped the depth of their financial problems. Strike one was borrowing $3 million to buy a condo that might be worth $2.5 million in this market. Strike two was thinking he could support his mother and brothers at the same time. He had no interest in whiffing at whatever happened next.

CHAPTER THIRTY-EIGHT

By 6:45 P.M. MoMA's atrium buzzed from a curious mix of celebration and consternation. The fifteen-piece band rocked all eight levels of the museum, their upbeat tempo belting into every corner, every crevice. The crowd was ready to swing and let their hair down. Ready to drink and talk moneyman trash amid Monet and all the greats. They had come to fête Cyrus Leeser for his many contributions to the world of art. They were ready to blow it out because one thing was sure. Every man and woman in the building sensed trouble on the horizon.

"Is Harry Winston in bad taste these days?" a slender woman asked her friend. She sparkled in black sequins and a vintage necklace assembled from thirty-five emeralds, a mix of thirty-eight round or marquise diamonds, and all kinds of platinum elbow joints.

"We got barbecue risk," remarked a young money manager across the hall.

"What the hell is that?" his buddy asked. That was the problem with jargon from the gods. Speakers needed to stay current on their metaphors.

"Somebody always grills better. Same thing with investment performance. Somebody always has better returns."

"In my opinion," a third god observed, "hedge funds are an endangered species."

"Hey, you masters of the universe," bellowed the bandleader, three hundred pounds all powdered, pressed, and packed inside a black tie. He flirted with the crowd, held them rapt with bright eyes the size of silver dollars. "You say the markets are bad. You say times are tough. Well, here's a little help from Jackson and Jefferson and maybe a Ben Franklin or two." With that his laughter resonated through the cavernous atrium as the band played "Dead Presidents" by Willie Dixon.

Inside the ladies' room Bianca studied her reflection in the mirror. Not bad for forty-eight, she decided. She fussed several dark hairs into place, sipped from her martini, and swore never to go blond no matter how much Cy insisted. As her eyes drifted lower, Bianca examined the faint hint of lace and smiled at Dorothy Parker's classic line: "Brevity is the soul of lingerie."

The evening had taken forever to arrange. The details consumed her: guest list, catering, gift bags, invitations, floral arrangements, sound systems, who would speak, who would emcee, what she would wear, what Cy would wear, who would come and how much they would pay, which would be a thousand dollars per head minimum no matter how much Brazilian whoop-ass required to shake loose donations in these tight, tight markets. The execution of perfection went on and on. April, the month she first tackled the project, seemed like yesterday.

Bianca had no idea whether Cy noticed. He showed zero interest in her black Heidi Weisel off-the-shoulder jersey dress. He did not care about her long hours combing Bergdorf Goodman for their big night at MoMA. She could have done without all the preparations, the hobnobbing, and the gilded—or was it gelded—life of social philanthropy.

Tonight was Cy's thing, not hers. He wanted the acclaim. Bianca preferred a good book, comfortable pajamas, and popcorn in bed. She hated mascara and regarded most makeup as a total waste of daylight. She would trade Heidi Weisel for loose-fitting capris any time, anywhere. If only Cy paid attention. If only he agreed to a few rounds of counseling.

A vigorous flush interrupted Bianca's reverie, and Lady Dana of Deerfield Drive burst from the stall. She was not a Lady in the British sense of royalty. It was more of a hunting title conferred by Greenwich glitterati. A jogger sighted her in a tree one morning with crossbow and quiver full of arrows. In full hunting regalia, topped by a deerskin cap, she was waiting for the return of several does that ate $75,000 worth of plants on her property.

"Damn, you look good, Bianca," admired Lady Dana, snugging her Versace into place.

The two women exited the bathroom and returned to the party, to Bianca reigning supreme among men and women in black, to the haut monde of New York, Greenwich, and London, to a crowd so elite, so nonpareil that Page Six of the *New York Post* sent three reporters to cover the event, each with a photographer in tow. Society *sgarristas*—not made men from the mob but women made to perfection—swarmed Bianca.

"It's great what Cy and you have done for MoMA," congratulated one.

"Your hair looks fabulous," said another.

"What a cute dress, girl."

Bianca sighted her husband working the crowd across the great room, dazzling and smooth with no apparent worries about the market and with Nikki always nearby. His assistant wore a ruby red stud in her nose tonight, the stone subtle but the perfect foil to her shimmery black gown.

Martini glass in hand, Bianca watched Cy and wondered what happened to her marriage. "Our girls deserve better," she mumbled under her breath.

"What's that?" asked Lady Dana.

"Nothing," replied Bianca, bright and sassy and thoroughly heart-broken.

With the crowd noise gaining volume, Victor stood alone near the bar. He drained his green-apple cosmopolitan and wondered, for a brief second, why anybody bothered with scotch. Mercifully, the Dow had rallied over 400 points during trading hours. He ordered another cosmo, not from relief and certainly not to celebrate a market rebound. This cocktail was all about resolve—his.

It was time for LeeWell Capital to man up, take its losses, and go to cash. Lee decided the dickhead Cusack had been right about Bentwing. The stock was a piece of shit, regardless of today's yawn-inducing rebound. The only issues were how to convince Cy, and, of course, how to execute the trades.

"What brings you here?" a woman asked.

Victor turned to find a tall, striking, golden-haired woman: late twenties, brown eyes, and a silk dress that fit like duct tape. The woman turned heads. She wore black stockings with seams running down the back of each leg. No doubt her lineage traced back to Aphrodite, the goddess of love and beauty who pulled double duty as the patron of prostitutes.

"Cy's my boss," he replied. "I'm Victor Lee."

"Well, Victor," she said in a voice reverse-engineered for seduction, "why don't you buy me a drink?" She took his arm, assuming they would storm the bar.

Her touch surprised Victor. He missed the cues, the sexy voice. He was still engrossed in her back-seamed stockings. "Drinks are free."

"I'd like a glass of white wine," the golden-haired beauty replied, "and for you to tell me something delicious."

"What for?" Victor asked without thinking.

"Oh, a challenge," the woman observed, brushing up against him. "I like that."

Victor, surprised by the contact, missed her cues and said, "You sure about the wine. You seem a little shaky."

"It's okay if you forget my name," the golden-haired woman said, blinking, turning, her face a confused sneer. She left Victor with his thoughts about Bentwing and the seams of her black stockings.

It was drizzling outside.

Across town Emi Cusack rushed through the gates. She wore an Isabella Oliver gown, black trench coat, and red sneakers. She carried an umbrella in one hand and extra-large purse in the other, white pearls and black high heels buried deep inside. Emi invited attention racing out of the zoo and into the Bronx, showing six months and searching everywhere for a cab.

Her presentation, the last one before maternity leave, ran past five into the early evening. There had been no choice but to change at work. She could not race home, clean up, and return to MoMA in time to hug her dad and put on a good show for James. New York's traffic was a bear at this hour.

The mist morphed into rain as Emi stood on the street. Looking north and looking south, she scanned Southern Boulevard to no avail. There were no cabs anywhere. Nothing. Just Emi losing time, rain gaining strength, and night turning black.

Conrad Barnes never met Emi Cusack before. He knew trouble when he saw it, though, a pregnant woman alone in the Bronx. He doubted her red tennis shoes would help much. Ever the gentleman, Barnes marched to her side, momentarily leaving his younger companion behind.

"May I help you find a cab?"

Marge was in Florida, and Conrad was in heaven. He loved their Thursdays at the zoo, preferred them to senior Olympics inside the Westchester Mall with other walkers. But everything was different today, including the fact he had parked on Southern Boulevard because Parking Lot B was full.

Barnes had befriended a young nurse near Tiger Mountain—never would have happened with Marge around. They were eating out in a few minutes. Jumping in his car and driving into Manhattan for dinner, probably someplace on Avenue A. They would never run into Bronxville friends at one of the discreet haunts on the Lower East Side.

"You are so sweet," Emi replied. Tall and white-haired, Conrad looked like a walking billboard for madras-gone-wild videos taken at local country clubs. He also sported the most unruly unibrow Emi had ever seen. "But I'll be fine."

Barnes refused to leave. He raised his left hand and whistled between his teeth, his lower jaw thrust forward like a shopping cart. From the north end of the street, a yellow cab appeared.

"How'd you do that?" asked Emi.

"I'm on a roll," Barnes said, flashing the closer's smile that had propelled his career in pharmaceuticals. He held the taxi door open just as his young companion joined them.

The twenty-something woman was buxom and athletic. She was dressed in white with a cute figure and perfect auburn hair. Emi noticed a scar on the back of her left hand, puffy and damaged. The woman—Emi thought she might be the older man's daughter—wore a nondescript shade of lipstick. Her vibrant eyes shone Atlantic blue with help from tinted contacts.

Emi pulled her umbrella shut, threw her monster bag into the backseat of the cab, and said to Conrad, "Thank you so much." She fixed on the woman's ocean blues and almost said, "Take care of your dad," but thought better of it. There was something about the younger woman's body language.

A few minutes later as Rachel ducked into Conrad's sedan, she worried about the pregnant woman. The way she had looked at Rachel. The recognition in her eyes. That was the thing about face blindness. Few people know anything about it.

CHAPTER THIRTY-NINE

MOMA . . .

"It's been a long time," Cusack told his father-in-law.

"Too long, James. That's what our dynamic duo says." Caleb's corrugated forehead made him look like a man with galvanized opinions and one option—his.

"Anne and Emi?" asked Cusack, referring to mother and daughter.

"The same."

At five foot nine Phelps was neither short nor tall. His curly hair was neither black nor gray but still trying to decide. And his face was neither friendly nor hostile but clearly resolute.

"I'm glad you came," said Cusack as the band rumbled "But it's gonna take money," the refrain from a George Harrison song.

"Actually, you're not," Caleb started. "I know you're still pissed from December. I've had nine months to think about things, nine months to discuss our phone call with my daughter. And there are some things I should have done differently."

"Forget it." Cusack was unsure whether he meant his words or not. But it was the ambassadorial thing to say, one of those lessons drilled into his psyche during childhood.

"I'm buying the division of a public company. I slip one time, and the SEC stretches me across the rack until I'm six-four. Particularly because I'm announcing my candidacy in January." Phelps struggled with his words. He was not a man who apologized often, if ever. He held Cusack's eyes with his steely gaze.

"Why get your lawyers? A simple phone call would have done the trick."

"I listened to gunslingers, James, and made the mistake of not going with my gut. The only way to explain the lawyers, and this doesn't make it right, is I can't have public slips. Not even one."

"We all make mistakes," replied Cusack. "There's not a minute that goes by when I don't regret losing your money."

"Sunk cost," Caleb declared, and reached to shake Cusack's hand. "I'm glad you landed on your feet. Now, it's time for me to earn your trust."

Phelps believed the Berlin Wall had just collapsed, a fitting end to the family feud. Cusack felt the bricks crash down hard. He was buried up to his neck in secrets and other rubble.

"You must be Caleb Phelps," a voice boomed above MoMA's din, as the in-law peace negotiations came to a close.

"I am."

"Cy Leeser. I've heard so much about you." He sipped a single malt with his left hand and extended his right to shake.

"You're the man of the hour," replied Phelps, once again the politician.

"And I hear you're ready to announce your candidacy for governor of Massachusetts."

"It's not a well-kept secret," Caleb admitted.

Leeser shot Cusack a knowing glance and said, "I've gotta tell you, Caleb. I'm lucky to have your son-in-law on my team."

Cusack smiled crookedly, uncertain what to say but thinking his boss could skip rope better than tarantulas.

"My daughter's lucky to have him."

"That's an interesting deal you struck with Hartford," Leeser said. "I think we can do some business together."

"We think that division fits our operations like a glove."

"From what I hear," Leeser continued, "you're the heat on Boston's waterfront."

"We own a few properties around the New England Aquarium."

"I'd love to get the personal tour."

"Let's set something up," Caleb offered. "Middle of next month?"

"Done. The sooner, the better."

Shit.

"Hey, Cy, Caleb. There's Graham Durkin," Jimmy said. "I want you to meet him."

Within fifteen minutes Cyrus Leeser, Graham Durkin, and Caleb Phelps became new best friends. It was like the party stopped, and no one else in the atrium mattered. Cy wanted to do business with Caleb. Caleb wanted to cultivate Graham, as an out-of-state patron for his gubernatorial campaign. And Graham wanted to learn more about MoMA from Leeser, who said, "We can use somebody like you on the board."

"You made Cy's day," Nikki told Cusack.

The two had drifted to the side, one of those spontaneous cocktail sidebars. Nikki remained attentive, however, in case her boss needed anything. For the last hour he mostly needed single malts.

"You know, Caleb," the billionaire said, "my brother-in-law can be helpful."

"Why's that?"

"He's the president of the Massachusetts Police Association."

"That sounds like a good excuse for a speaking engagement," Leeser offered Phelps, jumping at the connection. "I'd be happy to host a dinner in Boston."

"That's awfully kind," Caleb replied, sounding more and more like a politician every minute.

"But one thing," Graham said. "I know my brother-in-law. There are only two words that get his attention."

"And they are?" Caleb beckoned.

" 'Family values.' "

"If you guys know my son-in-law," Caleb said, "you probably know where I stand on decency and ethics."

The three men turned toward Jimmy and Nikki, both standing on the periphery. Almost on cue Emi joined the group. She was relieved to spot her husband's two-star pin amid the sea of black ties and faceless strangers.

"How are you, honey?" greeted Caleb, who hugged his daughter. Patting her stomach with a dad's affection, he added, "See what I mean about 'family values'?"

"Did I miss something?" asked Emi, kissing her husband square on the lips.

"We missed you," Jimmy replied.

Leeser watched, eyes aglow, sipping his drink. He enjoyed the minireunion of father, daughter, and porn star. He was in command, surrounded by hundreds of admirers. His plan was working. It was only a matter of time before Caleb Phelps stepped up to the plate and solved the problem with his stupid hedges.

Cy had no idea the next thirty minutes would shake his control of Cusack. That help would come from Bianca—and at her expense. That his wife, for all her time and effort venerating Cy Leeser with help from the rich and famous, still took counsel from Dorothy Parker on most everything:

"If you want to know what God thinks of money, just look at the people he gave it to."

CHAPTER FORTY

FIFTEEN MINUTES . . .

After the emcee's introduction, Cy embraced the microphone like a hungry lover. The paparazzi and three, maybe four hundred from society's crème de la crème whooped and cheered in his honor. Savoring the moment, Leeser waited for their applause to fade. He showed the patience of a peacock on full display.

You'd think Leeser walks on water, one of the journalists scribbled on her pad.

No one watched more closely than Bianca, bestselling author, mother, and the hurricane force behind the festivities. She clapped among throngs of the rich and the stunning, surrounded by the usual suspects of fashion from Armani to Narciso Rodriguez.

Cy was on display, but everyone knew Bianca owned the night. She had done the heavy lifting, the rustling of papers, and the hustling of pocketbooks. The truth was, Mrs. Cyrus Leeser no longer understood why she bothered.

Last night Cy scoffed at Bianca. She had floated the notion of resurrecting her career as an author. "You think the world wants romance," sneered Leeser, "from a broken-down plagiarist who hasn't published in sixteen years?"

Bianca's eyes grew moist as she thought about their twins, wondering how to shield them. One of her Pilates buddies noticed the tears and handed Bianca a handkerchief. "I'm so proud of you, girl."

"Thanks, sweetie."

Bianca eyed her martini as her husband savored his fifteen minutes. Leeser extolled MoMA and the gods of Greenwich, naming people in the crowd who donated six figures in the name of good taste. He discussed the challenges of a train-wreck market, and at times, his speech vacillated between a pep rally for Hedgistan and a call to action:

"We're hurting. The markets are suffering this month. Some people blame us. They say hedge funds created the subprime mortgage fiasco. They say *we* gave birth to toxic assets."

To Cusack's ear, Leeser sounded like a Sunday morning televangelist with twenty lines open and operators standing by to take calls. Fire and brimstone. Full of shit.

"They talk about our greed. They blame us for the fall of Bear Stearns and Lehman Brothers. They say we're to blame for the financial troubles that face our country."

Bianca pretended to smile.

"Well, I'm here to tell you," Leeser roared, "it's hedge funds that make capital markets more efficient. It's hedge funds that rein in greed and force companies to work harder. We're America's watchdogs. We're the ones that insist on quality. And we're the reason this country is prospering."

The crowd hollered for Cy to continue. They nursed their cocktails and nodded their heads in agreement. They had no idea whether LeeWell Capital was making money or not. Only limited partners knew the value in their accounts, and even their knowledge was limited to the one-line statements mailed at the end of each quarter.

"Sure, we make a few bucks," Leeser acknowledged, "but hedge funds give back to society. And tonight, I challenge every person in this room to join me in giving more to MoMA."

A thunderous ovation rocked the building. Even Bianca cheered. But for all the things Leeser said that night, only one mattered. He began what sounded like a sweet tribute from husband to wife:

"You know, there's a good woman behind every successful man."

Bianca's ears perked up and her jaw dropped ever so slightly. For a moment, she fantasized things were okay. Wives turned and nodded in her direction. Husbands flashed her the big thumbs-up.

"We're here tonight," Cy continued, "because of my wife's Herculean effort. And I want to brag about her." Leeser paused to sip from his scotch.

Bianca blushed.

"This is an election year." Cy toasted a glass in his wife's direction. "We all know about Joe Biden's problems at Syracuse. And don't forget

Teddy Kennedy at Harvard. He took two years off after that little episode with his Spanish exam."

The crowd hushed. To a man and to a woman, they wondered where Leeser was going. Bianca shook her head, however, first to the left and then to the right. She knew. She knew exactly what to expect, and in that moment she would have traded her Heidi Weisel formal for a tortoise shell.

"Most of you know my wife loves Dorothy Parker. Maybe too much given that Bianca never finished college. It was more of a borrow than a steal, if you ask me."

Cy sipped his single malt, peaking in glory. The crowd gulped their drinks, watching in disbelief. Bianca gave her martini to a passing waiter and closed her eyes, praying her husband would stop.

"You can talk about Biden and Kennedy—the way they came back," Leeser continued in his staccato rhythm. "Those guys have nothing on my wife, who wrote ten bestselling novels. And tonight I'm pleased to report Bianca is two credits away from earning her degree at NYU."

Cusack nudged Emi, who nudged Caleb. The three clapped at the word "NYU," thinking it was the only way to salvage the dignity of a bestselling author outed for plagiarism. The crowd joined, relieved by instructions for what to do.

When the applause stopped Leeser said, "Honey, this is for you." He pulled out half-frame glasses and read from Dorothy Parker:

> *Some men tear your heart in two.*
> *Some men flirt and flatter,*
> *Some men never look at you,*
> *And that clears up the matter.*

"Bianca, we're all looking at you tonight," Cy boomed from the podium. Raising his cocktail glass, he said, "Let's give it up for my wife." Cy clapped, and people joined him. But the applause was muted, troubled rather than jubilant, eyes horror-show wide throughout the room.

Emi whispered to Cusack, "Talk about insensitive."

Bianca flashed a wan smile at socialites and reporters. Emi noted the tears welling in her eyes, however, and rushed to the stricken woman's side with a quickness that defied six months. She put her arms around Bianca and used Yaz as a battering ram all the way to the ladies' room.

A few minutes later, Cy was standing next to Victor Lee and Graham Durkin. Caleb was there, too, but he was speaking with a reporter from the *New York Post*. Cusack joined them just in time to watch a train wreck take out his biggest prospect.

Graham: "It's not my business, Cy. But is Bianca okay?"

Cy: "Sure. Why?"

Graham: "You humiliated her."

Cy: "I complimented her courage and grit."

Graham: "You implied she got kicked out of college for plagiarism."

Cy: "You're kidding, right?"

Victor drew close and whispered into Leeser's ear, "Maybe Nikki should check on Bianca."

Lee's interruption was exactly what Durkin needed. Using the band's booming rhythm as cover, the billionaire turned Cusack away from the group. "I need to cancel our meeting."

"Is there a problem?"

"Your boss is tone-deaf, Jimmy."

Cusack needed to do something, say anything that would salvage tomorrow's presentation. His biggest prospect was slipping away. When Cy discovered the cancellation, he would be pissed.

"The smartest people in my industry sometimes miss cues," explained Cusack, measuring his words. "They get too wrapped up in the markets. And tonight Cy blew it big time. But focus is what makes people good at managing money."

"Your boss can't focus," countered Graham, "until he sorts things out with his wife. You can take that to the bank."

"I'd love to show you our shop, the trading floor, our offices in Greenwich."

"Don't worry about it." Then, turning to shake Caleb's hand, Durkin said over his shoulder, "Just make sure to get me your father-in-law's coordinates."

"You got it, Graham."

"And I'll make sure we talk family values with your brother-in-law," Caleb added.

"You want to grab dinner with us?" Cusack asked, trying to salvage time with Durkin.

"No. I'm taking off," the billionaire replied. "Pass on my apologies to Emi."

"Should I get a car for you?" Jimmy asked.

"Got it covered," Durkin replied. He turned and walked out of MoMA's atrium.

Caleb turned to Cusack and said, "I don't know how to thank you, after tonight, after December. This introduction may be the best thing that ever happens to my campaign. Dinner is on me when Emi gets back. We've got some catching up to do."

The rain ended the same time as MoMA's festivities. The freshly bathed air was invigorating. It breathed new life into Manhattan's grime, a fine respite from the mandatory showers at the end of every day. Cool, clean, crisp—it was a perfect night to joyride with a seventy-something guy.

Rachel held the steering wheel with her right hand and fussed auburn hair with her left. She mashed down on the gas pedal, eighty, ninety, one hundred miles per hour, somewhat surprised by the car's acceleration on the upper deck of the George Washington Bridge. She looked at Conrad and laughed, her white teeth glistening and radiant underneath the overhead lights of the bridge.

Conrad looked skeletal. Like he was about to die, face ashen, his knuckles pressed hard against the dashboard. He was a bundle of nerves, every limb in his body rigid from Rachel's driving. His Mercedes, leather trim and fully loaded, closed like a cruise missile on an eighteen-wheeler.

"Pull over," he demanded.

"What's wrong, lover?" she asked, slowing, slowing, slowing in the middle of the George Washington.

"Don't stop here," Conrad screamed, cars honking and whizzing past. "I want to drive."

"Oh, puhlease," she said, sounding bored, as though she drove high-performance cars every day.

"I hate your driving," Conrad announced, too scared to measure his words, and unnerved by his wife's absence. "I need to go home."

"Bronxville can wait for what I have," she replied, winking at him, ignoring the road and hurtling to within five inches of a Saab's bumper before backing off. She weaved the fingers of her right hand through her hair.

"Would you keep your hands on the wheel?" stuttered Barnes.

"Maybe you're right," she said, pulling off the auburn wig, throwing it toward the Hudson, shaking her blond hair free.

"I'd kill for a speeding ticket," he muttered under his breath.

"What's that?"

"Nothing. Where are we going?" asked Barnes.

"To the Meadowlands."

"What for?"

"So you can check out my jets."

Conrad loved Marge. He cursed his mistake, the big adventure with this cross between a flirt and a nutcase. Barnes had no idea Rachel would snuff his fuse in forty-five minutes.

CHAPTER FORTY-ONE
FRIDAY, SEPTEMBER 19
BENTWING AT $32.27

Nikki walked into Leeser's office and placed an overnight package on his desk. The sides of the envelope bowed out half an inch. The contents were not heavy. Nor were they large. They were shaped irregularly—evident from the bend in the package. Something other than paper was inside.

Cusack, sitting in front of his boss, appreciated Nikki's interruption. Leeser had started the day in an absolute snit. He glanced at the package and thundered, "What do you mean Durkin canceled?"

"He told me last night," replied Jimmy, calm on the surface and an angry mess inside.

"Because of what happened with Bianca?"

Suck up. Bide my time. Get the video.

"Graham still wants to meet." Jimmy struggled to hide the white lie. "He had a fire drill back in Providence."

Leeser's shoulders relaxed. The storm clouds passed. "Your father-in-law won big."

"You bet."

"Did Caleb say anything about Bianca?"

"That she was upset," Cusack replied.

"Caleb doesn't blame me, does he?"

"No."

"She drinks too much. She's been drinking too much for sixteen years. Last night was just another example."

"Bianca looked sober," replied Cusack.

"Let me tell you something, Jimmy. A twelve-step program won't work for my wife. Bianca needs twenty-four. Now get out of here and schedule a meeting with your father-in-law."

After Cusack left, Leeser inspected the overnight package on his desk. It came from Hafnarbanki and was marked PERSONAL AND CONFIDENTIAL. The return address showed the name Ólafur Vigfusson.

"Well, Ólafuck," gloated Leeser, as he opened the envelope. "I'm glad you know when to capitulate."

Back in his office, Cusack toiled with the time sink otherwise known as Microsoft Outlook. He answered a few e-mails but deleted most. He never called Caleb, who was in meetings all day. Instead, he considered the videotape and speculated about the risks to his father-in-law:

Will Cy threaten Caleb?

After ten minutes of withering self-flagellation, Cusack phoned his real estate broker for more of the same. "Any nibbles on the condo?"

"Are you kidding? I haven't closed a sale in three months."

"I can't drop the asking price."

"I doubt it makes any difference," Robby said.

"Thanks for the encouragement, smiley."

Jimmy called Sydney next, his ex-assistant from Goldman Sachs and Cusack Capital. "How are you?"

"Been better," she replied with the kind of voice that says, "You don't want to know."

"What's wrong?"

"Jean Bertrand's running around with his teeth set like a stubborn mule."

"You almost sound like him," observed Cusack.

"If it's not one thing, it's another," she confided. " 'Sydney, I need this.' Or 'Sydney, I need that.' And when his door's closed, he's always, I mean always, screaming at some woman, 'Fuck you, darling.' "

"He talks to you like that?"

"No. I'm 'sugar.' "

"You want me to rough him up?" teased Cusack, trying to lighten her mood.

"Don't call him," she said, deadly serious. "He'll take it out on me."

"What for?"

"He's a freak about secrets."

"Plenty of that going around."

"Jean Bertrand blames me for everything."

"I don't mean to put you on the spot," said Cusack, twisting in his chair. "But has he lost any clients?"

"Not that I know of. The guy's a world-class bullshitter. He lies about everything."

"Bullshitters know how to survive," Cusack observed philosophically. "Which means you have a job until we figure out what's next."

"I gotta go," she announced, suddenly busy.

"Can I buy you lunch?"

"Just get me out of here."

"May I come in?"

Bianca Leeser stood in Jimmy's office doorway. She wore white cords, a blue oxford with one button open, and a battered Yankees cap. She looked different, but Cusack could not explain why.

"How are you?" He rushed round his desk to hug her hello. With a sweep of his hand, he gestured for Bianca to sit. He grabbed the other guest chair and pulled in close.

"Your wife is adorable."

"Thank you," Jimmy replied. "Emi said you had a good talk."

"It's amazing what we accomplish in the ladies' room."

"I know last night was awkward," Cusack said, "but whatever happened in college was a long, long time ago."

"I forgot one footnote," stated Bianca in a rueful tone.

"You don't need to explain."

"No. But I've been wearing a scarlet letter all my life. In some ways, I'm glad Cy outed me. Takes a load off."

"I hope things are okay." Cusack immediately regretted the comment, too much of an opening.

"They're not."

"I don't mean to intrude," Jimmy said.

"Dorothy Parker said, 'Union is spelled with five letters. It's not a four-letter word.' You know what I say?"

"No?"

"She lacks urgency. I should have left my husband years ago."

"What a nice surprise," greeted Leeser, as Bianca and Cusack walked into his office.

The words belied his tone. He sounded like a priest administering last rites. The phone rang before they could respond and preempted, perhaps, a confrontation between husband and wife.

"This is my conference call," announced Leeser, turning his back.

Cusack, feeling the air grow lousy with tension, asked Bianca in a low voice, "Would you like to wait in my office until he finishes?"

"You still have the names of all our contacts in Reykjavik?" Leeser growled into the receiver.

"No thanks," Bianca whispered to Cusack, as her eyes darted from one painting to the next. She pulled a pen and paper from her purse and said, "I'll be fine."

Leeser continued to bark on the phone. "You've got to finish that piece from the International Institute for Financial Transparency. Today, dammit."

The ranting and raving hardly bothered Bianca, who grew industrious despite all the commotion. She scribbled notes here and adjusted tallies there. She appeared thoughtful and, to Cusack's eye, the most curious thing. Peaceful. "What are you doing?" he asked.

"Taking inventory."

On the way out of Leeser's office, Cusack bumped into Shannon. Literally. The big man came to visit Cy, and the head of sales could not wedge through the door at the same time as the head of security.

Shannon looked past Cusack and spotted Bianca, pad in hand. He frowned and turned to Cusack. "How long will they be?"

"I'd give them some space," Cusack suggested. He paused and added, "Hey, do you have a minute?"

"I do now. What do you want?"

"To discuss a few things."

"Yeah, whatever, Cusack. Let's get this over with."

Suck up. Bide my time. Get the video.

"We got off on the wrong foot," Jimmy said when the two were inside his office. "I don't know if there's any way to clear the air, Shannon. But I'd like to try." He extended his right hand in truce.

"Why?" The big man scowled at Cusack's hand and made no effort to shake it.

Jimmy retracted his hand, not comprehending the depth of venom. "So let's cut to the chase then. I can't afford for that videotape to go public."

"Think I care?"

"Maybe not. But I have a favor to ask."

"You don't listen, man," the big man said, surprised by Cusack's persistence.

"Just keep it under lock and key, okay?"

"Not my problem," Shannon scoffed. "Nikki keeps the Mac."

"I don't know what you think about me. Or why. But LeeWell Capital is a small shop, and it would really help if we got along."

"Then stay away from your Geek friend," the big man instructed. "I've got a job to do, rich boy." He stood to leave and added, "One other thing."

"Yeah."

"You may be a plumber's son, Cusack, but I don't owe you shit."

"My family is off-limits, pal," muttered Cusack as Shannon walked out of the room.

Bianca tucked the inventory count into her purse. Scanning Cy's desk, she found the overnight package from Reykjavik marked PERSONAL AND CON-

FIDENTIAL." Her husband's back turned, Bianca reached into the envelope and pulled out a four-inch nail and handwritten note.

The note read:

Dear Mr. Leeser,

You may recognize this nail from your crate of Seventeenth Nail in My Cranium. What a generous gift to Siggi. I commend your choice of wine, which I had the good fortune to share. Seventeenth Nail is an excellent vintage, the taste dramatic if I say so myself. It gives me great pleasure to return this nail with the profound and personal hope you shove it up your ass.

Sideways if possible.

Too bad about Bentwing. Shorting and betting against companies— like war if you will allow me to paraphrase von Clausewitz—is an "act of violence, which in its application knows no bounds."

Yours sincerely,
Ólafur Vigfusson

Bianca examined the note, read it over several times, and checked the return address from Iceland. It sounded bad, and the preternatural curiosity of a novelist consumed her. When Leeser finished his phone call, Bianca put her business on hold and asked, "Who is Ólafur Vigfusson?"

"Siggi's second cousin."

"I like Siggi. How'd you piss off his cousin?"

"These damn Icelanders," hissed Leeser, "are crippling my portfolio."

"What about the secret sauce?"

"Screw you," snapped Leeser, "and don't you ever tell anyone *Night of the Living Dead Heads* was a bomb. What the hell were you thinking?"

"I don't see what the big deal is."

"I can't fucking hedge fast enough to protect my portfolio from these Icelanders. That's the big deal." Cy's face bloated with contempt. He finally said, "Ólafuck is about to get his. Mark my words."

You, too, thought Bianca. But she said nothing.

CHAPTER FORTY-TWO

There is no escape. Not even on Saturdays. The markets control the psyche of every man and woman in the money business. They occupy the mind like invading warriors that seize, plunder, and rape all thought courtesy of the Internet and other means of modern colonization. There is always the overhang of bad news, easy enough to find on cable twenty-four/seven.

Cusack forgot Bentwing as best as possible. He forgot Cy's preoccupation with Caleb and the videotape from the Foxy Lady. And he focused on matters at hand, breakfast for Emi.

He scrambled eggs with so much cilantro they looked green. He served seven-grain toast, dripping with enough butter to X out all the health benefits of wheat versus white bread. He placed fat juicy strawberries in the center of the table and squeezed what seemed like a thousand and one oranges. By the time he stopped frying steaks—Emi said no more bacon while she was pregnant—there was enough left over for three days of lunch.

"You can't get this at the Ritz," he said, admiring his handiwork on the table.

"Oh, I don't believe this," Emi said, eyeing *The New York Times*.

"Tell me."

She held up the paper, folded to display a man's photo. He looked to be in his seventies. "Do you know this guy?" she asked.

Cusack studied the man's face. "No, who is he?"

"Conrad Barnes."

"Never seen him before, Em."

"I have."

Cusack raised his eyebrows. His wife recognized people by names. Faces in print were a bigger problem than faces in person.

"How do you know him?"

"He helped me find a cab." Emi was never so bold. She usually hung back and waited for others to confirm identities. Not this time. "I was starting to panic. He whistled, and it was like magic. A taxi showed up from nowhere."

"You saw Conrad Barnes?" Cusack asked, doubt seeping into his voice.

Emi bristled ever so slightly. "Look at his face. What's the one thing you notice?"

"He's probably in his midseventies."

"What else?"

"His unibrow is a mile wide."

"Exactly," thundered Emi, who always combed features for striking visual clues.

"Plenty of guys have unibrows," replied Cusack. "Maybe I should grow one so you can spot me."

"Let's stick with the two-star pin," she laughed. "But have you ever seen one so thick and bushy?"

"You got me there," replied Cusack, still doubtful.

"He was the sweetest man. And now he's dead."

"That's eerie."

"It's gruesome," Emi said.

"What do you mean?"

"He burned to death inside his car," she reported. "He crashed on Washington Street in Carlstadt, New Jersey."

"I know that area," said Cusack, surprised. "I park there for Jets games."

"Are there any bars?"

"Redd's. But most of the buildings are industrial. Why do you ask?"

"Police think alcohol was involved," Emi explained.

"Happens all the time."

"He wasn't drunk when I saw him." She toasted her orange juice for effect.

"Redd's could fix that."

"He was with a younger woman," Emi continued. "I thought she was his daughter at first."

"So?"

"So the *Times* says Barnes is married and a longtime resident of Bronxville. I don't see a seventy-year-old guy driving all the way to New Jersey, getting drunk, and flipping his car." She paused and added, "Alone."

"You sound like *Law and Order*."

"Maybe. But I bet that woman was his mistress."

"Are you sure it's the same guy?" asked Cusack, growing more skeptical.

"I'd know his unibrow anywhere. And you should have seen the scar on that woman's hand."

Inside her one-bedroom on the Upper East Side of Manhattan, Rachel scraped lingering bits from a ravaged half of a grapefruit. With painstaking care, she spread a wisp of margarine onto a half slice of wheat toast. Coffee, no cream, was the one indulgence she allowed. And she downed cup after cup as she leafed through *The New York Times*.

When Rachel found the article on Conrad Barnes, she dialed her employer. "Did you see today's paper?"

"I'm glad we can move on."

"That may not be possible, Kemosabe."

"What do you mean?"

"A woman saw me with Barnes."

"Not my issue," he said.

"I don't like loose ends."

"And I don't need extra bodies."

"That's easy for you to say. I'm doing all the heavy lifting," Rachel complained. "And if the law gets me, you're at risk, too. I don't care who or where you are."

"Are you threatening me?"

"Stating facts."

"Do you know who she is?"

"No. But it won't be hard to find out." Rachel doubted many pregnant women visit the Bronx Zoo in formals. There had to be a trail.

"Do what you need to do. But one thing."

"Yes," she replied.

"Don't call me anymore."

CHAPTER FORTY-THREE

Nikki was slumped outside Leeser's office when Jimmy Cusack arrived. At 7:30 A.M. she was already a wreck, headset askew and hair disheveled. Even her nose stud lacked the trademark allure. Cy's visitors usually found Nikki warm, her command of the details reassuring. That morning her large-and-in-charge persona had gone AWOFL, which is the same thing as AWOL but more so.

"You're here early," Cusack remarked in his most pleasant voice. He lingered at her station, hoping she would speak her mind, hoping to make the guardian of Cy's computer his new best friend.

"I couldn't sleep," explained Nikki, her forehead a tangled knot of furrows.

"Everything okay?"

"You tell me. Are *we* okay, Jimmy?"

"What do you mean?"

"I have a girlfriend who was decruited by a global macro shop at Pickwick Plaza." Nikki was referring to a hedge fund located at offices around the corner from Greenwich Avenue.

"What's 'decruited' mean?"

"She was fired before she started," explained Nikki. "My job isn't what worries me, though."

"It shouldn't," soothed Cusack. "Cy needs you."

"Don't get me wrong," she continued, "I worry about car payments like anyone else." Nikki added with a wry smile, "Except you, maybe."

"You don't like my Beemer?" His car became the office joke after Greenwich Plaza's management towed it one day. They thought it had been abandoned.

"If you're making payments, honey, you'd better stop."

"Easy now," Cusack laughed. "What's bugging you?"

"Victor, for one," she replied.

"Another hammer attack?" asked Cusack, suddenly alarmed.

"Nothing like that. He's changing."

"What are you talking about?"

"He notices everything. And you know how his pants are always too short?"

"Waders," Jimmy confirmed.

"He pays attention to what he wears now. A friend of mine works at Randolphs. She told me Victor is living in the men's department."

"That's a good thing, right?" Cusack did not see the problem.

"I'm not sure. If Rod Stewart were a girl, Victor would look like her."

"I'll ask Cy if he's concerned."

"He's not in today," she reported.

"Why not?"

"He's taking the day off. Things are bad with Bianca. I heard that all his clothes ended up on the lawn again."

"We'll get through this, Nikki."

Up 369 points on Friday, the Dow plummeted 373 points by the close. Lee-Well's investors overwhelmed the phone lines. Cusack forgot the Foxy Lady video and his own financial concerns as the fund's panicky limited partners shotgunned questions with no right answers:

"Is my money safe?"

"Should we double up?"

"Is ten thousand eight hundred the market bottom?"

It was not until 7:43 P.M. when Cusack packed up to head home. He was exhausted. His mouth tasted like a sewer from all the caffeine. He had been speaking twelve hours nonstop, twelve hours of slugging down coffee, chocolate, and soft drinks, twelve hours of regurgitating the same empty words:

"We've never had a down year."

"We hedge the portfolio."

The one thing Cusack never said: "My boss is a liar and a snake no matter how good your investment results looked before this year."

Cusack shut down his computer. He thumbed his nose at 179 unanswered e-mails in Microsoft Outlook and started toward the etched glass doors of LeeWell Capital. He was already mulling over take-out with Emi—spring rolls, fried rice, Moo Goo Gai Pan, and other cornerstones of Chinese comfort food—when Nikki's private fax beeped.

It signaled an incoming message. Beckoned him to take a look. If beeps were visual, this one was a big, bold sign that read, "Please close your eyes, keep walking, and pretend you never saw what I'm about to print."

The fax machine sat on Nikki's desk outside Cy's office. A bank of stomach-high files barricaded it from view. Most days, Cusack would have continued out the door. And during office hours, Cy's assistant would have shuttled the document to her boss.

Nikki was gone, though. She left hours ago. The fax's ringtone reminded Cusack he was alone. It was as good a time as any to check for the Mac laptop with the video from the Foxy Lady. He tried every drawer in Nikki's bank of lateral files. They were all locked.

Cursing his bad luck, Cusack watched the cover page print. He listened to the document burp its way through the fax, the retching sounds of a dying technology. The firm Dillon and Henshaw, located in Paramus, New Jersey, was sending two pages.

Underneath the address, someone named Ron had scrawled, *For your files*. Cusack almost left. He hated paperwork. He stayed, not sure why, as the second page slowly bleated out of the fax. It proved to be a death certificate—cold, clinical, and indifferent to the message.

Manner of Death: The box for "accident" was checked.

Surviving Spouse: The name "Margery" occupied the space.

Medical Examiner/Coroner: Alexander Griswold had signed his name and certified the death.

When Cusack found the deceased, he read the name three times just to be sure his brain was operating on the up and up. The dead man was Conrad A. Barnes.

There was no question about the odds. It had to be the same guy Emi mentioned. The name was right, same spelling as the unibrow in the *New York Times* obituary. The date was right: September 19, 2008. Even the location of death was right: New Jersey.

Cusack stapled the two sheets and placed them on Nikki's chair. He turned off the lights and headed into the night. He wondered whether Cy had taken the day to mourn a friend's death.

Even a liar and a snake can have friends.

CHAPTER FORTY-FOUR

TUESDAY, SEPTEMBER 23
BENTWING AT $32.76

"Meet me downstairs in fifteen minutes, Ólafur."

Hafnarbanki's shares, trading at 625 kronur, had dropped more than 11 percent in two weeks. Hedge funds were not buying the stock. Nor was anyone else, not even the Qataris. Guðjohnsen had asked Ólafur to take a walk, away from wandering eyes and curious ears all through the office. There was a problem, and Ólafur knew it. But he had no idea what.

The chairman's face ordinarily remained expressionless, the kind of bland white mug used to serve coffee at diners around the world—even Iceland. Guðjohnsen appeared pensive today. Like he belonged upstairs in the office. "Where do we stand on your war?"

"LeeWell got the message," Ólafur replied. "Cy Leeser has lost over one hundred million dollars on Bentwing since January. When his fund collapses, no one from that godforsaken rat turd named Greenwich will ever short Hafnarbanki again."

The silver-haired chairman appraised Ólafur, eyebrows raised, as the two men walked through the streets of Reykjavik. The younger man found the chairman's expression curious. He had no idea what his boss was thinking. They walked in silence for two, maybe three minutes. Ólafur decided, *This is weird.*

Guðjohnsen finally asked, "Anything else I should know, Ólafur?"

"The Qataris love us. They're making money on the Bentwing short, and it's only a matter of time before their investment in Hafnarbanki pays off."

"You're pretty sure of yourself," noted Guðjohnsen.

"Our stock," affirmed Ólafur, "will bounce back."

"No," bellowed the chairman. He stopped walking. With eyes like gun sights, he fixed on his subordinate and repeated, "No."

"What do you mean 'no'?"

"You killed us," hissed Guðjohnsen between clenched teeth.

"What are you talking about?" Ólafur lost all awareness of people in the streets. For a moment, he thought his boss daft.

"Your heat-seeking missiles," the chairman cursed, "came back and locked on Hafnarbanki."

Ólafur said nothing, stared blankly.

"Have you ever heard of the International Institute for Financial Transparency?" asked Guðjohnsen.

"No, sir."

"I pay you to know these things," observed the older man, shaking his head. "But because you don't know, I'll explain. The Institute is a financial services firm that publishes research reports, including a few on Hafnarbanki."

"So does Merrill Lynch."

"The Institute released a report last Friday," the chairman continued, "that landed on the desks of editors-in-chief at *Morgunblaðið*, *Fréttablaðið*, and *DV*."

"Okay?" Ólafur kept his words short. They could sink him later. He avoided the temptation to say, "Unknown research houses send their reports to everybody, including Iceland's newspapers."

"The Institute sent the same report to every member of Parliament."

"What did it say?"

"The usual, Ólafur. Fifteen pages of leverage ratios and portfolio analysis. I wouldn't be surprised if they did a copy-paste job from Merrill Lynch. Except for one thing."

"Which is what, sir?"

"Page seven examines our relationship with Sheikh Fahad Bin Thalifa."

Ólafur felt his knees buckle.

"The report says his investment in Hafnarbanki makes no sense. That our relationship with him is too cozy. That the timing is suspicious."

Ólafur clenched his fist and kicked at the sidewalk, frustrated by his loss for words.

"The International Institute for Financial Transparency," continued Guðjohnsen, "questions whether we negotiated a backroom deal at the expense of our depositors. That's what every member of Parliament is reading today."

"*Anzvíti!*" Ólafur exclaimed, which is a cross between "damn" and "bastard" in Iceland. "Who are these people?"

"I doubted you'd know. According to my sources, a hedge fund from your 'rat turd named Greenwich' owns the Institute. The fund uses it to release nasty research on stocks they short."

"We'll expose them," the younger banker cursed. "We'll bury them."

"I told you," grimaced Guðjohnsen, "you already buried us."

"What do you mean, sir?"

"My phone is ringing off the hook with reporters or friends in Parliament. I expect a criminal investigation to start any day."

For the first time in his career, Ólafur understood what it meant to get his ass kicked. He said nothing, tried to regroup, and wondered what Sun Tzu would have counseled.

"Fix your problem," the chairman growled. "Our loan to the Qataris totals thirty-eight billion kronur."

"My problem?"

"Need I remind you," Guðjohnsen continued, his voice growing angry and loud, "the loan is non-recourse. The sheikh can default and we're stuck with Hafnarbanki's shares."

"You approved that loan, sir."

"That's not how I remember it." Guðjohnsen waited for a few suits to pass as he squared off with his subordinate and rubbed his hands in a washing motion. "If the state prosecutor cries fraud, you're not taking me down."

"The Qataris will work with us." Ólafur suppressed his temptation to throw a punch at the seventy-year-old man.

"They're already working with *you*."

"What's that mean?" Ólafur shot back. He added, "Sir," to punctuate his question.

"The sheikh paid your cousin five million dollars for a painting."

"That was part of the plan to win Leeser's trust and get information."

"Or line your pockets, Ólafur?"

"It's not like that," he protested.

"I'll tell you what it's like. Your warning to hedge funds is shit. Our market value is down over four billion euros since January. And you sold a five-million-dollar painting to one of our most important customers."

"I can explain."

"Save your breath. I only need to know one thing."

The two men were now standing outside the 101 Hotel on Hverfisgata, the place where everything began to unravel. The junior banker, after a long game of silence ping-pong, asked, "Which is what, sir? What do you need to know?"

"How you intend to clean up your mess."

CHAPTER FORTY-FIVE

LEEWELL CAPITAL . . .

"Shut the door," Cy ordered Victor.

The words "meeting" and "beating" had become synonymous at Lee-Well Capital as the markets crashed. Leeser returned Tuesday morning and summoned Cusack and Victor into the conference room first thing. He sipped coffee from an Andover mug, gripping it so hard his knuckles turned white. He chambered hollow-point words that mushroomed when they hit, exacting maximum damage on the soft targets of ego and personal pride.

Cusack assumed his boss had taken Monday off to attend a funeral for Conrad Barnes. Or to focus on Bianca, who had converted the front lawn into Leeser's personal closet. But if there was lingering sadness or problems at home, Cy never revealed either. He was neither happy nor depressed. He was calm, a technician. He appeared oblivious to the Bentwing shorts, like he had found new resolve from three days off.

"Okay, ladies," said Leeser, with take-charge persona. "I pay you to think. Not to lounge with your pants around your ankles, hoping for some personal growth."

Lee winced. Cusack shifted uncomfortably.

"Jimmy, I want you to take another run at New Jersey Sheet Metal."

"They put us on hold. You know that."

"I don't give a shit. You're the one with cash flow problems. So earn your keep. Make some calls. Set up some meetings. There's big money when people flip out. Get us in front of every dollar we know, and that goes double for Durkin."

"You got it." Cusack felt his ears go red.

"Is Caleb on our calendar yet?"

"Working it. We canceled two dates already because his schedule keeps changing."

"Stay on it, Jimmy. I don't want a problem with my loan payment come February."

The color drained from Cusack's face. His ears stayed red.

"Your turn," announced Leeser, turning to his head trader. "Is there activity on Planet Victor this morning?"

Lee shrugged his shoulders. The gesture was more "here goes" than "screw you." Then he shocked both his colleagues. "Well, for one, I'm in Cusack's camp. I say we sell everything in the portfolio and go cash."

Jimmy whipped around, surprised.

"What about Bentwing?" asked Cy.

"You sit on the board. We can't sell until the middle of October without running afoul of the SEC. But when the time comes, when the window opens, I'd blow out Bentwing, too." Victor finished by asking, "What do you think, Cy?"

"That yours never dropped."

Lee's eyes widened. The rebuke caught him by surprise. He said nothing. His hands fumbled for the hammer, which was nowhere to be found.

"When Eddy or Numb Nuts wants to trade, offer market color, or whine about their wives," Cy continued, "you swagger. You attack. You pour on the insults until they're bawling on some shrink's couch over their pathetic little lives at that joke of an investment bank formerly known as Merrill. Same for Goldman and the other cretins. We don't work here. We fucking own Greenwich."

Cusack and Victor both stared at their boss. His face was burning fiery red. The veins in his neck throbbed with enough 911 intensity to scramble a dozen paramedics.

"Why?" asked Jimmy. "What's the point?"

"If you act like a loser in this market," explained Leeser, "you'll be the first to get fucked. I know. I've been here before. So cowboy up, ladies. We're not selling a damn thing."

"Glad to see the confidence," pouted Victor. "Care to explain why?"

"You think this is sharing circle, Vic?"

"I'm just asking," he replied.

Cusack detected the slightest quiver in the head trader's voice.

"If you must know," crowed Leeser, "I cured our problem with the hedges. Now get out of here and make me some money."

On the way back to their offices, Cusack turned to his boss and said, "Sorry to hear about Conrad Barnes."

Cy paused for a moment and said, "Come into my office."

"What's on your mind?"

"Do you know Conrad?" asked Leeser.

"No. I was here late last night and saw his death certificate. I assume he's a friend."

"How'd you see my fax?" Cy knew the machine was hidden deep inside Nikki's workstation.

"The pages sailed." Cusack decided his white lie deserved a trip to confession. "I picked them up off the floor."

"Conrad and I had business dealings from time to time."

"I'm sorry for your loss. Emi said he was a good guy."

"Does she know him?"

For just a second, Cusack thought Leeser was losing his take-charge vitriol from the conference room. "No. But he helped Emi catch a cab to MoMA the night of your party. She recognized his picture in the Saturday *Times*." Cusack absently rubbed the two-star pin on his lapel. "My wife was probably one of the last people to see him alive."

"That's creepy," Leeser observed.

"That's what Emi said."

"Where'd she see him?"

"The Bronx Zoo. Emi's a scientist there."

"I see," said Leeser.

"His death sounds gruesome."

"The family's pretty choked up, Jimmy. I'm helping his wife sort out their estate."

"That's really nice."

WEDNESDAY, SEPTEMBER 24

BENTWING AT $32.86

Inside Café Oliver on Laugavegi, Mr. Ice drained a shot of Reyka. "Get your money out of Hafnarbanki."

Siggi said nothing. His jaw never dropped. His Siberian-blue eyes, usually in a perpetual state of alarm, never grew wide with surprise or fear. And he did not ask, "Why, cousin?"

Ólafur ordered a second round, even though his cousin was still nursing the first. "I'm in trouble and may lose my job any day."

Siggi blinked, watching his cousin shatter like glass. "What happened?"

"Nothing worked. Nothing at all."

"Your plan with Cy?"

"Doesn't matter, Siggi."

"Your shares in Hafnarbanki?"

"Sold them yesterday and today." The stock closed Tuesday afternoon at 580, down another forty-five kronur.

"I'm sorry," Siggi said.

"Every bank in Iceland is on the verge of collapse. Hafnarbanki can't keep your money safe anymore."

The banker drained his second shot in as many minutes. When he ordered a third round, Siggi waved off the bartender, who shrugged her shoulders and returned to the other patrons.

"What's your problem?" Ólafur snapped. "I just gave you great financial advice. And now you're cutting me off?"

Siggi had never seen Mr. Ice so vulnerable. "I closed my account at Hafnarbanki last week."

Ólafur did a double take. "You're kidding. Why?"

"My dealer friends in London spooked me."

"What'd they say?"

"The krona is shit, and they won't take it anymore. Last year, we could buy one euro with eighty-eight kronur. Today, it takes one hundred thirty-nine."

"What'd you do with your money, Siggi?"

"Wired it someplace safe."

"Where?"

"Bank of America."

THURSDAY, SEPTEMBER 25

BENTWING AT $33.67

Rachel Whittier looked at her watch under the streetlight's amber glow. It was 8:15 P.M. She crossed Gansevoort Street in the Meatpacking District, the area of New York City sometimes known as "MePa," and slipped into the evening shadows. Rachel spied Emi Cusack leaving the building with a gaggle of friends, all with boxes in hand.

Septuagenarians were easy targets. They lived solitary lives, ate every night at six P.M. never fail, and seldom ran into people. Many of them talked way too loud, their decibels a built-in LoJack for finding the aged. It was far more difficult to monitor Emi Cusack's moves. She was either working at the Bronx Zoo, meeting her husband, or gabbing with friends.

Plus, she was lucky. And tonight hardly justified the risk. Emi Cusack in public. Emi Cusack accompanied by a throng of women. Emi Cusack in the middle of a baby shower. "How can I hip-check you into traffic," Rachel cursed from the shadows.

She dialed her employer and said, "I'm staring down the barrel of a dilemma."

"What is it now?"

"She's in the middle of a baby shower, Kemosabe."

"Not my problem," he said, and clicked off.

FRIDAY, SEPTEMBER 26

BENTWING AT $32.77

Victor brooded at his trading station. There were three new LCD panels, his stash of pharmaceuticals underneath. Noticeably absent was the claw

233

hammer. It was safe, tucked away in a drawer and buried beneath a tangle of gadget cords, jar of moisturizer, and half-empty box of Wheat Thins.

"Damn," Victor mumbled. "You had your chance, Cy." The Dow was trading over 11,000 again after yesterday's brief rally. Thursday had been the perfect time to get safe.

But there would be no going to cash. There would be no taking of losses. There would be only one thing—the swaggering around the Street. "Confidence," Cy had preached. "We're on top of the world. You betray fear and somebody will nail-gun your balls to the mat."

Victor dialed Numb Nuts at Merrill Lynch. "Got any color on the market?"

"Strong opening," the trader replied. "Congress will probably inject massive amounts of money into financial institutions. I say we rally on expectations."

"Keep going." Victor leaned forward in his chair and rolled his head in a big, wide circle, making ready to strut his stuff and exude the confidence that Cy demanded.

"Not much to add. But you should sell and pay off debt ASAP." With that, the Merrill rep stopped talking and waited for Lee's reply.

Recognizing his cue and seizing the moment, Victor cowboyed up with all the bravado and bluster he could muster. He grabbed his pills and said, "Let's do lunch, Numb Nuts."

Victor had an idea. He doubted his body parts would be nail-gunned to the mat. Unless, of course, Cy found out.

CHAPTER FORTY-SIX

MONDAY, SEPTEMBER 29
BENTWING AT $28.87

There are plenty of alpha males outside Hedgistan. Emi sipped her bottled water and stared at the grassy slopes of the Baboon Reserve. She regarded *Theropithecus gelada* as a magnificent species, her favorite exhibit at the Bronx Zoo.

Gelada baboons grow two feet tall, give or take a few inches. They weigh anywhere from thirty to forty-five pounds. And their thick, black manes stick out straight. Like defibrillators zapped them. Like electric current is still buzzing through the hair.

Males are especially vibrant. Their chests have bright patches of red skin, shaped like hourglasses and surrounded by snowy tufts of white hair. They look fearsome when roused.

Emi loved to eat lunch here in Somba Village, to sit outside and break from her work with reptiles. It was unseasonably warm for September 29, the perfect day for catching rays.

"Herpetology" comes from the Greek word "*herpeton*," or creeping animal. The study of reptiles had seemed like such a smart career choice during college. Emi could always distinguish their countless shapes and colors. Through the last few months, however, she had grown tired of snakes and crocodiles. Her head was no longer in the game.

Emi looked at her sketchpad and realized she had drawn Yaz. Fat little cheeks. Wisps of hair. Eyes closed in the happy sleep of newborns. She reminded herself, in that moment, that she would be a mother in two months. The thought made her happy.

She had checked out long ago from her career and her reptiles and her other distractions from Yaz. Almost by instinct, she looked up to see if anyone was looking. There was a blonde, three tables over, peering at her. The woman had green eyes and red fingernails. She looked through Emi, or pretended to look through her, and shifted her eyes to the hilly range on the other side of the patio.

Emi wondered if the woman was staring at her.

Rachel rubbed her right hand, watching Emi Cusack chew a ham-and-Brie on wheat. *Why do people eat that crap,* she wondered, *when the hot dogs smell so good here?*

She knew the Bronx Zoo created special challenges. Visitors could turn the corner at any second on the tree-lined grounds and catch her in the middle of an insulin injection. Long-range sniper shots were easier—but disgusting. The notion of a headshot, splattering somebody's grits against the wall, made Rachel nauseous.

There was an art to contract killing. Rachel fancied herself the Andy Warhol of assassins, a cleaner with a select client base of one who avoided guns and other plebian methodology all too common in her line of work. She had standards.

It was more challenging, better from a career perspective, to disguise executions as natural deaths. Or tragic accidents. There was that decapitation two weeks back, unplanned of course, but the police never suspected foul play. "Poor Barnes lost his head," Rachel mused to herself.

Of course, the Bronx Zoo offered unique options. No problem to hip-check a pregnant woman into the animals. The question was which cage. Rachel deemed polar bears the most reliable of all predators. Without much encouragement, they would rip Emi to shreds. *Ursus maritimus* stood eight feet tall and weighed over a thousand pounds. They looked so cute, the white fur more eye-catching than the razor claws. Even better, they ate seals.

"Emi Cusack is shaped like a seal," Rachel smirked under her breath.

The African wild dogs were another option. Known as "painted dogs," a reference to their mustard and brown-black markings, they hunted in packs. In the wild, the dogs could run at speeds up to forty-one miles per hour for as long as one hour. A pack could easily catch a pregnant woman lumbering through the grassy fields. Emi Cusack, it seemed, was always visiting the dog exhibit.

The chase, one pregnant woman and a bunch of snarling hounds, sounded better than NASCAR. But Rachel decided against the dogs. They made the most annoying sounds. They did not bark. They squealed like pigs. The other problem was size. At best, the dogs weighed sixty pounds each. She needed something big and mean, something like polar bears.

Rachel realized, to her horror, that she had been staring at the mark. Now Emily Cusack was staring back. The pregnant woman stood, crumpled her brown-paper lunch bag into a ball, and walked toward Rachel with the clear intention of making contact.

It's too soon, Rachel cursed herself, behind a wide and welcoming smile.

"What a beautiful day," remarked Emi. She spoke with the patrician accent indigenous to Beacon Hill. Her kind intonation would serve as either a greeting to a friend or a pleasant hello to a stranger. Rachel had no way of knowing. But Emi had worked years to master that inflection. Her tones were the perfect way to mask prosopagnosia and draw out a response.

"You brought a picnic."

"Sure did," Emi laughed, radiating the warmth and inner glow unique to women in their third trimester. "I work at the zoo. Do you need help finding an exhibit?"

"The Nile crocodiles."

"What a coincidence," said Emi. "I'm heading over there now."

"May I join you?"

"Of course."

"Is it true," asked Rachel, "that their jaws exert more than two thousand pounds of pressure per square inch?"

"You've done your homework."

"That's me," Rachel said. "I pride myself on preparation."

Cusack was battling a different kind of predator. His assailant did not stalk septuagenarians, either asthmatics or grand dames from the Colony Club. It had never orchestrated the spectacular auto crash of a seventy-two-year-old man looking for adventure. His predator was fearsome, nevertheless. It was ruthless. And it was lunging forward, savaging everything in its path.

Fear is the serial killer of money. The House defeated Bush's $700 billion rescue package, and the Dow crashed 778 points. The world panicked and sold everything possible, no longer caring about losses but only trying to protect whatever was left—somehow, some way. Investors wondered whether any financial institutions remained solvent.

Cusack broke from the action, away from the craze of incoming phone calls, and texted Emi's cell phone: *I'll be home late.*

He had no inkling about the predator stalking Emi. No clue the battle between Hafnarbanki to the north and LeeWell Capital to the south was sweeping his face-blind wife into the cross fire. The war had turned personal long ago with Shannon's videotape. Now it was lethal.

CHAPTER FORTY-SEVEN

"Jimmy, I'm freaking out."

Seven-thirty in the morning was too early for anyone to come unglued, especially Sydney. Cusack's former assistant was bulletproof on most days, a rock of can-do attitude. Today was different. She was stammering. Sydney sounded like the survivor of a defeated army. Like she was waiting for the victors to mop up whatever remained.

"What's wrong, Syd?"

"I need help."

"Can't you just tell me? The market's having a nervous breakdown."

"So am I."

Cusack's stomach soured, his thoughts shifting to Jean Bertrand Bouvier and the sublease at the Empire State Building. He said nothing for a minute, and Sydney finally pleaded, "Please."

"I'm on the way."

"Good. Because all hell will break loose when people show up for work."

"What do you mean by that?"

"Just get over here," urged Sydney.

Cusack ignored the view from the sixty-first floor of the Empire State Building. Nothing looks spectacular when a $1.2 million fiasco arrives from nowhere. Jimmy surveyed his old office and glanced where Sydney's cubicle once stood. He looked inside the conference room, now empty of the oak table, all ten chairs, and even the fifty-two-inch flat-screen television.

There were no phones. There were no computers. Only Mr. Coffee remained, Emi's purchase from Walmart. Jean Bertrand Bouvier's shake-and-bake hedge fund shook and booked in the middle of the night.

Sydney stared at Cusack, her brown eyes in shock, her brunette hair mussed, her face showing the toll from the last few hours and more likely the last few weeks. "I have no idea what to do," she said.

"Let's start with Jean Bertrand. Did you call him?"

"He doesn't answer his cell phone."

"What about the maintenance people, Syd?"

"They say Jean Bertrand sneaked out last night."

"Somebody saw him."

"I know, Jimmy. But you know what he's like. The guy can charm the venom from a rattler."

"Damn, you sound like him," said Cusack.

"Sorry."

"So, nobody's heard from Bouvier? Are there any numbers to call, anything?"

"No, and we won't hear from him." Sydney spoke with absolute conviction.

"Why's that?"

"He missed payroll last Friday," she reported.

"You're kidding. Why didn't you call me sooner?"

"Jean Bertrand said it was a computer glitch, and he'd square things up this week."

"You believed him?" asked Cusack.

"He took the office out for a steakhouse dinner and ordered seven-hundred-dollar bottles of wine like money was TP."

"Talk about the last supper."

"Not funny, Jimmy."

"Not meant to be."

"What should I do now?"

Cusack's stomach began to ache, like he might retch any second. But he looked at Sydney, rock-solid reliable through the years, and said, "Here goes. Call building maintenance on your cell. Get them to station somebody outside the office. Nobody in and nobody out until the police arrive."

"Got it."

"Where does Bouvier keep client assets?"

"Bank of New York," replied Sydney.

"Tell your rep there's a problem," he said. "No wire transfers and no trades until further notice. Okay?"

"Got it."

"Call the police, Syd. Tell them to get over here."

"Do you think something happened to Jean Bertrand?"

"No," said Cusack. "I think that Creole cretin skipped in the middle of the night and took everything that wasn't nailed down."

"Asshole."

"Do you know," Jimmy asked, "his accountants or lawyers?"

"My computer is gone, and that's where I keep their phone numbers."

It can't get any worse.

Louis Armstrong begged to differ. He interrupted, singing "La Vie en Rose." It was the ringtone Cusack reserved for Emi.

"Can you talk, James?"

"Not now," he replied. "I'm at the Empire State Building with Syd."

"Why aren't you in Greenwich?" asked Emi.

"Long story. Do you mind if I call you back, sweetie?"

"Somebody's stalking me."

Cusack forgot Bouvier. His face tensed, and he asked, "Are you okay?"

"Creeped out is more like it."

"What happened, Em?"

"Some woman was staring at me during lunch yesterday."

"Did she say something?" asked Cusack.

"No. But she had this funny look, like I didn't recognize her."

"Do you know her?"

"That's what I thought at first," admitted Emi. "I talked to her, and she was nice enough."

"But?"

"Call it feminine intuition. She had a creepy vibe."

Cusack checked his exasperation. "I don't see the stalking part."

"I didn't either at first. The two of us walked over to the Nile crocodiles. And you know how people stand too close sometimes, the way they violate your body space?"

"Did she touch you?" asked Cusack, concern replacing exasperation.

"No—"

"But what?"

"It's hard to say."

"Did she grab your bag or something? What'd she do, Em?"

"Is this twenty questions? I don't know what she did. She was creepy, the way some guys are greasy. Okay, James? I forgot about her until this morning."

"What happened?"

"I spoke with Tina."

"Who's Tina?"

"She works in tickets," explained Emi. "And this morning, Tina said, 'I'm glad you found your friend.'"

"The stalker?"

"Exactly," she confirmed. "The woman stopped by the zoo last week and asked all kinds of questions. According to Tina, the woman is a 'long-lost friend who wants to surprise me with a baby gift from Tiffany.'"

"What did Tina tell your stalker?"

"Everything she knows about my schedule here," replied Emi.

"What made Tina think it was okay?"

"She saw us walking yesterday."

"Jesus, Em. This is creepy. Give me ten minutes, and I'll leave for the zoo."

"Why don't you go back to the office?"

"Because I might smash a chair over Shannon's face."

"Smitty, it's me," said Cusack. "I've got a big problem."

"What now, Jimmy?"

"Bouvier skipped town last night. Took everything that wasn't nailed down."

"Anybody know where he went?"

"Not yet," Cusack advised his lawyer.

"That's trouble," Smitty stated. "Remember Litton Loan Servicing?"

"Of course," replied Cusack. "Get to the point."

"You don't have forty-five days. Your condo is gone, pal."

"What are you saying, Smitty? We're talking about my lease at the Empire State Building. The condo payment is not due until February."

"I doubt you own it another month, especially if you don't find Bouvier."

"Why?"

"Remember the terms of your mortgage note?" asked Smitty.

"Of course not," barked Cusack.

"Start with the Empire State Building. You personally guaranteed the lease payments. I bet Bouvier is two payments behind. You are technically in default on the lease."

"I have a million-dollar problem. I know that."

"No. You have a four-million-dollar problem, Jimmy. You signed a cross-default clause on your condo. Because you defaulted on the lease, you triggered a default with Cy."

"Why'd I agree to that clause?" asked Cusack testily.

"For one, you had no choice. For another, Cy insisted on an early warning device. You make one annual payment every February. He wanted a heads-up in case there's a problem. Now there's a problem."

"But Cy has to go through all the foreclosure proceedings," argued Cusack, "same as Litton."

"I doubt it, Jimmy. He's not a bank. My guess is he takes the keys to your house."

"He'll own it?" Cusack suddenly felt nauseous.

"You may be able to stall for a while. But not forty-five days. You're negotiating with your employer. When all is said and done, you'll pay rent to Cy Leeser."

Cusack slumped. Loss of face. Loss of money. Loss of cash flow and somebody stalking Emi. Leeser was pulling all the strings at the office. Now he was pulling them at Jimmy's home.

"What are my options, Smitty?"

CHAPTER FORTY-EIGHT

WEDNESDAY, OCTOBER I
BENTWING AT $28.42

"No, Graham. Invest now, and you catch a falling piano."

Down 778 points on Monday, the Dow rebounded 485 points Tuesday to close the quarter. As Cusack and Durkin spoke Wednesday morning, the markets were tanking, giving up yesterday's bounce like a torn trampoline. Same story, different day.

Cusack no longer cared. The office door was wide open. He wanted out of

LeeWell Capital. Wanted out of this freak show now. Never mind Leeser's instructions: "You're the one with cash flow problems. So earn your keep." It was time to go.

"Is something wrong?" asked Durkin.

"Just the market," replied Jimmy, eyeing the sonogram of Yaz. "Can we meet later this month?"

"I'll put my assistant on the phone. Set something up."

"Will do, Graham."

Cusack hung up thirty seconds later. Leeser could kiss his ass. So could Shannon, the stalker, and everybody else out there. Fingers laced behind his head, the POW pose from World War II, Cusack gazed outside his office door. Nikki was returning to her workstation, purse in hand.

He eyed her handbag for the longest time. It was leather, nothing flashy. Nikki bought it from Saks, at least four figures. Or she paid a street vendor ten dollars for all he knew. When she sat and disappeared behind the bank of lateral files, Cusack knew exactly what was necessary. Time to take a page from Leeser's playbook, the one that said: "We fucking own Greenwich."

"Hey, Nikki," Cusack hollered ten minutes later. "Spread the word. Lunch is on me."

"What's the occasion?"

"The world is losing money. Hedge funds are collapsing left and right. But I booked a major appointment this morning and want to celebrate." Cusack doubted he had ever been more charming.

"Planet Pizza?" she asked, referring to a spot just around the corner from Two Greenwich.

"No way. I already ordered from Glenville Pizza. Two meatballs. Two pepperonis, extra cheese. One salad. Two veggies. One everything, hold the sardines. And enough sodas to wash all the salt and grease back to Manhattan. But I have a problem."

"There's always a catch." Nikki raised her right eyebrow. She looked wary, but playful and hip in her ruby-colored nose stud.

"My conference call starts at noon. Can you get the pies?"

"May I take your car?" she asked.

"Absolutely not. There's a trick to cranking the engine, and I don't want you stuck in Glenville with our lunch. Besides, this is a celebration. Get Shannon and take Cy's Bentley."

"What if he says no?"

"Are you kidding? You're the one person on earth who can make Shannon smile. It's all about you," Cusack said. "Your mission is to save the global capital markets: one car, two people, and eight pies at a time."

"I'll get Shannon. You need a nap. Or something."

"Just bring me back a Mountain Dew and tons of caffeine."

"You sure it's necessary?" Nikki shook her head, bemused and smiling wide.

"I paid for everything, all the drinks, everything, including a tip. Disavow any knowledge of your wallet."

"Is there anything else, Jimmy?"

Forget your purse.

Five hours ahead in Reykjavik, Siggi closed early and met Ólafur at the bar. "They what?" exclaimed the mild-mannered gallery owner.

"You heard," Ólafur replied listlessly. He downed a shot of tequila, his sympathy drink of choice. "Hafnarbanki fired me." The banker flagged the bartender and said, "Another."

"After all you've done."

"It doesn't make any difference. Hafnarbanki won't last another week. Yesterday, Guðjohnsen spent the day with investigators behind closed doors."

Siggi lowered his voice and scanned the bar. No one was listening. "Who turned them onto you?"

"Cy Leeser."

"What about his troubles with Bentwing?"

"What about them? I made money on the short but lost my ass on Hafnarbanki." Ólafur downed the second shot.

"You sent a message to Greenwich."

"I sent a hiccup in a hurricane. And now I have no job."

Siggi appraised his cousin, bent, drunk, shattered, slumped, his skin going sallow from too much sauce or not enough sun or whatever stress picked at him. Ólafur looked like a beat dog, whimpering with a broken tail between his legs. The sight stirred something in the meek art dealer, opened the faucet on more adrenaline than he had ever known throughout his entire mild-mannered life on a mild-mannered island away from the gore-or-get-gored world of trading desks.

"Fuck you, Ólafur."

The unemployed banker looked up with the sour grimace of a man kicked in the testicles. "Excuse me?"

"You're Mr. Ice. You're the one who says, 'The only victory that matters is the last one.'"

"What do you want from me, Siggi? I'm probably going to jail."

"I can't change whatever you did, cousin. I can't get your money back or keep you out of prison. And one thing's for sure. I can't sit around and watch you snivel your way through shot after shot of tequila. You're coming to work for me. And you start right now. Right fucking now," he bellowed, "by acting like a man."

Ólafur almost scoffed from force of habit. Siggi was a man of taste. He never exuded power or authority. But his cousin had been cool as ice during the Raphael scam. "What are you talking about?"

"I need your help."

"What kind of help?"

"I'll get the bill, and then we're buying you a ticket," Siggi replied.

"Where to?"

"JFK," the gallery owner answered. "We're going to New York."

"What for?"

"To meet my client," Siggi said, inspecting his cousin's face, more mottled than ever. "You won't believe what she does for a living."

"What's our job?"

"To rip out Cy Leeser's Achilles' heel."

Ólafur studied his cousin with shock and awe and plenty of newfound admiration.

At 11:59 A.M. Cusack donned his headset, which was more persuasive than talking into a receiver. He punched buttons and paced the floor. He mustered all his strength for a sales call unlike any in his career. It started with one question:

"Buddy, who's on the phone with us from New Jersey Sheet Metal?"

Over the next fifteen minutes Cusack nodded and gesticulated. He patrolled his modest office, throwing his hands up in exasperation or pumping his fists in triumph. He stormed. He danced. He uttered every line he could remember, cliché or god patois that made no sense:

"I'm talking an Elliott Wave Five. This is opportunity knocking."

"You liked the market at twelve thousand. It's a steal at ten thousand eight hundred."

"When Greenwich needs portable alpha, the hedge funds see us."

Cusack bobbed and weaved, pausing every so often to listen and catch his breath. To take a timeout. There was no one on the other line. And it was difficult to pretend nonstop as he waited for Nikki to leave, watching her every move like a three-eyed hawk.

Shannon appeared at 12:15 P.M. on the nose. Nikki slipped on her jacket. Cusack pumped his right fist for good measure, and she finger-waved in return. The big man scowled, as Jimmy gave them both two thumbs up.

No purse. Nikki was not packing.

Thirty seconds of eternity ticked by. Jimmy waited, still talking, still selling, still staking out his claim to an Oscar. That was when his worst fears materialized. Nikki came back.

She reached under her desk, grabbed her pocketbook, and fished out her wallet. With both palms up and a perplexed face, Nikki signaled, "How's it going?"

With both palms down and a gleam in his eye, Cusack rocked left, then right, and signaled back, "The weight of the free world hangs in the balance."

Twenty minutes max until they return.

Cusack waited five to be safe. He strolled casually over to Nikki's cubicle, checked to make sure no one was watching, and shoved his right hand into her purse—something he would never do with Emi's handbag. He dug out her keys, put them in his pocket, and returned Nikki's purse to the same spot. That's when Cusack heard the speed-bag voice. "Hey, Jimmy."

"What's up?" asked Cusack, wheeling around, struggling not to redden.

"I heard you on the phone," Leeser said. "That's exactly the chutzpah we need. Who was it?"

"New Jersey Sheet Metal."

"Did you make any progress?"

"We're picking up again after lunch." Cusack clenched his fist as a show of determination.

"Nice work. And I'm thrilled you're buying lunch."

"I was afraid," Jimmy admitted, "you'd be angry. I know lunches aren't your thing."

"Should have done it myself."

Thirteen minutes.

Cusack walked toward reception. He waited forever at the elevator bank. Waited. Waited. Waited. The elevator arrived. Stopped at every floor. Somebody said, "Local." Nobody laughed.

The doors opened. Cusack marched through the building's lobby, checked left and right in the parking lot for Cy's Bentley, and headed for Greenwich Avenue.

Eleven minutes.

Jimmy peeked over his shoulder one last time and sprinted for Greenwich Hardware. Halfway up the street he ducked around a nanny pushing a stroller with an older woman in tow, probably the mother.

A few seconds later, he was standing in line, waiting for a beefy carpenter to order a pound bag of nails. Lumberjack shirt. Fifty pounds on the wrong side of fat. "Do you have any twelve-D nails that come with a three head?"

"They only come with a three-and-a-quarter head," the clerk replied. Gray hair. Balding. Big smile and earnest.

"Nah, man. I need a three head."

Seven minutes.

"Ten-Ds come with a three head. You need a three head, I got ten-Ds in three weights."

"I need the twelve-D length."

"Then you get a three-and-a-quarter head."

Lumberjack Shirt scowled, and Cusack said, "Guys, I'm in an awful hurry to get a key made."

Clerk and carpenter turned, both men annoyed. Lumberjack Shirt asked, "Think I care?"

"Twenty dollars say you do." Cusack held up a crisp Jackson.

"You're right about that." Lumberjack Shirt snatched the bill and told the clerk, "Help my new friend, Gordie."

"Hey, I could use one of those, too," Gordie the clerk protested.

"Cut my key, and I'll fix you up," Cusack promised. He reached into his pocket and found not one file key on Nikki's ring, but three. "Check that. I need three."

"This will take time."

"Time turns your Jackson into a Lincoln," advised Jimmy.

"I'll get her done."

Grinding. Cutting. Seconds, seconds, seconds. Cusack sprinted out the door with three fresh keys and fifty dollars less, no change.

Three minutes, thirty seconds.

Cusack had never been the fastest guy on Columbia's football team. Nor the slowest. He sprinted down the Avenue, racing toward Two Greenwich before Nikki and Shannon returned. His heart beat like a stopwatch.

One minute, thirty seconds.

He walked into the lobby, panting and sweating. Pouring from his brow. He checked the room again, controlling his lungs en route to the elevator. Dodging the gods with take-out lunches.

Fifteen seconds.

Nikki and Shannon entered the building. The two were talking and laughing, Shannon carrying the boxes of pizzas, each one stacked on top of another. They steered toward the elevator.

Cusack noticed Shannon's eyes. He saw the big man's gap-toothed smile disappear behind a tight-lipped grimace. He saw his own blurred reflection in the smoky chrome of the elevator doors. He was inside. They were outside, waiting for the next car.

The doors opened, and Cusack burst into the lobby. He pushed into Lee-Well Capital's reception area, and from under her headset, Amanda called, "Hey, thanks for buying lunch."

"My pleasure."

At Nikki's workstation he dropped a pen, accidentally on purpose, and pulled her purse off the desk as he bent down. Key ring out. Ring inside purse. Bag on desk. Cusack stood up, his lungs still burning from the run, and prepared to turn around. That's when he heard a familiar voice.

"Hey, Jimmy."

Cusack jerked around to find Victor Lee.

"Thanks for buying lunch," said the head trader.

"Don't mention it."

"Did you get something light?"

"One salad. Two veggies."

"You're the best," Victor said. And pointing to the desk, he added, "Nikki shouldn't leave her purse out like that."

"You got that right," Cusack agreed.

"It looks like a Birkin knockoff."

"Okay, Victor."

In that moment Nikki joined them, Shannon trailing her with the pizzas. "Follow me, boys." She led all three men into the conference room, where other employees were already waiting.

"We have Jimmy to thank for this meal," Cy Leeser announced. After the clapping stopped, he said, "Just don't eat so much you fall asleep this afternoon. We have work to do."

Amanda raised her hand, daring to ask the forbidden question from the last pizza party. "Does this mean we can turn up the heat, boss?"

No one said a word. Leeser squinted at one face after another, leveling on every pair of eyes in the room. It wasn't until he broke into a broad grin that everybody laughed. The markets down, down, down—it was the release LeeWell Capital needed.

There was only one person who didn't laugh: Shannon. Cusack bit into one of the greasier slices of pepperoni extra cheese, and the big man said, "You forgot something."

"Greek olives?"

Shannon held up Cusack's pen. "I found it at Nikki's desk."

"Thanks," Jimmy replied, sounding happy.

The big man said nothing. Mack face. Cold eyes. No smile. Shannon's callous expression reminded Cusack what he already knew. Digging Cy's computer out of Nikki's files would not be easy. The head of security was there every step of the way.

CHAPTER FORTY-NINE

A flicker of light, the distant bang of a backfire, and even the passage of time all contribute to the basic problem of breaking and entering. Every change, no matter what or how minute, drills the senses like a do-it-yourself root canal. It is impossible to escape the anticipation of getting caught, especially when you have no practice rummaging through locked files and fishing out a video with your sad-sack puss mushed against four naked lap dancers from the Foxy Lady.

Cusack shifted uncomfortably on his Aeron chair. He pretended to answer e-mails. He pretended like he gave a damn the market lost nineteen points today. He had been pretending for the last hour. The waiting, the vigilance, and the erring on the side of caution were all wearing thin. He was sick of pretending.

LeeWell Capital was far from silent, even at 8:20 P.M. on a Wednesday night. There were fifteen flat-screen televisions, each one ranging from forty to fifty-two inches, all tuned to the talking heads. CNBC and Fox Business were still dissecting the day's trades, still warring over airwaves to win the hearts and minds of investors everywhere. And no one, no one, was there to listen.

No one except Cusack.

Nikki had been the last person to leave. That was forty minutes ago. Cusack stood and began walking through LeeWell. He peeked inside every office. He inspected the kitchen and found the screaming eagle atop the cappuccino maker right where it belonged. He checked the pool room. He even inspected the sauna to ensure the coast was clear.

Cusack eyed Nikki's filing cabinets, each with three drawers. He pulled out the three keys from Greenwich Hardware and unlocked the first file. Pushing the meticulous folders left and right and checking over his shoulder all the while, he probed for the Mac laptop with the Foxy Lady video. No luck.

He rifled the second file, showering each drawer with alpha waves as though the power of positive thinking would lead him to the Holy Grail. Nikki kept a few extra pairs of shoes and an unopened pair of stockings in one drawer, the only clutter among the otherwise pristine organization. But no computer, nothing.

The Mac was not in the third filing cabinet, either. Cusack cursed his luck and stared blankly at the green hanging files, one after another. Each one packed with fat sheaves of paper. Soon, Nikki would need another lateral file just to hold all the papers. Cusack closed the drawer and stared at the keys.

What a waste.

His sprint to the hardware store was a bust. So were the pizzas. The Foxy Lady video was still out there, still likely to surface at the most inopportune time. That's when an image triggered in his brain. Something inside the last file. Something he saw.

Cusack opened the last drawer and inspected the contents. There were a total of eight sections, approximately six inches each. Every section contained records for one person. And there it was. There was the connection that sparked a second look.

"Barnes, Conrad" was the first file tab.

Cy Leeser was helping a widow with her husband's estate. But last week, he had dismissed the importance of the business relationship. "Barnes and I had business dealings from time to time."

Six inches of carefully labeled paperwork felt like more than "business dealings from time to time." For the moment, Cusack forgot all about a Mac laptop and the ambient sounds from the after hours. His curiosity took over.

Jimmy scanned seven other names in the drawer. Conrad Barnes was the only one he recognized. All eight names contained the same three tabs: UNDERWRITING; PURCHASE AND SALE; and CERTIFICATES. Nikki had arranged her files with perfectionist care, labels typed, consistent divisions for each person.

"Underwriting" conjured up investment banking transactions. So did

"Purchase and Sale." Cusack peered at the drawer for what seemed a month of Sundays. And then he understood.

Or at least he had a hunch. He was staring at the secret sauce. He was staring at answers that had eluded him ever since day one at LeeWell Capital, ever since he gagged on the 30 percent concentration in Bentwing Energy. Cy's fanatic secrecy, his indifference to Qatari shorts and his strange preoccupation with Caleb Phelps—it was all there in front of him. Why some creep was stalking his wife. Why Leeser was holding him hostage with video clips, not to mention an overleveraged condo in the Meatpacking District. Why Shannon was a dick. Maybe Victor, too. Why Leeser had lied about *Night of the Living Dead Heads*. And why some cloak-and-dagger Samaritan named "Daryle Lamonica" was warning him to get the hell out of Dodge and "beware the Greek."

Cy Leeser, Jimmy decided, hedged risk through private deals. He solved the age-old problem of stock tickers, which reported bad decisions with the cold consistency of Chinese drip torture that repeats, "Stupid, stupid, stupid," every second, every trade. Private deals were less transparent and took more time to value. At last there were answers, all wrapped up in tidy files courtesy of Nikki.

Cusack found a pad in Nikki's middle desk drawer. He scribbled down seven names—he knew Conrad Barnes by heart—and made a mental note to Google them later. His watch read 9:10 P.M.

Jimmy reached for Conrad's Underwriting file. But he heard a muffled noise. Or was it his imagination, fear wrapping his senses like an octopus handshake?

Cusack yanked six inches of paperwork from the middle of the drawer and closed it. He never checked the name. Anyone would do, anyone other than Conrad Barnes. Leeser might dig through the records any day to help the widow.

First one key. Then another. The last one. Jimmy locked all three lateral files. The rustling grew louder. The noise was real.

Cusack grabbed his list of seven names. He double-checked Nikki's desk one more time. No way he'd repeat his earlier mistake with the pen. He scooted across the hall into his office and dropped the six inches of paper underneath the desk. He grabbed his briefcase and turned to his door.

Cleaning crew?

Not a chance. Jimmy Cusack glanced up to find his worst nightmare.

Shannon. The big man closed fast, his eyes blazing, his perma-scowl angry and contentious. Cusack braced for the long-simmering confrontation.

"We gotta talk, Kemosabe."

"What is it now?"

"Have you been watching CNBC? I about strangled on my heart to-day."

"You can't watch the market. It'll drive you nuts."

"But, Kemosabe," Rachel persisted, "this reminds me of when Daddy told me Santa got killed in the war."

"I have no idea what you mean."

Shannon thundered across the floor. He screeched to a stop, blocking Cusack's exit from the office. The big man's bald head, brighter than the chrome bumper of any eighteen-wheeler, gleamed under fluorescent lights that showered fatigue from the long day. "What the fuck are you doing here?"

"Going home." Cusack smiled crookedly. He yawned, struggling to stay calm, and stepped around Shannon.

The big man shifted and blocked Cusack's path. Old-school intimidation.

"Is there a problem here?" Jimmy demanded.

"Security is twenty-four/seven," Shannon announced, cocky and self-important with drill-sergeant swagger, like he was smelling his own musk.

"So is prospecting. But for the record, I feel safer knowing you have an eye on things."

"You got a smart mouth, rich boy." Shannon stepped closer, violating Cusack's body space, inviting him to push his way through. Any closer, and it was a rugby scrum.

"Why don't you join me for a beer and a crash course in personality?" Cusack taunted, smiling crookedly, not flinching, not backing off.

Shannon did not advance. Or give any ground. "What were you doing at Nikki's desk today?"

"Buying pizza for the office. You got a problem with that?"

"What were you doing at Nikki's desk tonight?"

"Walking past it. You got a problem with that?"

"Let me clue—"

"No, Shannon. Shut up and follow me." Cusack turned and stormed back to his office. He dumped the entire contents of his briefcase, satchel construction, onto his desk. From the corner of his eye, Cusack saw that the six-inch file had slid into view underneath his desk chair.

"Knock yourself out," boomed Cusack, pulling his bottom desk drawer wide open for effect, "so I can do my job." The file drawer obscured Shannon's view of the paperwork and the all-caps label that read HENRIETTA HEDGECOCK. Cusack swept his arm, big-time flourish inviting the head of security to poke around.

"You finished?"

"No. I'm just getting started. And I wish you'd leave my family and me the fuck alone. I don't care about Cy's trade secrets."

Shannon blinked. His scowl faded, and his face turned sly. He picked up the list of seven names Cusack had scribbled. "Who are these people?"

"Prospects," Cusack snapped.

"You always take notes on Nikki's stationery?"

Shannon smiled wide, not friendly, but a gap-toothed semi-gloat. He held out the letterhead like a banner. It read, *From Nikki's desk.*

"You know Nikki. She's always there with a piece of paper when I have a moment of brilliance."

"Not much action there, Cusack."

"Nice shot. Why don't you inspect my office and make sure all your bugs are working, so I can go home."

"Pack your bag, rich boy."

Cusack loaded the sprawl from his desk back into his briefcase. He left his file drawer open. "You need anything else before I go?"

"Just doing my job," returned Shannon.

"Whatever."

"By the way," Shannon added, "you might consider what to tell the boss."

"That I'm staying late and busting my ass to bring in dollars."

"I hope he buys it," Shannon said, doubting, shaking his head from left to right. "He knows you've been looking through office files."

"What do you mean?"

"See that dome?"

Cusack eyed a reddish dome on the ceiling. He'd thought the fixture was a smoke detector. With a sinking feeling in the pit of his stomach, he suddenly grasped the big man's meaning.

"Say cheese, Cusack. That's our eye in the sky. Cy has a new video for his collection."

"An empty office makes for riveting footage," Jimmy bluffed.

"Hah." Shannon sneered. "First porn, now Cy has you stealing trade secrets."

CHAPTER FIFTY
THURSDAY, OCTOBER 2
BENTWING AT $26.80

Siggi leaned over and clinked glasses with Ólafur. They were sitting on Icelandair 613, destination JFK Airport. The two men drank Diet Coke as they waited to take off for New York City.

The gallery owner had long dreamed of a big score, a sure thing. Now it was within reach. And it would make him richer than he ever thought possible, though not so rich as Ólafur once thought. Those long bleak days from childhood, Siggi and Ólafur mending torn fishing nets for their fathers, were fading from memory.

Siggi drifted back to the Nordic chic bar inside Hverfisgata's 101 Hotel, the place that made this windfall possible, the place where Icelandair 613 really originated. He wondered what Cy Leeser and his friends were thinking the night they all met in Reykjavik. But the moment passed.

"You packed everything, Ólafur?"

"Yes."

"Black tennis shoes, black workout clothes, and dark sunglasses. Your suits won't do any good where we're going."

"Everything's in my carry-on bag," Ólafur confirmed.

"Get some sleep on the plane. I've arranged for the truck to meet us at the airport."

"Are you sure I can't return to Iceland with you?" The banker looked at Siggi hopefully, as though asking for permission.

"With your legal problems? I think it's best for you to wait until things cool off."

"Okay," Ólafur agreed, his bluster long gone.

"Good. Not another peep, cousin, until we reach Greenwich."

Eight A.M. Cusack's eyes burned bright red from tossing and turning all night. His sandy hair resembled a plate of spaghetti. News stories scrolled across his thirty-inch LCD screen, promising another grim day for investors. And here he was, ready to walk the plank.

Leeser would arrive soon. He would check his e-mails or voice mails and find the inevitable report from Shannon. That's all it would take, Cusack imagined, for war to erupt inside LeeWell Capital.

Cy: "Get the fuck out of here."

Cy: "You owe me three million bucks."

Cy: "Breaking news on Caleb Phelps. Porn star son-in-law accused of stealing trade secrets. Film at eleven."

Cusack could not return the stack of paperwork under his desk. Not with Nikki sitting at her workstation. And what difference did it make? Leeser possessed a second video—the head of sales snooping through filing cabinets and stealing trade secrets.

Nikki was so organized, so methodical. Cusack assumed Henrietta Hedgecock's paperwork was a template, more or less, for the files of all eight people and the secret sauce. It was also evidence, all the excuse Cy needed to fire his ass. Maybe even sue.

Jimmy checked his office door. Nobody was looking, not yet anyway, not that he cared. It was the principle. Curiosity about the secret had consumed Cusack since April. And even though his short stint at LeeWell Capital was screeching to an end—any minute now—there were answers at his fingertips. Cusack needed to know.

He pulled out the folder marked CERTIFICATES. The paperwork contained the usual collection of sedatives made from tree pulp: notarized signatures, instructions for where to deliver documents, and a note from some company named Wealth Solutions LLC based near Times Square.

Underneath the note, Cusack found a death certificate for Henrietta Hedgecock. Again, the details were cold and clinical.

Manner of Death: Accidental drowning.

Surviving Spouse: None.

Medical Examiner/Coroner: Peter von Maur had signed the death certificate.

Cusack grabbed the Purchase and Sale file and found more mind-
numbing documents—purchase price, schedule of payments from LeeWell
Capital, and wire instructions. He leafed through the stack of papers, his
eyes darting to the door every so often. He hoped to answer one question:

What are we buying?

When Cusack picked up the Underwriting folder, he found his answer.
It was not what he expected. Nor did it make any sense. Jimmy dialed the
one person he never expected to ask for help.

"Phelps here."

There was a time when Jimmy Cusack hated his father-in-law's voice.
After the December ambush, Jimmy carped to Emi, "Your father sounds
like a flat EKG."

Not now. Not since the night at MoMA. Not since Emi Cusack bro-
kered a peace with her mother's support. Those two words, "Phelps here,"
boomed sweeter than Roy Orbison.

"I need your help."

"What's wrong, James? You sound like hell."

"Up late." Cusack glanced at Henrietta Hedgecock's file. "What do you
know about life settlements?"

"It's an evolving industry."

"What do you mean?" Cusack checked the door.

"'Life settlements' are when owners sell life insurance policies—ones
already in place—to third parties. Usually to people they don't know. The
practice gained notoriety in the 1980s with AIDS patients, who needed
cash to pay the high cost of medical care."

"Viaticals."

"Right," Caleb acknowledged. "Treatment for AIDS has improved, and
the terminally ill aren't much of a market these days. But the practice of selling life insurance policies—from owners to people they don't know—
caught on. And life settlements are flourishing."

"Who sells the policies?"

"Anybody who needs cash."

"But insurance policies have cash values," continued Cusack. "Why not withdraw the money and keep the life insurance?"

"When people reach their seventies," Caleb explained, "it's possible to sell existing policies for more than their cash value."

"Got it."

"Sometimes families buy more insurance than they need," Phelps continued. "Rather than allowing policies to expire worthless, brokers arrange sales on behalf of their clients. Larry King sold two or three policies with death benefits totaling fifteen million."

"Why would he sell them?"

"Nobody turns down free money, James. Not even Larry King."

"Who buys life settlements?" asked Cusack.

"Hedge funds. Warren Buffett. Anybody who wants a return."

"Are you in that business?"

"We originate more life insurance in New England," Caleb replied, "than our three biggest competitors combined. But I won't sell insurance on my life to people I don't know. And I won't do it for clients."

"Question," said Cusack, checking the door again for Leeser, "do hedge funds invest in life settlements to protect their downside?"

"It's insurance, not alchemy. You can lose money."

"How?" objected Cusack. "Everybody dies, right?"

"If somebody lives too long, you might pay more for the policy than what you get in death benefits. First, there's the down payment for the policy. Then, there are the annual premiums that can go on and on."

"Oh, of course." Cusack flipped through the Certificates folder. "And the average life expectancy is what, eighty-six?"

"Depends. Rich people live longer."

Hedgecock was seventy-six when she died.

"Why all the interest, James?"

"Call it research for now," answered Cusack. "I need to ask one last question that might be a little insensitive."

"Okay."

"Have you ever thought about selling your company?"

"I just bought one," Caleb said.

"But would you sell your business?"

"Everything I have is for sale. Except my family. Now I'm really curious." It was Caleb's turn to press.

"I'll call you back."

Cy Leeser was standing in Cusack's office door.

Victor Lee looked at his terminals. The market was already down 200 points, down with no bottom in sight. Just down, down, down. All three screens bled red tickers.

"Dammit, Cy. I told you to sell," Victor mumbled to himself. His three junior traders stared at their LCDs.

Lee looked at the Premarin underneath the terminals and wondered whether the estrogen had been such a good idea. True, he read the markets right. True, he cut trading expenses down to nothing. Maybe women were better traders over the long term. But he hadn't thought about a woman in weeks.

"Where's my hammer?"

Victor glared at his LCDs, then at his junior traders. "All right, boys. I need a show of hands. The Dow's over ten thousand. Who thinks it hits nine thousand before eleven?"

All three boys raised their hands.

Leeser coiled on the guest chair inside Cusack's office, waiting, watching, and biding his time. Every so often he clenched his teeth, and the ripping blue veins of his neck bulged like garden hoses. His words came out soft and slithery, every *S* hissing longer than necessary. He was hard to hear but there was no mistaking his serpentine venom.

"You were checking Nikki's files for prospects?"

"Wait here," bellowed Cusack with no hesitation. He erupted from his chair and stormed from the room like a bad mood. His sudden exit surprised Leeser, left him slack jawed and wide eyed.

Cusack returned a few seconds later. He said nothing but placed the photo of Cy's daughters on his desk, taking great care to ensure the twins were facing their father.

"Oh, I get it," sniped Cy. "You think LeeWell Capital is a commune. Nikki's files and my desk—what else are we sharing, class?"

"This way *even you* can understand," Cusack jabbed back. Pointing at the photo, he growled, "What would you do if somebody threatened your girls?"

"What's this got to do—"

"Answer the question," Cusack barked. "What would you do?"

"Kill 'em," Leeser replied, no hesitation, no emotion, no pulse, no volume. "You'll understand when you're a dad."

"Anything to protect them, right?"

"Right."

"Because they're family," bellowed Cusack.

"Right."

"So why are you hosing mine?"

"What are you talking about, Jimmy?"

"Your video from the Foxy Lady."

Leeser's face softened. The veins of his neck relaxed, and his eyes grew sly. "That's why you're snooping through Nikki's files?"

"I don't care about your insurance policies. I want the video."

Leeser tilted on the back two legs of the guest chair. His brow wrinkled for a moment, his forehead bunching in deep furrows of concentration. "It's time," he said, his demeanor turning pensive, "you know. You need to know."

"Know what?"

"We invest in life settlements."

"I don't care."

"Would you take just a moment and work exceptionally hard to shut the fuck up?" asked Leeser, barely raising his voice. "Or did you skip that class at Wharton?"

Cusack shut up.

"How much do you know about life settlements, Jimmy?"

"Enough."

"Life insurance is a noncorrelated asset class," Leeser stated, resorting to the inscrutaspeak of Hedgistan. "People die no matter what the markets do."

"I don't care."

"Hear me out."

"Fire me. Whatever you need. But spare me the lecture, and give me the video."

"Maybe you're the one who needs help understanding." Leeser spoke softer and slower. But he delivered every word with more poison than the last. "You smile and nod your head. You suck up and listen to what I say. Because that cross default clause in your mortgage puts you on the street today—if I give the word. We clear?"

"I don't care." Cusack took the gut punch, struggling to sound defiant, surprised Cy already knew about his lease problems.

Leeser poised for a split second before striking. His words were faint, hardly a whisper, but more sinister than a serpent's tongue. "Nothing like malfeasance to fuck up medical insurance. Your wife hasn't had any complications, has she?"

Jimmy could not breathe, the air gone, bitch-slapped from the bottom of his lungs. After a long and withering silence, he reached for his bag and started to pack. He grabbed chargers from one drawer, pens and loose items from another. It was the only way to busy his hands, the only way to stay in control.

How about I rip your nose out your ass?

Leeser watched Cusack tuck Yaz's sonogram inside his jacket. He studied his employee impassively, almost clinically. And as he considered Cusack's impending departure, he grasped the enormity of his mistake. Cursed himself for things spiraling out of control.

When Cy finally spoke, he raised his voice, though not in anger. With enough outward contrition to moisten every eye in the Vatican—and no internal remorse whatsoever—he said, "I'm sorry, Jimmy. It was a crappy thing to say. Cool off and listen. I'll give you the video."

Cusack stopped packing.

"I offset risky investments with life settlements," explained Leeser.

"Whatever," said Cusack, his head still spinning. He was unsure whether the video mattered.

"Give me five minutes," said Leeser, retreating and less hostile. "I buy insurance policies tiered across different ages. Sixty-eight. Sixty-nine. Seventy. See what I mean?"

"You ladder ages. Someone is always dying, and LeeWell gets paid on a regular basis. I get it." Cusack feigned indifference but his thoughts had returned to the video.

"Right," Leeser confirmed. "We can't lose."

Not according to Caleb.

"LeeWell Capital owns the policy on Conrad Barnes?" asked Cusack.

"Right."

"Life settlements aren't really a hedge, Cy."

"Twenty million buys time on our margin loan with Merrill. Sounds like a hedge to me."

"I'm tired of dancing around the issue," replied Cusack, immersed in the conversation again, finally understanding the preoccupation with his father-in-law. "You want to buy Caleb's company?"

Leeser measured his words carefully. "I should have been more direct. Your father-in-law has a great business."

"His business. Not mine. I'm not involved."

"Once he's elected governor of Massachusetts, he can't run his agency."

"He has competent people."

"It's not the same, Jimmy. His operation will atrophy unless he's at the helm."

"If you want to buy Caleb's business, pick up the phone and call him."

"I planned to fire you for stealing trade secrets," Leeser said. "I was wrong. And I'm sorry."

"Just give me the video."

"I already said you can have it. But I need a partner. Not an adversary."

"I don't understand."

"We can put this deal together. You and me. Take tomorrow off, Jimmy. Think about how we buy your father-in-law's agency. Come back Monday, and we'll talk."

"But what about the video?"

"The Mac's at my house."

"Can we get it today?" asked Cusack hopefully.

"No. I checked into the Delamar Hotel."

"Why?"

"I can't have Bianca throwing my clothes out the window every time she gets a feather up her ass. Half of Greenwich thinks my estate is a drop zone for the Salvation Army."

"I'm sorry, Cy."

"Look, I'll get you the video by Monday."

"That's great news."

"You help me," Leeser prodded, "and I'll help you. I'm a generous guy."

Cusack said nothing.

"Returning that video is a show of good faith." Leeser's demeanor turned warm and conspiratorial. "Now it's your turn to help me buy Caleb's company. And think about all the perks."

"What perks?"

"You can fire your father-in-law for pulling the plug on Cusack Capital."

"How do you know about that?"

"I don't lose. And that means knowing everything about everyone." Cy stood up to leave, walked to the door, and turned as though struck by one last thought. "By the way, Jimmy. Do you have something for me?"

Cusack reached under his desk and pulled out the paperwork belonging to Henrietta Hedgecock. "Is this what you mean?"

"Exactly," Leeser confirmed. "See you Monday."

CHAPTER FIFTY-ONE
FRIDAY, OCTOBER 3
BENTWING AT $26.48

Emi inherited Caleb's gift for feisty New England clarity. She operated at her level best when confusion ran amok. While others deliberated and scratched their heads to sort things out, she swung her opinions like gnarled two-by-fours. "Cy Leeser's not reliable. You can't trust him."

"I need to play along," argued Cusack, more inclined toward diplomacy. "A few days and we get the video."

"Don't get your hopes up. It's fifty-fifty whether that guy even shows for his own funeral." Emi left for work, but the two agreed to continue their discussion over lunch at the Bronx Zoo. She still had no clue about their iffy finances.

Cusack grabbed his laptop and trudged to a greasy spoon on Hudson Street, home to the fastest wireless in Manhattan according to signs in the window. He introduced himself to the $7.99 special, a platter full of greasy steak, rubber-soled eggs, and home fries that made him wonder whose home turned potatoes into felonies. It was like breakfast arrived on a shingle, which did not help the worries gnawing at Cusack's stomach.

"How is everything?" asked the waitress. She splashed coffee while loading Cusack's cup, which was okay because the bursts nailed Cusack's sleeve instead of his computer.

"Special." He read *The Wall Street Journal* and *The New York Times* online. He needed to decompress.

When Cusack reached inside his jacket for money, any attempt at decompression stopped. He found the list of seven names from Nikki's files. Instead of paying the bill, he ordered a doughnut and things got interesting.

Henrietta Hedgecock was the first name Cusack Googled. *The New York Times* had printed her obituary in late April, about the same time Jimmy started at LeeWell Capital. Hedgecock was one of New York City's foremost socialites. An avid swimmer, she drowned in a pool after suffering a seizure. Seventy-six years old at the time of death. Fifteen million dollars, Cusack recalled, in insurance proceeds to LeeWell Capital.

Cusack Googled Conrad Barnes next. He was not hard to find given the spectacular crash in the Meadowlands two months ago. Barnes was a bastion of the Bronxville community, a guy who made it big in pharmaceuticals.

The following five names generated too many Google hits. Cusack found John Emery, Joshua Kendall, Robert Miss, Francis Rotch, and John Ranney. But he could not be sure whether he found the right people.

Harold Van Nest was a different story. He was a fixture in the Harvard community, fêted by half a dozen charities for his philanthropic largesse. He died of natural causes back in December, but *The New York Times* obituary did not elaborate.

Cusack cursed himself for bungling the opportunity to examine Nikki's files. In less than twelve months, Cy Leeser had collected three major death benefits. Jimmy never saw the size of Harold Van Nest's policy, but he assumed the man was wealthy given all the fanfare. If the policy paid $20 million at death, Cusack guessed that Van Nest sold it for at least $2 million. Maybe more.

The estimate reminded Cusack what his father-in-law said: "Nobody turns down free money, James. Not even Larry King."

Jittery from too much coffee, Cusack ordered another cup anyway. His thoughts began to drift. And he found himself blaming Google—the Internet boot camp for ADHD. Before long Cusack forgot the Web and focused instead on Bianca's haunting words from the bar.

Bianca: "Did Cy tell you about the time he bet against oil?"

Cusack: "No."

Bianca: "Lost his ass."

Bianca dubbed her husband the Wile E. Coyote of hedge funds. But collecting $55 million dollars in twelve months—20 from Barnes, 15 from Hedgecock, and 20 from Van Nest—was something else. It made Cy brilliant. Or lucky. Eighty-six was the average life expectancy, which meant the three policies paid about ten years early.

Cusack called the one guy who knew numbers better than anyone else in Hedgistan. The one guy who saw patterns that eluded everyone else. And the one guy he trusted like a deck of fifty-two suicide kings.

Geek pulled off his Coke-bottle glasses and rubbed his eyes. He had worn a hole in his pants over the last three weeks. His knee pumped like a piston. His right leg rubbed against the side of the desk with every downstroke of the Dow. He expected the markets to plummet another hundred points before the day was out. "I called a dozen times. You still pissed?"

"Yeah, fuck you, it's out of my system and I need your help." Cusack gunned his words in one long sentence without breathing.

"How bad are things at your shop?"

"Never mind. What's the market connection between December of last year and April of this year?"

"You," Geek replied without hesitation.

"I'm not kidding."

"Me either. Cusack Capital blew up in December after your banks bombed. And you joined LeeWell in April. The Dow started the month down five percent."

Geek's words hit Cusack like an anvil from thirty feet. "That's it. I can't believe it's so simple."

"What's 'it' Jimmy?"

"Bentwing dropped like a rock at the end of August."

"Can you bring me into your quadrant?" asked Geek.

"December, April, and September—those months all followed bad markets."

"The Dow was up during July and August."

"Bentwing got smoked," replied Cusack.

"Sounds six sigma."

"That's what I say. Too many coincidences," Jimmy agreed. "Do me a favor."

"What's that?"

"Stay away from LeeWell Capital. I'll tell you everything next week."

The red-haired woman—baseball cap, burly sweater, dark sunglasses—drew from her cigarette, long and glorious and altogether satisfying. She filled her lungs, savoring the hot vapor, remembering the cafés of Paris where the fumes billowed in great clouds of secondhand nicotine. It was the perfect day to smoke, a crisp autumn afternoon at its best, even though Rachel Whittier now had a problem.

A hornet's nest in the outhouse, she thought.

Dirt lodged in Rachel's eye. Or maybe her contact lens slipped. Rachel turned away from the baboon reserve and blinked out the chocolate-brown lens. She popped it back in place, fussed with her sunglasses and wig, and told herself to pay attention.

Emi was eating lunch at Somba Village. Most days she would finish and hike back to the World of Reptiles, past a cutoff to the brown bears and the big white polar. It was that junction, home to *Ursus arctos horribilis,* where Rachel Whittier would dry-gulch Mrs. Emily Phelps Cusack, seven months or so pregnant.

Rachel patted her purse and the syringe inside. Doing Cusack was a good thing. Made her feel better. She remembered how good it felt to stand over the lifeless body of her father, her words back then: "I got the rigor-mortis touch, old man."

Emi looked at her watch, not once but a dozen times. She stared at her brown lunch bag. She fidgeted for a while and then, losing focus, disappeared into a silent reverie of gelada watching.

Rachel reached into her handbag and pulled out a pair of light fall gloves, taking care to hide her motion from the pregnant woman. Just once Emi glanced in her direction, a look that chilled the nurse. Rachel never knew when she would be made, disguise or not. But Emi drifted past Rachel, and there were no telltale signs of recognition.

That was when Jimmy joined his wife for lunch. Rachel closed her eyes in exasperation, and shaking her head, she said in a voice so low no one else could hear, "You're lucky, girlfriend." Given the couple's animated discussion, it looked like Cusack would never leave.

The color drained from Emi's face. "Is there anything else?"

"Isn't that enough?"

Emi appraised her husband. He was a stranger. She lowered her voice and said, "I hate secrets."

"Cusack Capital was *my* fuckup."

"We have no life if you hide things from me."

Emi had no idea what to add. Of all Cusack's revelations over the past fifteen minutes, the coincidences at LeeWell were the most unnerving. Three life insurance policies. Three bouts of financial loss. And three untimely deaths.

It was Jimmy who broke the silence. "I want more for our baby than Somerville."

"Your childhood didn't hurt you."

"I want more."

She paused, again, and measured her words. "And I don't want Yaz visiting his father in jail."

Three tables over a red-haired woman glanced up from her book at the word "jail."

"What do you mean, Em?"

"Life settlements. Too many people died too young."

"It may be a coincidence," he said. "The people all died of natural causes according to their obituaries. I have a hunch and nothing more."

"Life settlements sound scummy."

"Warren Buffett invests in them."

"My dad doesn't," Emi replied.

Cusack drank a Coke. The two sat in silence for a while.

"Barnes wasn't drunk," Emi said, breaking the silence, "when I saw him."

"He had plenty of time to tie one on."

"I think we should call the police."

The red-haired woman looked up from her coffee.

"And tell them what, Em? That I'm suspicious. That seventy-year-olds die when the market tanks. That you've been stalked by a woman with a scar on her hand?"

"Her scar is hideous."

The red-haired woman, grimacing, stood up and walked to the Somba coffee counter. She ordered another cup of coffee and returned.

"The police will run from you," Cusack announced, his voice firm but uncomfortable.

"Why?"

"Prosopagnosia. Lawyers will tear you up in court."

"Quit your job, James."

"That's a no-brainer."

"Afterward, we go to the police," she asserted.

"There's no proof those deaths are anything more than a series of unfortunate coincidences."

"I don't care. The whole thing is creepy."

Cusack smiled crookedly, not sure what to say. He finally replied, "I'll resign on Monday. But no cops."

"Why go to the office?"

"To get the video."

"It's not worth the risk, James."

"It's a bigger risk if I don't go."

"What do you mean?"

"Let's say the insurance policies are more than a coincidence. I don't want Leeser coming after us."

"That's why we go to the police," she said.

"No way. They investigate but drop the case due to insufficient evidence. Label us as goofballs. And we wake up one day with Shannon standing over our bed. That scares the shit out of me."

Emi's eyes turned glassy and wide—more grouper than sapphire blue.

"I resign," he continued, "and we act like nothing's wrong."

"What about that woman with the scarred hand?" Emi asked.

"Surveillance. I think she works with Shannon. And I think she goes away when LeeWell Capital goes away."

"But you're resigning. If you're right about the insurance policies, Cy will suspect you immediately."

"Not when I tell him I'm joining your father's business."

"What! You said that would never happen."

"I'm not taking one dollar from your father. But I'll do anything to protect our family until the coast is clear."

"Will Cy buy it?"

"The way I sell—yes." Cusack leaned forward and pretended to address his boss. "'My resignation, Cy, is the next logical step. I join my father-in-law, kick the tires from the inside, and then we buy his operation. You and me, Cy. What's better than an inside job?'" He smiled crookedly to punctuate the sales pitch.

"I don't know, James."

"'Cy, I can't think of anything sweeter than giving Caleb Phelps a pink slip. I'll deliver it myself.'"

"I don't know," Emi repeated.

"In the meantime, don't walk alone. Don't go anywhere by yourself, including the bathroom. And whatever you do, make sure your cell phone is with you at all times. If you see the woman with the scar again, we go to Plan B."

"Which is what?" she asked.

"Call the police. Otherwise, we pretend everything is normal."

"I trust your instincts," Emi consented.

"What can happen?"

The red-haired woman sipped her coffee.

"Remember when you said, 'Not my problem'?"

"I also remember asking you to stop calling me."

"Now we have a problem."

"You sound like my wife," observed Leeser, suspecting it was another money call from his partner. "What is it now?"

"Cusack suspects you."

"That's crazy," argued Leeser. "The kid wants to buy his father-in-law's company with me."

"He's resigning on Monday, you idiot."

"You sure about that?" Cy sounded skeptical.

"The Cusacks spent the last forty-five minutes discussing life insurance at LeeWell Capital."

"What do they know?" asked Leeser, growing alarmed.

"Enough to be suspicious. Enough to question our life insurance policies."

"Oh, shit. That's a problem," he agreed.

"But one we can handle."

"And how's that?"

"After I finish with Emi, we take Jimmy Cusack for a ride in your helicopter."

"A ride, where?" asked Leeser.

"As far over the ocean as you can fly. To a place where he gets an anchor for a parachute and nobody notices."

"No way. That's your job," protested Leeser. "That's what I think."

"And I think you're a few bricks short of a load. The Cusacks can tie you to those insurance policies."

"But you're the one that handles these situations. Why me?"

"One: You can fly. I can't. And we don't have time for something more creative. Two: I've been thinking about our arrangement. There's no insurance on either of the Cusacks, and I'm not working for free. And three: The police will link Cusack to his wife's death when he disappears."

"Why's that?"

"It's always the spouse."

"Great." Cy found the logic unsettling.

"You sound thrilled."

"I'm not." Leeser balled his right hand into a fist. And rubbing it with his left hand, he added, "But it is what it is."

"You worry too much. We've got the element of surprise."

"You sure they didn't recognize you?"

"Jimmy Cusack," explained the limited partner, "never saw me before."

"What about his wife?"

"Have you ever heard of prosopagnosia, Kemosabe?"

"No. What's that?"

"Emi Cusack won't know what's happening at the polar bear pen," explained Rachel, rubbing her hand, "until it's too late."

CHAPTER FIFTY-TWO

As twilight shadows dappled the grounds outside, Bianca shuffled through the great room of her Greenwich home. Restless and alone, she stewed underneath a vaulted ceiling with eight-by-eight beams. The surrounding walls once played host to cubists, modernists, and other "ists" that shared no common denominator other than the heft of their price tags. But that was last week.

The explosions of color were gone. So were the ephemeral whims of Cyrus Leeser and his well-hung checkbook. All that remained were a few picture hooks, scattered here and there. They held nothing other than the ghosts of her husband's social aspirations, like the five-child corporation that never happened.

Cy was gone, out of her life, out of their 19,000 square feet of Greenwich hell. The last sixteen years were a bust, everything except for the twins. Bianca had tried. For chrissakes, she had tried. "You gotta know when," she told herself. "You gotta know when."

A glass of mineral water perspired on the table to Bianca's left, beads of condensation rolling like snowballs to the coaster underneath. A MacBook Pro rested on her lap. She reminded herself there was work to do.

Bianca studied a small square centered horizontally on the upper edge of her laptop. With equal parts amusement and apprehension, she appraised the deep circle inside the square. Her eyes glimmered. Her full-tilt lips twisted into a broad grin that stretched from ear to ear as she savored the sweet elixir of revenge.

"I can do this."

The camera on the MacBook Pro eyed Bianca—her breathtaking mocha-and-cream complexion; the happy crow's-feet, alluring with the seductive appeal of experience; and the dark hair, untainted by bleach, much to her husband's annoyance. The camera found the massive fireplace behind Bianca and the surrounding walls, curiously empty throughout the sprawling house. When Bianca spoke, low echoes accompanied every word.

"You may know me as Bianca Santiago, author of ten bestselling romance novels," she said. "But I doubt you know me as a desperate housewife. And I'm not talking about the sitcom where everybody's laughing."

Bianca sipped her water.

"There are many ways to suffer through an empty marriage," she continued. "For years, I sacrificed everything for my husband's career. Blamed myself when our home wasn't perfect. When dinner wasn't right. When he disappeared with younger women or watched the same television show downstairs that I was watching in our bedroom. I found every excuse to take responsibility." She paused and leaned into her laptop. "You know what I mean?"

Her eyes widened. The MacBook lens caught more than a woman's image. It caught an unruly mob of emotions—love and hate, strength and vulnerability, joy and fear. In front of the camera Bianca returned to the populist woman, to the author whose pen flowed nonstop with the stuff of romance and good cries. She turned charismatic, a winning voice that resonated near and far.

"Why did my husband lose interest?" she lashed out, the question rhetorical. "Is it me?"

More water.

"Let me ask you something. Do you hate workouts at the gym?" From nowhere Bianca produced a bowl of ice cream and ladled out big spoonfuls, one after another. She savored the Belgian chocolate as the camera, frame by frame, recorded every mouthful.

"Well, ladies," she said, "nobody tells this old girl I'm 'past my shelf life.'"

In that moment Bianca morphed into the consummate politician. "It's time we work together." Her rhetoric fierce, she exuded power. She bubbled, all charm and winsome personality, a woman who knew her friends. "We won't be taken for granted. We won't bear children for our husbands. We won't trade our careers for diapers, while our husbands cavort around the globe. Eating what they want. Unzipping their flies for whom they want. We won't watch passively from the sidelines as our husbands leer at younger women."

Bianca paused for effect. She stared into the camera, cool, commanding, and charismatic. She added, "We won't allow them to betray us in public for all our friends to see. We need each other."

Putting the ice-cream bowl aside, Bianca adjusted the MacBook forward on her lap. She leaned into the camera. And with the all-powerful brawn of feminine charm, she said, "And I need you." She waited in silence for her words to register. "Nobody tells me I'm 'one divorce away from cougar' and gets away with it. Ladies, meet my next ex-husband."

Bianca reached down and produced a nine-by-twelve headshot of Cyrus Leeser. "Call him Cy. Note the sculpted chin, the piercing black eyes, the long black hair."

More water.

"Ladies, are you suffering? Are you withering under an endless storm of expectations? Are you like me?"

Bianca leaned forward—powerful, breathtaking, and conspiratorial for the camera.

"I'm serving divorce papers on Monday," she explained. "Would you help me give notice? Would you e-mail my husband and tell him what you think about guys who control-freak their women into submission? Cy's e-mail is cy@leewellcapital.com. Let's see what happens." She added Leeser's cell, fax, and office phone numbers, repeating them twice for good measure.

Five minutes later, YouTube had Bianca's entire rant—a masterpiece of unbridled emotion. She uploaded the clip under the title "Bianca Santiago's Husband Is an Idiot Scumbag." Simple and to the point.

Inside the mammoth great room of their Greenwich estate, Bianca surveyed the empty walls. She sat back and smiled to herself. She liked Siggi. She liked his cousin Ólafur. They did good work. She hoped her movers were just as competent.

Somewhere in the wilds of Montana, a forty-something housewife watched a YouTube clip. The woman was a lifelong fan of Bianca Santiago's. Read every one of her books twice. Yearned for another installment, even all these years later.

At times the Montana woman rocked back in horror. Other times she laughed out loud. When the clip finally ended, the woman sat back and considered what she had seen. She thought about Montana's bitter and desolate winter, just around the bend.

"I'm in," she finally uttered in the darkness of her cottage.

She forwarded the link to twenty-two friends with the short message: *Let's join Bianca's tribe.*

———

Somewhere in the money canyons of Manhattan's Upper West Side, a mother of three sipped her glass of chardonnay. She knew how to mobilize people. After all, she was a high-school drama mama. Used to be a publicist. Missed her career. She wondered if any of her girlfriends knew the remarkable lady from Greenwich.

She sent the YouTube link everywhere: nine women in book club number one; seven women in book club two; sixteen friends that cycled through the Columbus Avenue divorce bar on Thursday nights with white wine spritzers in one hand. And that was only the start. She could enlist several women from her Pilates and yoga classes, too.

"I'm in, Bianca," announced the mother of three.

SUNDAY, OCTOBER 5
MARKETS CLOSED

By that morning, Bianca's video had gone viral. There were over 2.6 million hits. The average rating was four stars. There were 759 comments, starting with one labeled "Bianca's brigade."

Female comments outnumbered male remarks about eight to one. A few men quipped about "MILFs and cougars." But angry responses flamed them into submission. The fervent missives, women to women, beseeched all ladies to demand respect—or else.

"That's it," announced Siggi. "We're done."

It was dark outside. Ólafur wiped perspiration from his brow with the sleeve of his black sweatshirt. "I'd love to see Leeser's face when he walks into his office tomorrow."

"Bianca wants to see that expression, too," observed Siggi. "She is one pissed-off woman."

"You got that right, cousin." He asked hopefully, "Can we hit a bar, sort of a mini celebration for old times' sake?"

"No, Ólafur. We need to return Bianca's key."

CHAPTER FIFTY-THREE

Cusack hopped into his black-and-blue Beemer and rattled all the way to Greenwich—indifferent to the car's knocking. He marched through the parking lot, the six-figure imports unwashed and unkempt, curiously flaccid during the ugly markets. He pushed through the etched-glass doors of LeeWell Capital.

"It's a good thing you're here," reported Amanda the receptionist. "Today is what our traders call a 'shit show.'"

"What's wrong?"

"Hang on, Jimmy. Cy Leeser's line," Amanda announced to the caller in her receptionist voice, shades of CNN. She paused, listened to the caller, and finally said, "Let me take your number so he can get back to you."

Amanda returned to Cusack. "Cy hasn't stopped screaming all morning."

"About what?"

"Hang on," she repeated, holding up one finger and grabbing another call. "Mr. Leeser needs to call you back, ma'am." Amanda frowned at the response.

Cusack, sensing an extended conversation, headed back to Nikki's cubicle. Her phone rang, and he noticed the console resembled Times Square at night. Lights. Lights. Lights.

Nikki picked up the line, listened attentively, and said, "No, he won't call you back." And with that she slammed down the receiver.

"What's going on?"

"Cy's phone is ringing off the hook," she said. "Lots of angry women."

"Is he in his office?"

"He's in, all right." Nikki's tone rang with a careful-what-you-wish-for intonation. "I wouldn't go in. He chewed Victor out something fierce."

"About what?"

"Not sure. But Victor stomped off to the men's room and didn't come out for thirty minutes."

"Oh."

"No kidding. I sent one of the guys to check on him."

"Why's Cy so angry?"

"See for yourself."

Rachel paid the driver and hopped out of the yellow cab. Black hair, black lipstick, black pants, and black jacket—a few black tats and she would be a damn Goth. The irony, Rachel mused, was she had no need for the disguise. Emily Cusack would never recognize her. Unusual in the cleaning business.

There were always visitors to the Bronx Zoo. Rachel worried about them. She had studied the grounds, walked every square inch around the polar bear compound. But all the surveillance, her dogged and unrelenting search for blind spots, could never eliminate the risk. Somebody might be watching from the distance. And these days, it seemed like everyone had a camcorder on hand. Or a cell phone with video camera.

Rachel relished the taste. Thrill—her heightened sense of risk—smacked of salt and sweaty endorphins after a killer workout. Her skin tingled. She heard everything, a dog barking, feet shuffling on the pavement, an engine backfiring in the distance. Faces became photos, which she stored in her memory. She saw every flash of movement, every turn of the head.

Hunting. Hunting. Hunting.

Rachel's fingertips morphed into human sensors. She anticipated every change around her. Inside her head, she journeyed to the familiar zone. To the netherworld where she went from good to great. To her second life as a "cleaner." To the place where no avatar was needed.

At the zoo entrance on Southern Boulevard, Rachel paid the cashier. She walked through the gates and checked her knapsack one last time. The 100-unit syringe was loaded and primed for action. So was the pink trophy from Henrietta Hedgecock's purse. So were the hot dogs. All twelve of them.

"Where are you, Mrs. Cusack?" Rachel asked in a low whisper as she hiked toward the World of Reptiles.

Cusack poked his head inside Leeser's office. He did not detect the noise, the rapid-fire sonar pings, not at first anyway. The walls caught—no, they snared his attention. They engulfed his internal musings like a fisherman's net, wrapping round and round him, choking him until one question repeated over and over:

What happened to Cy's paintings?

The walls were empty. Gone were the paintings and the drawings, the vast expanse of portraits and landscapes fighting for space with abstracts everywhere. Gone in the middle of the night. Even the Picasso was gone, the master's sangria-soaked meanderings nowhere to be seen. Gone like yesterday. The picture hooks were the only items left. They lined the walls like tombstones, testaments to majesty that had once been.

"Bite me," Cy snarled into his landline, and slammed down the receiver.

Behind him, the computer pinged like a submarine's sonar every five seconds. The sound reminded Cusack of old World War II movies. He could almost see navy crews waiting in silence as Nazi destroyers dogged through the murky seas and dropped their lethal charges.

Ping. Ping. Ping.

Cy's BlackBerry loomed uncomfortably on his desk. Like his computer, the smartphone also announced the arrival of angry e-mails with pings. Cy had selected the same sonarlike ringtone. Or perhaps he had never changed the factory settings. The BlackBerry pings rang crisp, and they rang sharp. They rang every five seconds—though always a second earlier, or a second later, than the pings from the computer.

Ping. Ping. Ping.

The pings came in waves. They filled the room: first the lead pings from the computer; and then the echo pings from the BlackBerry; or vice versa. Every angry e-mail announced its arrival twice, all with rambling variations of the same vitriolic message.

E-mail number 1,314: *What about your children, Asshole?*

E-mail number 3,025: *Hey, butthead, don't show your face in Venice Beach.*

E-mail number 5,911: *Did you mail your check?*

Cy's landline rang yet again, and he snatched the receiver from its cradle. "What?" His brow furrowed as he listened. "Bianca said what?" He listened a few minutes more and slammed the receiver into its cradle.

He turned to Cusack and barked, "What do you want?"

Ping. Ping. Ping.

Leaning forward on his desk, distracted and preoccupied, Leeser did not wait for a response. "My wife just sabotaged me in a way you can't imagine."

"She took your paintings?" Cusack deliberated over what impressed him the most, the empty walls or all the pings.

"Worse," he confirmed. "She jammed our communications. Our phone circuits are overloaded. Don't work worth a shit. I must have twenty thousand e-mails by now. And my BlackBerry is fucking useless. I can't hear myself think. There's a goddam call-waiting signal every time I'm on the phone. Or a text message every time I fucking dial. So what do you want anyway?"

Cusack ignored the bad timing. Leeser's distractions, he decided, might even help. "Our conversation from last Thursday. That videotape from the Foxy Lady. Okay to finish our discussion?"

Ping. Ping. Ping.

Inside the Bronx Zoo Rachel turned left at an intersection, instead of taking the right toward the World of Reptiles. It was an instinctive decision, the feral change of plans common to all predators—choices they make but cannot explain. Emily often started her days inside the long, meandering building named Madagascar, home to the Nile crocodiles.

The detour required only ten minutes, a quick jaunt through the shadows of Madagascar, a search-and-destroy mission among obscure carnivores such as the mongooselike fossa. It would not take long to find a pregnant woman inside the building. The crowds had yet to arrive, and Rachel could save herself the trouble of doubling back later. Dressed in her Goth garb, Rachel disappeared into Madagascar's interior blackness. Just to be safe, she reached into her bag and pulled out a pair of black leather gloves.

As the corridors zigged and zagged, cool and foreboding, Emily was nowhere to be seen. Rachel checked the Nile crocodiles and their limestone caves. Not there. She checked around the tomato frog, so named for the astonishing red that belongs in every painter's palette. Not there.

Rachel decided the building was empty until she found the hissing cockroaches, *Gromphadorhina portentosa.* The roaches were indigenous to Madagascar. No doubt they would thrive in Manhattan like a hundred million others, give or take.

There in the shadows, Rachel Whittier eyed a pregnant woman walking quickly in the opposite direction. "Gotcha." She smirked.

Outside Leeser's office, Victor paced back and forth. First to the left. Then to the right. Huffing at every turn. Every so often, he peered into his boss's office to check if Leeser and Cusack were finished.

"Victor, why don't I call you when they wrap up," Nikki offered.

"How long, do you think?" He inspected her over the bridge of his horn-rimmed glasses.

"No idea."

"I can't wait that long." Victor stormed into Leeser's office, five foot six inches of unbridled fury, still smarting from that morning's confrontation with his boss.

"We need to talk." Lee plopped down on the guest chair next to Cusack.

"Not now," rejoined Leeser. "No dwarves allowed."

"The market's dropping like a rock and you're busy?" the head trader scoffed, ignoring the shot. "We'll see nine thousand any minute."

"Everybody 'wants to talk,'" growled Leeser. "I've probably received a thousand calls from angry women. They want to talk. There are twenty thousand e-mails on my computer. People I don't fucking know 'want to talk.' I can't figure how to turn off all these goddam pings. And now there's you, Victor, and you, Jimmy. You 'want to talk.' Who goes first?"

"I do," demanded Victor. "If we don't sell right now, not tomorrow, not an hour from now, but right now, Merrill will call their loan and puke out our positions. They don't care if you sit on the board of Bentwing. Merrill will sell sloppy, and pretty soon everybody else will know and start puking out their own positions. Puke. Puke. Puke. You gotta do something."

"Anything else?"

Ping. Ping. Ping.

"Yeah," Victor declared. "We sell now, or I quit and go somewhere that understands talent."

"And Jimmy," Cy said, resting his left thumb on his right thumb, coiling his index finger around his lip, "what about you?"

"We should speak in private."

Victor shrugged his shoulders and shook his head. "I'm not going anywhere."

"Come on, Jimmy," taunted Cy. He was distracted. "There are no secrets among friends."

Ping. Ping. Ping.

"Okay," said Cusack. He stood up and reached his hand over Leeser's desk. "Let's buy out my father-in-law."

CHAPTER FIFTY-FOUR

LIFE IN THE FAST LANE . . .

"What are you talking about?" Leeser recoiled from shock, from expectations that Cusack was about to resign. The boss no longer had eyes. Stinger missiles had replaced the pupils, and they were taking aim.

"What's wrong?" asked Cusack, confused by Leeser's reaction. "You said, 'I need a partner. Not an adversary.' Let's get started."

No reply.

"Caleb's a careful guy," Cusack volunteered. "But I think he might sell his company."

"Really?" said Leeser.

"Excuse me," interrupted Victor Lee. "What about me?"

"Maybe you should leave," Cy replied, quietly, not so much in control as in a state of confusion.

"Leave?" yelped Victor. "I've been here three years. And you're making *him* a partner."

"We can discuss it later," replied Leeser.

"I'd rather discuss it now," Victor squawked, his voice rising. "Cusack over me! What happened to loyalty?"

"You just threatened to quit."

"I'm the head trader. I make the sacrifices. I think outside the box." Lee shook with rage, with the yawing motion of a bobble-head doll.

"What sacrifices? What are you talking about?" demanded Cy. He was annoyed and perplexed. He was mashing the Off button on his Black-Berry. "These pings are driving me out of my fucking mind."

Shannon appeared from nowhere. Large and menacing, LeeWell's head of security heard the ruckus from down the hall. Walking into the office, he asked, "Is there a problem, boss?"

The woman scrambled, fast for being pregnant. Rachel remembered Emily as taller, not so round. But deep inside Madagascar, the inky lighting and shadows played tricks with silhouettes.

The pregnant woman turned one corner and then the next. Fast, with purpose. Her movements became frantic.

Rachel wondered if Emily recognized her. It was impossible. Rachel concealed her scar. The Goth look would fool anyone, especially someone with prosopagnosia.

Too soon to use the insulin syringe. The bear pens were too far a hike. People responded to the drug in different ways. Emi might collapse from the massive shot within seconds. That would blow everything. Or she might turn belligerent and aggressive, before succumbing to the drug.

"Bobby, where are you?" screamed the pregnant woman. She hustled around the corner and found her son inside the Spiny Forest. He was three, maybe four years old.

"What are those?" he exclaimed, pointing at the ring-tailed lemurs.

The mother, who looked nothing like Emi Cusack in the eerie glow from token lights, bent down and hugged her son. "Don't run off on me like that," she scolded. And she hugged Bobby some more.

"I saddled the wrong pony," Rachel cursed to herself.

"We're fine," Cy advised Shannon.

"You sure, boss?"

"But do me a favor and ask Victor to join you."

"Whatever," the head trader sighed, rising to his feet. Juiced on 1.25 mg of Premarin twice a day, Victor tramped across the room. At the doorway, he called over his shoulder, "You make me feel like an old cow, and I don't like it."

"Close the door, Victor."

Cusack sat back in his chair. The theatrics over, he focused on Cy. "I'm pumped. You too, right?"

"I don't know what to say," admitted Leeser, looking through Cusack.

"Emi's on board," Cusack added. "I had to work it out at home before saying yes here."

"You got that right. Otherwise you get your paintings stolen and underwear scattered across the lawn." Leeser's words sounded bland and indifferent, preoccupied.

"Are you sure everything's okay?"

"Yeah," he grunted, his mind elsewhere. "It's this thing with Bianca."

"I hate to ask, but did she give you the video?"

"No," he admitted, blinking. "Bianca still has my Mac."

"Do you mind if I call her?"

"That might be best," Cy replied, distracted. "Can I borrow your cell phone?"

"Is yours broken?"

"Sabotaged. I'll return it in an hour."

Cusack flipped his cell phone to Leeser, who grabbed it and walked out the door. Jimmy sat alone in Leeser's mausoleum, surrounded by empty walls, and wondering what had just happened.

In the parking lot underneath Greenwich Plaza, Cy marched through the sea of four-wheeled imports. There was enough money in cars to rival the GDP of a small Caribbean nation. When Leeser found his Bentley, he gunned the engine and dialed Rachel's cell phone. His wheels screeched as he pulled out of the lot.

One ring. Two rings.

The voice mail picked up, and Rachel's trademark recording purred through the airwaves. "You missed me." No invitation to leave a message. Nothing else. Just a beep.

"Call me now," Cy thundered. "Now, Rachel."

Leeser turned onto I-95 heading south toward the Bronx Zoo. He dialed again.

Rachel, her black sunglasses on high beam, trooped through the courtyard en route to the World of Reptiles. When her cell phone rang, she did not recognize the number. The caller went into voice mail. The issue could wait, whatever, whoever it was. She had a job to do.

The blinking message light piqued her curiosity, though. Made her wonder whether it was a new client, somebody other than Cy. He was grating on her last nerve.

Outside the Amazing Amphibians exhibit, the phone rang again. Same number. It rang as Rachel stalked past the Bronx Zoo store. More voice mail. Three messages now.

By the time Rachel reached the Dancing Crane Café, it was clear the caller would not stop dialing. This time Rachel answered. "Yes."

"It's about time you picked up," snapped Leeser.

"You sound like a lizard on a hot grill, Kemosabe." She could not help but add, "I wish you'd stop calling me."

"Have you finished your business?"

"No," answered Rachel.

"Good." Cy exhaled, sounding relieved. "Abort everything, now."

Rachel turned left on the path. "Abort. What are you talking about?"

"Cusack didn't resign."

"What difference does it make?"

"Don't you see?" snapped Leeser. "They don't know. Cusack wants to buy his father-in-law's company."

"I know what I heard," countered Rachel. "They know."

"You're wrong."

"No way," she snorted, her voice low, barely audible, but loud enough to register anger.

"Then why didn't Cusack resign?"

"It doesn't matter."

"I'm telling you, Rachel. Something's fishy. If you strike now, we have problems." He added cautiously, "No telling what the police will do."

"Emily Cusack can ID the scar on my hand."

"Wear a glove. You're the one who told me about prosopagnosia."

"Not worth the risk."

"I order you to leave her alone, Rachel."

"You're ordering me. I don't think so," barked Rachel, locking horns. "I've yet to receive one dollar from LeeWell Capital. All I get are your promises about my partnership interest. So don't go telling me, 'I order you.' I'm doing Emily Cusack to settle my nerves."

"I'm sorry," retreated Cy. "But we've got to think straight. Otherwise, this thing will bite us in the ass."

"Like you say, Kemosabe, 'not my problem.' I have no links to your employee's wife."

"Just wait. I'm on my way."

Rachel held the cell phone away from her mouth and faked the crackling sound of static. "You're breaking up, Cy."

"Back off. I'm telling you, back off."

More fake static.

"You're breaking up, Cy." Rachel punched the End Call button on her cell phone. This assignment had turned fun. She loved the challenge. She loved asserting her will, just to spite Leeser.

Cy heard dial tone and cursed, "You stupid . . ." He didn't bother to finish the sentence. He stepped on the gas pedal.

Back at the Bronx Zoo, Rachel Whittier saw Emi Cusack leaving the World of Reptiles. This time there was no mistake. Rachel adjusted her sunglasses and began stalking the target.

CHAPTER FIFTY-FIVE

LEEWELL CAPITAL . . .

Bianca pushed through the etched-glass doors. She wore crisp blue jeans and a baggy black sweater, by no means Greenwich couture, but comfortable and appropriate for the weather. She had a tall man, six one, maybe six two, in tow.

He was buff, ten years her junior. He wore an off-the-rack suit, a dozen or so natural fibers beyond plastic bag. And he carried an almost-leather briefcase from one of the office supply superstores. Just above the right eyebrow, his forehead looked like it once played catch with something other than a baseball. Maybe a glass pitcher from an Irish bar.

Amanda stood up from behind her reception desk. "It's nice to see you, Mrs. Leeser."

"Hey there, sugar," Bianca greeted, warm with no hint of business whatsoever. "Where's my husband?"

"He stepped out."

Bianca rolled her eyes, exasperated. "Do you know when he'll be back?"

"No, maybe Nikki knows."

Bianca pulled out her cell phone and dialed Leeser. His voice mail reported that it was full and not taking messages, which she took to be a good sign. Bianca turned to the tall man and said, "Come on, hun." And the two pushed inside LeeWell's inner sanctum.

"Do you know when Cy will be back?" Bianca asked Nikki.

"He didn't say where he was going."

Bianca cocked her ear around the corner of Leeser's doorway and listened to the rapid-fire pings from arriving e-mails. "Been like that long?"

"All morning," Nikki reported.

"Nice," exulted Bianca, now looking inside the office and admiring the empty walls Siggi left behind. "But I can't reach Cy," she complained to Nikki and the man by her side.

"That's because he has my phone," Cusack announced, walking out of his office, where he had been paying attention.

Bianca hugged him hello and asked, "What's your number, hun? We've got papers to serve." Bianca nodded toward the tall man.

Cy mashed his foot on the accelerator, hard as he dared. Seventy miles per hour. Sometimes eighty. Every once in a while he throttled back. The cops loved to ticket Bentleys. Six-figure cars brought extra bragging rights back at the station houses.

Jimmy's cell phone rang, and Leeser thought, *Why not*. He answered, "Yeah."

"Do you like my present?"

"Where the fuck is my art?"

"Our art," Bianca corrected, smirking from ear to ear. "And I understand you've heard from the fans of a 'broken-down plagiarist who hasn't published in sixteen years.'"

Leeser flipped her the bird, long distance, straining to check his anger. "Where are you?"

"At your office with the marshall."

"Marshall," bellowed Leeser. "Why'd you get a marshall involved?" He really needed to stop Rachel.

"We have the papers right here." Bianca was onstage now, acutely aware that Nikki and Cusack were hanging on to every word. She added, "Where are *you*?"

"I have some business in the Bronx. I'll be back in an hour, and we can talk."

"Since when do you have clients in the Bronx?" asked Bianca.

Cusack's eyes widened. He mouthed the words, "Where in the Bronx?"

"Just give me an hour," Leeser pleaded, trying to buy time. "We can sort this out. And I'll move back into our house."

"You mean my house."

"Your house?" The words angered Leeser. They confused him, too.

"Unless you forget," Bianca replied, "Roundhill Road is under my control. It'd be a shame if you were arrested for trespassing."

"I pay the mortgage. My lawyer will kick you out by the end of the week."

"Don't bet on it. Remember our estate planning?"

"Yes." Leeser stepped on the gas pedal, now doubling as a release valve for his fury.

"A trust holds the estate for our girls," explained Bianca. "You wanted it. You were the one who said, 'Everybody else in Greenwich has a trust.'"

"So?"

"I'm the trustee."

"Just hold on until I get back from the zoo. We can work this out." Cy frowned and added, all oil and nose pores, "For our twins, babe."

"Don't you dare attack me with our girls," she replied dismissively. "Finish your business and get back here. What are you doing at the zoo anyway?"

This time Cusack mouthed, "Bronx Zoo?"

"Forget about it," snapped Leeser.

"The Bronx Zoo," said Bianca while nodding yes to Jimmy, "strikes me as the perfect place to showcase your hedge fund."

"Hey, the bitching hour came early," barked Leeser, no longer able to control his temper. "You used to wait until I got home."

"Say hi to Emi Cusack," said Bianca, winking at Jimmy.

"What makes you—"

Bianca cut Leeser off. She had grown tired of their game. "Cy, there's only one takeaway from this conversation. Dorothy Parker said, 'The two most beautiful words in the English language are "cheque enclosed." Think about it." She clicked off her cell phone.

"What's wrong?" Bianca asked Jimmy.

"What did Cy say about Emi?"

"Nothing," she replied. "Just that he's driving to the Bronx Zoo."

"Did he say why?"

"No, Jimmy. Why are you so upset?"

Thirty minutes ago Cusack had wondered how to get the Mac laptop from Bianca. Now he no longer cared. "I need to ask you something. My question may sound odd. But I want you to think long and hard before you answer."

"Okay?" Her eyebrows arched high with concern.

The stress was beading off Cusack like sweat. "Have you ever seen Cy hanging out with a woman with a bad scar on her hand?"

"Sounds like one of my novels."

"It's not fiction."

Cusack stared at her, waiting, his thoughts shifting to last Friday's lunch with Emi. That afternoon the couple had agreed Cusack would resign. They changed tactics over the weekend, however, after confiding their suspicions to Caleb.

"Let me reconnoiter with my friends in the insurance industry," he had said.

Bianca finally replied, "No, Jimmy. I can't think of anybody."

In that moment Cusack remembered the red-haired woman from Somba Village. He never noticed a scar. But she could hear their conversation, no question. Cusack blinked once, and his alarm bells exploded.

Emi's in trouble.

Without warning, Cusack pushed through Bianca and the tall, gangly marshall. Nikki glanced up from her bank of files. Cusack burst past her, lunging, lurching, his feet scrambling for traction, desperate for pace, for acceleration.

"What got into him?" Nikki gasped, as Cusack's slipstream sucked her tower of paperwork and sprayed it through the air.

"My husband," Bianca answered, not missing a beat.

Jimmy blasted into the reception area. Headed for the etched doors of LeeWell Capital. At that exact moment, Shannon towered in the office doorway. He loomed in front of Jimmy Cusack, a large, hulking, menacing presence.

Cusack lowered his shoulder, shades of glory days from Columbia football, and plowed through Shannon. Caught him by surprise. Bowled him ass over elbows.

"Out of my way."

Shannon's head snapped against the jamb. He collapsed on the floor. He wheezed, "Ugh," as the Berber carpet greeted the back of his neck, "Hello."

Cusack reverberated from the impact. Saw stars and did a 360. Pain surged through his shoulder from contact with the human wrecking ball.

Elevator.

Ground floor.

Cusack pushed through a cluster of dour-faced gods, the lobby usually empty at this hour, and burst into the gray October day. Twenty seconds later he was pumping the accelerator of his blue Beemer, screaming, "Shit, shit, shit."

The motor turned over and over. Grinding. Not catching. The "adventure in precision physics" had run its course. Cusack tried the ignition once. He tried it a dozen times. No angle of the key worked as the engine ground round and round, deader than a med-school cadaver.

He smashed the dashboard in frustration. He turned the key one last time. Besmirching BMW. Beseeching St. Jude. Swearing and hoping for a miracle. The old engine hacked to life. It resurrected not in glory but with the throaty knock of a smoker's cough.

Three minutes, and Cusack was flying down I-95. His speedometer hit eighty, ninety, one hundred miles per hour. Over and over, he checked the rearview mirror. He expected to see troopers any minute, their flashing blue lights. He waited for sirens to erupt. He wondered if his Beemer would lose a muffler. Faster and faster, he drove—his foot crushing the gas pedal.

Why did I give Cy my cell phone?

Cusack cursed himself. Once. Twice. A thousand times. Checking the rearview mirror, he spied a car closing fast. There were no sirens. There were no flashing lights. It was a white Audi. Jimmy stared hard and recognized the driver. He knew that perma-scowl anywhere.

Shannon was on his tail, sneering, gaining.

CHAPTER FIFTY-SIX

BRONX ZOO . . .

The pregnant scientist walked west toward the Dancing Crane Café. The Goth-garbed cleaner walked east toward the World of Reptiles. In twenty seconds the two women would collide, and Rachel would make her move. Emi paused, however, to speak with a colleague.

Rachel stopped at the Bug Carousel. Through black sunglasses, she pretended to study the long-legged praying mantis. She hardly noticed the ride's figurines. She had zero interest in the bombardier beetle or firefly. And forget about the ladybug.

Rachel rooted through her black bag, which now reeked from twelve hot dogs. She bypassed the 100-unit syringe, fingering this way and that for the pink trophy from Henrietta Hedgecock. Her cell phone vibrated and interrupted the search, though. It was Cy again.

She ignored the call, just as she had ignored his last five attempts. Leeser was becoming a thorn in her side. He was obsessive, compulsive, and flat-out wrong. There was no mistake. Emily Cusack could ID Rachel. She was going down today, baby and all.

Rachel decided to visit Cy later, talk things over and hold what her daddy called a "sit-down." She hated surprises. She hated debates midway through the game. Last-minute deliberation was unprofessional. The more she thought about Leeser's interference, the more he annoyed her.

Instead of reaching for the cell phone, Rachel pulled the pink C2 from her bag. Tasers, she decided, were more persuasive than syringes. Small, trim, and light, the C2 was shaped like a bent twig, no more than six inches long. The pink trophy looked like nothing special, like a load of empty postholes, but people were terrified of getting zapped.

Rachel had fondled the weapon a million times. She studied instructional manuals until she knew every feature cold. The pink personal protector was easy to use: Slip back the protective slide on top, aim using the laser pointer, and mash down the trigger button with your thumb.

The Taser fired two small probes, each attached to fine fifteen-foot wire lines. The probes could pierce clothes two inches thick and microwave the target a new hairdo. They delivered 50,000 volts, half the power of most stun guns. But Rachel's personal protector zapped for thirty full seconds. That kind of power would drop anybody, especially a woman seven months pregnant.

One problem. Rachel hated to take chances, and the C2 was a big one. With each firing, the gun rained confetti traceable to the owner. The debris, according to Taser, prevented the wrong guys from using the gun for the wrong reasons. What if police connected the confetti to Henrietta Hedgecock, a woman who had drowned back in March? Would they ask questions? Would they investigate the insurance policy that LeeWell Capital owned?

"I hate loose ends," Rachel told herself.

Still, the C2 made a compelling threat. It was more menacing than a syringe, no matter how long the needle or what the injection. Rachel knew the one threat guaranteed to make any mother comply:

"How'd you like me to Tase your baby?"

Rachel doubted Emily would scream. She doubted it would be necessary to fire. A simple, unequivocal threat and "Come with me" would do the trick. Rachel liked the mental image: two probes and 50,000 volts discharging into a swollen belly. The pregnant woman would seize, before tumbling backward into the ravine. And the polar bear, primed with twelve hot dogs, would finish the job.

Emi was walking west again.

Jimmy had not called. Emi was a knot. She wondered what was happening at LeeWell Capital. Whether James had convinced Cy about working together. How long it would take her father to find answers. She willed herself to go through the steps, to behave like everything was fine. She rubbed her bulging stomach and said, "I haven't heard from you either, Yaz."

On this crisp October morning, students all in school, there were few visitors to observe a pregnant woman cooing to her tummy. The moms with strollers and kids with snotty noses were nowhere to be seen.

The only other person on the path was an athletic woman power-washed in coal. She wore black gloves, black pants, and black lipstick that looked like a hostile makeover from a Goth. Ever the scientist, Emi Cusack wondered why so harsh. The inky colors clashed with the woman's delicate features.

Emi reached into her purse and pulled out a cell phone. The woman in black stopped and looked over her shoulder, deliberating whether to retrace her steps back to the Mouse House.

"That's weird," muttered Emi, getting a busy signal at LeeWell Capital, staring at her phone with a confused look.

The Goth woman was walking again, drawing near, opting against the Mouse House. She was taking off her black gloves. She was holding something in her hands, something cute and pink. There was something on the back of her hand. White. Puffy. A scar.

The scar.

Emi turned and punched the numbers to James's cell phone, petrified but in control. Just as she was about to punch the little green phone button, the icon that actually dialed the numbers, she heard a familiar voice:

"Emi Cusack," the man called. "I thought you might be here."

Relieved—she glanced at the smiling man and burst out, "I need your help." She knew the voice but could not place it. Not yet, anyway. Emi felt the Goth woman crowd behind her.

"It's Cy Leeser," the man said, putting his arm on Emi's shoulder, cheek-kissing her hello, smarmy as a can of WD-40. "What's wrong?"

"What are you doing here?" Emi recoiled from Leeser's touch. Shivers flossed her vertebrae. And she cursed herself for flinching. She wondered if Cy had noticed.

He did.

"You're awfully jumpy," observed Leeser.

Rachel, he realized, had been right. He could smell the pregnant woman's fear. She was no different from the CEOs of his portfolio companies. An open book. Easy to read. Leeser berated himself for missing Cusack's ruse earlier that morning.

"Don't scream, sugar," Rachel interrupted from behind, her voice matter-of-fact. "I'll zap that baby into labor right here on the spot. I'm holding fifty thousand grade-A certified volts."

"You wouldn't." Emi grabbed her stomach in horror, protecting Yaz by instinct.

"One peep," the nurse grinned, "and I'm plugging a fifteen-foot extension into your umbilical cord." She brandished the Taser to punctuate her words.

Emi's eyes widened. Her jaw hung slack. She studied the puffy white scar on the back of Rachel Whittier's hand. It was the same scar she had seen when Conrad Barnes hailed a cab with a woman forty years his junior.

"I was wrong," Leeser acknowledged to Rachel.

"You've got some 'splaining to do," Rachel told Emi. "Why didn't your husband resign?"

"We talked to my dad over the weekend," explained Emi, mustering whatever bravado she could find. "His people are running a check on eight of your insurance policies right now. It's only a matter of time."

"That's a problem," snapped Leeser. He looked stricken.

"I bet the authorities are on the way now," Emi threatened, bold and brave and petrified to the core.

"Doesn't matter," Rachel noted, addressing Leeser and gliding with the predatory stealth of a big cat. "First Emily. Then her husband. It's always the spouse, Cy. We stay on plan."

"But Bianca's back at my office with a marshall."

"What's that about?" asked Rachel. She prodded Emi in the stomach with the Taser, and the three began walking toward the bear pens.

"Bianca's divorcing me."

"Doesn't matter," Rachel repeated. "There are two people who can ID us. Maybe three if they really talked to Caleb Phelps. We need to check boxes one and two before we deal with anything else."

"Cy, what's wrong with you?" gasped Emi. "There's no way out."

"Let me worry about that," scoffed Rachel.

"Why, Cy?" Emi was looking for compassion, somewhere, anywhere.

"It is what it is," Leeser replied, treating Cusack's wife like just another trade.

"Where are we going?" asked Emi.

"Leave the questions to me," ordered Rachel, "and tell us about the polar bears, Emily. You can personalize our tour."

"What smells like hot dogs?" asked Leeser.

Rachel started to answer. But the sounds of Louis Armstrong stirred the poison air. He was singing "La Vie en Rose."

CHAPTER FIFTY-SEVEN
HUTCHINSON PARKWAY . . .

"Come on," screamed Cusack.

He pounded the steering wheel of his Beemer. Both fists. Traffic on the Hutch had slowed to a crawl. The construction just ahead, backhoes and orange pylons closing off lanes, snared all drivers heading south. Beefy guys in hard hats everywhere.

Cusack had no cell phone. He had no proof anything was wrong. But he knew. He knew beyond all doubt. Something had gone bad. And Emi would not recognize danger until it was too late.

What in the dense hell was I thinking?

Great clouds of black smoke belched from the Beemer. Back on I-95, when the speedometer needle had edged over 110 miles per hour, the engine went "clack." Now his ancient Beemer, a relic from the last century, coughed and sputtered with a noise resembling "Woo, woo, clack. Woo, woo, clack." The engine clanged with a death rattle all its own.

"Come on."

Cusack eyed the heat gauge on the dashboard. The needle wasn't touching *H* for hot, not yet anyway. But the pointer headed in that direction.

He checked the rearview mirror. Black fumes ballooned from his engine's exhaust. Cusack eyed Shannon through all the smoke. The white Audi trailed two cars back, stuck in traffic just like everyone else.

Up ahead, a police officer waved traffic past orange-and-white sawhorses with blinking yellow lights. There were only three cars until the end of construction. Only three cars navigating through orange pylons that turned two lanes into one. The drivers slowed anyway, rubbernecking at the road repair. The cop, skinny as a rail, with black sunglasses, blew his whistle and flapped his arms like a maniac. He commanded drivers to get moving.

Two cars. Cusack rolled down his window. One car.

My turn.

Cusack almost floored the gas pedal. His Beemer would launch from the snarl, shoot forward like water through the nozzle of a hose. He held back, though, eased down on the brake and leaned out the window. The engine pounded with the woo-woo-clack noise.

"Move, move, move," the officer screamed, fierce in his black aviator sunglasses.

"See that white Audi two cars back?"

"What about it?" the officer hissed.

"The driver's got a gun."

"What are you talking about?" Alarm registered in the cop's voice.

"Big black guy. He was waving a forty-five at me on I-95. Tried to force me off the road."

"Are you sure?"

"Call for backup," instructed Cusack. "I've never been so sure of anything in my life."

"Pull over." The cop pointed to the breakdown lane.

"Fuck you," snorted Jimmy. "The guy's got a gun."

This time Cusack gassed the Beemer, which burst forward like a howitzer's shell. From his rearview mirror, he watched black exhaust blanket the trooper. Even through the haze, he saw the cop unhook a latch holding his pistol.

On the open road Cusack's Beemer rumbled forward. It gained speed. Sixty, seventy, eighty miles per hour—the engine rattled like it would explode, growing louder and more fierce as the pistons pumped. The needle on the thermometer hit *H,* and then some. Steam poured from the hood.

Woo, woo, clack.

Cusack did not care. He planted his foot on the throttle, forcing his car to dig deep. Only three miles to parking lot B at the Bronx Zoo. Smoke poured from the exhaust. It billowed from the hood, where the wipers hid. Shannon was nowhere in sight. Cusack was flying.

Until he wasn't.

The Beemer's engine was losing power. Up ahead, Cusack could see exit six. He could see parking lot B. He would run the last half-mile. He pulled into the breakdown lane and looked in his rearview mirror, making sure he could open the car's door. What he saw horrified him.

Shannon was back. The human Mack truck parked just behind the blue Beemer. He burst from his white Audi and ran toward Cusack.

Jimmy sprang from his car and crouched in a boxer's stance. Circling. Ready to throw a haymaker. On the highway, cars raced past the two men. When Shannon and Jimmy were no more than five feet apart, one car full of college students thundered past the two men.

"Fight, fight, fight!" they hollered out the window.

"That was a cute trick back there," yelled Shannon, his bass tones cutting through the din.

"I don't have time for you," Cusack yelled back.

"In my car," the big man ordered.

"Get away from me," yelled Cusack, turning toward the parking lot. "Before I kick your ass."

Shannon grabbed Cusack's shoulder.

Jimmy whirled around, cocked his arm, and threw a knockout punch from the ghost of Jack Dempsey. He aimed at the big man's face, at the gapped teeth that looked like a broken zipper.

Shannon hardly moved. Did not flinch. With his massive left paw of a hand, he caught Cusack's fist and absorbed every ounce of power like a sponge.

"Knock it off," Shannon ordered. He controlled Cusack with his left hand, crushing Cusack's fist like a vise, bending back the wrist, bringing the smaller man to his knees.

"My wife's in trouble," Jimmy gasped, uncertain what to say, bending lower and lower under the big man's power.

Shannon eased his grip, allowing Cusack to stand. "I know."

"Say what?" asked Cusack. He was confused. Shannon was no longer crushing his hand.

"Get in the car."

"I need to help Emi."

"We'll reach her faster if you get in my car."

"Who the hell are you?" Cusack demanded, heading toward Shannon's Audi.

"I'm the cavalry. But you can call me Daryle Fucking Lamonica."

CHAPTER FIFTY-EIGHT

HOLD ME CLOSE AND HOLD ME FAST . . .

"Hello." Leeser answered Cusack's cell phone, silencing the Louis Armstrong ringtone.

Nothing.

"Hello."

Nothing.

Leeser scrutinized Emi, his eyes like slits, hers round and ripping with the "guilty" look of a mug shot. He clicked off the phone and reached out his hand, palm up. "Let's have it."

"What?" She pretended not to understand.

Rachel reached into Emi's coat pocket and pulled out the phone. Emi had punched in Cusack's number before Cy and Rachel nabbed her. She pressed the Dial button, cell phone buried in her pocket, and connected with a nightmare.

"See what I borrowed from your better half." Cy flashed Cusack's Black-Berry. His coal eyes glowed, more from anxiety than triumph. His long black hair, always so carefully coiffed, had gone on strike. It dangled in his face, ruffled and askew.

"Where's James?"

"Waiting his turn," gloated Rachel.

"We need to move." Cy glanced at his watch and then scanned the paths. Nobody was in sight. He was nervous. Anxious to move along. Field operations were never his thing.

Emi tried to stall. Anything to buy time. Anything to attract attention. But how? She dragged her feet, lumbered from the weight of her pregnancy.

Rachel poked Emily in the ribs with the Taser. "Stop acting like a seal."

"I need to pee," snapped Emily. It was the only excuse that came to mind.

Leeser rolled his eyes.

"Keep walking," instructed Rachel. "You'll pee your brains out in the polar bear pen. The bladder's the first thing to go." The familiar instincts had returned. Rachel was toying with her prey.

"I need a bathroom," Emi insisted.

"Shut the fuck up," Leeser barked, his voice taught and strained. "Or I'll fucking zap you myself." He looked left, right, and checked everywhere. Fieldwork was not his thing.

Rachel shrugged her shoulders. "I really wanted a primer on the polar bear."

"Let's get this over with," snapped Leeser.

Shannon roared past parking lot B, thirty miles per hour too fast. The Audi rumbled up to the admissions gate, scattering visitors left and right. Cusack and the big man bounced out of the car and raced through the zoo's entrance.

"What's wrong with you?" a woman scolded. She was pushing a stroller.

"Hey, what are you doing?" yelled one of the attendants. She was dressed in a zoo uniform. "You can't park here."

"Take care of it," Shannon shouted. Never breaking stride, he flipped his keys to the uniformed woman.

"This isn't valet parking," she barked, snatching his key ring from the air.

"Call the police," screamed Shannon. "We need help fast." He never stopped. Never broke stride. He hurdled the turnstile, hundred-meter style, leading into the Bronx Zoo.

"Do you know Emi Cusack?" Jimmy asked an attendant.

"She's the scientist," she replied. "Pregnant, right?"

"Have you seen her?"

"She works at the World of Reptiles."

"I know," Cusack responded, unable to mask his annoyance. He broke into a run.

"She likes to eat at the Somba Village," the woman called.

"You guys need to pay," another employee hollered.

Shannon and Cusack raced full bore. They turned left at the World of Birds, Bison Range off to the right. Tiger Mountain, and they turned left again.

Shannon never broke a sweat.

"We split up at the bears," Cusack panted. "You go left to Somba Village. I go right for the World of Reptiles."

"Roger that."

They abandoned the plan immediately. In the distance Cusack saw Emi, Cy, and a woman dressed in black. "There they are," he panted, air heaving from his lungs.

Shannon darted forward, leaving Jimmy in a cloud of dust. "Come on," he growled over his shoulder.

Cy, Rachel, and Emi marched past the grizzly pen. Every other second, Leeser pushed Emi from behind. "Pick up the pace."

Two massive bears lounged in a pool shaped like an oversized hot tub. One bear's flank was turned to the other. The second grizzly scrubbed the first one's back. Emi hesitated for a moment, only to feel the cattle prod from Rachel's C2 Taser.

"Down the stairs," ordered Leeser.

Rachel gestured with her pink stun gun. A couple emerged from a small seating area to the left. Rachel poked the Taser into Emi's side. The jab hurt, but nothing like the excruciating pain of 50,000 volts electrocuting baby Yaz.

Emi winced. Said nothing. The three walked down the stairs. No one was in sight outside the polar bear pen.

Leeser spied the bear. It was white. It was huge, at least one thousand pounds of raw feeding power.

"What's wrong with that thing?" Cy muttered.

On the left side of the pen, the tall lanky polar bear walked to one cave. It retraced its steps and walked to another. Over and over the bear checked the caves, back and forth, first one then the other, as though locked in a stiff-gaited OCD trance.

"Maybe Osama bin Laden is hiding in there," replied Rachel.

"Push her in," demanded Leeser.

"We need the hot dogs," Rachel replied.

Emi blinked, unsure what to expect.

"Make this fast," Leeser snapped, "before anybody gets close." He scanned the perimeter for gawkers.

The three walked along a split-rail fence separating visitors from a ten-foot ravine that prevented the polar bear from escaping. The bear could descend steep stairs into the ravine. But it could not climb out of the ten-foot gully into the open zoo. Nor could visitors who fell in.

Rachel trained her Taser on Emi the whole time, never losing focus, never veering, not once. She reached into her black bag and pulled out two of the hot dogs. With a quick, underhand motion, the cleaner tossed them onto the stairs leading to the great, ten-foot ravine.

The polar bear stopped checking the caves. The giant beast raised its long snout to the air, sniffing something foreign. It bellowed once and bounded for the stairs in long, gangly strides. Drawing closer and closer. Fangs glistening in the morning light.

Leeser could not believe its speed. "Push her in."

A twig snapped.

"That thing can outrun the beaters on an electric mixer," whistled Rachel, checking for the source of the noise, delaying on purpose.

Emi and Rachel had seen the polar bear charge before, Emi as a scientist and Rachel during practice runs. Emi's heart beat like a bongo drum. Rachel burned with anticipation.

"Watch this, Kemosabe," the nurse crowed, proud of her animal trick, the way she wrenched the bear from its cave ritual.

In a flash the polar bear seized the hot dogs and sucked them down. Gnawing. Gnashing. Gulping in frenzied motion. It raised its massive head to the three gawkers as though to say, "More. I want more."

Rachel spied two women at the grizzly pen. They turned and walked away.

"Okay, Emily," taunted Rachel. "What's it going to be?"

"Push her in," Leeser barked. "And let's get the fuck out of here."

Rachel paid no attention. "The easy way or the hard way?" she asked Emi.

"What are you talking about?"

"You're stoic," observed Rachel, still checking the coast was clear. "I'll give you that. Not even a quiver of the lip."

"You got three seconds to jump," bellowed Cy. "Or we fucking Tase you in the gut, in which case you're falling anyway. You make the call."

CHAPTER FIFTY-NINE

Polar bears, otherwise known as *Ursus maritimus,* are the world's largest walking carnivores. In the wilderness adult males reach 1,500 pounds, about twelve times the weight of an average Great Dane. There are reports of some bears tipping the scales at a ton.

They require four or five pounds of fat every day just to survive. Their stomachs, however, hold much more—up to 20 percent of their body weight. Grown males can ingest up to 300 pounds of meat. That's like a 180-pound man eating 144 quarter-pounders in one day.

Ringed seals, which weigh about 120 pounds, are the favorite meal of *Ursus maritimus.* On land the bears stalk the seals, creeping closer and closer, white fur, arctic ice. When their prey is fifteen feet away, the polars charge furiously. They nab the seal heads, clutching and tearing and gnawing with four fearsome canines.

These canines are longer, sharper, and set wider apart than those found in other bears. The extra space improves the ripping motion and makes it easier to peel flesh from bones. The other thirty-eight teeth don't get in the way.

With seal heads lodged deep inside four canines, the polars flip their quarry through the air, end over end, to safer spots on the ice. *Ursus maritimus* eat the skin and fat first, followed by the meat. They rinse frequently in the nearby arctic waters. Things get sloppy with all the blood and blubber, the chomping and crunching of forty-two teeth, the matting of white fur under the gush of entrails.

Watching polar bears feed is a fearsome sight.

Rachel waved the C2 Taser toward the polar bear and ordered, "Move it, sugar."

"Is it money you want?" Emi begged Cy.

"Hurry up because early don't last all day." Rachel poked Emi in the flat of her back, and pain shot up the pregnant woman's spine.

"How much is enough, Cy?"

Rachel smacked the back of Emi's head and said, "Get on with it."

"You do that again, lady, and I won't be able to help you."

Rachel prodded her with the Taser.

Emi picked one leg up over the split-rail fence, then the other. She moved stiffly, slowly, trying to devise Plan B. She peered down the ten-foot gully, trembling, too afraid to scream, uncertain what was worse—50,000 volts or the bear's teeth. She eyed the polar bear.

The polar bear eyed her back and licked its chops, a long pink tongue slathering round its snout of forty-two teeth: four canines, twelve incisors, sixteen premolars, and ten molars.

Yaz kicked deep inside the womb as Emi studied Rachel, trying to find some way out of this mess. She could feel her knees buckling, her balance giving way.

"What kind of woman are you?" Emi demanded.

"The last one," snorted Rachel, "you'll ever see."

On the other side of the split-rail fence, Leeser chafed from the chitchat. "Come on, Rachel, push her in."

And Rachel Whittier nudged Emi Cusack closer to the edge of the ten-foot ravine with her metallic pink stun gun.

"Use your fucking syringe," instructed Leeser. "Do something. We gotta go."

Emi screamed.

A freight train flashed behind the two women. Something dark. Something black.

The Taser tumbled from Rachel's hand, skittered into the bushes. The bag full of hot dogs flew from her shoulder. Emi slipped. And a woman tumbled into the ravine. She went down butt first with a sickening thud.

Somehow, she righted herself and yelped like a seal.

The polar bear roared. Its bellows drowned out the woman's screams. The sound carried for miles, the fierce thunder of violence in the wild.

Ursus maritimus charged down the stairs, its movement clumsy on the steep incline. The polar bear skidded. Its massive hindquarters scooted under forepaws.

The creature rolled, ass under elbows, but just for a moment. It regained footing. It stormed toward the screaming prey. The polar bear opened its mouth wide and angry, wide enough to swallow a seal head, all four canines glistening under the October sun.

Every animal in the Bronx Zoo—painted dogs to gelada baboons—pricked their ears. They sniffed. They waited. They smelled death wafting through the air.

The woman turned. She legged it, polar bear on her tail. She was slow off the mark, her ankle twisted from the fall.

The bear lunged. It struck like a guided missile. Its powerful jaws engulfed the woman's head. And they locked. For the first time in a long, long time, the polar bear savored the satisfying crunch of teeth against skull and oatmeal.

CHAPTER SIXTY

SECONDS EARLIER . . .

Emi teetered backward and started to fall. Rachel sensed motion and whipped around. It was too late.

Shannon grabbed Emi with his left hand. He jerked hard. Just in time. The pregnant woman sailed past him onto the safety of the landing. Landed in the brush.

"Dammit," screamed Leeser.

Shannon's right arm slammed against Rachel. She flipped from the impact, arms windmilling, grabbing, searching. Shannon reached for her arm but missed.

Rachel crashed into the ravine.

"Fuck you," screamed Leeser, a murderous rumble rising from the back of his throat. He charged Shannon's back.

LeeWell Capital's head of security was a massive target of opportunity. Vulnerable, poised on the brink over the polar bear's ravine. His back turned to Cy. Exposed to the blow that would send him over the edge.

———

Cusack, three steps behind Shannon, launched at Leeser. Shoulders low, he flew through the air and speared him. He blasted against the money manager, whipped him off to the side like a sack of laundry.

The two men crashed the fence hard. Cusack's head cracked against the railing. The impact dazed him. Round and round they rolled. Leeser came up on top.

He punched Jimmy with a crushing blow to the cheekbones. Left. Right. Fists like his voice, the double-punch rhythm of a speed bag. Something cracked. Cusack's face started to give way. It felt like a cantaloupe that had gone rotten and all mushy.

Leeser clambered to his feet and ran. A small crowd had gathered. He pushed through, some people gawking, but most gaping into the ravine where the massive bear was chewing Rachel Whittier's scarred right hand. Her head looked like hamburger. The crowd, so late to arrive that morning, screamed in horror.

Cusack was dazed. Losing consciousness. Face pulpy.

He shook his head, waking even as his brain screamed, "Sleep." His ribs pulsed. He glanced at Leeser running through the crowds and up the stairs.

"James," screamed Emi. Blood trickled from his cheekbone. His jaw was already swelling, his right eye beginning to shut. She lumbered for him.

Cusack struggled to his feet. His face twisted more crooked than ever. He hugged Emi and ran, wincing, shedding the grogginess. At the top of the stairs, Cusack sighted Leeser.

Cy glimpsed left and scanned right, confused by the zoo's directions. Even the staff found them bewildering. He darted toward Somba Village.

Pain. A thousand knives ripped through Cusack's face. Another thousand ripped through his side. He was out of breath. He had cracked two ribs from his crash against the rail. He legged it anyway.

Cusack flew across the clearing, the grizzly pen to the left. One of the two grizzlies bellowed and raised an arm. Visitors parted as Cusack chased after his boss.

Leeser cut through a wide corridor, high walls and open at the top. He raced through a booth with glass panels for viewing into the Baboon

Reserve. He exited into the seating area at the Somba Village. A handful of mothers chatted with each other as they checked their baby strollers every thirty seconds to ensure all was okay.

Cusack, younger by fifteen years, caught Leeser. Flinching from the pain, Jimmy grabbed Cy's left shoulder and spun him around. With an uppercut from the right, he hammered Leeser's left jaw with torque and a fist resurrected from the old neighborhood.

Leeser's head snapped. But he caught himself. He popped Cusack's nose with a quick jab. Blood squirted everywhere. Cy, the better boxer, turned to run.

Jimmy, the better runner, caught his boss and threw a wild right. He somehow nailed Cy's nose, mushing cartilage against cheek, and the fight was on. The two men circled. Cusack squared, blocking the direction Cy had been running.

Mothers everywhere, nowhere to be seen thirty minutes earlier, scattered from the area. They pushed their baby carriages, to the left, to the right, anywhere to dodge the melee spoiling their morning at the Bronx Zoo.

"You got shit," taunted Leeser, his nose trickling. He circled and jabbed again.

Cusack slipped most of the shot. Not all. Leeser's fist knocked hard against his ears. The glancing blow stung like a thousand bald-faced hornets. Jimmy concentrated, summoned his old neighborhood. He was back on the streets of Somerville.

"Nothing," repeated Leeser, circling left, his head bobbing and weaving.

Cusack jabbed once and popped Leeser in the mouth. He jabbed again and connected. The two blows cracked smart and sharp, but not hard enough to take Leeser down.

Cy wiped the gruel of snot and blood from the bottom of his face. His coal-black eyes burned, angry and crazy. "After this is over," he sneered, "I'm coming back for your wife. Think she'll recognize me?"

"I do now," replied Emi. "Love your long hair, Cy."

"Huh," Leeser stammered.

Emi stepped through a crowd of mothers, circling, dialing 911 on their cell phones by the dozen.

Cusack saw the opening. He popped Leeser's head to the right with a quick jab. He followed with a right hook. Through the pain of the two quick blows, he heard three words from his wife.

"Stand back, James."

That's when a muffled bang rocked Somba Village. Everyone in the village gasped. A few mothers flinched. Most stopped talking on their cell phones as a startled silence swept through the park.

CHAPTER SIXTY-ONE

SOMBA VILLAGE . . .

Two probes sailed through the air. Thin power lines trailed behind. The C2's specially marked confetti burst from the Taser, raining triumph across Somba Village and echoing like a firecracker. The tiny missiles whizzed toward Leeser's groin, found their mark, and completed the circuit. He lurched backward from the impact.

Cusack turned to see his wife, her lips pursed, her face masked in concentration. She focused on the target and ignored James. Leeser's head jiggled like a jackhammer, his eyes rolling white and inside out as one probe landed to the left of his zipper and one to the right.

Emi had never read the online manual. She had no idea the probes could penetrate two inches of clothing. Nor did she care about the other specs. Her sole objective was to point a pink pistol.

Fifty thousand volts jolted through Cy Leeser's unhappy gonads, the thirty seconds an eternity of current. The electricity pulsed through the fine lines. It surged and buzzed, crackled with the hideous sounds of a frying crotch.

"Bull's-eye," thundered Emi, furious and angry but steady as a surgeon's hand.

With his muscles spasming from the electricity, Leeser toppled backward. He collapsed over a wire barrier and into a shallow gulch, which separated the Baboon Reserve from the rest of the park and made visitors wonder why the geladas never escaped.

After thirty seconds, the pink C2 Taser spent its electrical load. Leeser's body shuddered in the water. He quivered and jerked and miraculously staggered to his feet. He was stunned. He was spent. He was alive. He lurched unsteadily up the rocky slope, tripped, and fell to the ground—out like an empty light socket.

From the top of the hill a band of six or seven geladas roamed down the slope in Leeser's direction. One was a male. The rest were females. They all moved toward Cy with purpose, with something on their minds.

"Do they bite?" asked Cusack. He moved toward the railing. He was ready to hop the fence, slog through the water, and carry Leeser back to safety.

"Totally harmless," replied Emi. "They graze on grass."

The baboons circled Leeser, who lay on his back, his eyes closed. The male darted left then right and made a funny face.

"What's it doing?" asked Cusack.

"See how he's flipping his lips?" replied Emi. "That's what geladas do when they're unsure about something."

From the left side of the Cusacks, two mothers pushed their strollers toward the railing. The danger was over. But the women parked their babies well shy of the fence and walked forward. A redheaded woman pointed at Leeser and asked, "Isn't that the guy from the YouTube video?"

"Absolutely," replied an auburn-haired mom.

Redhead: "How can you be so sure?"

Auburn hair: "See for yourself." She held out her iPhone for the redhead to inspect an Internet photo of Leeser.

One of the geladas squatted over Leeser's face and urinated great yellow streams into his black hair, slick and suddenly greasy, growing wetter by the moment. The once-immaculate locks turned ragged under the shower of kidney mousse, mixed with twigs and other debris from the hillside.

A big bass voice boomed behind Emi and Jimmy. "Are you folks okay?" It was Shannon, bruised but not beaten.

"We're fine," replied Emi.

"Your baby?" the big man asked.

"Fine," Emi echoed, rubbing Yaz instinctively.

"I suppose you have questions," said Shannon.

"Yeah," agreed Cusack. "Who *are* you?"

Emi watched Leeser like a hawk. He was moving. He was struggling to his feet. "He'll get away," she warned.

"Oh, I don't think so," replied Shannon, his eyes turning toward Leeser. The big man was calm, his voice a deep and soothing elixir, his arms like tree trunks. "The police will arrive any second."

"What makes you so sure?" Emi demanded.

"I phoned NYPD," Shannon said, "and told them to beat feet over here."

At that exact moment, almost on cue, a new voice joined the conversation. "We're here now."

Shannon, Jimmy, and Emi turned to find two blue-uniformed police from NYPD. One was short and broad like a plank, the other tall and lean as a willow. The short cop was the one who had spoken.

The tall cop asked, "Is he the problem?" The officer pointed to Cy, who was standing unsteadily and grimacing like he had swallowed bad milk.

"'Problem,'" parroted Emi. "You could say that. That bastard tried to throw me into the polar bear pen."

"What did you do?" asked the shorter officer.

"Tased his lights out," she said, sounding matter-of-fact.

With that, the two officers hopped over the fence into the gelada reserve. They waded through the ravine. They cuffed Leeser and read him Miranda rights as a crowd gathered. Try as he might, Leeser never managed to stand entirely straight. When he walked, he limped.

"What happened to the woman dressed in black?" asked Cusack.

"Her name is Rachel Whittier," answered Shannon. "And let's just say she lost her brain housing group."

"But who is she, Shannon?" Emi insisted on knowing.

"We believe Whittier was Leeser's paid assassin. We know she's an investor in LeeWell Capital."

"Why didn't you shut them down sooner?" asked Cusack.

"We didn't have anything that would stick."

"That still doesn't explain," Jimmy continued, "who you are."

"I'm with a private detective agency," explained Shannon. "Several insurance companies have suspected Cy Leeser for some time. They hired my firm to investigate. We never had anything solid. Until today."

"But how do you know about Daryle Fucking Lamonica?"

"Your brother Jude is in Iraq with the Hundred and First," replied Shannon.

"What's he got to do with LeeWell Capital?"

"I was in Iraq, too."

"Do you know Jude?" asked Cusack.

"No. But I learned about him during my background checks on you. I called my army buddies in the Hundred and First for information."

"Anybody ever tell you he has the disposition of a pit bull with gout?"

"Heard it all the time," laughed Shannon. He gestured to the two-star pin on Cusack's lapel. "So we never forget."

"So we never forget," echoed Emi. She smiled at the hidden meaning.

"Your brother," explained Shannon, "is a big-time Pats fan. Knows the franchise history, everything about the team—scores, players, won-lost records against opponents. He references Daryle Fucking Lamonica every so often."

"Lamonica isn't exactly a household name."

"Raiders fans might take issue," contended Shannon.

"You a member of Raider Nation?"

"Born and bred in the Bay Area." Shannon smiled broadly. "I used Lamonica's name to signal help was on the way. Never thought you'd confront me in front of Cy."

"The letter. The call to Emi. You've been watching my back?"

Shannon smiled a yes.

"You knew Leeser was buying life insurance policies and killing the insured?" asked Cusack.

"Not at first. We thought he was clean-sheeting."

"What's that?" Emi raised the question, but her eyes never left Leeser.

"It's a type of insurance fraud," Shannon explained. "People buy life insurance without disclosing their illnesses."

"Like not disclosing you have a heart problem," said Emi. "Or AIDS."

"Exactly," the big investigator agreed. "Usually, third parties buy 'clean sheet' policies right after they're underwritten. Their returns are huge because the insured die soon afterward."

"The difference," Cusack observed, "is that Cy purchased insurance policies from people who were healthy."

"Or their ailments were known," clarified Shannon. "At least one of his victims had asthma. His death was the one that really made us suspicious."

"Why's that?" asked Emi.

"It was a twenty-million-dollar policy," answered Shannon. "It's hard for third parties to buy policies that big."

"And it's no coincidence that Em's father is in the insurance business," observed Cusack.

"Right," agreed the big man. "We think Leeser began killing people as early as 2002 and 2003, when LeeWell Capital first suffered market losses."

"Did he kill his partner?" asked Emi.

"We don't think so," replied Shannon. "But there was a ten-million key-man policy on Stockwell."

"Bailed Leeser out?" asked Cusack.

"'Made' him who he is today." Shannon used his fingers to quote the word "made." "The insurance payment was like a how-to guide the next time LeeWell Capital had a problem."

"Those first few years were tough," Cusack observed. "Bad years for the markets."

"Right," agreed Shannon. "The fund was far smaller then. Leeser started his business with fifty million dollars under management. A few five-million-dollar policies could make a big impact on performance."

"But we started the year at eight hundred million in total assets," countered Cusack. "It's harder to affect performance."

"Right," Shannon confirmed, "which is why the Bentwing shorts created absolute havoc. Leeser was losing so much money the life insurance payments couldn't fix his problem fast enough."

"The market is picking up where the Qataris and Icelanders left off," Cusack noted. "I don't see the Dow's slide stopping any time soon."

"What's this got to do with my father?" asked Emi.

"Leeser needed bigger and bigger life insurance policies," explained Shannon, "to affect his performance."

"He hired me to get to Caleb?" asked Cusack.

"I'm sure that was the plan."

"Bastard," Emi decided.

The two policemen, Leeser cuffed and in tow, passed the trio at that moment. The Greenwich money manager looked disheveled, wet from the gulch and baboon piss. His hair was matted, riddled with leaves from rolling across the autumn ground.

"You got nothing," bellowed Leeser, again, as he walked past. "You wouldn't have a job, Cusack, if it weren't for Phelps." He trudged ahead, defiant and angry.

Jimmy ignored Leeser. "I'm still surprised," he ventured to Shannon, "you didn't nab Cy sooner."

"He's cagey," the big man replied. "Cagey about everything. He wanted a huge fund, for example, but borrowed money instead of finding new investors. He thought they'd ask too many questions."

"That explains all the debt," said Cusack.

"James had less to do with finding investors," said Emi, "than buying my dad's company?"

"That acquisition was a dream come true," replied Shannon. "But we think Leeser initially wanted to source life settlements through your father."

"Why'd you film me at the Foxy Lady, Shannon?"

For the first time ever in Cusack's memory, the big man looked uncomfortable. Out of character. Almost remorseful. "I'm sorry," said Shannon. "We were getting close. And Cy was leaning on me hard. It was either film you or blow my cover. I bet Bianca will—"

"I'll call her," interrupted Cusack, moving on. "What about Victor?"

"What about him?"

"Is he involved?"

"We weren't sure at first." Shannon shrugged to emphasize his uncertainty.

"And now?" asked Cusack.

"We don't think so."

"What about the weird behavior?"

"You tell me," said Shannon.

"What's that supposed to mean?"

"It's a hedge fund thing," the big man replied.

"What are you talking about?" Cusack was confused.

"Victor read that women make better traders."

"I remember the article on his desk," agreed Cusack.

"He's taking estrogen tablets, Jimmy."

"Is he crazy?" exclaimed Emi.

"Maybe he needs an intervention," Cusack offered helpfully. "You know. For hormone abuse."

Emi looked at her husband. Shannon studied him, too, Cusack's bloody face, his bent nose. The big man finally said, "Let's take you to the hospital and get you checked out."

CHAPTER SIXTY-TWO

Victor Lee was frozen. He lacked Cy's approval to sell. He was paralyzed in a "tough tape," Street jargon for bad markets. Just as he predicted, the Dow had already fallen under 10,000. Cy's lack of focus would cost Lee-Well Capital plenty—and something even worse:

"My bonus."

The capital markets, it appeared, were hacking up phlegm from too much leverage and too many bad loans. News stories scrolled nonstop on the left LCD, one after another, each reporting the demise of Western civilization. On the middle panel, LeeWell's portfolio prices confirmed all the doom and gloom to the left. And on the right, CNBC's talking heads filled the screen. They took turns panting about the latest disasters.

Victor grabbed a spray bottle of Windex and began wiping the right LCD. He needed Leeser's permission to trade. Cy was the general partner. Cy called all the shots. Cy was the one who insisted on all the debt. Lee hoped cleaning would make him feel better, that getting rid of dust was his antidote for a bad move. That was when CNBC broke the story that changed his life.

"Just when you think things can't get worse," the anchorwoman reported, "we have bizarre news from the Bronx Zoo. A woman is dead, the victim of a polar bear attack. Authorities have arrested Cy Leeser, an emerging star in the hedge fund industry."

"Ack!" exclaimed Victor, dropping the Windex.

"That's right, Erin," agreed a reporter from the Bronx Zoo. "We have a film clip of the bear's attack, recorded by a visitor to the zoo. The footage is disturbing so we caution viewers."

"What does the polar bear have to do with Cy Leeser?" Erin asked the on-site reporter.

Victor Lee never heard another word. He was too busy. He had all the authority he needed. He dialed Numb Nuts over at Merrill Lynch and barked, "Lose ten thousand shares of Bentwing Energy at the market. Call me when you're done." Then, he dialed Goldman Sachs and HSBC and all the other houses he used to book trades. The message was always the same, "Sell."

"I'm back," Victor announced inside the trading room, eyeing the Windex streaks on his terminal. "I'm bigger and fucking better than ever."

"Let me drive you to the emergency room?" offered Shannon.

"No thanks," said Cusack. "I'm fine. We'll grab a cab."

"What about your car, Jimmy?"

"There's a tow truck coming."

"What will happen to LeeWell Capital?" asked Emi.

"Who knows?" replied Shannon. "It'll shut down. Insurance companies will sue. And families of the victims will file civil lawsuits."

"Like the ones against O.J.," observed Emi.

"Exactly," the big man replied. He smiled to reveal the gap between his teeth. In that moment Emi and Cusack forgot the fierce expression superglued to his face.

"You should smile more often," observed Emi.

"And why's that?" asked Shannon, looking perplexed rather than fierce.

"Because I'll never forget your face for as long as I live."

"And that's saying something," observed Cusack. Both Emi and he laughed.

"What?" asked Shannon, confused.

"It's a long story," explained Cusack. "Are you coming into the office tomorrow?"

"Probably. Assuming the police let us in."

"See you there."

Emi kissed Shannon good-bye with a monster peck on the cheek and said, "Thanks."

When Cusack and Emi were alone, she asked, "Why are you going into the office tomorrow?"

"The clients know me. It's my reputation. I've got to clean up this mess before moving on. And I've done it before."

"I wish you'd forget about Cusack Capital."

"That's what your dad says."

"See. He's not all bad," Emi added impishly.

"I know. I know," Cusack acknowledged. "I need to speak with Graham Durkin, too."

"Why?"

"We have a good rapport, and he's always asking for market advice."

"What are you going to tell him, James?"

"To put his money under a mattress."

"Yeah, right."

"I have another idea, Em."

"You can tell me while we're on the way to the emergency room."

It was dark in Reykjavik. Siggi was sitting at his desk, getting ready to close the shop. He stared at the small line drawing by Picasso, the one from Leeser's office. Soon, probably Thursday or Friday, the other paintings would arrive. All 427 of them. All crated, labeled, and sealed for the journey to Iceland.

The phone rang. It was Ólafur. He had stayed behind in New York. "Did you hear what happened?"

"Settle down, cousin. And take it from the top," commanded Siggi.

"Leeser was arrested today. Something happened at the Bronx Zoo. Apparently, he tried to push a pregnant woman into the polar bear pen. But someone else fell instead and got eaten." The ex-banker spoke fast, really fast.

"Slow down, Ólafur. And tell me what you're talking about."

"That's all I know. You should ask Bianca. She was awfully sweet last Friday."

"Good idea," said Siggi. "I hope she's okay."

"What I don't understand is why she's selling all her paintings through you."

"What do you mean, cousin?"

"For one, Cy is your client," explained Ólafur.

"Was," the gallery owner corrected. "Which, quite frankly, is what I told Bianca."

"If you don't mind me asking," Ólafur persisted in a humble voice, "why you? Why not a dealer in the USA?"

"I have a Web presence."

"So does Sotheby's."

"I have Russian clients."

"So does Sotheby's."

"But Sotheby's is in the USA. Leeser's wife is divorcing him. She wants everything out of the country. Gives her more leverage in the settlement."

"Now you're talking, Siggi. Wish I were there to toast you."

"When are you coming back?"

"Not for a while," the ex-banker sighed, sounding down and despondent but not completely out. "Chairman Guðjohnsen is about to sacrifice me to the authorities."

"The FME suspended trading on our stock market today."

"I heard," said Siggi, thinking FME was an odd acronym for Iceland's Financial Supervisory Authority.

"Parliament seized control of Landsbanki. Glitner will fall next and then Kaupthing. It's only a matter of time before Hafnarbanki goes."

"How does this affect you, Ólafur?"

"The regulators want blood, cousin. And Guðjohnsen will give them me."

"What about your lawyers? What do they say?"

"That Guðjohnsen's powerful. That he owns half of Parliament. That I'm fucked."

"What can you do?" asked Siggi.

"That's why I'm calling. I need to speak with Bianca."

Their conversation ended ten minutes later. Siggi hung up with Ólafur, pleased by the discussion. "My cousin's back. And he's meaner than ever."

CHAPTER SIXTY-THREE

MONDAY, NOVEMBER 10

BENTWING AT $19.81

Leeser lounged on his bed, bare feet bolstered by an extra pillow. He read Friday's *Wall Street Journal*, which had arrived only one hour ago. He cursed the late delivery. He cursed his six-by-ten room—two cots, toilet, concrete floor, and a monstrous roommate named Babe, who could block moonlight from the window had there been one. Leeser's closets in Greenwich were bigger than this cell. He cursed his 19,000-square-foot house, too.

A trunk, approved by the prison bulls, sat at the foot of his bed. Inside the trunk were cartons and a few beat-up cigar boxes. And inside the cartons and the boxes were cigarettes, lots of cigarettes, every brand, every taste imaginable. Filtered. Unfiltered. Camels. Even a few 120 mm Virginia Slims.

Cy Leeser hated cigarettes. Never smoked one in his life. He would rather eat dirt and run his nails down a chalkboard. Cigarettes were, however, the currency of choice inside prison.

"Fucking lawyers," he cursed, not caring whether his roommate replied.

The judge, a woman, refused bail. Called Leeser a "flight risk." He regarded her as the antithesis of intelligent life. Be that as it may, she was the one in control. His trial would not start until sometime next year.

The bed over him sagged under Babe's enormous bulk. Someday, Cy feared, the mattress would give way. It would come crashing down, all three hundred pounds of padding and fat ass smothering the life out of his lungs.

"Hey, Cy."

"Yeah, Babe."

"I bet you a carton of cigarettes the Patriots whip the Jets on Thursday."

"Where are you going to lay your hands on a carton of cigarettes?"

"My old lady is bringing them."

"What kind of odds, Babe."

"What do you mean, 'odds'?"

"The Pats whipped them last time."

"So."

"So if the Jets win," said Leeser, "you should pay me three cigarettes for every two. If the Pats win, I'll pay you one for one. Sound fair?"

"I don't know." Babe shifted his bulk as he wrestled with the decision. "I don't know shit about no odds." He tossed and turned, and the cot groaned.

"That's fine. No odds. No bet."

"Okay, okay. I'll do it."

"Some things never change," mumbled Leeser.

"What's that?"

"Don't worry about it." Cy had plenty of time to explain.

Back in Greenwich, Victor eyed his three LCD screens. He saw a stock tick upward and immediately punched the speed-dial button to Merrill or whatever they called themselves these days.

"Short another ten thousand Bank of America at nineteen."

"Thanks a lot," groused Numb Nuts. "You sure?"

"I'll take a report," Victor said, "when you're done." He expected the trader to sell the shares and call back with the execution price.

"Short ten thousand Bank of America at nineteen," the trader from Merrill confirmed and clicked off.

Victor eyed the rows of desks across the trading floor. His office at Greenwich Plaza no longer looked like LeeWell Capital. The snooker table was gone. So was the screaming-eagle coffee machine. Only the sauna remained. And the office temperature was set to seventy degrees Fahrenheit.

Victor Lee Capital.

Lee liked the sound of his firm's name. Everything had come together so quickly: paperwork, his team of traders, even $200 million of funds to manage. He had called every one of LeeWell's investors, saying, "I'm your best chance to stop further losses." Some bit in the worst market he had ever seen. Victor Lee Capital was the fastest hedge fund of all time.

Sally Williams shot Victor the bird.

He shot one back.

Gwen Dickinson thought it was funny. She shot each of them the bird. Back to back. Boom. Boom.

Victor smiled and waved the three-fingered salute in a circle.

Edie Smothers hated to be left out. She smoothed each of her eyebrows—first the left, then the right—with the bird.

Victor laughed at his team, with his team. They all laughed. Their portfolio was short everything, already up eight percent on the month.

"You ladies are adorable."

Lee reached into his drawer that served as a burial ground for extension cords. He rooted round and round all the wires until he found his hammer. It took a while to untangle the mess. But at last, when the hammer was free and clear, he tossed it into the trash basket—confident about one unassailable truth.

Women make better traders.

CHAPTER SIXTY-FOUR

There was a knock. Freddy and Ginger, the dachshund dance duo, sensed trouble. They ripped to the front door and barked at the menace, trembling with all the ferocity their eleven-pound bodies could muster. Or perhaps they were yapping at him for being late. Freddy and Ginger knew who it was.

So did Bianca. These days the mailman arrived every afternoon between four-thirty and five. He always brought four biscuits, two for each dog, and delivered at least three dozen letters.

The snail mail paled relative to Bianca's e-mails. She received about a thousand every day. They arrived at all hours. Some were short and to the point. Others were long, rambling diatribes that included the occasional picture or two.

"Hi, Mark," she said. "More letters?"

"More letters," he confirmed, handing mail to Bianca and biscuits to Freddy and Ginger. "Your fans must love you, Mrs. Leeser."

"I know two dachshunds that love you," she said, as the mailman returned to his delivery truck. It was parked in the driveway behind Leeser's Bentley, which she planned to sell.

Bianca looked at all the letters and smiled uneasily. She relished her new direction. She regretted, however, the driving force behind her newfound success. There were just too many miserable marriages out there, like hers.

The cavernous home was empty now. The paintings were gone. So was most of the furniture, either sold or placed in storage. Soon she would be gone, a new resident of Manhattan. Her life had grown so complicated since Cy's arrest.

The evening of October 6, Bianca drove to Andover and worked the phones. She called therapists the first half of the trip. Her primary objective was to protect her girls.

Afterward, Bianca called her lawyers. Then she called real-estate agents. She wanted out of that house in Greenwich. She was not concerned about the bad market or whether she could keep proceeds from the sale. The thought of Cy Leeser, what he had become, made her sick. Bianca called her literary agent from fifteen years ago, and after listening for thirty seconds he said, "Here's what we need to do."

The effort paid off day one. Bianca never expected, however, the incoming call from Siggi's cousin and Cy's nemesis. Ólafur had been a stroke of luck. He offered to tell her everything about the feud between Hafnarbanki and LeeWell Capital.

Sure, he wanted revenge for the short that took down his bank. More important, he wanted to expose the role of Chairman Guðjohnsen in print through a bestselling, international novelist. But Ólafur had no idea about Bianca's discussions with her agent when he called.

Bianca's Web site, "Trophy Wife Revenge," was not a hit. It was a sensation, generating 359,000 visits every day. Her blog mixed revenge fantasies with nuts-and-bolts advice about how to avoid verbal abuse. The forum was becoming a way of life for women toiling in loveless marriages.

She embedded her infamous YouTube video on the home page. She invited guest bloggers to submit techniques for her online column, "Getting Even With a Scumbag Husband." And she even posted her recipe for spaghetti Bolognese, made with '61 Chateau Latour, and included a picture of Freddy and Ginger with their testimonial, "We love it."

Next came a two-book deal. Bianca's agent advised her to forget romance novels for the time being. Sure, she could make a living. Her ten novels, sizzling and steamy, still sold today. But the publishers wanted nonfiction. They wanted a memoir worthy of an Oprah interview. They wanted research. They wanted a tell-all, unrivaled in the history of modern literature. Cousin Ólafur, his willingness to help, offered an interesting angle to say the least.

The public yearned to read everything about Cyrus Leeser, the man who made Enron's execs look like saints. Her memoir would no doubt become an instant bestseller, an exposé of greed without conscience. She had signed the contract yesterday. It came with a six-figure advance and the requirement she tell everything about her life among the hedge funds.

Who are these gods of Greenwich?

Bianca sat in a leather chair, one of the few items remaining in her living room. She looked at the massive fireplace, reached down on the floor, and grabbed the remote control. She clicked once, and the gas-fired logs burst to life.

The fake logs were Cy's idea. Bianca hated them most days. But this evening, she savored their warmth. She grabbed her Mac—brand-new because Cusack pressed her for the old one—and decided it was time to begin the memoir.

"My husband is Cyrus Leeser," she typed. "He will soon be my ex-husband. But he is everything the late Dorothy Parker desired in a man. Cy is 'handsome, ruthless, and stupid.'"

CHAPTER SIXTY-FIVE

MONDAY, DECEMBER 1

BENTWING AT $21.35

Jimmy leaned back in his Aeron chair. The hoary wooden floors of his condominium, once tagged for industrial use, groaned as he shifted his weight. Cusack considered the days ahead and smiled.

The Beemer was parked outside—just in case. Emi could deliver any day now. He was ready. For a moment, he visualized what would happen.

Emi: "It's time."

Cusack: "I'll get your bag."

Emi: "Okay, Pops." He could almost see her stadium-light smile, enough wattage to moisten the eyes of most GE engineers.

These days, Emi seldom called him "James." It was always "Pops" or "Daddio," although she preferred "Pops" by a margin of two to one over "Daddio."

Cusack envisioned himself carrying Emi's bag, shepherding her to the Beemer, and speeding off to the hospital. Richard Petty, David Pearson, and Bobby Allison—NASCAR had nothing on him. Over the past weekend, Cusack drove the route and timed himself just to be sure.

On the ride to the hospital, Emi would probably ask for the two hundredth time, "Are you sure about the name?"

They had settled on Bart Phelps Cusack. Emi insisted on the Phelps part. Throwing in surnames had been her family's tradition ever since the *Mayflower*. Cusack agreed, though he secretly hoped the decision would go extra innings and end with a miracle victory. He loved "Yaz" and doubted they would ever call his son anything else.

Cusack resisted the temptation to buy a new car. Instead, he paid a garage to renovate the Beemer. The old clunker sported a new engine, new radiator and air-conditioning, new tires, and new paint job—retro styling with a metallic tan body, white roof, and shiny chrome. The car boasted a new lease on life, and the overhaul cost less than the latest models.

"Caution" was the watchword. The markets were flailing. Even though Cusack's own financial fortunes had turned better—a modest uptick—he preferred to be careful. There was no certainty his improved fortunes would last. Plus, he had new obligations to consider.

Yea.

At that moment Emi interrupted her husband's thoughts. "It's time," she said.

"What do you mean?"

"Do I need to spell it out on paper?" she asked, her sapphire-blue eyes dancing with mischief. She paused and added, "Daddio."

Cusack's heart began to pound. His eyebrows raised high. Adrenaline and excitement and an emotion he could not identify surged through his being. "You sure?"

"My water broke."

Five weeks earlier, Graham Durkin called Cusack on his cell. "Can you talk?"

"Always," replied Cusack.

"What are your plans?"

"What do you mean?"

"Are you looking for a job?"

"Short term, I'm shutting down LeeWell Capital."

"Are you joining Victor Lee?"

"You know about his fund?" asked Cusack. Durkin had never invested with LeeWell Capital. There was no reason for Victor and the billionaire to be in touch.

"I keep my ear to the ground."

"It's nothing personal, Graham. But Victor is a whack job. No way I'm joining his operation."

"You're not a fan of estrogen pills?"

"You know about that?" Cusack's eyebrows arched high in surprise.

"I hear he ran numbers on the benefits."

"Your sources must be good."

"Look, Jimmy. I'll cut to the chase. You know money, and you've already made me a bunch."

"By pushing you away from LeeWell Capital?"

"No. But that's one reason I want you to work for me. You put my interests ahead of your own. It makes me think I can trust you."

"How did you make money?"

"Remember DOG?"

"Of course, it's the perfect stock right now. It goes up when the market goes down."

"I backed up the truck," said Durkin. "I'm up twenty-five percent and wondering what to do."

"Do you have much money at risk?"

"Enough to be uncomfortable."

"Book the profit," Cusack advised with complete conviction.

"See what I mean? I need somebody to run my finances. And I want that somebody to be you."

"DOG is one idea that worked. My investments don't all work out. And we hardly know each other."

"Look, Jimmy. I've done my homework. I know all about Cusack Capital and checked you out with my buddies from Goldman. I bet you have a few problems with your lease obligations."

"I'll figure something out." Cusack tried to sound cool. But he knew where this conversation was headed. It was that time again.

"Can you be in Providence tomorrow?"

Two weeks later, Cusack and Graham inked a deal. There was a small signing bonus and enough paperwork for Cusack to refinance his mortgage until he sold the condo and moved someplace more modest. Even better, Durkin agreed to establish a presence at the Empire State Building and insisted they rehire Jimmy's assistant from his days at Goldman Sachs and Cusack Capital—Sydney.

It was still early. But Jimmy and Graham had already discussed Bentwing. They liked the idea of building a strategic position in alternative energy companies. At $21.35 the stock looked like a steal, a victim of the games that short sellers play.

"Your water broke?"

Emi nodded yes, her face a roaring bonfire. Without warning, she winced and grabbed her stomach. "We gotta go."

Cusack leaped from his Aeron. Suddenly, he was everywhere. He squeezed past Emi, who was standing in the door. He ran down the hall and grabbed Em's coat from the hall closet. "Where's your bag?"

"By the door where you left it."

"Oh, right. Where are my keys?"

"Check your pockets."

"Oh, right."

"You ready to go?" asked Emi, trying hard not to snicker now that the contraction pain had eased. She waddled through the short corridor to the family room.

"Let's roll," Cusack replied, and raced back to help his wife.

In the elevator Cusack studied Emi intently. "Are you okay?"

"No different than any other mother in the history of mankind."

When they were outside Emi hugged Cusack's right arm, her overnight bag slung over his right shoulder. Together they marched toward the retro tan-and-white Beemer, the couple energized by December chill and the adventure ahead. Ever the gentleman, Cusack opened the passenger door for Emi and helped her inside.

Cusack jumped in the car behind the steering wheel, smiled crookedly, and said, "Here we go."

"Here we go," echoed Emi.

He turned the key in the ignition, hoped for the best, and smiled crookedly as their Beemer fired the first time.